and ... the balcony rail. "A new struggle has begun! A new day has dawned in the world order—*let there be no mistake!*"

The skeleton turned away briefly, motioning behind him, and then turned back to face the terrified crowd.

"This is the price of the old—*the bill has come due!*"

Four human bodies appeared on the edge of the balcony, thrashing. As they were thrown over, and as the ropes attached to their necks brought them up short, kicking as they hung, I recognized them as the top Soviet leadership— among them, the head of the KGB, the foreign minister, the head of the army, and the Premier. It was a sickening display.

Lenin leaned down to look at them until the bodies were still. Then his hard fist went up again.

"This is the price of defiance!" The white skull's jaw split into a monstrous grin, mirrored faintly on the shroud of Lenin's ghostly features. He held up his hands to the skeletons surrounding the Square.

"Destroy them all! Let them join the masses!"

———

"Bizarre brilliance. *Skeletons* is a wild and ingenious weird fantasy by a master stylist. . . . I highly recommend it."

—Joe R. Lansdale

Don't miss other spine-tingling horror novels
from Bantam Books by:

SKELETONS

Al Sarrantonio

FALCON ™

BANTAM BOOKS
NEW YORK • TORONTO • LONDON • SYDNEY • AUCKLAND

SKELETONS

A Bantam Falcon Book / June 1992

FALCON and the portrayal of a boxed "ff" are trademarks of Bantam Books,
a division of Bantam Doubleday Dell Publishing Group, Inc.

ISBN 0-553-29754-6

Published simultaneously in the United States and Canada

Bantam Books are published by Bantam Books, a division of Bantam Doubleday Dell Publishing Group, Inc. Its trademark, consisting of the words "Bantam Books" and the portrayal of a rooster, is Registered in U.S. Patent and Trademark Office and in other countries. Marca Registrada. Bantam Books, 666 Fifth Avenue, New York, New York 10103.

PRINTED IN THE UNITED STATES OF AMERICA

RAD - 0 9 8 7 6 5 4 3 2 1

For
my three babies:
Beth,
Tim,
and
Mikey

SKELETONS

Prologue

The earth revolves around the sun once every 365.2 days. Along with the sun, the other eight planets, and all the various debris including comets, asteroids, and detritus of our planet such as satellites, the earth revolves around the galactic plane, that is, the core of our own Milky Way galaxy, once every two hundred million years.

Which means, if there was a certain area in the galactic plane composed of strange plasma, space fog, unknown gas particles, or whatever, the earth would pass through it once during each revolution around the Milky Way's galactic core—in other words, once every two hundred million years.

There was.

It did.

1

The inner diary of
Claire St. Eve

1

Today something happened to me.

Mrs. Garr, my counselor at Withers, has said that I am like a seed closed tight and ready to grow. She says that I am mute because my voice, too, is locked inside the seed. She says she is a gardener, and that she is trying to find the right kind of soil, the right sun, and right water to make me sprout.

Today, for the first time, I felt the seed shiver.

2

This early summer day at Withers Home for Women, in Cold Spring Harbor, New York, started like any other day. All of us up at six-thirty, the donning of drab uniforms, washing and brushing, a half hour of calisthenics in the gym with Mr. Cary. Then breakfast in the prison-like cafeteria, rows and ranks of benches and tables, no talking permitted, the stacking of trays, back to our rooms. An hour of meditation, they call it; aloneness, I call it. Then therapy, followed by lunch, again eaten in silence.

Then, the television room.

The tyrant Margaret Gray, the oldest tenant of Withers Home for Women, was waiting there, because that is when we are finally left alone. As always, she waited until Priscilla Ralston, her eighteen-year-old toady, put on the television to the religious channel, waited until Priscilla had regained her chair. Then she moved quickly to the front of the room, climbed a chair, and turned to face us.

"We'll learn," she said, her thin hand closing into a bony fist, her eyes darting the room, daring anyone to contradict. Even her voice was hard and mean and thin. "We'll watch and learn."

She climbed down, stood under the television like a sentinel, making sure all eyes stayed on the set. Everyone remembers Laura Paine, the girl whose eyes were scratched out. Laura was big, nearly twenty, knew how to laugh. She came to Withers last summer, nearly a year ago, and was blinded a month later. She had an alcohol problem, and beautiful blue eyes. For three weeks she put up with Margaret Gray's television tyranny, then got up one day, pushed Margaret aside, and put the soap operas back on. The other girls cheered. Laura smiled, stood sentinel where Margaret had been until Margaret left the room. We watched the soap operas the whole week.

Then on Friday morning Laura didn't appear for breakfast. They found her in her room, fists pressed tight to her scratched-out eyes, drunk. The staff said she had smuggled the liquor in and done it to herself. Priscilla Ralston told one of the other girls that Margaret Gray had held a knife to Laura's eyes, which Laura thought were her best feature, and made her drink until she passed out.

According to Priscilla, Margaret had said, "If thine eye offend thee, pluck it out," and then slashed Laura's eyes while she lay unconscious.

When television time ended at four, we went back to our rooms for more enforced loneliness. At five I saw Mrs. Garr for an hour.

Mrs. Garr took me to the window of my room. The

cool late-afternoon summer breeze blew across me. She made me look out at the rolling grounds, the playing field, the little cemetery with Mr. Cary's cottage nearby, and beyond, the glint of water, a red boat on Long Island Sound, through the trees.

"Don't you want that?" she said, standing behind me, squeezing her hands on my shoulders. "Don't you want to run through the grass and shout, or jump in the water, take it all in and blow it all out again like a whale?"

I looked up at her silently, and she squeezed my shoulders harder.

"Oh, Claire, I want you to flower so badly." She turned me around, held my hands in her hands, and looked deep into my eyes. "You're almost sixteen years old," she said. "You've never spoken a word. But there's nothing wrong with you. Your vocal cords are fine. You're intelligent, and your written work is as good as a college student's. You perform your tasks well. You get along with the other girls, here.

"But it's like all of you is inside that seed. Like you haven't started to be alive yet. Like you're . . . waiting for something." Mrs. Garr's frustration showed in her voice. "You're going to speak when you're ready, Claire. I know it. I want you to begin to live."

Mrs. Garr waited for my response, but I only looked at her until she finally put my hands down and walked away from me, balling her hands in frustration.

"That seed's going to break open," she said, leaving my room.

At six we ate dinner, followed at seven by more television, with Priscilla playing her part of putting on the funny shows, and Margaret Gray marching up to change it to the religious channel. Margaret held court until ten, when we all marched to the bathroom, again to wash and brush, and then to bed. Mrs. Garr stopped at my room, her form outlined in hall light, to say good night before closing the door.

And there I lay quietly in bed, and slept, until sometime in the night I awoke, and something happened to me.

I sat up in bed.

Like a breeze from the window, something washed

over and through me. I felt a tingle from my fingertips crawl down deep within me, and there was a leap inside me.

I rose, and went to the window.

Outside, I saw shapes in the darkness moving over the hills near the trees and water.

Someone screamed.

And then I heard much noise around me, and Mrs. Garr threw open the door to my room.

"Claire, hurry," she said.

And then she marched into the room and took my arm, pulling me out into the hallway, and there were more screams.

2

The Memoirs of Peter Sun

1

This was to be the greatest of all rallies. Think of it: the finest day of all our lives, delegates from Asia, the Third World, North and South America, Australia, Europe, even Cuba. I saw with my own eyes this morning, as the sun rose on Red Square, on the tents that had been springing like flowers there for the past week, held down on the corners with rocks, a crowd in excess of what was expected. Did I say a hundred and fifty thousand? More like two hundred thousand. Maybe more. Up to a point I thought I knew what to say to them all, to open the greatest single day on earth in the cause of democratization.

And me, a humble man from humble Cambodia, a land raped repeatedly for thousands of years, a country still laced with Khmer Rouge and nearly as bad Pnompenhists, chosen to open the proceedings. The Moscow leadership would even come out to greet me. There wasn't an unfriendly soldier in sight.

But when the sun rose on that assembly, on all those thousands and thousands of tents and bedrolls, those hundreds of thousands of different faces, it was too much for me, I suddenly *didn't* know what to say, and I had to get away.

As I left the stage there was Jon Roberts, from the United States, sixties headband around his forehead, long hair held in place. "Like Woodstock," he said, smiling almost naively, though he is not naive, only too young. "I'll make breakfast. Pancakes in Red Square."

"I'll be back," I said, suddenly unable to keep my breath, suffocated by the fact that it had all actually happened, that all these speakers from around the world, great thinkers and scientists and writers and musicians, had actually come here, to this place, to celebrate democracy.

"Don't go far," he cautioned, frowning. "Peter, Paul, and Mary go on in twenty minutes, the CNN people will be here in less than an hour, you know they want—"

"You handle CNN," I said, patting his shoulder. "You can do it, Jon."

"But the media, you know how important all this shit is—"

"You handle that part," I said. "You're better at it."

"Be back by noon, dammit!" he called after me. "You *have* to be back by noon to speak—"

"I promise," I said, turning away to push through the crowd.

Some of them recognized me, and though most made a path, there were those who needed to shake hands, to talk. Finally I reached back into my backpack, found my sunglasses, put them on, veered right, head down. Soon no one recognized me. I watched as I walked: a sea of human picnics, families rising with the sun, which now pushed up over the square. It was cold here even on a July 1st morning, at this time of day. But already you could feel the mist, the dew, dissipating. I saw nothing but smiles.

This is remarkable, I thought to myself. This is truly remarkable.

It took me nearly a half hour just to get out of the crowd. And then, suddenly, I could breathe. There were buses, the big, boxy, clanking things the Russians still make, and I was able to catch one leaving the city. I had to be out somewhere with dirt under my feet, farmland, at least for a little while. The bus clanked along, wheezed to a stop, listing to one side as passengers entered, rolled along, and within forty minutes we were out of Moscow.

2

With all of its martial trappings stripped, the Soviet Union is a beautiful place. And in July the wheat, what there is of it, begins to sprout and climb. I knew I had arrived at what I wanted when I saw a field of this stunted gold, and got the driver to stop. He assured me that another bus back to Moscow would be by in an hour and a half and would get me back to Red Square long before noon. "I know you," he said thickly, smiling, showing one lost tooth. He poked me hard in the chest. "You're a good man. And you speak Russian!"

"Yes," I said.

He poked me again. "I'll be here myself for you in ninety minutes, deliver you myself."

I nodded thanks, wishing my sunglasses were bigger, and slouched out of the bus, a few passengers following me with their gaze as the bus lurched off.

Soon there was dirt under my feet. Just off the road there was a strip of rocky gravel and, past that, blessed soil. I removed my shoes, rolled up my pants, and moved into it. The first rows were hardened by sun and packed by weather. Stunted ranks of wheat chaff brushed against my shins.

There was a newly tilled patch of ground behind the wheat field, most probably for potatoes. I moved into it. I had found what I sought, freshly turned soil moving between my toes. This is what I had needed.

"The true democrat," a philosopher had once said, "is the farmer who tills the soil."

I lay down with my back against a soft furrow and lay looking at the sun. It had been a long road leading me to this one, and the previous nights had been hectic and filled with excitement. I pulled out a many-folded piece of paper from the pocket of my denim jacket and looked at it. The words I would say, inspired by the writings of Abraham Lincoln, suddenly looked fresh and viable again. I knew I could say them, and believe them, after all. The other words I had thought of saying, which would unmask me as the fraud I was, must stay unsaid, at least for the moment. Too much was at stake for the confessions of one man to destroy it. The words on this paper would do.

I refolded the paper and put it back in my pocket.

I was suddenly tired, being here. I closed my eyes and slept.

There followed a foolish dream, a world of pink and blue petals where children danced and the sun was always warm and the rain was warm and new flowers bloomed each day. And, as I lay in a bed of petals and watched this world, a tingle washed over me, and a lovely, dark-skinned girl walked toward me through the petals smiling. She held out her hands, opened her mouth, and said a single word. The dream went on and then, finally, ended.

3

When I opened my eyes, I knew by marking the height of the sun that I had slept nearly too long. I rose, dusting myself, and marched back toward the road. In the near distance I saw the bus, like a sleeping beast, at the side of the road.

At the edge of the potato field I tripped over something and fell.

I picked myself up and looked briefly for the rock that must have caught my foot.

There was no rock, but rather, sticking up from the soil, the skeletal remains of a human hand, fingers splayed. The bones were bleached very white, but seemed covered with a ghostly mist of human form—

The fingers of the hand moved, jerking back and forth.

"You must come with me," a voice behind me said.

I am not in the habit of being startled, but this time I jumped back, into a defensive stance, turning as I did so.

It was the bus driver, who had made his way to me

through the field. "Please come," he said, looking at the skeletal hand fearfully.

"I'm not dreaming?" I said, dazed. "What I'm seeing is real?"

"Yes. Please."

I followed him through the ranks of low wheat, looking back at the spot where the human hand had been. Now there was not only a hand but a skeletal arm pushed up out of the soil.

"Wait," I said, taking hold of the driver's arm.

He crossed himself, turned back toward the bus, begging me to come with him.

"It's happening all over," he said. "We must go."

I stood my ground. It occurred to me that I *must* be dreaming, my other infantile dream balanced with this dream of strangeness. The day was still warm and pleasant, there were no blue and pink petals underfoot but pleasant wheat chaff nevertheless.

"This is not real," I said.

"It is," the driver said. He stopped, and looked as if he had lost his moorings. "At the last stop on my route there were two skeletons waiting next to the road. They attacked my passenger, an old woman named Mrs. Borogrov, as she left the bus. They used their jaws like weapons, biting into her. She mewled like a cat. I closed the door on one of them as he tried to enter the bus, catching the bone arm. I beat at it until he retreated, pulling the arm out of the door. The other passenger, an even older woman, tried to escape through the back door of the bus and they pulled her out and threw her to the ground. Mrs. Borogrov was not moving by then. I saw blood covering her face. There is an old cemetery thirty meters off the road in that spot, and I saw other skeletons climbing the low fence, coming toward the bus. They had my other passenger on the ground by then and were hitting her with anything nearby. One of them lifted a stone and brought it down on her head—"

I took him by the arm and shook him, realizing that he was in shock.

"You must come with me," he said. He stumbled back toward the bus.

I looked back at the field, seeing a nearly complete

human skeleton pulling itself from the ground. There was something nearly invisible, a more human shape, surrounding it, like a vague shroud, but the impression mainly was of a collection of human bones in human configuration yanking themselves to a standing position.

The form looked at me with its skull, opened its jaw soundlessly, and began to stride toward me, cakes of soil dropping from its joints.

I moved back toward the bus, finding the driver already sitting in his seat, waiting for me. His eyes were glued to the skeleton approaching us.

"In," he said, his hand on the door handle, waiting to close it.

I jumped onto the bus, and the driver immediately pulled the door closed. The engine coughed once, then roared into grumbling life. The driver threw it into gear.

I moved into one of the front seats and looked out the dusty window. The skeleton had begun to run toward us, and reached the road as we pulled out, standing in the plume of dust the rear wheels kicked up. In rage it bent, searched the ground, and found a large stone, which it hurled at us, hitting the rear window.

"Mother of God," the driver said, his eyes alternating between the road and the rearview mirror. "Mother of God."

"I must be dreaming," I found myself saying, out loud.

"The whole world is dreaming," the driver said. "The whole world, finally, is mad."

"Was there anything before this happened?" I asked. "Did anything happen before this started?"

"There was a kind of pleasant feeling, like something washed over me, just before," the driver said.

"I felt that, too," I said, remembering the tingle that had washed over me in my dream.

Behind us the skeleton had begun to walk calmly in our direction, in the center of the road.

*   *   *

4

For fifteen minutes, the madness retreated. We saw nothing but countryside, far houses dotting the low hills, a summer day. I thought perhaps I had been dreaming after all, had somehow boarded the bus back to Moscow and fallen asleep, to awaken now at this normal time. Only the driver's nervousness, his darting glances to either side of the road in watchfulness, peering even into the other cars on the road, made me think otherwise.

"You must do something," he said abruptly.

"What do you mean?"

"You must do something to stop this. I'm sure you can do it, you were able to get them to have that meeting in Moscow, to bring all those great men and women from around the world. You can make all this stop."

"Perhaps it was only something that happened outside of Moscow. Perhaps your government can take care of it."

"The government," he spat. "But I hope you are right."

Almost immediately he said, "Mother of God." We were at the outskirts of Moscow. A huge crowd had appeared ahead of us, off to one side of the highway, and as we approached we saw that what had appeared to be a mass of white shirts was in fact a crowd of skeleton figures.

"The National Cemetery," the driver said, in awe.

There, to the left, at the perimeter of the city, the sprawling National Cemetery seemed alive. I have visited others like it, such as Arlington National Cemetery in the United States, but this is on a vaster scale. There were many heroes of the Soviet revolution, many dead bodies to bury, and many of them were interred here.

And now it was alive, acre upon rolling acre, with white stick figures, moving en masse toward the center of Moscow.

Ahead of us a car screeched to a halt, the driver climbing out to stare at the spectacle in wonder. The bus driver cursed, sought to veer around him, caught the rear fender of the car with the bus and pushed it into the man, who went down.

"You must stop to help him," I said.

"Look."

The driver had slowed, but now we saw, breaching the embankment on the side of the highway, five skeletons. They stood and approached the man, who rose, holding his leg. One of the skeletons held a garden hoe aloft, and brought it down on the man again and again.

The other skeletons turned their attention to us.

"Shit," the bus driver said. He pushed the accelerator. But we only moved the car in front of us farther.

"The fenders are locked."

The driver put the bus into reverse. But already there was a line of cars. He hit the front one. There was a muffled shout. The bus driver nevertheless continued to try to back up. I heard more crashes and moved down the aisle of the bus to the broken back window to see cars sprawled all over the road, turning the highway into a parking lot. As far as the eye could see, skeletons were climbing up the embankment. Many bore crude weapons. Close by I saw a skeleton jab a long length of wood into the open window of a car, bending to see where he poked. There were muffled screams around us.

"We're getting out!" the bus driver shouted. He threw the bus into forward and veered hard to the right. We nearly tipped over the embankment. But the driver pulled the bus hard to the left and kept us on the highway. Cars in the opposite direction had now come to a halt. In front of us a few cars still moved into the city, but the roadway was becoming covered with a flow of white skeletons.

One of them tried to block the bus by jumping straight in front of it. The driver picked up speed and hit the skeleton. It went down. Peering through my window, I tried to see what became of it, but it was lost in a mass of moving white behind us.

As the cemetery drew away behind us, the number of skeletons thinned, and soon we were free of them.

"Perhaps Moscow is safe," the driver said. It sounded like a prayer.

5

We drove on until, a few blocks from Red Square, we could go no farther. And now, suddenly, the Red Army appeared, a phalanx of olive-green uniforms with red markings pushing all traffic off the road. The bus driver pulled over as a line of trucks passed, heading toward the outskirts of Moscow.

"This is the end of the line," the driver said apologetically.

"That's all right."

The driver opened the door, and I saw the fear on his face as I passed him.

"Are you going to stay?" I asked.

The battle going on in him was evident on his face. He reached out to take my shoulder, stood out of his seat. "I promised to deliver you, and I will," he said. "You'll be able to stop this madness."

I said nothing.

As we left the bus there was more noise than I could have imagined. Off in the distance I heard the crack of a rifle shot, then what sounded like a mortar. A plume of thin smoke rose from the east. Around us was chaos, soldiers trying to direct a swarm of aimless people. There was no panic, but rather a kind of pushing uncertainty. "What is it?" one man said next to me, to a woman who accompanied him. "What could it be? Is it the Americans? Is there war?"

"It's the Chinese!" another man said, with certainty in his voice. "The bastards have finally attacked."

"I'll bet it's the Germans," a woman close by said. "I always knew Germany would fight again."

"Why don't they tell us something?" the first man, the one with the woman, said. "Why do they always keep us in the dark?"

During all of this conversation the bus driver and I were trying to make our way through the crowd toward Red Square. The general movement seemed neither toward nor away from the square, but rather a kind of gelatinous stasis.

"Come with me," the driver said as another explosion, closer, definitely a mortar, went off, sending our

close companions into another round of frantic speculation. "It's definitely the Americans—only they have the
technology to sneak up on us like this!"

"No, they wouldn't, it's got to be the Germans!"

The driver pulled me through our immediate knot
of people and soon we had crossed the street. "We'll go
through GUM," the driver said. And, indeed, we now
managed to stand in front of the huge department store,
mere feet from the front entrance.

Pushing and jostling, we managed to make it to the
revolving doors. But they would not move. There were
people in them trying to make it to the outside, but the
weight of those already on the street in front kept them
from leaving the store.

"Go back, dammit! Don't you see who I have with
me?" the driver yelled. With a fierceness I had not yet
seen, using both shouts and gestures, he managed to
empty the doors so that we could push through.

"You first," he said, occupying the door behind me
and keeping constant pressure until we were through.

The crowd had, indeed, recognized me, and made a
respectful path. The driver took my arm and brought
me on, until one young woman stopped me and said,
"What is going on? Do you know?"

I started to tell her about the skeletons, then said,
merely, "No, I don't know."

There was fear in her eyes, but she said, "The army
will handle it. They always do."

Those around her seemed to concur.

The driver rushed me through the store. What might
otherwise have been a pleasant shopping trip was turned
into a surrealistic, fast-motion tour—a blur of strangely
out-of-place consumer goods tastefully arranged on polished tables, a waxed floor clacking under our feet. Sales-
persons stood nervously at their counters, suddenly
without anything to do. Small groups of them talked in
whispers. Outside, two mortars went off, and suddenly the
whispers became louder.

"Closer, definitely closer," someone said.

Another, duller explosion.

"Ah, the army is driving them from the city!"

"Driving *who*?" one clerk said, grinning nervously.

"Whoever it is!" his friend answered.

We moved through the entire store, approached the next block. There was chaos outside these doors, too, but not as great. The general movement here was away from the sounds of gunfire, toward Red Square. We pushed our way through the doors and out into the crowd.

"Stay with me," the driver said. "I know all the back ways."

He did. It might have taken us hours to get to Red Square through the slow-moving throng, but after five minutes of working through the crowd, we had crossed the street and entered another building. This one was deserted. We passed a long bank of open elevators and reached a guard in a small booth. He was listening attentively to a radio, ear cocked, and ignored us.

"What do they say?" the bus driver said, stopping.

The guard continued to ignore us. He was old, perhaps a pensioner with connections, and there was a look of sullen, concentrated fright on his features.

"What—" the bus driver repeated, reaching out to the uniformed old man, but the guard abruptly turned the radio off.

"It's bullshit," he said. "All bullshit." He tried to look blissful, but the hard look of fear stayed in his eyes.

"What did the radio say!" the bus driver yelled, now taking the old man by his lapels.

"They say what they always say," the guard said. "Stay calm, go to your homes, the situation is under control." His face collapsed, the false look of bliss gone. "Oh *God*, the last time they said that, the Germans, the tanks, my Vanya taken away . . ." He put his face down into his hands and began to weep.

"Come on," the bus driver said, pushing me on.

We passed out of the building onto the next block, which was nearly empty. "One more over," the driver said. Through another building, this time not a soul to be seen, but a vague rumbling sound intensified as we approached the far door.

"This will take us onto the square through the wall, past Lenin's tomb," the driver explained.

"Tell me your name," I said.

He looked around at me, startled.

"What is your name?" I repeated.

Suddenly he was bashful. Almost comically, he stopped and bowed. "I am Victor Volokovsky, at your service," he said.

"Thank you, Victor," I said.

If anything, his bashfulness intensified. "You're welcome." He stood with his hands in front of him. "It is a pleasure to serve you. You are a great man."

I smiled and reached out to squeeze his shoulder. "I doubt it," I said. "But I appreciate what you've done for me."

"It is what *you've* done—" he began, but a loud explosion nearby startled him from his gratitude and he took my arm and said, "We keep moving."

The low rumbling was the murmur of the huge crowd in Red Square. I caught a glimpse of it as we entered through the Kremlin wall, passing the huge mausoleum there that held the remains of Lenin. As we passed I told Victor to stop.

"Shouldn't there be some sort of guard there, in front of the tomb?"

His eyes widened. "Always. There is a contingent of color guards. They march constantly. And the door is always locked."

The door was not locked now, but stood wide open. As I approached it Victor held back.

"Perhaps we shouldn't," he said.

"Come with me."

Reluctantly, he joined me. We went in.

The hairs on the back of my neck stood up. The tomb was empty. The long glass case holding Lenin's body was open, the heavy glass cover pushed aside. There was broken glass on the floor.

"Mother of God!" Victor said, backing out.

I followed him. Soon we had made our way out into the square.

The crowd from the morning was still there, but not by choice. They seemed trapped by the larger crowd outside seeking to enter the square. I saw little evidence of the army. A few hatless soldiers tried to push their way through, but were pinned in place.

The huge stage set up under the Kremlin balcony

was empty. I was about fifty yards away, with little hope of reaching it. Studying the front of the stage, I found the figure of Jon Roberts by his headband. He was trying to keep order in front of him. He seemed to be struggling with a microphone that wouldn't work.

Part of the crowd had found its way toward us, pressing from behind, and we were slowly being pushed forward.

"I have to get to that stage," I said to Victor.

He looked pensive. Then his face brightened. "I have one more trick."

Shoving our way, he led me back to Lenin's tomb. We entered and went past the empty casket to the back wall. Victor stopped, began to talk to himself, closing his eyes.

"Where, where," he said.

"What are you looking for?" I asked.

"There was a television special," he said. "A tour. They showed some of the secrets of the Kremlin. There is a set of tunnels underneath Red Square. One of the entrances is here, in the tomb. I remember it clearly. And I believe there is an exit somewhere near your stage—ah!"

He moved to the right, his hand falling on the handle of a barely visible door. He twisted the handle up and down, to no effect.

"I was stupid enough to think the door would be open," he said dolefully.

"Thank you for trying," I said. "I'll just have to fight my way through the crowd."

"I'll fight with you!" Victor said. He walked to the foot of Lenin's open casket, chose a large sliver of heavy glass, pulled off his jacket, and wrapped it around the lower part. "If I have to, even though you wouldn't approve, I'll cut my way through—*Mother of God* . . ."

His eyes went wide, staring into the casket. Gingerly, he reached down, pushed the satin lining aside, widening a hole.

"Quickly, help me!"

Between the two of us we soon lifted the bottom out of the casket, exposing a gaping hole. Cold air washed up and over us.

"It must lead to the tunnels!" Victor said. A hint of smile crossed his face. "Those sly communist bastards even left Lenin an out after he was dead!"

He climbed up over the rim of the casket, lowered himself gingerly down into the hole, feeling around.

"There's even a handrail," he said. Soon he had climbed down to the point where his head disappeared. "It's all right!" he called up. "Come down—there's even enough light to see by!"

I climbed down after him.

I found myself on a solid, dry floor. For a moment I saw nothing. Then my eyes adjusted, and I saw Victor in front of me, peering ahead. There was dim, shifting light ahead. As we approached it the muffled sounds of the huge crowd outside began to filter down to us.

"Must be a grate above," Victor said, and sure enough we soon stood below a grate set high above us. It was nearly covered by shifting forms and let only a little light in.

"It must be quite easy to see, without a crowd above," Victor said.

More dull, faraway booms sounded in the distance, and the crowd above reacted by shifting first one way, then the other.

Victor moved ahead, into the tunnel.

I followed.

We walked perhaps thirty yards before reaching another grate. This one, too, was covered with shifting forms. The mortar sounds from above were more regular now, though still distant.

"I imagine the army is making some sort of stand at the entrance to Moscow," Victor said. For a moment I remembered the maggotlike horde of skeleton figures we had seen streaming from the National Cemetery toward the city.

"This is not what I had in mind for today," I said.

"No, it's not, is it?"

We moved on.

The next grate had a ladder built into the wall leading to the surface. But it, too, was hopelessly jammed with bodies. I estimated we were getting close to the stage. The next, as I had secretly hoped, was under the stage itself—but had no ladder.

"Let me boost you up," Victor said, and he stood rigid, feet splayed, hands against the wall, as I climbed onto his back and then stood upon his shoulders.

"I can't reach it," I said, my straining fingers just failing to touch the bottom of the grate.

"Does it look like it can be pushed up?" Victor asked.

"I don't see anything holding it down."

"Good. Come down for a moment."

I lowered myself from Victor's shoulders and followed while he marched back to the last grate, the one with the ladder. The mortar firings were constant now, but still far away.

Victor climbed the ladder and began to poke up through the grate at the feet of those standing on it.

"You there! You!" he shouted.

Someone above yelled, "They're down below! They're coming at us from below!"

There was shouting, and a general movement away from the grate. Victor tried to push the grate up, but more bodies were jostled into standing on it. Then, someone carrying a cane fell across it and he was unable to get it up.

"Help me! Help me!" someone cried above as Victor grabbed at a piece of clothing.

"Listen to me!" Victor shouted.

Above, a face turned to stare down at him. "Oh, God, please no!"

"I'm not going to hurt you!"

"Let me go!" the figure above pleaded. "They're stepping on me, kicking me—owww!"

"*Listen to me!*" Victor shouted, putting his face up to the grate. "You must help me—do you know who I have down here?"

"I don't want to know—stop it! Stop it!" the figure above turned away to shout at someone on top of him, waved up feebly with his cane.

"Look at who I have down here!" Victor shouted.

The head turned back, the eyes looked down at me.

"This is Peter Sun," Victor said with authority. "He's

the only man who can get us out of this mess. Do you understand?"

"My God! My God!" the figure above said. The eyes stared down at me. "It's true! Help him! We must help him—*get off of me!*"

The figure above struggled up, stood for a moment, then squatted down to look back at me.

"Mr. Sun, we'll help you!"

The figure stood back up, began to shout, "Get away from the grate! Mr. Sun is down there! Let him up—get away from the grate!"

The shouting was interrupted by the first nearby explosion. The man above was silent for a moment, then put his face back down to the grate.

"A bomb has fallen in the square! There are people hurt!"

"Please get me out of here," I said.

"Yes! Get away! Get away!" The cane was waved around, but there seemed to be just as many bodies on the grate as ever.

The man with the cane bent quickly down. "I'm sorry—I can't make them move—ohhh!"

Another blast sounded nearby.

"Give me your cane!" Victor shouted up at the man.

"Another bomb, nearby! People are screaming!"

"Your cane—give it to me!"

"Oh, God help us!" the man said, trying to move away with the crowd. His cane momentarily slipped into the grate and Victor grabbed it.

"What are you doing!" the man above shouted. "Give it to me!" He tried to yank the cane up through the grate. "Give it to me!"

"I need it to get Mr. Sun out of here!" Victor shouted. "I can help Mr. Sun with it!"

"What? Oh, yes. Oh, God . . ." the man said, suddenly letting go of his cane before being pushed away from the grate by the crush above.

Victor pulled at the cane, getting it halfway down before it was caught by kicking, falling bodies above. Another face stared down at us, pressed against the grate, shouting painfully, "Help me!"

Victor tried to work the cane free, then suddenly broke it in half.

"It will have to do," he said.

I stood looking at the face crushed against the grate above.

"Help me, help me. . . ."

"There's nothing we can do," Victor said, drawing me away.

Reluctantly, I turned and followed him to the grate under the stage.

"Now up on my shoulders again, and push it open with this," he said, putting the broken cane in my hand. "It should be long enough."

I mounted his shoulders again and pushed at the grate, which immediately rose up. It slipped once, but the second time I was able to work it to the side, snugging the end of the cane into the middle of the grating and making an opening.

"Now's the hard part; I'll have to boost you to get you through," Victor said.

"What about you?" I asked.

He was silent for a moment. "I'll have to go back to the tomb. I'll watch you work your magic from the crowd."

I reached down to take his hand. "You're a good man, Victor Volokovsky. But I have to warn you, I don't think there's anything I can do."

"You will try."

"I'll try, yes, but—"

He smiled, squeezing my hand firmly then letting it go. "I know," he said. "But I'm proud you took my bus."

"I'm proud to know you, Victor."

"Go," he said.

He boosted me up off his shoulders, holding my legs up with his strong hands while I grasped and then held the top of the grating hole. I pulled myself out. When I looked down, he had already gone. I heard his retreating footsteps down the tunnel.

I was indeed under the stage; and there, unbelievably, was Jon Roberts when I emerged, pacing in front of a shrinking cordon of soldiers, the still-clear stage behind him.

"My God, I don't believe it!" he said, hugging me. "Where—"

"There's no time," I said. "Are any of the guest speakers still here?"

"Gone," he said. "They fled when the first shooting started. They were sure the Soviets had decided to turn this into another Tienanmen Square. I still don't know what the hell's going on. But I decided to stick it out. There's all kinds of rumors, but the army guys look as scared as anybody." He laughed. "Some jerk even said the place was surrounded by *zombies*."

Before I could answer, he went on. "Look," he said, taking hold of my arm and steering me toward the steps leading up to the stage, "I think I've got the main mike working now. You're the only one who can calm them down, Peter."

Another mortar round went off, landing on the far side of the square. Jon flinched, then looked hard into my face. "Do it," he said.

Never feeling more helpless, or more false in my thirty-five years, I walked slowly to the center of the stage, watching Jon until he had checked a group of cables, finding two he wanted and connecting them, and gave me a signal.

"Please," I said. Immediately there was some reaction from the crowd in front of me. Eyes turned to the stage. Miraculously, the shelling had stopped. The wave of attention spread, and now I felt that rush of purpose I had so often felt before crowds, a Svengali-like power, sweep through me and over them. Much of the screaming stopped, and I saw people bend to help their neighbors up.

"Please help those beside you," I said.

The injured were carried toward the back of the crowd. Miraculously, there was near silence.

"Today was to be a great day—" I began. But that was as far as I ever got, for up around us on the buildings and Kremlin wall surrounding Red Square I saw a horrible sight. A line of white skeletons, shoulder to shoulder, rose as one. Now the meaning of the cessation of shelling became evident.

The army had been defeated.

Jon ran to me across the stage. "Peter—" he said, then looked up. "My God, what is it? Is this some sort of joke?" He put his hand on my shoulder, and at that moment a shot rang out. I even saw the rifle from which it came, the puff of smoke from the barrel of a gun borne by a skeleton directly across the square.

I felt a splash against my face and was sure I was hit. But in an instant of recognition I realized that it was Jon's blood that had hit me. His eyes were wide with surprise even as he collapsed, the lower part of his face torn away. He said nothing and dropped, falling from the stage.

I had seen death before, had seen it worse than this. But now I was paralyzed. The crowd had yet to react, and I knew I must say something to them, stand here even if it meant my life. But even as the words froze in my throat there was a sound from behind and above me. I, along with all the others in the square, turned my attention to the balcony of the Kremlin, from where so many Soviet leaders had reviewed their troops and spoken to their people. A loud, booming voice, a Russian voice, now came from there, commanding attention.

"Silence!"

An instant thought went through me: that this was, after all, a trick of the Soviet establishment; that all of these skeletons rising from their graves were tricks of technology, weapons to defeat the democratization we all, Jon and I and all the others who professed so highly to believe in it, thought was inevitable here and all throughout the world. Perhaps the totalitarian regimes had their own plans. Power does not pass easily, the saying goes; though it resides in the heart, its manifestations can be in the softness of blankets and pillows or in the hardness of steel. Was this, then, a trick, a weapon?

I looked up, and waited.

The balcony seemed to be empty. Around it the tops of buildings in Red Square were thick with rows of skeletons, bearing weapons. I saw a battery setting up a mortar in one spot, and other large guns being readied. In my heart I began to be sick, and knew the words I would say now when the time came.

"Silence!" came the commanding Russian voice again.

And then, at the edge of the balcony, leaning out over the crowd stiffly, appeared a ghost from history.

It was Lenin himself. On quick examination he was a skeleton like all the others, but the more one looked, the more that faint shroud I had noticed on the bony figure in the potato field became defined and visible. Like a ghostly etching on the air around the skeletal figure, the features of Lenin appeared: the sharp beard, the piercing stare, the hard face and clenched fist. It was a skeleton holding Lenin's body opaque as air around it.

"Listen to me, bourgeoisie!" he shouted. His voice rang out around the square with booming authority from every loudspeaker. The huge crowd was electrified by fear and shock.

The skeleton raised its clenched fist and leaned out farther over them. "A new struggle has begun! Let there be no mistake! The proletariat will triumph, the worker will triumph, the masses will triumph! The comfortable bourgeoisie will be trampled into the ground. All workers will share in the blessings! The worker *is* the state—the state *is* the worker! A new day has dawned in the world order—*let there be no mistake!*"

The skeletal fist came down hard on the balcony. Lenin turned away briefly. He motioned behind him, then turned back to face us. When he spoke again, the voice was lower, but just as hard.

"This is the price of the old—*the bill has come due!*"

Four human bodies appeared on the edge of the balcony, thrashing. As they were thrown over, and as the ropes attached to their necks brought them up short, kicking as they hung, I recognized them as the top Soviet leadership—among them the head of the KGB, the foreign minister, the head of the army in his uniform, and the premier, who was to speak before me today. Though I had seen its like before, it was a sickening display, four bodies kicking their life away yards below the very spot where they had held such high sway for so long.

Lenin leaned down to look at them until the bodies were still. Then his hard fist went up again.

"This, then, is the price of defiance!" The white skull's jaw split into a monstrous grin, mirrored faintly on the shroud of Lenin's ghostly features. He held up his hands to the skeletons surrounding the square.

"Destroy them all! Let them join the masses!"

Gunfire erupted. I ignored the bullets hitting the stage around me, took the microphone, and shouted, "Please! Watch your neighbor! If you watch your neighbor, you will stay calm!"

Only the word "Please" got out before the microphone went dead, and I saw a skeleton holding the severed halves of the mike's cable as another aimed a rifle at my head. I was sure the shroud surrounding the skeleton who had broken the cable held Jon Roberts's features.

I dropped to my knees as the shot sounded. Now, out in the crowd were many skeletons who had moved in from the streets. Mortar rounds went off in all directions. The air was filled with smoke and screaming.

I crawled from the stage and dropped to the square. A woman lay at my feet, a bullet hole neatly over her left eye. As I stared at her the skin and features of her face began to fall away to dust, revealing the white skull beneath. All of her body melted away; I saw her ankles above her shoes become white bones. Faintly, her former features came into ghostly view around the bones, and I saw the shadow of her real eyes blink open as the polished skull turned its eye sockets on me and the jaw clacked open.

"Kill him!" she shouted, reaching her bony hands up at my throat. "Kill him!"

I jerked away as she rose. Her clothing clung to the just-glimpsed ghost of her body. In direct light, though, even this close, it looked like a movie skeleton was wearing those clothes.

"Kill him!" she screamed, leaping at me. I felt the pressing tingle of her ghostly hand, then the rub of a bony finger on my neck. I pushed back into the crowd, turned, and ran away from her. Almost immediately I ran into another skeleton, who swung a rifle butt at my head. I jerked away from it and found myself back near the stage.

"All of them!" Lenin shouted. I looked up through a clearing in mortar smoke and saw the communist leader turn away. Below the balcony the four dead human bodies had turned to writhing skeletons. As I watched, the former premier grabbed the rope with his bony hands and pulled the noose from his neck. He began to climb the rope up to the balcony, the other three behind him.

The smoke rolled in. Close by I heard the scream of a man. I reached into the smoke as an arm appeared and pulled the man toward me. It was the old man who had given Victor his cane. He seemed dazed, but unhurt.

"You . . ." he said.

"Yes," I said. "Come with me."

I ducked beneath the stage, pulling the old man after me. He was hobbled, but able to move. We went to our hands and knees. In front of me a haze of smoke blew aside, revealing a prone human body, a man in a brown suit and wearing glasses with a bayonet thrust into his neck, beginning to decompose to skeleton.

"Hurry," I said.

We crawled past the body and found the open grate. I pulled the old man to the hole and lowered him down.

"It will be a few feet to jump, so be careful."

I let him go, and heard him hit with an ooof.

Quickly, I followed.

"My cane," he said, picking up the remnant of broken staff that still lay on the floor. "My uncle Mikhail gave me this cane," he said dreamily. "It was of the finest wood."

"We must go," I said.

"My uncle Mikhail—"

I took the cane from his hands. "If we don't go, we will die."

"Perhaps we should," the old man continued dreamily. "Did you know I was a schoolteacher before my pension? Twelve-year-old boys. I taught them history, about Lenin. None of us knew we would live to see Lenin, did we? Perhaps I am asleep. I wonder where my twelve-year-old boys are now." He looked at me pleadingly. "Don't you know how to stop this? Weren't you supposed to do away with Lenin and all of them, bring democracy to the world? What have you done! You've made it worse!" He grabbed at me angrily. "Give me my cane so I can beat you—look what you've done!"

He began to weep, turning away from me in the near dark, back toward the grate opening.

I took him by the shoulders gently and turned him around. "Come with me. It's possible we can escape."

"My boys. Those poor twelve-year-olds, seeing this." For a moment his eyes cleared and he seemed to find reason. "You're right," he said. "We must try to survive."

"Good."

I walked on, at a slower pace than I wished in deference to the old man, who limped behind me. He would not let me help him. I paused at the laddered grate and looked up. A body lay across it, writhing, nearly covering it. Though the screams and explosions were muffled down here, it was not hard to realize that a great battle was taking place above.

I walked on.

When I came to the next grate, I looked back, but the old man was nowhere to be seen. I called out, and heard a muffled gasp somewhere behind me.

I ran back and saw the old man just falling to the ground at the hands of a skeleton, the brown-suited figure I had seen earlier. He had shaken off most of his real clothes, but a torn arm of a shirt still clung around one skeletal arm, and almost comically, his black glasses still clung to the faintness of his features around his skull. He had thrust the bayonet from his own neck into the old man's chest, and now pulled it out as the old man collapsed lifeless to the floor.

"And now *you*," the brown-suited skeleton said to me, in an almost hearty voice.

He lunged at me, brandishing the bayonet. I pulled the old man's broken cane out and fended the blow off. The skeleton dropped the bayonet. As he bent to retrieve it I lay the cane across the back of his head. He went down, tried to rise, and I hit him again. This time he lay still.

The bones of which he was composed crumbled to fine dust, and the faint outline of his body dispersed. Only his glasses and the bit of torn sleeve remained.

"So, the dead can die," I whispered.

This was not the first man I had killed. I had hardened to it long ago. Only the faintest feelings of remorse filled me, despite my sober preachings of peace. I briefly thought of the bus driver, of Jon Roberts, the others who had looked at me for salvation. What if they had known of my other lives? What if they had known of the things I had been? Would they have paid such homage to me then?

I didn't know whether to laugh or feel shame.

"Must die . . ." a voice said close by as a hand slipped around my neck.

It was the old man who had owned the cane. He had come back to skeletal life. He was quite strong, and with momentary panic I saw the glint of the bayonet he had retrieved as he brought it around in front of me to cut my throat. Instantly, I threw my elbows back into his bony chest and threw him off balance.

He let go of my neck and I came around on him with his own cane, beating him to the ground. He threw his hands up in front of his face.

I hesitated in fear, seeing the outline of his features covering the horrible empty skull. But my hesitation lasted only a moment before I brought the cane down again and again until he was still and had turned to dust.

Hearing movement down near the open grate under the stage, I retrieved the bayonet, held the cane close to me, and ran the length of the tunnel until I reached the opening under Lenin's tomb.

I cautiously climbed out of the casket and entered the tomb. The building was empty. Outside, the sounds of battle raged.

I went to the vault door and looked out. Overhead I heard the scream of jet engines and saw three planes fly over in formation. There was a streak of fire and one of them was hit, the wing shearing off. As its mates roared on, the hit plane tumbled to the ground like a broken toy. I heard the thud of its explosion as it hit the ground. A black plume of smoke rose over the city.

I thought of the fields outside the city. I knew that the only possibility of survival was to reach a more unpopulated area. In a flash the question came to me that for the first time shook me to my core:

My God, was this happening all over the world?

My ruminations were interrupted by another pass by

the two remaining jets. This time they each dropped a load of bombs, before veering off away from the city. Another streak of fire chased one, but the possible hit was dwarfed by the much louder explosions of the plane's bombs going off, in a line from left to right in front of me, leading right into the middle of Red Square. The ground shook beneath me. I heard a crash as part of Lenin's tomb behind me gave way and collapsed upon itself.

Almost immediately, another squadron of planes appeared and executed the same maneuver. Two of them were hit as they disgorged their bomb load, and one of them screamed toward the earth so close by that I could look into the cockpit of the plane to see the writhing form of the pilot. It was a skeleton. Before the MIG slammed into the center of Red Square behind me, the pilot ejected, shot in a high arc before his parachute brought him to earth to a jerking halt, and settled him gracefully to earth. I saw his dangling skeletal legs as he disappeared behind the Kremlin.

There seemed nothing to do but get out of Moscow. It was clear that, at least locally, the Soviet army was beaten. But the Soviet Union was a huge country. Though the vision of the skeleton rising from the potato field intruded, I could not help but recall again the feel of soil between my toes, the smell of earth. . . .

I made my decision, and began to walk.

6

Keeping close to the buildings, I made my way east, toward the perimeter of the city. Once I dodged into a doorway when a caravan of army trucks drove by, four in number, the drivers all skeletons. In the open rear of the last truck was stacked a pile of human corpses, some of them on top melting to skeletal remains as I watched, clacking into new life.

I had gone perhaps a half mile when a car, a Soviet-made sedan, screeched out between two buildings in front of me and stopped. The passenger door was pushed open.

I drew back, pulling out my bayonet.

It was a young woman.

"You won't last five minutes on the street. Get in."

I got into the car and slammed the door.

"I know who you are," she said.

I sat looking through the windshield and said nothing.

"I watched you in the square, trying to calm the crowd. Not many men would have stayed on that stage."

"I failed."

She snorted. "In what? Don't you see what's going on? Nobody can stop this. The whole world is going to fall apart."

"Is it happening all over?" I asked.

"Everywhere." She pulled the car out hard into the road, turned it east, stepped hard on the gas pedal. "I know some side roads, there's a chance we can make it to the countryside."

For a moment she didn't speak, but drove. We passed through a succession of alleys, always heading vaguely east. Once I saw a glimpse of the main road, clogged with traffic, puffs of smoke rising here and there from burning vehicles.

"How do you know what's going on elsewhere?" I asked.

"The radio. There was news from Britain, from Spain, from America. The television was working for a while, but then it just started to play martial music. You know the way they do. Then a test pattern came on. Then nothing. The radio was still working when I left, but not much was changed. If we could find a shortwave, there would be more, I'll bet. We had a shortwave, but it broke. We couldn't get parts."

She made a deft turn as another convoy came past. The head truck slowed, the skeletal driver glancing at our car, but then drove on.

"It's the tinted windows," my companion said, smiling. "I'm glad my father got them. He really had no choice, there's no such thing as options in Russia. You take what they have."

"This is your car?"

"My father's. He's dead now, so I suppose it's mine."

"I'm sorry."

"About what?" she said.

"About your father."

She laughed, a strained sound. "He was alive this morning. This is the way the world is now, isn't it? He went to visit my mother's grave. Once a week he went. He was there when it happened. My mother killed him when she rose. The two of them were in our apartment waiting to kill me when I escaped from Red Square. We were very lucky to have our own apartment, not have to share it with five or six others. My father was a big government man."

I realized now how hysterical she was. She was trying very hard to hold it in, to be hard, but her hands began to shake on the steering wheel.

"I really am sorry. . . ."

She turned her face to me. There were tears brimming in her eyes. "Why? I killed them, of course. I hit them both with a broom, and then a shovel, until their bones fell apart. They were talking to me all the while, telling me that soon I would be with them again, when Father killed me with the ax he kept in the closet. That was the ax my grandfather used in Stalingrad, in 1942, to hit dogs with, so they could eat them. The Germans almost had them starved out, but they ate anything they could get their hands on to survive. My father must have told me that story a hundred times."

She turned back to the road, taking a turn out of an alley much too hard before straightening the sedan.

"You did the right thing," I said quietly.

"Did I? Did *you* ever kill your relatives?"

I was silent, not telling her that at one time I had.

"Did you ever see what little there was of your life die in front of you?"

Again I was silent.

Suddenly she laughed harshly. "I thought of something funny. If Lenin is alive again, then surely Stalin is, too. And the czars. Won't that make a fine mix? I wonder how they'll handle things. And Peter the Great, too, and Catherine. The two Greats. What a mix, right? Think about it, my grandparents are alive again, too—Stalin had them killed in one of his last purges—"

She broke down, weeping. The car veered dangerously.

She jerked the wheel hard to the right, sending the car into the wall of a building. We hit hard. I braced myself, head down, my shoulder hitting the dashboard. When we had stopped, I looked across to see that the young woman had been thrown forward over the steering wheel, her head hitting the windshield, breaking the glass. There was a run of blood down the front of the windshield, pooling over the hood.

I felt for her pulse, which was weak.

"Coming, Father . . ." she whispered.

Her pulse stopped.

I had to push hard to get the passenger door to open at all. The girl's body had begun to stir, her flesh falling away to nothingness. The skull head swiveled around to grin at me.

I pushed at the door with my knee, managing to get it open a crack. I felt the girl's hand on my shoulder.

The door would not move. And now I smelled gasoline.

I tried to roll down the window and it went halfway, then stopped.

The girl reached across with both hands and was tearing at my shoulders, trying to get at my face. When I turned briefly, her head was inches from my own. Her lower body was still pinned by the wreckage, but she was squirming, trying to get free, trying, at the same time, to bite me.

I used my arm to batter at the glass in the stuck window, and finally it shattered, sending pieces everywhere. I pushed my head out and pulled my body free. The smell of gasoline was intense.

The young woman screamed after me. She caught at my legs and for a moment held them in a hard clasp until I kicked back and knocked myself free. I dived out of the car, fell to the pavement, and got up, stumbling away as the car caught fire and then exploded.

The young woman shrieked, then suddenly pulled herself through the window. She was burning like a wax candle. I was reminded of the self-immolation of Buddhist monks. She lay on the ground, then picked herself up and staggered toward me. After a few steps she stumbled, fell, and burned on the ground, shrieking. Abruptly, her bones fell into a pile of dust and the fire was snuffed, even as I heard her final scream fade.

I turned and lurched away as a military jeep roared around a far corner and sped toward the wreckage of the car.

I hid in an alley while a skeleton got out, examined the wreckage, then climbed back in, drove slowly past me, and was gone.

7

An hour later I was near the edge of Moscow. The National Cemetery lay two miles to the north. I emerged from the shelter of tall buildings and walked through a neighborhood of houses and low apartments. I kept to the shadows. From nearly every dwelling came screams and shouts; figures, mostly skeletal, peered from windows and open doorways.

And now night was falling.

How long had this been going on, then? I had seen the first skeleton drag itself from the earth this morning. Here it was early evening. A mere matter of hours, and already so much destruction had occurred. I welcomed the lengthening shadows as friends and continued east.

As a nearly full moon rose three hours later I found myself in the beginnings of farmland. Moscow, to the west, was lit with fires from horizon to horizon. Occasional explosions, dulled by distance, sounded. Other villages and towns to the north and south were lit by smaller fires, accompanied by smaller sounds. An occasional jet roared high overhead, and all at once a fleet of fifty or more planes sped east, high above me. Their vapor trails made silver etch lines to the luminous moon.

True darkness came. At last I found my hiding spot. An untilled field was bordered by a deep ditch. A shallow stream ran by it, which proved to be brackish. A hedge of early blueberries grew nearby, which only made me realize how hungry I was.

I gathered as many as I could and crawled down into my hiding place, a ledge of hard dirt above me.

A dog sounded nearby: a growl followed by a mournful whimper. I felt suddenly lonely, and more than willing for the companionship of a dog.

"Here, boy," I said gently, raising myself from my hiding place.

It stood not five paces from me—the skeleton of a dog, starkly outlined in silver moonlight.

The skeletal beast howled and leaped at me.

I held my arm up, batted it aside, and quickly drew my bayonet and hacked into it.

The ghost dog huffed once and evaporated to dust.

Checking the area around me carefully, I once again settled myself into my hiding place.

So even the company of a dog would be denied me. Fine.

I would deal with this as I had dealt with everything in life. I would eat what was on my plate.

In spite of my fear, I laughed, thinking of Peter Sun, this latest and perhaps best mask I had worn. I had worn many masks. Who would I be now, in this newest of worlds? Philosopher? Assassin? Jester?

For a moment I let my life wash over me—there was pain, and some joy, and much shame. I thought of my childhood in Cambodia in the 1970s, my time in Thailand, my years in America, at Yale University. I thought of where I was now.

Who will you be next?

Whoever it was, I would be alive.

I wrapped myself in the night and, unafraid to live, slept.

3

From the Second Life of Abraham Lincoln

1

I ... awoke.

There was a memory fading behind my eyes. A theatrical play. Laughter. The loudest part I remember. And then something louder, the sound I heard all too many times around Washington, around the Union the past four years. A gunshot.

Into me, no doubt. Did I feel it? I felt something, like someone slapping me hard on the back, the way Joshua Speed, my old friend from Springfield, used to do. "Go at 'em, Abe!" he'd say. It made me sad to deny him a position in the administration, but even in politics, as my aunt used to say, things can't be too obvious. A man can't use lightning to chop a log, that'd be cheating.

So I'm awake. Now I remembered. The play, *Our American Cousin*. Ford's Theater. My God, is Mary all right? Poor Mary, she was always afraid of this kind of thing. Was she shot, too? There must have been more than one assassin, they did have those guards outside the box, didn't they?

Then ... the memory faded.

Where was I?

I was most definitely not in my box in Ford's Theater. No bunting here. Only a box in the dark, by the feel of it. My God, did they bury me alive? Was I shot, and pronounced dead, and buried, and me still with the world? What in God's teeth was wrong with these men! Maybe they let that George McClellan pronounce me dead, he'd take to that job quick enough.

At least I could breathe. And move, a bit. My, but I felt stiff and sore. And the back of my head ached. I should have been panicking now, but somehow I could only think of something comical, a picture of me in here all dead and buried with my headache, and poor Mary out there with one of her migraines because I'm gone.

I worried about Mary.

Well, it was time to test my waters. So I lifted my elbows up and tried to push on the door. These big elbows of mine got in their own way, and finally I had to put my arms out straight, next to my body, which felt as if it had been dressed in the damn wool suit, the expensive but itchy one, and then lay my palms up flat against the roof of my little house and push up.

Oddly, it felt like my hands were soft right down to the bone, and that the bones themselves were doing the pushing.

But darned if it didn't work! Up went the door on its hinges, at least a few inches. Must be in Springfield, I thought, because the dirt in Springfield is at least soft from all the rains. Or maybe they plunked me down in Washington, like I didn't want, where you could just about float a casket away in the swampy, mosquito-infested muck they called the nation's capital.

The nation . . .

My God, what was happening to the Union? Five days after Appomattox, what in hell would happen to Reconstruction with *Andy Johnson* at the helm? Not to be slapping myself on the back too hard, but *Andy Johnson?* My God, Andy was a good man, and a necessary man— but he was also a *sot*, to be plain, and a damned southern one to boot! And with his temper! The Congress would eat him for breakfast, and leave nothing for lunch!

My old bones creaking like they'd never creaked before, I pushed that casket door all the way open. It fell back easily, and no dirt, Illinois or otherwise, fell on me.

A burial vault.

And not too dark, thank God. A little light filtered in from a glass cut in the roof overhead. I stood up slowly and hit my head. The coffin was set into some sort of wooden receptacle. Felt nice and smooth, like mahogany or walnut. Lord, did those long bones of mine ache.

There were the dusty remains of flowers scattered about, which puzzled me. Hadn't I only been in here a few days at most? I picked a flower up, felt it turn instantly to dust. Well. Perhaps the drying actions of vaults.

It was best to take things as they came.

On trying to maneuver myself out of that receptacle, I found a silver plate on a shield attached to the coffin which read:

ABRAHAM LINCOLN
SIXTEENTH PRESIDENT OF THE UNITED STATES
BORN FEB. 12, 1809
DIED APRIL 15, 1865

I chuckled on reading that. Not so fast, I thought. Some fancy engraver might have to make himself a new plate to fix that last date! It was the kind of work I didn't mind him doing at all.

I got myself out of that receptacle, and finally stood tall and straight, listening to every bone in my body crack itself like a good set of knuckles.

Still feeling the stiffness work itself out of me, I surveyed my little stone house. They hadn't done bad for me. There were the dusty remains of evergreen branches on the floor of the vault. My, they'd gussied my afterlife house up like the floor of a Kentucky cabin. There was just enough light to study the two huge doors that held me in.

I didn't like the look of those doors, solid as two tree stumps. And the stump is the part you don't cut down.

I lifted my hand to scratch my beard, and got what I'd have to say is the shock of my short new life.

In the dim light I could see through my hand to the bones beneath.

I quickly pushed the sleeve of my fancy shirt up and studied my arm. Bones, surrounded by the merest hint of me. I found that if I turned my arms a certain way in the light, I became more visible, but never more than a trace. If I felt my arm, it felt solid enough to me, unless I squeezed hard, in which case I felt straight down to bone. By the looks of me I was little more than a walking skeleton.

Well.

I had to sit down and think about that one. The edge of the casket's receptacle was as good a place as any.

Thinking further, I turned, just able to study myself in the polished wood of the casket. The light was very dim, but what I saw unnerved me quite a bit.

I saw my own skull, with the shadow of a bullet hole in the back of it.

Again, turning my head in the light this way and that, I could make out bits of me. It was certainly me, all right, ugly as ever. What had they called me during the first presidential race? The Ape? Well, I'd never been much to look at. But this skeleton business made me considerably less attractive to look at, I had to admit.

I tried my smile, saw the barest hint of my own lips giving their melancholy grin, and mostly, behind it, the bone white of a smiling skull.

My, my.

Damned if this didn't give me the shakes. But I didn't let them last long. No sense in that. The only sense was in getting to the "nub" of the question. What was it Billy Herndon always said about me? He said I was given to thinking more than any man in America. Perhaps this was true. I just couldn't see the sense in keeping all the gloss and trappings on a question. Take all the gloss away, strip off the trappings, and you had the real idea to hold in your hand. Then you could study it plain and simple. None of that fanciness for me, thank you.

Well, that was the only thing to do now. Think it out.

The first and most logical thought was that the Bible thumpers were right, and that the Armageddon had come. Isn't that what they promised, that the dead would rise? Yes, but if so, they had also promised they would rise up to heaven. This vault didn't feel much like heaven to me. I had no doubt I'd find Springfield just outside those heavy doors. And while I'd liked Springfield well enough, it sure wasn't any heaven.

So what had happened? My second thought was a selfish one. Perhaps *I* had been raised from the dead. Old blasphemer that I was, I couldn't think in any more than joking terms that I'd somehow raised myself from the dead, or that someone had done it for me. I had as big a sense of self-importance as the next man—except for that fool McClellan, whose dose was considerably larger than any man's I'd ever met, including Stephen Douglas—but I couldn't believe one man, even me, was that important to the Union or anything else to be singled out for this honor.

Maybe science was involved? Maybe those fellows who had built us those iron warships, all those new guns, and come up with all those new ways of killing had come up with a way of doing the opposite?

I thought of five, then ten, then twenty possibilities. The plain fact was I didn't have enough facts to go on. I needed more, needed more true things to hold in my hands and study. I needed newspapers to read, and things to see with my own eyes before I could puzzle this one out.

So, sighing heavily, I stood, stretched those long bones of mine out, and prepared to do battle with the two stone doors of my little prison.

To my surprise there was no battle at all. When I put my hands on the doors, there was an inside latch and they opened easily, producing an opening of blinding sunlight.

Shielding my eyes, I stepped out into the world.

2

It was a cool, dark, moonlit night. Late spring, by the feel and smell of it. And though there were subtle differences from my remembrance, I knew this place. Oak Ridge Cemetery, sure enough in Springfield, in Illinois, in the United States of America.

For a moment I was overcome with being alive.

Whatever the circumstances, I surely *felt* alive. Almost too much so. I had an amount of energy I don't remember possessing at least since I was younger. Almost *too* alive. I nearly swooned and had to sit down.

I turned to look at my stone vault. It was really rather pretty in the moonlight, and well kept, two columns and a big-bricked front. I let my eyes play over the greening hillsides rolling away from my stone house. This was definitely Oak Ridge Cemetery, certainly Springfield.

My eyes finally sent their startling message to my brain: every grave around me, every vault and tomb, was opened to the sky.

I was not the only one come back to life.

3

I studied the hillside below me. I saw a flow of skeletal figures making their way to the iron-black gates of the cemetery. With all my thinking, I was apparently late in making my escape. Unblocking my view from the corner of my little vault, I now saw that there was a massive exodus of skeletons from this place, figures streaming from every direction to the exit.

Using my hill as a general's perch, I studied the four corners of Oak Ridge and saw the same thing: open graves, open tombs. The city of Springfield beyond looked changed, yet felt the same. Obviously it had been some time since I'd been interred. But how long . . . ?

I was startled by the appearance of a machine near the entrance to the cemetery, far below. A wagon, made of metal. In the back were shovels and a wooden casket, very plain. So the inventors had been at work after all. And no horse pulling it! Remarkable. But understandable. It moved along a thin road bordering the cemetery and seemed headed for the exit until it came in sight of the crowd of skeletons. Suddenly it stopped, and then began to go backward.

The skeletons on the edge of the mob saw it and pursued. Two of them hopped onto the front of the truck and pulled a door open, dragging a man out. The wagon stopped moving. Another man was pulled from

the other side. At this time I also noticed the coffin on
the back of the truck open, and a skeleton climb out,
frisky as a kitten.

The two men had been thrown to the ground, and
as I watched, the skeleton from the back of the truck
lifted a shovel and leaped from the truck. As his fellows
held one of the men down the skeleton beat him with
the shovel until he was still, then turned his attention to
the other man, whose cries I could hear from where I
stood.

My first reaction was to stop this mad violence and
force the skeletons to let the two men go. Wasn't this the
right action to take? I had never liked mob rule. But
something visceral held me back. It seemed *right*. Not
only that, but I felt a bloodlust arise in me that frightened me. Not only did these two men deserve to die,
they *had* to die, if possible. They were the *enemy*. Which
was a very strange way for me to feel. Not in all the years
of the great conflict which divided this Union did I want
to see a man die. In all the battles did not one death of
one Confederate soldier bring me joy; certainly, from not
one of my orders of refusal to stop the execution of a spy
or deserter did I ever feel satisfaction. But that was just
what I felt at this moment: immense satisfaction. Not only
that: I wanted to join in the melee—to kill the living myself.

These were repulsive feelings, but I felt them.

And now a remarkable thing happened below. As
the cries of the second man ceased I saw the first rise in
a new life. His flesh fell away, and he was now one with
his skeletal brothers. Soon his companion joined, too,
and the two of them remounted their wagon, urging others to get in the back, and the wagon made its way slowly
to the front gate. The skeletons there parted, cheering,
and others climbed on board as the metal wagon moved
through the gates, out of the cemetery, and toward
Springfield. Other skeletons, not content to wait their
turn to get through the gates, were climbing the
wrought-iron fence in various spots, like white bony insects.

Though part of me longed to follow, a greater part
told me to hold back. Josh Speed once said I had a quick

mind, but this, I countered, was not true; as I said many times, I am slow to learn and slow to forget. In this case there was much to learn, and I couldn't see rushing about it like those others down below. They sought only to get out of where they were. To me the question was, why?

There were those buried here in Oak Ridge whom I had known. I did not have to walk far to stand before the open grave of one I had known and dearly loved. Remembered grief overcame me in looking at the name on the little gravestone: WILLIAM WALLACE LINCOLN.

My little Willie, who had died of fever. I still remember the pony we kept in the White House stables, and which he loved to ride, the little codger. His death broke Mrs. Lincoln, and it almost broke me. Even the pony had died only months later, in a stable fire.

His hole was empty, the ground churned up where a little body might bore up and through. I found myself, lost in long-ago grief, fallen to the ground, digging through that dirt, saying, "Willie? Willie?" until I found his coffin, sure enough, open and empty.

I stood, shaking with a new emotion. Would I actually see him again? And Edward? And all the others I had known here and in Kentucky and Indiana and Washington? All the many ones, both dear and remembered in fondness, who had been taken away by time and the Greater Power?

This was a truly overwhelming idea.

I sat on the ground, momentarily overcome with the greater idea of it. *The dead risen.* What did this mean? Was it, indeed, the Judgment Day?

I stood myself up. This was foolishness, allowing myself to wallow in idle speculation like this.

Letting my hand fall on the cold corner of Willie's gravestone, I turned and walked down the hill, determined to find newspapers, to find books with facts.

I determined to learn just what the world had become.

4

From the decidedly unexemplary life of Roger Garbage

1

I mean, what the *shit* has been going on tonight? Have you ever seen anything like this? I just hope my friggin' batteries hold out. I mean, music's music, right? I mean, you never know. Here I am, minding my own business, listening to tapes at thirty thou feet like they used to pay me to do, the sons of bitches, and *bammo*, next thing you know I'm in the middle of a war. And if we're in the middle of a war, it might be hard to get batteries, right?

Are these batteries in correctly?

Oh, hey, what about the Vomits? I mean, I can always hope they're dead, can't I? Maybe the first friggin' bomb landed on their friggin' bus, and *boom*, there goes Roundabout Records' meal ticket. Carl Peters's first-class flights, the videos in his plane seat, the whole nine yards down the drain. One can hope, right? Heh, heh.

Hey, what the hell's this pilot doing? He's not gonna *land* in the middle of this shit, is he? What the—

Good. Just a little announcement on the loud-speaker. "We'll be circling for a little while longer, ladies and gentlemen." Right, until we run out of friggin' fuel. I wonder what the dumb bastards back in coach think of all this, the ground-to-air fire below us, the streaks of fire-works light and little puffs of popping smoke ten thou feet below. They figure out if we come down into that it's good-bye Roger and Co.?

The cows.

So I can only hope the friggin' Vomits are dead. 'Cause I know I am. The big flight home to get fired. And I hope Carl Peters, ol' Carly boy, went with them. Bammo, right into an abutment or something. Hey, I mean it would probably be a month before they cut off my ex-pense account, I could have some serious fun during that time, while all the funerals and shit are going on.

How long these batteries last?

No matter. Got a whole case full of 'em. Double-A's up the wazoo. Turn off the machine, I'm sick of listening to it anyway. I wish that bitch stewardess would come by, I need another vodka and lime to wash the tingle of that coke out of my sinuses.

No matter. Ring the little buzzer thingy . . .

Hey, miss? Another vodka and lime. And you got any more of those chips?

Bitch, she looked at me like I'd just kicked her off the toilet while she was changing her tampon. No matter. She'll have a special place in my heart, the bitch of the skies, Carol I think her name is, I'll find out who she is and have her fired. These big airlines don't want trouble in their first-class cabins, I've done it before. They'll just kiss her ass good-bye and she'll be selling Chanel No. 5 behind a counter by next Friday.

Oh, the power of the expense account and here she comes with that drink—

Uh-oh, there goes the plane. What the—oh, she spilled the drink on me! Shit! You know how much this suit cost, you bitch? That's Chilean leather! Don't you sit down, you get me a friggin' cloth or something!

Jeez, her face is kind of pale.

"Look out the window," she says.

Fine, I'll look out the window. So what, it's the

ground I see. Which means that friggin' pilot made one heck of a turn. We're not supposed to be over this far, are we? That's the lights of L.A. down there, all right, and look at all the fires. So what's the pro—

Oh, right, the wing. So the friggin' engine's on fire.

Another puff of smoke below, and the plane rocks and then straightens.

"This mean we'll be landing on time?" I say to the bitch, who has stood up and straightened herself out.

She stares at me and shakes her head, and walks away.

"Hey, how 'bout another drink!"

Shit, I'm enjoying this. Ol' Carly, I hope he's dead, damned if I'll give him the chance to fire me like he was going to. I guess I owe that cow Rita something for passing that along when I called in yesterday. Did she really expect me to make it with her tonight? Jeez, I just thought *being* with the cow was payment enough.

Give me the ax, huh, Carly boy? We'll see about that, *dude.*

Uh-oh—

2

Later, as they say. Seems we made another unscheduled dive. This one I kind of saw, the ground spinning outside my window like some friggin' Bugs Bunny cartoon. Lots of screaming from back in the cattle car. But ol' Cap'n Bob, whatever his name is, he pulled us through, got us straight again.

Hurray for Cap'n Bob!

Where's my drink?

The stewardess, what's her name, Carol, she comes by but not with my new drink. By now the old one's drying on my leather pants. Jeez, I can still smell vodka.

"Hey, where's my—"

But the bitch tells me to put my seat belt on and go down into crash position. She even says please. So I say, "Blow me," which gets not much of a reaction, and she reaches over to put the belt on me. At which time I push her hand away, saying, "Not a *hand* job, honey, a *blow* job," which makes her lose her cool and start yelling at me. At that moment the cabin door opens and Cap'n Bob himself comes out, and he's almost as pale as ol' Carol.

"What's the matter?" he says, in clipped Cap'n Bob tones.

Carol says, rather shrilly, "He won't put his damned belt on!"

"Put it on, and get down," Cap'n Bob says, but at that second the plane does a doozy drop and Cap'n Bob loses all interest in me as well as all the color in his face. He pulls his way back to the cabin. Carol, the moozer, now weeping, has decided to go back to coach to help some of those poor suckers save their skins, which is just fine with me.

"Bring me another vodka and lime!" I yell back at her. "And screw you all, I lost my job anyway!"

And then, suddenly the plane is very quiet and the lights go out.

I know this one, I've seen the *Airport* movies. Right now I bet ol' George Kennedy is on the ground fighting to get us down.

Jeez, I do wish I had that one more drink, just to get me over the top. Look at that, we're on our side again. Another puff of smoke. I know now why it's so quiet. We've lost the engines. Shit, if only I could see and we were straight, I'd do another line of coke.

And then the lights come back on.

Cheering, from the back. I'm the only one in first class, so I give a little cheer myself, to hold up my end. That's just what Carl is going to say to me, "You didn't hold up your end, Roger."

"Hold this, Carl," is what I'm going to say to him.

Screw the Vomits, screw Roundabout Records, screw all of it.

The lights go back out.

We're going down!

Weeeeeee! I've never been in a tumbling DC-10 before. Is this pitch or yaw? Actually, it's rather better than Disney. The cattle in coach don't think so though, they're screaming enough. I yell back at them to shut up, but at this point I don't think I can be heard. It's as good a time as any to stop talking and snap on the Walkman again, listen to one of the Vomits' promo tapes I won't be pushing anymore:

> *Oh, yeah, my-yi-yi baby*
> *She's as fine as cotton candy,*
> *If she's so fine*
> *How come her name is Andy?*

That's enough. I mean, this shit is almost saved by Brutus Johnson's guitar, but not quite. That was something Carly boy and the rest of them never understood, that the Vomits didn't have much and weren't going to get much more. It was guys like me who were going to keep them going, pushing those tapes on the college stations, getting those major media deejays high, the only kind of pure payola left. And that was one of the reasons he was going to put my ass in the can? For *helping*?

"Miss," I shout into the dark, spinning cabin, "I'd like that drink now!"

Fu you, Carl.

Okay, maybe just a little more Vomits before we hit the ground, so let's fast-forward:

> *In the darkness*
> *I think I love her*
> *Reach out to her*
> *Kiss and squeeze her*
>
> *Then the day comes*
> *And the light comes*
> *And I see her*
> *Ooooo Ooooo baby*
> *You're so* ugly.

Enough again!

And then . . . we're not falling!

I can hear that left engine, the one on the other side of the plane, kick in. It feels like being on a boomerang that suddenly goes straight. The lights blink, come on. I see ol' Carol stumbling toward me, stop a couple seats behind, bend over, and throw up. Not too cool, Carol.

Maybe I should let her listen to this tape. They'll dock you for sure, babe. Have to keep the seat covers clean.

You know, she's not such a cow after all. Maybe she'd like to make it before we crash and burn: go out on a high.

"Hey, Carol," I say, but then she stumbles forward as the lights go out yet again and falls across me, crying. I can almost *feel* the ground, very close.

"Who the hell was shooting at us?" I say just before the plane hits.

3

Lands, rather. I don't know how Cap'n Bob did it, but he managed to get us on a runway in a reasonably horizontal position. Speaking of Carol, before I can try to get horizontal with her, she's up and off me, obviously glad to be alive.

Stewardess-bitch mode clicks in again, and she's all efficient.

"Maybe *you'd* better look out the window this time," I say.

She does, and her eyes go bug wide and she gives a little screech.

Coming toward us on the tarmac where we've come to rest, slightly angled on one half-collapsed landing gear, is not the rescue party ol' Carol expected. Me, I'm sure it's just the coke and amphetamines and vodka I pumped into myself making me see what I'm seeing. There's a whole armada of airport vehicles—a fire truck, two or three of those little rumbly luggage carriers, a sedan with a flashing light on top—racing toward us, all manned by *skeletons.* For a moment it's just too silly, and I have to laugh.

"Grateful Dead, man!"

Carol has backed off and is lurching toward the cockpit cabin.

The cabin door opens and Cap'n Bob appears as the first shot rings out. These skeleton freaks have guns and are firing them at us!

"Is it Halloween?" I ask. They ignore me, so I take

the time to gather all my things—Walkman, tapes, batteries—into my briefcase. In the back of the plane the cattle are starting to stampede.

"If they hit the fuel, the plane will blow," Cap'n Bob, in his Cap'n Bob voice, says. "Get the chutes out the opposite side. We've got to get everyone away from the fuselage."

Cow Carol nods and moves off toward the back. Behind Cap'n Bob, in the cabin, I see Navigator Ned and Copilot Pete pulling their headsets off and getting set to abandon ship.

"It's bad," Cap'n Bob says to me grimly, perhaps not noticing my grin. "It's like this everywhere."

I nod, giving him the response he wants, and he moves past me toward the back of the plane. As Copilot Pete passes me he says, very efficient, "Better get ready to move, sir," and I try not to laugh and say, "Aye, aye."

They move past me to the back of the plane. As the curtains are pulled aside I see organized chaos, people in the aisles, and then a faint whoosh as a door or window pops and one of the escape chutes begins to roll out and inflate.

I look out my window, seeing the skeleton people now parked close by, out on the tarmac, formed into shooting ranks.

"Jeez," I say, moving toward the cabin of the plane, stopping to check the bar in its curtained panel and scooping five or six little vodka bottles out, putting them in my leather jacket pocket.

I enter the cabin.

Oooo, boy, just like a big toy. I close the door behind me, put my briefcase down, sit in the captain's big chair.

"Cap'n Bob, up up and away!" I yell, wondering briefly where the intercom switch is so I can let them all hear it as they leave. Yawning, I look out the right side of the plane and see the skeletons in firing position, waiting patiently.

"Time for snoot," I say.

I pull my briefcase up on my lap, get out my bag, cut a line of coke with my best credit card. As the Alaskans say, don't leave Nome without it. As the Pope says, don't leave Rome without it. As the faggots say, don't be homo without it.

Then out with Mr. Straw, up into Mr. Nose.

I jump a little, hearing gunshots, but my curse at spilling some of the coke is tempered by one of the neatest special effects I've ever seen.

Another jet has tried Cap'n Bob's same trick, but this cap'n of the skyways doesn't quite make it. My eyes track just as a ground-to-air missile scoots up to hit a jumbo jet as it's making its crooked approach. The damn thing is bent in half with the explosion like a broken aluminum-foil tube. It seems to hang there in the night with the explosion for a second, then spins lazily down, fire boiling up and down the fuselage until the whole thing hits the runway about a mile away and goes up into a big ball of orange. Our own little jet is shaken.

Now, the skeleton boys outside begin to fire.

I hear the pops, hear the screams. Languidly, I swivel out of Cap'n Bob's chair and over to Copilot Pete's. On the far side of the plane the cattle crowd is running for their lives. The race is over nearly before it begins. I see one village idiot with his carry-on bag clutched in his hand go down. Amazingly, when the shadrool gets up, having only been winged, he *still* has the carry-on clutched in his hand. The second shot gets him almost immediately, though, and he lets go of the bag now because he doesn't need it anymore.

He's not alone in meeting the tarmac. It's definitely Custer's Last Stand. There's Carol the cow, and she's made it almost fifty yards before one hit spins her around and the second hits her below the neck. She can't decide where to clutch, but the third shot puts her out of the vodka-and-lime-making business forever. She falls in a heap.

Plenty of heaps. I decide it's time for one of those vodkas and pull it out of my pocket. I'm twisting off the little cap when who but Cap'n Bob reappears.

"Out of the way!" he screams at me. I think maybe he's lost his professional cool.

"I'll have to tell your boss," I say, offering the little bottle out to him. "I thought it was bad policy to yell at passengers. Have a drink! You might as well fly loaded. Enough of your pilot brethren do."

He looks at me as if I've landed from Pluto, pushes my hand away. "I'm going to try to lift off," he says, throwing himself into his chair, starting to flip switches.

"Why?"

"It's a massacre out there! Did you see what they did to those passengers? I've kept some on board, I might be able to get away, fly to an island or something."

I shrug and move out of his way, taking my briefcase with me. As I saunter out of the flight cabin there's all kinds of craziness going on in the rest of the plane: people running up and down aisles, a lot of shouting and weeping. Someone's trying to come back up the emergency ramp, someone else doesn't think it's a good idea. "We're taking off!" the one on the inside says, as if that explains it. A rifle shot hits the one trying to get in, a suit type with crooked glasses, and that seems to decide things because he reaches for the back of his neck where a big gout of blood has popped out. He lets go of the top of the ramp and slides down out of sight.

I finish my vodka, put the empty on the nearest seat, and reach in for another one. A casual look back at Cap'n Bob tells me he's trying, but not getting too far.

I tilt the bottle up, emptying it in one long swallow, put the empty next to its brother on the seat, and dust my hands.

Looks like it's time to save ol' Roger's skin, I say to myself, because the ol' Roger danger radar, accurate without fail, has begun to go off in my head.

Saw this in a movie, once. I walk into the curtained partition in first class where they keep the bar and the food dolly, a little elevator set into the bottom of the compartment that brings all that hot, good, nutritious first-class airline food up from the galley. There's a little button on it that at first does nothing. I'm thinking maybe the power's gone out, but then it bumps to a stop and I pull the little door open. Not too big inside, but when I pull all the aluminum trays and shelves out, it's just right for me and my briefcase.

Which is just in time, because some of those skeleton dudes have made their way up the ramp and are shooting into the cabin. And now I notice a curious fact, that when one of my air compadres goes down, he soon makes a reappearance as one of the bone men, everything flaking away to leave just that cartoon skeleton. And there's something else from weirdland: up close, these bone boys aren't all bones, but part ghost, too, since I can see the faint outline of something human when the light hits them the right way.

But enough idle thoughts: it's into the elevator, pull the little door closed, and wait for whatever.

I've got a plan, of course; always do. They didn't call me "The Shark" at Roundabout Records for nothing. They also called me "The Shit" and "The Weasel" and "The Whackhead," but none of that bothered me. "Pustule" bothered me a little, but what the fu, I was getting paid for it.

So what's the plan, Jan? When in doubt, wait it out. I really don't think the boneheads are gonna blow the plane while they're on it. Hell, they might even need it later. What they're gonna do, from observation, is off everybody in sight. And, to continue the scenario, once they off everybody, then everybody is gonna be just like them and they'll all go away. Is that Cap'n Bob I hear yodeling a scream close by? Could be. There's just enough room in here to reach in and uncap another of these fine baby Gilbey's—

Damn! Spilled it on myself! I'm as bad as the cow! Jeez, I'd like to scream a little. These leather pants are taking a beating, I hope the bonies didn't get Rita yet; she's got to reconnect me to that tailor friend of hers and get me another pair of these beauties.

Jesus, is that an *engine?*

Oh, Christ, they haven't gotten Cap'n Bob yet after all. I hear him hooting in glee in his little cockpit, the dumb little shit, and one of the engines is fired up! He's gonna kill us all now, for sure!

Then, the blat of an automatic weapon sounds close by. Cap'n Bob screeches like a woman and then, mercifully, the plane is shut down.

Wish I could cut a line in here.

One more little bottle of vodka—careful this time, ol' Roger—and, ah, it's time to take a little nap, to the sounds of rat-tat-tat and the mopping-up going on outside, and the words of that Vomits lullaby singing playfully in my head:

> Go to sleep,
> Go to sleep,
> Go to sleep, little bitch,
> You got what you wanted
> You took what you wanted
> You got what you wanted
> So now go to sleep. . . .

And they really thought these suckers could make it without a guy like me?

4

Awake to blessed silence. I'm no dumb shit, so I give a long listen before opening the door. They may have left somebody on the plane, but I doubt it. They probably searched all the way through it, and if they haven't found me by now, I'm one free dude. So slowly I open the door, uncramp the legs—damn that spilled vodka smell!—and roll out into the aisle like a baby, pulling my briefcase after me—

Nothing.

Darkness, the ambering down of the plane's batteries giving the aisles that night-light look, and outside: still nighttime!

All right, I didn't sleep the night away. With this brush-head look of mine, maybe I can blend in with the boneheads.

So up and down the aisles. Nothing but luggage here, I doubt there's anything worth taking in any of them. A couple of piles of dust, but my boot does away with those.

A look out the windows: nothing. The airport seems quiet from here; in the near distance the terminal is lit up, but there doesn't seem to be much going on. Then in the sky I see the line of a plane, lights blinking, dropping for a landing. There's no antiaircraft fire at it, it three-points down, rolls across my own runway in front of me, toward the terminal. Nothing weird about that.

Is it over? Did I dream the whole thing?

Nah, I don't think so.

If I had to guess, I'd say that plane was full of bone-heads.

So back to the galley, my former prison cell. No food worth eating here; all the trays I pulled out to get into the box are spoiled, that fine *au jus* gravy turned to so much brown tar. But up above, on the bar, a big basket of those chips I asked the skycow Carol for. So fill up the pockets, take a few gin bottles since the little vodkas are gone—

What's that sitting behind the little snorts—a bottle of Stoli?

My God, this must be my lucky night. And not a little one, either, the real thing, the full liter, and unopened. Was this Cap'n Bob's secret vice? Did ol' Carol keep it for her best passengers? I wonder how ol' Carol looks dressed in bones.

Ah, Stoli, Stoli . . .

I dump out the little little gins; it's me and my big vodka bottle and I'm ready to roll.

Standing out of the open doorway by one of the slides, I take a peek out into LAX night. Doesn't look too bad. A few stars through the overhead muck; must be a good night in L.A. Were there any parties I was supposed to go to? There's always the nightclubs, if nothing else is going on. Though the bonies have probably been there by now. It's up into the Hollywood Hills for me, I guess. But I can't resist a look at downtown, before I go.

I think I've even got a good, safe way to do it.

Ol' Roger, ol' Shark, always thinking.

Okay, out we go.

The slide isn't as firm as it should be; in fact, it must have been popped with a few bullets 'cause it's pretty much flat and gives me a drop straight down. But luckily there's a little air in the bottom and it saves my fanny.

And I don't drop the Stoli, thank God.

Now I saunter through the airport. It's not as clear as I thought overhead; in fact, it's started to drizzle. Those stars I thought I saw were airplanes, and now one of them is landing and it's time to lay low. The sucker drops in and taxis on past me. Sure enough, in the lit cockpit I see a couple of boneheads manning the controls. Headphones and everything.

As my father used to say, the world is changing, son. Right, Dad.

It's a longer walk than I thought to get where I'm going. Why don't they put these Rent-A-Car counters out by the far runways, in case you need them? If there's a suggestion box by the Hertz desk, I just might drop a note.

Finally, though, once having to hit the tarmac to avoid one of those luggage mobiles manned by a boner, I reach the place I'm aiming to get at.

It's dark and deserted, just the way we like it. The parking lots are full. What I want is a new 'vette with the top down. What I need is something different.

It takes me almost a half hour to find it: a Lincoln Town Car with darkened glass on the windows. A real godfather-mobile. It takes me another twenty minutes to find the keys in the office.

And then, as I'm walking out to my new purchase, someone's coming into the lot.

Easy enough to hide, just pick a car and squat. The figure passes not five feet in front of me.

To my wonder, it's not a bonehead, it's a California girl, and not too ugly.

"Hey, sis," I say.

She jumps nearly out of her tank top, turns at me, and goes into some Ninja-turtle-type stance. All I do is grin. She moves in closer and I let her see how harmless I am: just a geek in leather pants and leather jacket, open-neck shirt, earrings, buzzhead. Normal California businessman.

"Who are you?" she hisses.

"What you see is what you get." I shrug. "And if I were you, sis, I'd crouch a little lower. Somebody else is clacking this way."

She goes immediately flat and quiet. At least she's that smart. I've already moved way back in the shadows, around the grille of the car.

It's a bonehead, this time, automatic slung over one shoulder. He's just close enough where I can see he's not as fearless as he seems. All bones, he looks scary; but when I get a load of the ghostly outline that goes with it, I see the fat couch barnacle he was, beer gut hanging over the stretch pants. The T-shirt, just visible, says, GO LAKERS.

What a dope.

But sis isn't so smart after all. The fat skel is nearly past when she rushes out at him, catching him from behind. She produces a long TV-offer-type knife and then plunges it in.

The skeleton cries out a little and nearly gets the Uzi around on her before collapsing.

Soon, next amazing thing: the bony body, ghostly T-shirt, beer belly, and all, turns to a pile of dust.

So.

"World's changing, son," I say.

She's back in front of me instantly. She does seem to know how to use that knife, and she's got it up in front of my face.

"I asked you who you are," she says, in a movie-tough tone.

I push her hand away, but maybe she's nuts after all and willing to cut me. The Roger danger radar has begun to go off again.

I ease back on the smile, make it more friendly. "Sorry," I say. "Been a tough night. My plane was shot out of the sky, then everybody in it was murdered by skeletons. Call me a kook, but I'm not quite myself this evening."

She untenses, just a bit, just to the point where my radar stops blaring and tells me she might not kill me after all.

"Take it you've had a rough one, too?" I try.

"Yes." All at once she unwinds, lowers the knife to her boot, where it disappears into a sheath somewhere. She looks at me, grim but not murderous. "Real bitch of a night."

I venture a short laugh. "Right."

She keeps looking at me. Suddenly I know I have had a bad day because normally I would have smelled cop all over her the moment she appeared. I consider it unwise to offer her a snort of cocaine, as I was about to do.

"I'm Roger," I say, holding out my hand. "I work for Roundabout Records."

She looks at the hand, then suddenly takes it. "I'm Marianne. Until two hours ago I was a cop. Now I guess I'm just a human being."

"I knew you were a cop," I say, grinning, because she would have stopped being weary in a few minutes anyway and started getting suspicious of me. It's another radar I have. "Undercover, right?"

"Highway Patrol," she says. "Actually, I was at home when this shit started. Just heading out to work. When I got there, half the station was already dead. Bodies all over the place, coming back to life as . . . those things. Streets were swarming with them."

She had more, so I let her catch her breath, go into shock for a moment, do the tough-cop thing, and come out of it.

"I've been killing them ever since."

"Jeez," I say, putting, I think, just the right amount of sympathy into it. Actually, I want to yawn.

The sincerity thing must have been what she wanted, because she breaks down for a moment.

"I never actually *killed* anybody on this job. And now I've done nothing but kill for the last eight hours."

"I was in the air when it started," I say, trying to figure out a way of getting her to go away. "Must have been hell here on the ground."

This time I *do* yawn, but she doesn't catch it.

"It was," she says. She runs her hand back through her hair. She's not ugly at all, but I know the type. She's got a boyfriend who's a bodybuilder or something, and spends a lot of time on the beach, maybe surfing, and if I put a hand on her, she'd whip that knife out and cut it off at the wrist. "There's fighting going on all over L.A.," she says. "All the main highways are blocked with wrecked cars. There's National Guard units out fighting in Torrance and San Pedro. *Jesus* . . ."

She collapses into a weeping wreck, which is good because my radar has gone off again and I have time to react, but she doesn't. I get down flat and roll under the nearest car as two boners appear, walking casually, as if they were at the mall. One of them has a rifle, the other a kind of yard tool that looks like a middle-class machete. I don't wait around to see what their ghost images might look like: I see bones and I roll.

Ol' Marianne hears them, too, but it is already too late for her. Weeping never pays. She turns and spins and kicks one of them, but the one with the machete brings it down on her and cuts her clean across the back of the neck.

She gasps and goes down to one knee, but keeps fighting. This is a tough cop lady. She actually has her TV knife halfway out of its ankle sheath before the boner with the machete hits her again, taking half her friggin' head off.

Gross me out.

You don't have to be Einstein to see what's going to happen next. But the two boners, bless their knobby heads, save my butt by dragging the dear deceased cop away as she's turning into one of them. The machete one, I see as they pass under the parking lot lights, is actually some kind of farm worker, by his ghostly image. Nice backhand, Juan.

So I climb up and get into my Lincoln Town Car, quiet as can be, rev the beauty up, praising that kitten engine, and pull out.

But I don't make it out of the parking lot, naturally. Once a cop, always a cop. In the rearview mirror I see ol' Marianne, now an official skel, pushing aside her two bonehead comrades and dashing after me. Damned if she isn't going to catch up, too, so I throw the smooth transmission of the Lincoln into reverse, timing it perfectly, and run the bitch down before she can get out of the way. Inside that luxurious interior I hear the faint crunch of bones, and when I pull away, peeling rubber this time, there's a neat little pile of dust behind me, already scattering in the faint Santa Anas. Juan and his buddy are still standing where they were, properly puzzled.

5

By the way, thanks for the traffic info, Marianne.

I stay away from the freeways, and it's not long before I have confirmation of what the cop said. Wrecks everywhere. Even the exit ramps are blocked. So it's think-back time, a bit of nostalgia about my good ol' days, growing up the only white boy in my part of East L.A., and all those back roads come back to me.

What was another of ol' Dad's quaint sayings? "Get me a fresh needle, son."

Amazingly, no one bothers me. It's just assumed I'm one of the boneheads. What few humans I see are either running for their skins into dirty alleys or in the process of being boned. I'm sure there's lots more hiding in cellars or attics, not to mention the sewers. In the middle of one street I see two boneheads beating up on a third bonehead. They're just skeletons until I get real close. Curious, I slow down to watch the action as their outlines come into faint view under the streetlights. Looks like two druggies pounding a third. As I watch they hit him real hard with something like a cosh and he's down on the ground, then turns to powder.

So. Even the dead kill the dead.

Then it's time to hightail out, because druggie one and two have turned their attention to me, their skeleton eye sockets following me, jaws creaking up and down. Can skels drool? I know what these guys want, the Town Car, so it's time to burn some more rubber and move on.

Up into the Hollywood Hills, which rise into view in front of me after another half hour of twisty turns and back roads, dodging wrecks, fleeing humans, and skels chasing them like Keystone Kops.

The Hollywood Hills: still lit up like the movies, magical, probably still mostly what it was. Even the "H" on the Hollywood sign is the only one that's been hit by mortar fire, attesting to the mostly intactness of phonyland.

My kind of place.

I rev the engine, heading straight for it, and finger

open my briefcase with my right hand to pull out my prized bottle of Stoli.

It's time to party.

I wonder what the rest of the world is doing tonight?

5

The inner diary of
Claire St. Eve

1

At first I thought Withers Home for Women was on fire. We had fire drills, sometimes in the middle of the night, but the look on Mrs. Garr's face was not one of calm. She looked terribly upset. As she grabbed my arm it suddenly occurred to me that my life was about to change. That tingle that had washed over me had made that seed begin to grow. It both elated and frightened me. Perhaps this little room, and this big, terrible place, would be no more. I think I actually smiled.

Mrs. Garr looked at me, and a pitiable look came onto her face.

"Oh, Claire," she said, "I'll take care of you," and pressed me close to her.

Out in the hall there was chaos. I kept looking for hoses, for water pails. I thought of the shapes I had seen outside near the trees and water and thought they must be firemen. Where were they? Why did I hear no sirens?

Then a siren did go off. Many sirens, from the one on the pole just outside the Withers grounds to at least two others I could distinguish in nearby Cold Spring Harbor. That meant the fire must be huge.

But where was it? As Mrs. Garr dragged me through the halls I saw nothing but confused, frightened faces. Then another siren went off, a large one even farther away, and I thought perhaps an even greater calamity had come. War? We had had those drills, too, mostly the sit-in-the-hall-with-your-head-between-your-knees kind. My elation faded, leaving only fear, and I stopped dead in the middle of the hall.

Mrs. Garr bent down to look into my face. "Don't worry." She held me to her again, but I felt no comfort. The fear in Mrs. Garr's own eyes was enough to tell me that this was no mere fire.

Then we were heading into the cellars. All of the chaos in the halls turned out to have purpose. Ragged lines were pushing their way toward the two huge open green doors that led to the basement. We had had one drill here, when I was very young. The drill had been for nuclear war.

Behind us, somewhere deep in what should have been the emptiness of the building, I heard the sound of breaking glass. What would that be? Had a bomb fallen? I waited for the flash of light, the blast against the building that blew us all away to dust, but nothing came but another shattered pane. The firemen? Who were those figures I had seen by the water and trees? Russian soldiers landing?

Our turn came, and we were jostled through the big green doors and down.

There was mumbled talking, but I picked up nothing. Then someone came close in the dark with a pair of headphones and Walkman, and I heard a snatch of radio: an announcer saying very loud that there was fighting in New York City, that there were reports of fighting in Chicago, in Miami, in Atlanta . . .

The headphones moved away from me in the dark. I had only Mrs. Garr's guiding arms to show me the way.

Behind us there was a loud crash, near the doors, and yelling from that direction.

"Close the doors!" someone shouted. It sounded like the vice-principal, Mrs. Carmody. Then an unmistakable voice, the booming of Mrs. Page, the headmistress, rose above all the murmuring.

"Be quiet!"

There was instant silence.

"Mr. Cary," Mrs. Page boomed out, "close those doors immediately."

We heard a sound at the top of the stairs. Then in the darkness we saw a crack of light as one door was pulled back and then slammed. I heard Mr. Cary, the gym teacher, grunting with effort.

"I . . . can't get it to close, Mrs. Page."

"Do it!" Mrs. Page roared.

"I—"

Then the door at the top of the stairs was thrown in, showing a huge rectangle of hallway above. Into this stepped something, fully illuminated, that at first made me want to laugh.

A human skeleton.

Mrs. Page had jostled her way through the crowd of boarders toward the stairway, and stopped near Mrs. Garr and me. I heard her audibly gasp.

"Mr. Cary!" she shouted, but Mr. Cary needed no urging, and threw the door closed on the specter. Mrs. Page pushed past us and tramped up the steps, and in a moment she and the gym teacher were pushing fiercely at the door. Something on the other side pushed back.

There sounded a loud snap, and the door was locked into place.

Mrs. Page roared, "The crossbar, Mr. Cary, the crossbar!" I heard something metallic slide across the door.

"Done," Mr. Cary said, panting.

"Residents," Mrs. Page announced from the top of the steps, in the dark. There was utter silence. "We are in the midst of a crisis. I am sure the authorities will handle it. In the meantime this is what you will do. You will remain utterly at ease. You will listen to your elders. You will above all listen to me. There are provisions down here, and I doubt we will have to stay long. Do you understand?"

Her rising inflection at the end of this speech was something we all understood; the iron voice of command. There was a wave of assent that ended with a girl near me saying, "Yeah."

"All together!" Mrs. Page screamed.

"Yes, Mrs. Page!" came all voices in a single voice.

"Very good. You, Mr. Cary," she said to the gym teacher, "will guard the door."

"Yes, Mrs. Page," Mr. Cary said halfheartedly. I could almost feel her glare at him in the dark before he repeated, with much more enthusiasm, "Yes, Mrs. Page!"

"Good."

I heard the clop-clop of her making her way down the stairs.

There came a loud dull bang on the cellar door.

"Mrs. Page?" Mr. Cary called out in the dark.

"Ignore it."

"Yes, Mrs. Page."

"The end is nigh!" came another voice in the dark. "Let the wicked forsake his way, and the unrighteous man his thoughts; and let him return unto the Lord!"

"Margaret Gray," Mrs. Page said sternly, "be quiet."

"And after these things I saw another angel come down from heaven, having great power; and the earth was lightened with his glory!"

"Amen!" answered Priscilla Ralston's voice.

"Ms. Ralston! Ms. Gray!" Mrs. Page commanded.

"And he cried mightily with a strong voice," Margaret Gray continued, "Babylon the great is fallen!"

"Mrs. Carmody," Mrs. Page ordered, "shut that woman up!"

I heard scuffling in the dark, and then Mrs. Carmody's voice cried out. Someone breathing hard pushed through the crowd, nearly knocked me down.

"Stop that woman!" Mrs. Page shouted.

At the top of stairs Mr. Cary gave a cry.

"Repent!" Margaret Gray shouted from the darkness at the top of the stairs. "Turn yourselves from your idols; and turn away your faces from all your abominations!"

"Amen!" cried Priscilla Ralston.

Mr. Cary shouted again, and then I heard the bar scrape against the door, heard it drop in the dark.

"Stop her!" Mrs. Page shouted, adding to Mr. Cary's own protests.

The door flew in on its hinges, showing Margaret Gray, rail thin, standing tall.

"Enter, angels of the Lord!"

She stepped back, leaving the doorway filled with skeletons.

At once everyone began to scream.

Mr. Cary appeared in the doorway above, trying to block the entrance of the creatures. One of them held something aloft, a large piece of cut glass, it looked like, and slashed it down at him.

He cried out and fell.

Margaret Gray moved back down the stairs, pushed her way back through the crowd. Her face was radiant.

At the top of the stairs the skeletons hesitated.

There were four of them. One stepped in, tentatively, lowered its head to look down into the basement. Its movements were reptilian, almost.

It backed up, barked a laugh, said something to the others, and went away.

While the others blocked the entrance Mrs. Page once again bulled her way through the crowd of girls. She stopped at the bottom of the steps and looked up. Mr. Cary was halfway down, panting, holding his right side.

"Mr. Cary," Mrs. Page said, "you make your way back to Mrs. Carmody. She'll take care of you."

Before Mr. Cary could speak, Mrs. Page stood and climbed the rest of the steps. At the top she faced the skeletons squarely.

"*You* will leave immediately!" she shouted in her most commanding voice.

The creatures stepped back, then one of them leaped forward, brandishing a long sliver of broken glass.

Mrs. Page stared intently at the specter for a moment, then gasped. "Mr. Carlucci!"

"That's right," the skeleton said. "Caretaker at Withers, 1904 to 1980."

"When you died . . ." Mrs. Page gasped.

"Hah!" the specter cried, and slashed Mrs. Page across the face.

Mrs. Page screamed, threw her hands to her face, and the other skeletons leaped upon her then, forcing her down onto the steps. I saw her legs kicking from beneath the pile. I heard her scream once, then say, "Girls!" before a second scream was followed by silence.

The room had compacted away from the stairway. Weeping girls were squeezed toward one corner.

Mr. Cary still lay panting at the bottom of the stairs. Now the skeletons were upon him. He shouted once, hoarsely, and was silent.

At the top of the steps the reptilian-looking skeleton who had left reappeared, carrying a large, dull red spouted can.

"Leave," he said, and the other skeletons abandoned Mr. Cary's bloodied body and remounted the stairs.

The one with the can twisted off the spout top and came halfway down the steps, pouring liquid out as he retreated to the top. He produced a box of matches, lit one, and dropped it onto the stairway.

"Have a hot time, ladies." He laughed, and the others laughed, backing away from the doorway. Above, out in the halls, there was still noise, the sound of breaking glass.

The entire top of the stairway roared up into flame. The cellar began to fill with dense smoke, and those girls not screaming began to cough.

"Repent!" Margaret Gray's voice came from the back of the room. "Repent!"

"Run with me, Claire," Mrs. Garr said, close by.

To my surprise she ran straight at the stairway, pulling me up after her.

As we reached the flames I felt her nearly lift me off my feet, cradling me against her. I felt the world go blindingly hot around me, felt flame against my arm—and then we were out of the fire, tumbling to the floor in the hallway upstairs.

"Up, Claire, quickly," Mrs. Garr said.

She yanked me to my feet and shoved me into a nearby door with frosted glass set into the frame. It was the ladies' room. The lights were out in it. She closed the door and held me against the wall as a figure passed outside.

The pressure of her hands on me loosened, and

I heard her gasp under her breath, "Oh, God, oh, God . . ."

Outside, down the steps, we heard the horrible keen of screaming. There was the roar of crackling fire, followed by a whump, and a larger scream.

Mrs. Garr held her shaking hands over my ears.

More figures passed by. One of them stopped in front of the frosted glass. I saw the shadow of a skeleton. The door opened inward.

Mrs. Garr drew me away from it, pressed me against the wall.

A skeletal head looked straight past us, into the room. This close, I saw a faint outline around the bones, could almost make out features. The skeletal hand reached for the light switch, inches from where Mrs. Garr and I stood.

Outside, another skeleton stopped, said, "Not in here!"

The skeleton with its hand on the light switch laughed, turned away, let the door close.

Smoke rolled in under the door.

I felt Mrs. Garr tense beside me.

Pressing me to stay where I was, she moved away from me into the darkness. She walked to the far side of the room, stopped in front of the long window there. Quietly, she raised it up a few inches.

I had pressed one of my own hands over one ear, my other ear against the wall, to block out the screaming that came from the cellar outside.

Another whump sounded, and most of the cries were silenced at once.

Across the room Mrs. Garr motioned for me to come to her.

I found that I couldn't move. I was rooted to my spot against the wall.

Mrs. Garr came to me, gently pulled me toward the window.

"We have to climb out," she whispered.

At this part of the building the ground below sloped down to the underground garages, putting us effectively two floors up.

"I'm going to lower you down," Mrs. Garr said.

I looked out into the night. There was a short stand of bushes seemingly a great distance below. To the right a pool of light illuminated the tarmac in front of the garage doors. There were cries off on the grounds, and now a pair of skeletal figures ran by in the short distance, toward the playing fields.

Mrs. Garr bent down and looked into my eyes.

"You have to, Claire."

I hesitated, then nodded.

She helped me climb out on the sill, then lowered me over the side, holding me by my arms, then my hands.

I looked down; the bushes still looked very far away.

Mrs. Garr let go of my hands.

I fell, closing my eyes, and landed in the midst of the bushes. I felt a burning tear up one side, but my legs hit firmly and I rolled down onto the ground, unhurt.

Above, Mrs. Garr was looking down at me, then out over the grounds. She made a quick motion and disappeared into the bathroom.

Three more figures appeared, closer, walking toward the garages. When they got into the pool of light, I could distinctly make out the smoky outlines that surrounded their skeletons. They were Mrs. Page, Mr. Cary, and the old caretaker, Mr. Carlucci.

They stopped under the light, talked. Mr. Cary laughed. He then pulled up one of the garage doors and the three of them entered.

Above, Mrs. Garr reappeared.

She climbed out over the edge of the bathroom window, lowered herself, and let go.

She landed beside me, hard. She rolled toward the building, pulling me with her into the bushes, as Mrs. Page reappeared at the garage door, looking around. She looked above us at the open window of the bathroom. I looked up, too. Flames were shooting out into the night.

Mrs. Page went back into the garage.

Mrs. Garr was rubbing her ankle, wincing. Carefully, she stretched her leg out, moved the ankle one way, then the other.

"Thank God, it's not broken," she whispered.

She held me close as another sound came from the garage.

In the pool of light appeared the back end of Mrs. Page's car, a big black sedan.

The car backed out, turned, and pulled away to the right.

Mrs. Garr was standing, helping me up, when Mrs. Page came out of the garage and saw us.

For a moment both Mrs. Page and Mrs. Garr stood frozen in spot. It was then that Mrs. Garr saw the shadowy outline around Mrs. Page's skeleton and said, "Mrs. Page?"

The specter ran at us, out of the garage light, and leaped at Mrs. Garr.

Mrs. Garr was thrown to the ground. Making a panting sound, the skeleton beat at her with its fists. Mrs. Garr threw it aside, tried to rise. Her ankle collapsed as Mrs. Page jumped onto her again. The skeleton held her down, reached for a nearby stone, and raised it to strike her.

There was another, larger rock, nearby. I picked it up, raised it with difficulty above my head, and brought it down on the skeleton's skull.

I saw a fissure of cracks in the skull break away from the point of impact, and Mrs. Page collapsed, then evaporated into a mass of powder.

Mrs. Garr rose. "We have to go, Claire," she said. "We'll go to my house, find my husband."

I followed her limping form toward the open garage.

2

Flames were licking from nearly every window of Withers by now. The screams had been silenced. Off away from the grounds sirens still wailed, and I heard the sound of distant honking horns and police sirens.

Mrs. Garr and I entered the garage.

It was empty.

"Oh, God," Mrs. Garr said. Then she turned to me. "We'll have to be very quiet, Claire, and get to my car. It's around front, in the main parking lot."

I nodded.

We set off, keeping close to the building.

As we rounded the far corner Mrs. Garr held back. I caught a glimpse. The grounds in that direction were covered with skeletons. I saw one specter help another from a broken cellar window. Both were charred, covered with soot.

"The other way, Claire," Mrs. Garr said.

We walked back past the garage and circled around the far side of Withers. We kept as close as we could to the building. High above, fire had reached the top floor. There were crashes. The stone walls where we walked were warm to the touch.

We reached the front of the building, stopping once to hide from a single passing skeleton. I looked out across the open lawns to the parking lot, far in the distance.

"Can you run, Claire?"

I nodded, wondering if Mrs. Garr could run, with her ankle.

She could. The area before us looked deserted, and we set off briskly, Mrs. Garr hobbling slightly, holding my hand.

Out of breath, we made it to the parking lot. Mrs. Garr fitted her key to her car and I got into the front seat next to her.

We pulled out of the lot, heading down the long, tree-lined drive. Behind us, Withers burned mightily, fire pushing up at the sky. I noticed for the first time that it was a beautiful night, that the moon and stars were out.

As we approached the front entrance Mrs. Garr braked to a halt.

"Oh, my God."

The massive gates of Withers had been closed and locked. Completely blocking the road, even if the gate had been open, was the crashed remains of Mrs. Page's huge black sedan, still steaming.

Two skeletons, Mr. Carlucci and Mr. Cary, appeared in our headlights, walking toward us. Mr. Carlucci held a tire iron in one hand.

Mr. Carlucci laughed. "Going somewhere, ladies?"

He pointed to Mr. Cary. "The old bastard didn't tell me he couldn't drive."

Mr. Cary put his skeletal hand on Mrs. Garr's windshield and said, "Get out of the car."

On my side of the car Mr. Carlucci brought his tire iron down, cracking the window.

Mr. Cary's skull grinned.

Mrs. Garr threw the car into reverse.

Mr. Carlucci threw himself on the hood of the car and brought his tire iron down again on the windshield.

Mrs. Garr stepped on the gas, pulled back fast, then turned the wheel hard.

Mr. Carlucci was thrown off. He hit a tree next to the road, hard, and collapsed into a pile of powder.

Mr. Cary was running toward us from the front entrance, shouting, "Stay where you are!"

Mrs. Garr turned the car around, back toward Withers, and put her foot on the gas.

"Pray, Claire," she said. "Pray that the back gate is open."

We roared past the main building, skirted the playing field, and drove past the small cemetery. Under the night sky the graves were all open and gaping.

There at the end of the cemetery was Mr. Cary's house, a small, neat cottage. Another short drive, hemmed in close by trees and underbrush, brought us to the gate.

It was closed, and locked. High on its iron bars was a sign of polished brass that said, WITHERS HOME FOR WOMEN.

"What will we do!" Mrs. Garr said.

Suddenly she seemed to reach a decision.

"Get out of the car, Claire," she ordered.

I obeyed. I stood on the side of road while Mrs. Garr backed the car up, turned it to the left, and drove it into the underbrush between two large trees. I watched the brush spring back up after the car disappeared. In a moment the car was hidden, and Mrs. Garr and I were making our way to Mr. Cary's house.

3

The house was a small, pleasant-looking place with a rock garden out front and flower boxes on the front windows. We followed a stone path up to the porch, and Mrs. Garr tried the door.

It was locked, and so was the window off the porch.

Retreating to the rock garden, Mrs. Garr returned with a rock and smashed it through the porch window. She reached in, unlatched the window, and raised it up.

She climbed in, and in a moment had opened the front door for me.

The lights in the house were off.

"I was only in here once, for tea with Mrs. Cary," Mrs. Garr said, "but if I remember, the cellar was off the kitchen—"

We heard a sound in the back of the house, down a hallway we were passing.

Mrs. Garr went quickly to the living-room fireplace, took the poker from its cradle.

She entered the hall in front of me.

A cat ran out past us from a bedroom.

We both jumped.

Another sound came from the room at the end of the hall.

Mrs. Garr pushed the back-room door open with the long poker.

A gunshot sounded, splattered plaster in the hall above our heads.

A voice shouted, "I'll kill you, stay away from me!"

Mrs. Garr called out, "Mrs. Cary, is that you?"

"I know who you are, stay out, I'll kill you!"

"Mrs. Cary, please, we can help you."

"Let me see your hand!"

Mrs. Garr slowly stretched her hand out into the bedroom door opening.

"It's a trick—let me see the rest of you!"

"All right," Mrs. Garr said. She turned to me. "Stay where you are, Claire." She stood and moved slowly out into the bedroom door opening.

The voice from the bedroom broke down into weeping. "Oh, *God* . . ."

Mrs. Garr called out, "It's all right, Claire." I followed her into the bedroom. There in a corner behind the big bed cowered Mr. Cary's wife. A handgun lay in her lap.

"Don't cry," Mrs. Garr said. She went to Mrs. Cary, knelt down, and held her. "It's all right now."

"They came, they were all around!" Mrs. Cary cried. Her trembling hand pointed to the window. Outside was a clear view of the cemetery. "Out there! I saw them! They rose up out of the ground, and they came to the house, knocked on the doors, they kept rising out of the ground. . . ."

"It's all right," Mrs. Garr said, holding the old woman.

"What about my John?" Mrs. Cary said suddenly. She had stopped crying and looked intently at Mrs. Garr. "You know my John, he was down at the school—what happened to him?"

"Mrs. Cary . . ."

"He's coming, isn't he? He'll be here soon to help me? He's always here when I need him—"

She had risen, letting the gun drop to the floor, and tried to walk out of Mrs. Garr's grasp to the bedroom door.

"No, Mrs. Cary, stay here. Come into the cellar with us." Mrs. Garr hesitated, then said, "John will be along later."

"Will he?" Mrs. Cary said, brightening. "Yes, of course he will. He never leaves me alone for long. He's always there for me."

Mrs. Garr said quietly, "Yes, of course. My husband, Michael, is always there for me, too."

"Then let's get into the cellar!"

Mrs. Cary rose and walked briskly to the doorway.

Mrs. Garr followed, picking the handgun up from the floor, and put her arm around my shoulder. "Come on, Claire."

4

We went to the cellar. Mrs. Cary went ahead of us, turning on lights. "There's a place in the back that John set up, just in case." She sounded unnaturally happy. "John is always thinking ahead. When we first moved here, he stocked us with cans of food and water. He never trusted those Russians, ever since they tried to put those missiles in Cuba." She looked around at Mrs. Garr and smiled. "He'll be proud of himself now. He's probably one of the only ones who was ready."

She pulled a light chain. We stood in front of what looked like a wall. But there was a handle in it. With some effort, and help from Mrs. Garr, Mrs. Cary pulled it open, revealing a small, dry little room with shelves of canned goods along one wall, another shelf with a lantern, a small cook stove and first-aid kit, a pile of magazines, a little row of books, two cots, even a little writing desk with an old, nicked chair.

"There's a pullout door on the bottom right with a portable toilet in it," Mrs. Cary said. "The waste gets stored behind it, down in a limed pit that John dug out." She smiled. "Oh, John is so smart! Even the air is filtered, and then are plenty of batteries if the electricity goes out. Best of all it can be locked from the inside, and no one on the outside can get in without John's key." She looked at Mrs. Garr. "Do you like it?"

"Very much," Mrs. Garr said. "Why don't—"

"Let me just go upstairs and close the cellar door," Mrs. Cary said. "Then I'll be back."

"All right," Mrs. Garr said.

Mrs. Cary went up the stairs, and in a moment we heard her upstairs, then heard the front door open and close.

"Oh, God," Mrs. Garr said, and I followed as she ran upstairs.

Mrs. Cary was on the front walk, heading for the road toward Withers.

"Mrs. Cary!" Mrs. Garr shouted.

Mrs. Cary stopped and turned. "It's all right," she said. "I'm just going to get John."

"But—"

"I know." Mrs. Cary smiled. "I knew from the way you looked at me. But he's never left me alone."

"Mrs. Cary—"

The old woman waved, started to walk toward the road again. "You don't understand. I've never been without him." She stopped again, looked back at us. "If I find him, I'll bring him back here."

She walked on, and soon was out of sight.

"God," Mrs. Garr said.

We went back to the cellar, went down into it. Mrs. Garr checked everything in the little shelter, then pulled the heavy door closed. There was a lock on it with a turning mechanism, and she turned it and tested the door. She turned to me with a tired but hopeful look.

"I think we'll be all right here, Claire."

She stared at me for a few moments, then came and held me. She began to cry. "Oh Claire, Claire, I hope my own husband is all right. . . ."

After a while she was calm, and lay on one of the cots. I lay on the other, and soon I was asleep.

5

I was awakened by Mrs. Garr. Outside the shelter door there was a scratching sound.

"Claire, get behind me," Mrs. Garr said.

She sat me back against my cot and got in front of me, holding Mrs. Cary's handgun.

"Mrs. Garr, are you in there?" came a voice from outside the door.

Mrs. Garr said nothing.

The voice said, "It's me, Mrs. Cary." She sounded just like she had before.

Still Mrs. Garr said nothing.

"Let me in, Mrs. Garr. I know you're in there. Please let me in."

"Did you find John?" Mrs. Garr said.

There was a pause. "No, I didn't find him. I'm very scared. Please let me in."

I looked at Mrs. Garr, who had not made a move toward the door.

"*Please,* Mrs. Garr. I think someone's coming." The scratching at the door resumed.

Mrs. Garr held the gun in both of her hands, and they were trembling.

"*Oh, God, Mrs. Garr! They're out here! They're all out here coming toward me! Please! Please let me in!*"

Mrs. Garr jumped up to open the door, but froze as another voice sounded outside.

"Doesn't matter," the new voice said.

"All right," Mrs. Cary's voice said calmly.

There was a rattling sound in the door, and the turning mechanism on the lock turned and the door swung open.

Mrs. Garr pressed back against me, held the gun up.

Mr. and Mrs. Cary, both skeletons, stood in the doorway. Mr. Cary held an ax in one hand.

"I told you John was smart," Mrs. Cary said. "He was the only one who had the key for that door."

Mr. Cary's skull's mouth opened in a shout and he charged into the room at us, swinging the ax.

Mrs. Garr pulled the trigger of the gun.

She was slammed back against me. There was a loud sound in the room. Mr. Cary collapsed where he stood, the ax dropping into the pile of dust he had become.

"*What have you done!*" Mrs. Cary screamed. "*My John! What have you done to my husband! Ohhhhhhhhhh!*"

Screaming, Mrs. Cary rushed into the room, her skeletal hands held out before her like claws. Mrs. Garr pulled the trigger of the gun again, but there was only a click as Mrs. Cary hit her. I felt one of her skeleton hands slide against my face, clutch the back of my head. There was a soft tingle, then the feel of bone. Mrs. Cary was screeching, trying to tear at Mrs. Garr and me both. I fell free as Mrs. Garr and Mrs. Cary fell to the floor. The gun fell, spun away to stop against the wall.

Mrs. Cary pushed Mrs. Garr down under her. She screeched. "*You killed my husband! You killed John!*" She scooped at the mass of dust that had been her husband and clutched it in her white fingers, howling. Suddenly she had whipped up the ax from the midst of the dust and swung it high overhead to bring it down on Mrs. Garr.

I picked up the gun in both my hands, holding it like I had seen Mrs. Garr do it, aimed it at Mrs. Cary, and pulled the trigger.

This time there was another loud bang. I fell back. My hands shaking, I dropped the gun.

When I looked, Mrs. Cary was dissolving into dust, her back arched, bones below her neck shattered. She said, "John ..." and then was gone.

Tears were coming down my face, and I could not stop shivering. Mrs. Garr came to me, held me. "Oh, Claire, you did the right thing. . . ."

Mrs. Garr led me to a cot, lay me down, and covered me with a blanket.

She went to the front door, started to close it, then opened it again and went out. She searched the floor until she found a key on a key ring. She brought it back into the room, closed and locked the door.

"Now no one can get at us," she said.

She locked the door and stood over me. "Sleep." She kept the light in the room on. She lay on the other cot, and after a while I heard her breath even and she was asleep.

I sat up on my cot and turned to look at the two scattered piles of dust that kept Mrs. Garr and me company in our little cell.

6

From the second life of Abraham Lincoln

1

It was the best of times, it was the worst of times.

I was never much of a fiction reader. Billy Herndon was always trying to get me to read this and that, and I think I took a secret pleasure in not accommodating him.

But this Dickens fellow was all right, and I remember Billy reading those words to me sometime early in 1860 or so, just before the war started. Though it seemed to me, as things went on, that we were getting more of the worst and very little of the best.

Those words seem more appropriate these days.

Madness is what I first thought we were in the middle of. Seemed the whole world was plagued like mad dogs. There was a summer back in Indiana when I remember rabies sweeping through; seemed every other critter caught it. We did more hunting and less food eating that year than ever in my life, and I got purely tired of the taste of vegetables. One of the better things about the Confederacy during the war was that they had most of the vegetables, and so had to eat most of 'em.

The best of times, the worst of times . . .

Sure looked like madness to me, men made out of little but bones running the streets, hunting flesh-and-blood people down like dogs and then turning *them* into skeleton men. Not the kind of world you'd think to wake up to, not the kind of Judgment Day. I'd all but ruled that out as a possibility.

What, then, if not the Greater Power's doing, was the root of this thing? What, then, did it mean?

Some personal happiness for me, for one thing. Just seeing my old home in Springfield brought me that. I reached it just as dawn was breaking, after walking all night through the madness. I must say the sight of its boxy structure, the five windows in a line on the top floor—even the white fence out front seemingly unchanged, heartened me. But what was this? When I entered the front door, I discovered the reason the house appeared unchanged. It had been turned into a museum! With tasseled ropes strung across the rooms and "No walking" signs on the rugs. Glory be. I wondered what Mary would say to that.

And then there she was, walking in on me while I toured my own home, almost afraid to touch anything because of all those signs.

"Father . . ."

"Mary."

She walked right in the front door as I passed it on the way to the other side of the house, and we stood there like two courting youngsters for a moment before she rushed at me and held me around my middle.

"Oh, Abraham, what's happened? How can it be . . . ?"

"I don't know, Mother, but it is, and here we are."

She looked up at me, and as I was getting used to looking for features around all those skulls and bones, I saw her face. It was an old face, but it was as I had first known it so long ago, before all her fears took hold and little Willie and Eddie's deaths robbed her of her strength.

"My goodness, Mother, I do believe you're smiling."

She held me tightly. I must confess I was sorely unprepared for this return of the belle who had roped me.

"Mother," I said, holding her tight myself, and letting all those early memories come back to me.

"It's not the way I thought it would be, but it's just fine," Mary said, and then I looked behind her and there in the doorway were Eddie and Willie themselves, just as they had looked before sickness took them, and behind them stood my Tad, whom I hardly recognized, he was taller and older than when I had last seen him.

"You little codgers!" I bellowed, loud enough, I'm afraid, so that I startled Mary into letting go of me. But I was already at the doorway, scooping the two little boys up, one in either arm, pulling in Tad after them and marching them around to get the feel of them.

"Hello, Mr. President," Tad said half seriously, in his old lisp, giving me a salute.

"And you, Eddie, don't you have anything to say to your commander in chief?"

He put his little arms around my neck, and heavens if I didn't begin to cry myself at the feel of him, for it was him, all right, and no ghost.

"That's what I always dreamed, Abe, what I always wanted paradise to be, all of us together again," Mary said, and damned if she didn't break down and cry again, and the rest of us with her.

I thought briefly of the silliness of it, five skeletons standing in a museum bellowing, but the truth of it was, the more time went on, the less I saw the skeletons of all of us, and the more that faint ghost of what we were was all I saw.

"Well, Mother, I don't know if this is paradise, but it's sure what we've got."

"And," she said, "if only Robert were here, it would be complete."

"Robert!" I said, thinking of my firstborn. "Where is he?"

"I don't know," Mary said sadly. "The last time I saw him I was . . ." For the first time since she had walked through that door, I saw a trace of the melancholy that had so affected her. I shuddered to think that it might return.

"Well, Mother," I said brightly, "I'm sure he'll come back. He'll know where to find us." I put Eddie and Willie down, and already they were ducking under those tassels, looking for old places to play.

"Abe, do you suppose . . ." Mary said hopefully, giving me one of her do-it-for-me looks.

I looked down at her and smiled. "Mary, the house is *ours*, isn't it? And if they turned it into a museum, I can't see there's any other legal owner than the ones they museumed it for, do you?"

"Oh, Father!" Again she threw her arms around me. I can't say there wasn't a moment of tenderness between us. "Abe, I'm so happy, it will be just like it was."

Yet, hearing the clamor outside, the sound of intermittent violence, I wasn't sure it would ever be like that.

2

To my surprise, though, for a while it was. I was pleased, and not a little astounded, at the amount of respect accorded us in our rehabitation of the old house in Springfield. After the first days of violence and upheaval a kind of lull ensued, at least in our part of the world. I understood that those of our kind had more or less occupied the city, but that many humans were either in hiding or fleeing to other parts. What visitors we had those first days wandered in from the street, and I must say the shock they evidenced on seeing the former owner reinstated was comical to behold.

After a while we were mainly left alone. I found my time well occupied in reading and catching up on the world. A few walks to the local library, with Eddie and Willie in tow, gave me enough looks at encyclopedias and recent newspapers to at least give a taste of the startling changes the world had undergone in the last one hundred and thirty years. The greatest shocks were of the discovery of the advances of the scientific men. If they hadn't caused the recent event of which I was a part, they had certainly kept busy with plenty of other projects. The telephone, and especially the television, were startling new toys to me, and though we had neither in the house, it wasn't long before I had grasped their significance. Jet airplanes, the automobile, the advances in medicine—all of these were filled with wonder.

My education in the short run was most propelled, however, by a serendipitous discovery in the hallway of our Springfield home, which kept me busy for a time. It seems one of the museum curators, seeking to enhance the living history of the place, had installed in one of our old bookcases a complete set of leatherbound biographies of the presidents of the United States. I have to admit that those before me little interested me. But those who had governed after me provided me with a complete overview of the politics of the nation and the world since I had left it. I can't tell how many hours of every day found me in my study, slouched low in my chair, one long leg draped over the chair's arm for comfort, absorbing this living testimony. I even admit to reading the volume devoted to myself, by a fellow named Sandburg. I told myself it was just for reference, to gauge the accuracy of the other volumes, but I know it was out of pride. I came away from it embarrassed at his praise.

So passed our time in Springfield. Though we were ghosts, we still proved to have appetites of a meager sort. Though Mary complained of the lack of servants, she was perfectly content to cook on the serviceable stove the food which Tad and I brought home from our short forays into the neighborhood markets. It was interesting to me the way our food was ingested, the way it seemed to vanish on passing through our ghostly lips, leaving the bright skeleton within unblemished.

Mary had her house, and except for their rare walks with me, Eddie, Willie, and Tad were kept close out of Mary's fears, not all of them unfounded, of what could happen to them outside. But the boys, especially the two younger ones, found plenty of mischief to get into inside, turning what the curators must have thought priceless objects in our house into broken relics. Though Mary was especially happy during this time, I saw little signs of her old troubles, especially in her fear of leaving the house.

"We can't just stay in here forever, Mother. Like it or not, there's a world out there that won't stand still for us."

"Why not! We gave them everything once, we owe the world nothing."

"Mother—" I tried to reason with her.

"No! Please, Abe, soon Robert will come, and everything will be perfect."

"Mary, I can't live like this. It's like"—I tried to avoid saying it, but darned if the analogy wasn't perfect—"being back in my tomb."

We both knew her act well, the old clinging fear, and for a while I let it work on me, out of guilt and out of responsibility.

3

One day, though, soon after I finished the last of the biographies, I felt the roof of the house pressing down on me like a closing coffin, and I had to get out.

"Where are you going!" Mary said shrilly, seeing me put on my old stovepipe, which the curators had been kind enough to save for me.

"Just to the library, Mother," I lied.

"I wish you wouldn't even go there, something could—"

"Something could happen right here," I said, almost testily. I found an unaccustomed rage rising in me, one I had to fight to temper. "We could be flattened by a boulder from space. A madman could rush in off the street with a bomb. I must go out, Mary."

And not looking back, I doffed my hat and went out.

I didn't go to the library, but headed for my old law office. That, too, I had learned from my readings, had been preserved. I longed to see the place where I had worked. I was halfway there when a sound down the street made me turn to see what all the shouting was about.

"Papa! Papa!" shouted Eddie, running after me with Willie close behind.

The two of them stopped before me.

"Permission to follow, sir," Willie said.

"Does your mother know you're here?" I said sternly.

Willie smiled. "No. She's mending a suit of clothes for Tad. Got him standing on a chair."

"Well ..."

"Please, Papa, please!" Eddie implored.

"I promise we'll be good," Willie said.

"All right," I said, secretly glad for the company, "but you'll have to back me up with your mother later."

"We'll tell any fib you want us to!" Eddie said.

I laughed loud like a fool, right there on the street.

"All right, you codgers, let's all jump in the soup together."

To my surprise and delight, when we reached my office, Billy Herndon himself stood in the doorway to greet me.

"So it's true," he said. On the faint ghost of his dark-complexioned face was a mixture of disbelief, shock, and, I believe, relief.

"Why Billy," I said as Eddie and Willie ran into the office, hooting with pleasure at finding all the old papers to be scattered, objects to be broken, "I do believe you're drunk."

"Thank God I am, Mr. Lincoln," he said, closing the door behind us as we entered the room and locking it.

On Billy's desk, sure enough, was a quarter-empty bottle of bourbon, and next to it, in the wastebasket, were three other empty ones. The rest of the room was as I had remembered it, with many books stacked in haphazard piles, except for the addition of a television set, switched on but showing no picture, and a radio, on but only hissing.

"Do you sleep with these contraptions on, Billy?" I asked.

"They come on periodically," he said. He poured himself another drink as he spoke. "There's news from both sides. It's a way of keeping in touch."

"I see. . . ." I said.

"Mr. Lincoln, has anyone contacted you?"

I looked at him in surprise. "*Contacted* me?"

"There are people in Springfield, our people, some of them from the old days. There's a movement to get some sort of organization, to find some sort of leadership. . . ."

He stopped to drink the bourbon, and as always I was taken by the ghostliness of the act, only the shroud of human features taking part in the process, the bourbon going nowhere but through his lips, leaving his bright bony skeleton intact, uninvolved. The likker seemed to have its effect, though.

He stood tall and thin, looked at me with his piercing black stare. "Don't you know what I'm talking about, Mr. Lincoln?"

"No, Billy, I don't."

"There's another war! Us against . . . them!" Again he stopped to pour a drink.

"You don't seem too taken with the idea, Billy."

"How could I be! How could anyone be! Do you know how . . . *bizarre* all of this is?"

"Yes, I do," I said. "I've been puzzling it out ever since it happened."

"What's to puzzle out?" he nearly shouted. Even Eddie and Willie stopped their rifling through my desk long enough to stare at him.

He lowered his voice and looked at me conspiratorially. "Mr. Lincoln, the scientists, the human ones, have said the earth has gone into some sort of cloud in space. There was a lot of discussion of it on the television before most of their channels went dead. There's been some broadcasts from our side, too. To me it's all talk. The plain fact is, we were dead and now we're alive. *All* of us. Everyone back, from the cavemen through Genghis Khan. Even Stephen Douglas!"

"Douglas!" I laughed.

He saw the humor of his own juxtaposition of Genghis Khan with Stephen Douglas, and laughed himself.

"But the plain fact is, Mr. Lincoln," he continued, "there's a fight brewing for who's going to run things. A big fight. And . . . good men are needed to win the fight."

I already saw where he was headed. I cut him off before he got there. "I'm not through puzzling this thing out, Billy. I imagine I'll be puzzling it out for quite some time—in solitude, if you don't mind."

"How can you say that?"

"Because it's the way I feel. And Mary ..."

"Mrs. Lincoln?" Billy said cautiously. They had never gotten along, since poor Billy had long ago made the mistake of comparing Mary, guilelessly, to a serpent.

"She's ... herself," I said. "She's been happy the past few weeks, Billy, and I'd like to keep her as happy as I can, within bounds."

He weighed my last words. "Which means you're not just going to hide in your home forever ..."

"No, I couldn't do that. But as for involvement, this war between the living and the newly alive ..."

"Mr. Lincoln, it's much more than that!" He knew he had my interest now and didn't reach for a drink.

"Tell me what you mean, Billy."

"There's war within our own kind! Think about it! All the evil men of history suddenly made alive again, along with all the good! Caligula, as well as Charlemagne. Cromwell as well as Washington. Napoleon—"

"Surely, Washington is more able than I—"

Now he broke off for another drink. "Washington is dead. Many of them are. There has been a lot of fighting already. The television reports have been horrible. A man named Hitler rose briefly in Europe, before he was cut down by the forces of Napoleon, who himself was assassinated three days ago. Alliances have been made and broken a hundred times. There's chaos on every continent. And of course the humans are still out there, attacking in small force, banding together, waiting...."

"This is impossible," I said, shaking my head. For the first time since I had awakened, the old despair dropped down toward me, crushing all the wonder of the last weeks, making me realize that it might be a different world, but it was still surely the same one. "Billy ..." I said slowly.

"Yes, Mr. Lincoln?"

"Have you noticed a certain ... viciousness in yourself, a quickness to anger, to violence, that was never there before?"

He paused to finish his drink. "I have. It's one of the reasons I've locked myself in here with these bottles."

"And have you noticed that though this latent anger is intensified when faced with humans, it exists toward those of your own kind, also—especially those who do not fit in with your own plans?"

"Yes."

"What do you make of this, Billy?"

"What do *you* make of it, Mr. Lincoln?"

"It's been one of the greatest puzzles to me, Billy. Human beings have always been a vicious race, but I believe we were saved by the temperance of thought." I smiled wanly. "If not the temperance of *likker*."

"Yes ... Mr. Lincoln," Billy said, returning my wan smile.

"But in these new circumstances, I believe we have something fundamental at work. In my reading the past few weeks, I came across mention of a man named Charles Darwin—"

"I have his book *On the Origin of Species* here, Mr. Lincoln!" Billy said, digging a volume out of the pile on his desk. He began to page through it, stopped, began to read.

I held up my hand to make him stop. "You know I don't have the patience for that, Billy. Thank Providence for the encyclopedias I found in the library. They gave me the kernel of it. This idea of the survival of the fittest."

"Yes," Billy said.

"I thought that a frightening idea, until I turned it around and looked at it. It makes perfect sense. We saw it all the time when I was growing up. An animal, a man, became sick, and died. Another, stronger one, lived on. If the sick ones did all the childbearing, there'd soon be nothing left. Everything's trying to better itself. If you look at it in that fashion, it's not a cold thing at all, but rather sound, don't you think?"

"I do, Mr. Lincoln."

"So I think that's what we have here. It reminds me of the man who had two stoves. One of them cooked things hot, the other warm. So one winter night he came in with his arse end frozen solid. He sat on the warm stove, and nothing much happened. Then he sat on the hot stove, and soon his arse end was unfrozen, and he was a happy man again.

"I think what we've got here, Billy, is a warm and a

hot stove. This war with the humans—well, that's a warm stove. This fight amongst ourselves, that's the hot one. We've got to go to the hot stove now and sit on it, or none of us will have arses left!"

"Exactly, Mr. Lincoln! The humans can be dealt with later. If we don't stabilize our own people, root out the tyrants from history, we'll end up with a country, and a world, in chaos. This is a unique chance to make the whole world safe for democratic principles, once and for all. . . ."

"There is, of course, a way to sit on both of these stoves at once, I think. . . ."

Billy looked at me expectantly.

I felt my stomach turning over. "This all sounds too familiar, Billy. And the cost in lives . . ."

"It will happen anyway, Mr. Lincoln, with or without you. And I'm afraid that without you what will happen will be a terrible thing."

I clenched my fist, watching the bones through my faint flesh form a claw. I still hadn't gotten used to this new appearance entirely, and it still frightened me, the new feelings I had. "But these feelings of violence, I fear they will get out of hand."

"They will, unless we rein them in."

I made a sudden decision. "No, Billy, I cannot. I cannot do this to Mrs. Lincoln, and frankly, I cannot do it to myself. I fear for the world, but it would take a hard man to do this job. I don't feel I have that hardness in me anymore."

"I think you do, Mr. Lincoln. I think you, of everyone, would find the balance in these new feelings, and put them to the public good."

"It would mean sending thousands, millions, perhaps, back to their graves, not to mention the millions of humans we would turn into our own kind." I hit my hand with my fist. "I *cannot* allow myself to do that. Not again . . ."

Billy put his hand on my arm. "Mr. Lincoln, if you don't . . ."

I held up my hand. "Enough, Billy." I turned to Eddie and Willie, busy breaking the points of our old preserved pens against the stove in the room. My heart

filled with satisfaction at the sight of them, even though
I was already forcing down the pride and lust for power
that Billy Herndon had awakened in me, along with the
guilt at knowing he might be right about me.

"Come on, you scamps!" I said to the boys, putting
my hat back on my head. I walked to the door and waited
for Eddie and Willie to run to me, shouting as they
scooted out of the office under my arm.

"We'll come and see you, Mr. Lincoln," Billy said.
"There are others who believe as I do. We'll convince
you, soon."

I pointed to the stove, which, being summer, wasn't
lit. "That stove is cold, Billy. Think of it as me."

And then I left.

4

They did come see me, a few days later. It was hell-
ishly hot, all of a sudden, the end of June and the first
heat wave of the year. I had prided myself on figuring out
the mechanism of the machines in our home that cooled
the air, providing much relief. We had no visitors and,
not having a television or radio, knew only that the world
immediately outside our home had quieted for the most
part. Now and then there was a ruckus in the street, but
no one came to bother us. Once or twice I went out for
a paper, but few new ones had been printed, and those,
sadly, provided scant news of the chaos that seemed to be
prevailing elsewhere in the world. I tired of reading old
news from the library. Mostly I played with the boys, and
sat thinking.

During these days Mary became even happier.
Though she had been older than me when she had
passed on, her features had regained their youthful glow.
I think she saw that some crisis had passed in me, and
that she would have me to herself after all. We ate meager
meals, and were content with them, though my one forag-
ing trip to the supermarket with Tad proved that foodstuffs were getting low on the shelves. In the back of my
mind this bothered me, and gave another portent of that
breakdown in order that seemed to be forming.

Billy Herndon and three others came after dinner while I sat on the porch admiring the fact that the sun, no matter what went on in the world, still went down in beauty like it always had. There was a sliver of moon up, and I enjoyed that, also. The mumble of Herndon and the others' voices stopped as they reached my gate, and they stood silent for a moment, unsure of how to proceed.

"Mr. Lincoln—" Billy began finally.

"Come in, gentlemen," I said, unhinging my long leg from the side of the rocker where I had let it dangle and rising. "We'll go into my study and talk."

As we passed into the house Mary appeared and clutched at me. "Father, what is this?"

"It's all right," I said, holding her close for a moment before releasing her. "Just some men come to speak with me. You remember Billy Herndon. . . ."

She gave Herndon a tight-lipped stare. "I do. . . ."

Billy bowed his head. I think he felt Mary's stare burn into him as we all went into my study.

I closed the door, feeling a pang at seeing Mary, obviously upset, stomp off into another part of the house.

"Sit down, gentlemen," I said. I moved to lift a pile of books from one chair, noting the vaguely familiar features shrouding the bones of one of Billy's companions, the thin face, the goatee. Of the two others one looked even more familiar, and the third I knew immediately as Stanton, my old secretary of war.

"Mr. Secretary!" I said warmly, clasping his hand. It was then I saw that his other wrist was manacled to the man in the goatee.

"What's this?" I said.

"Mr. President," Stanton said, not without warmth himself, but avoiding my question.

As none of the men made a move to sit down, I went behind my desk and sat down myself. I picked up a paperweight, a heavy glass globe which trapped a miniature White House inside, held it for a moment, placed it carefully back on the desk.

"I'm listening, gentlemen," I said.

The stranger who looked most familiar to me spoke up. He was an old man, in his eighties I'd guess, tall and thin, with the air of someone who has spent time in government service.

"Hello, Father," he said, "it is I, Robert."

"Robert!" I said. I made to stand up, then sat back in my chair, overcome with the fact that my son, the only one who had survived to manhood, now stood before me a full twenty-five years older in appearance than I. The last time I had seen him he had been a commissioned captain, at my own timid request, on General Grant's personal staff. He'd been twenty-two years old. "Robert, I can't believe it!" Now I did stand, came around the desk to clasp him stiffly. I had the unreal feeling of embracing my own grandfather. I stood back and looked at him. "Well, you certainly did make a go of it." I pointed to the door. "You march right out there and kiss your mother and brothers, immediately." I scowled. "Be gentle with your mother, will you, though, Robert? It *will* come as quite a shock."

"Yes, sir," he said. To my surprise he looked to Herndon first.

"It's best you're not here anyway," Billy said.

Robert nodded and left, closing the door behind him.

I turned my attention to Billy, who had a decidedly haggard look about him.

"You never were much for listening to your own temperance speeches, were you, Billy?"

"Things have gotten much worse in the past days, Mr. Lincoln," Billy said. "The United States alone is now split into five territories, three of them ruled by outright tyrants. The south, including Mexico, has been taken over by Aaron Burr, after fighting off, and eventually killing, Sam Houston. They're calling it the Second Alamo. Florida is ruled by Cortés. The northeastern section, including Maryland, Virginia, and Washington, D.C., is presently the most stable, with three territorial governors, none of them very strong, allied with a former president from the 1960s, Lyndon Johnson. There's word he's heartsick for Texas, doesn't have the stomach for what's happening, and would like to leave someone in charge and go south. Burr has promised him a governorship. Obviously, this stability could be shaken at any time, but we feel that if Johnson could be replaced soon, there's a chance of the continuance and growth of a democratic system. Most of the army is presently under Johnson's control. We think this will be our final chance to make something permanent out of the new order that's forming."

"That's all . . . interesting," I said, picking up my paperweight from the desk, holding it, putting it down.

"Mr. President," Stanton said. "Let me be blunt. Thomas Jefferson is dead, John Adams is dead, you already know that Washington was killed during the first days of fighting. Hamilton has apparently gone insane. Andrew Jackson has been seen in New Orleans, but he has reunited with his young wife Rebecca and has no designs on power. The later presidents we're not so sure about, though most of them, from what we hear, want nothing to do with the fighting or have not decided. Some of them, we feel, are not up to the task. A few of them are dangerous. In short, Mr. President, we think you're the only one for the job."

I began to speak, but Stanton cut me off.

"Let me finish if I might, Mr. President. There's more. The former leaders of the United States are not the only ones with designs on our territory. There are others, many of them extremely dangerous, in Europe, Asia, and what they now call the Soviet Union, comprising Russia and territories east. One of the ancient rulers of India has already slaughtered millions of Hindus. There are vast arsenals of weapons, some of them hideous in strength, poised for use or already used at various points around the globe. This is not a problem confined to the United States or even the Americas. And then of course there is the problem of the living. . . ."

"What the Secretary is saying," Herndon said, "is that once we stabilize the 'second lifers,' as we're calling them, there will of course be another fight with those who were already here. We know that as they are killed they become like us, which seems a relatively humane way of handling the problem. Coexistence is out of the question. You and I have already talked about this rage we seem to have against the living humans; apparently it is uncontrollable and we can only conclude there is a reason for it. They will not live with us; we cannot live with them. The only solution as we see it is to bring them over to us. This will be the war beyond the war. You seemed to realize all this already, when I talked to you."

"Yes . . ." I said, my heart sicker all the while.

"You do understand the urgency of this, don't you, Mr. President?" Stanton said.

I looked at him, at his manacled prisoner who stood mute beside him, gaze downward. One of the bones in his leg had been broken at one time, I saw.

"Yes, I understand. But unfortunately, I cannot help."

"Mr. President, this is impossible!" Stanton exploded. "Without you, there *is* no hope. Histories all over the world cite you, know what you did during the War Between the States. There is a man, Gandhi, who has tried to stop the bloodshed in India, who specifically mentioned you by name. He was cut down two days ago. You are *known*, you are someone who can be rallied behind. Mr. President," he said, overcome by emotion, "there is a train, waiting for you now, to take you to Washington. An aircraft would not be safe, we feel. Arrangements have been made with Lyndon Johnson to transfer power tomorrow, at noon. A former Supreme Court justice has been engaged. Television and radio will carry the proceedings around the world. You will declare that the United States of America is, as of noon tomorrow, a sovereign nation once more, and that, in fact, all nations are invited to join with it in a new, democratic order." There were tears in his eyes. "With you this can happen. Without you we have *nothing*."

A weight of sadness unlike any I had ever felt, even in the darkest days of the war, pressed down on me.

"Sirs," I said, taking my two friends, as well as the manacled stranger, in with my words. "I say no to you. I cannot, and will not, serve. Here is my reason. I have thought hard and long about this, and turned it every way, and searched the bottom of my heart. I have asked the Greater Power above for guidance, and felt I needed it, more than at any time in my existence. And this is my conclusion.

"Even if your cause is great, which it is, I cannot be

part of it. Even though any man of conscience, on examining that organ of truth, would conclude that this is the only path to follow, I cannot walk it with you. The fault is my own.

"I have thought that my reluctance stemmed from my inability to subject Mary and my family to further pain. I believe I told you that the other day, Billy. The truth is that duty would, as always, come first. If duty throws a path at you, your legs have to carry you.

"But the truth of the matter is I don't have the legs for the job, and am not able to walk that path. I would be a cripple, and a burden to you.

"The first time I had the strength for the job. I remember what it did to me, and to my family. But now the strength is gone."

I nearly wept, then. "I would be no good to you, gentlemen, alive or dead. I am hollow inside. I no longer possess the will to send men to their deaths in *any* cause. Though I sense this trait of violence in my new existence and agree with Billy that it was bred into us for a reason and for our betterment, I could not make use of it myself. I am too tired. And what I could not use in myself, I could not expect others to use on my behalf."

I looked up at them. Billy had retreated to the door of the room and seemed to be guarding it. He looked at me intently. Stanton, in the meanwhile, was unlocking the manacles of the goateed man and now stood away from him. The man stared at me intently, with surprising malice.

"Mr. President," Stanton said, "this is John Wilkes Booth, the man who assassinated you on April fourteenth, 1865, by putting a bullet into the back of your skull at Ford's Theater. He's the man who caused you, and the nation, so much pain, who robbed you of your life and the United States of America of its chance to properly heal."

I stared at the man and suddenly knew him. The actor. Mary and I had seen him many times on the stage. Carl Sandburg had named him as my assassin; he had broken his leg jumping from my box to the stage after firing the fatal shot.

I saw red anger in front of my eyes and heard myself

shout. *This* was the man who had tried to destroy the Union. I groped on my desk, came up with the heavy paperweight I had toyed with before, grasped it tightly. I saw nothing but absolute anger, and raised the paperweight over the cowering actor.

This—

Billy Herndon and Secretary Stanton were holding me. I was bent over double, and when I looked up, the door to the room had opened and Robert had entered.

"Is it over?" Robert asked.

"Yes. Your father will be fine," Billy said.

"Father," Robert said, "I have to tell you I knew—"

"It's all right," I said. "A man's got to know what he is—"

On the floor I spied the pile of dust the actor John Wilkes Booth had become; in the midst of it sat the bruised paperweight with the miniature White House caught inside, like a bug in amber.

I took hold of myself and straightened.

"It's in all of us," Billy Herndon said quietly. "And it's up to men like us to make sure the best possible world can come of it."

I put my hand on Billy's shoulder. "Yes," I said. "You're right, of course. I suppose sometimes a man can't, or won't, see the monkey he's got riding his own back. I had hoped . . ."

"You're the only man who can take control of this," Stanton said. "You're the only man all of us, all around the world, can rally around."

I turned away from them, and looked out the window, and put my hands behind my back.

"Mr. President?" Stanton asked.

"God help me," I said. For a moment I was silent. Then I said, "Robert, send your mother in. I must tell her it's time to pack for Washington."

7

The memoirs of Peter Sun

1

When I awoke in my ditch, I thought myself alone. But I awakened to find myself surrounded by bodies. Not bodies, exactly—rather, piles of clothing powdered with dead dust.

As I watched, snugged into my cutout in the side of my ditch, another pile of clothing fell from above, to land a few feet from me. It was then I heard the rough sound of laughter, the intercourse of two voices.

"That one will no longer bother anyone. What is the next crime?"

The second voice, more businesslike, said, "Looting. Stealing from the people's foodstores."

"Very well." The first voice made a grunting sound. I heard a gasp, a third voice, and then the first, rough voice laughed.

"He went to atoms easily, didn't he, comrade?"

"Dispose of him," the second voice said, testily.

"Very well."

Another pile of clothing, leaving a trail of dust, plopped down in the ditch.

"Next?" the rough voice said.

"Drunkenness. Hoarding."

"Very well."

The rough voice grunted, another pile of clothing came over to land in front of me.

Now there was a completely new voice above, a shrill scream. I heard what sounded like a struggle. The rough voice cursed, and then a fully clothed figure dropped into the ditch in front of me, fell to all fours, then rose. A skeleton's face looked straight into mine, startled. Its jaw dropped. Suddenly the figure, the vague ghostly outline of a woman's features shrouding its bone, looked up above and began to wave its arms.

"Comrades! Comrades! I've found—"

A rifle shot rang out, and the skeleton staggered back and then collapsed into dust.

The rough voice laughed. "She saved me the trouble of throwing her over the side."

"Continue," the businesslike voice said. "The next is a political dissenter. He was caught uttering antiparty slogans."

"Tsk, tsk." The rough voice laughed, then grunted. "I think two shovel hits for this one, for his terrible crimes."

Another dusty pile of clothing dropped in front of me.

"How about two at once, we'll make the job go faster?" the rough voice above laughed again.

Two more piles of clothing came over.

A rock loosened by my foot tumbled to the ditch and made a sound.

"Did you hear something, comrade?" the rough voice asked above.

There was silence, during which I held my breath and lay perfectly still.

"Nothing," the businesslike voice said. "Continue."

"Very well."

They went on for what seemed hours. Then, finally, the prissy, businesslike voice said, "We are finished."

"All right."

I counted to sixty, and was about to allow myself to move when a massive skeleton dropped down into the ditch in front of me, bearing a shovel, and began to study the piles of clothing and the far wall. He moved down away to my right, then turned, poking at the clothing with his shovel, and began to make his way down to me.

I snugged as deeply into my cubbyhole as I could.

"What are you doing down there!"

The massive skeleton stopped not four feet to the right of where I stood. The skull looked up. "I heard something before."

"Don't be foolish! Get up here immediately!" the businesslike voice commanded.

The skeleton's hand tightened on the handle of the shovel, and I heard it mumble a curse.

"What was that?" the figure above said. "What did you say?"

"Nothing, comrade," the massive skeleton said sullenly. "I'm coming."

He began to climb the side of the ditch, his foot at one moment snugging right into the floor of my cubbyhole as I watched, but then, to my relief, climbing on.

In a few moments, in the midst of much berating talk by the businesslike voice, I heard the roar of a starting vehicle, which then went into gear and pulled away.

Again I counted to sixty, then rolled out of my hole.

Cautiously, I climbed up the slope and looked over the top.

The road bordering the ditch was empty, and just disappearing behind a distant hill was an army truck.

I rested my back against the slope of the ditch and breathed deeply of fresh air, looking back at the place I had inhabited.

After a few minutes I pulled myself out of the ditch and, marking my way east by the sun, began to walk.

2

It wasn't long before I determined that I would not be able to get far by daylight, at least not near the road, which was periodically awash with traffic, most of it coming from the direction of Moscow. I kept close to my companion ditch, and on more than one occasion had to fling myself into it to avoid detection as a convoy rolled by.

All of these military vehicles were manned by skeletons, I noted, a fact that I found very disturbing.

Finally, spying what looked like a village ahead, I made my way off the road and approached it through trees.

The sight of piles of white dust as I approached told me immediately that some sort of local battle had taken place here. A cluster of empty-looking houses led into a small town square. There, surrounding a fountain centered by a statue of Lenin, were huge piles of clothing. Russian weapons, most of them World War II vintage, lay scattered about, along with hoes and rakes and crude clubs. Someone had fought here, but who? Human or skeleton?

"They were good people," a voice said behind me, startling me as I stood gazing at the fountain.

I went into a defensive posture, but the old, human woman who confronted me only smiled. She held a broom close to her.

"You won't need your fists against me, young man. I've seen much worse than you in my time, if you can believe it. The Germans, the pogroms, the camps. In other guises I've seen it all before. Yesterday was all of it rolled into one."

I relaxed slightly, still wary, and mad at myself for my tired carelessness.

"Are you alone here?"

She pointed with her broom at the piles of clothing. "Except for them. There are three of mine in there, my foolish son, a daughter, a grandson."

"What happened?"

Walking slowly, she went past me and sat on the edge of the fountain, laying her broom down beside her. "We fought, like we always do. And like always, we lost."

"The whole town?"

"All except me. They kept me alive, for revenge."

"The soldiers did this?"

She looked surprised. "Of course not. The skeleton soldiers didn't come until after the massacre. They rounded all the murderers up and took them away to join the army. They have plenty for their army now, I suppose. There was one army boy here yesterday, a human army boy, but he died with the rest of the town."

"Who did this?"

She pointed off over the rooftops with her broom. "They came from that direction, the graveyard, all at once. All the dead of this town. And they hadn't forgotten."

"Forgotten what?"

She looked up at me. "Why, how to be alive, of course. They hate us, you know."

I began to be impatient with this rambling old woman. I got up to walk away from her, but she made a quick movement and grabbed my arm, holding it tightly.

"If I'd known they hated us, I wouldn't have helped them."

I looked down at her. "What are you saying?"

"Forgive me," she said. Tears had come into her eyes. "Someone must forgive me. You get to be so old, you think you don't want life to end."

I stared down at her, waiting for her to go on.

"I helped them!" she said. "How was I to know they hate all of us, want all of us to be dead! They promised me life, if I told them where all of the hiding places were! They promised that all of the rest would be merely turned into those like themselves! How was I to know that my foolish, mad son, and all the rest, would fight them? How was I to know that!"

She clutched at me with both of her aged hands. "So they were grouped here by the fountain, the whole, living town, and the skeletons killed them once, and then killed them again! And they turned to this!" She let me go, picked up her broom, brushed at the powder with it. "I begged them to kill me, too, but they wouldn't! Now *you* must kill me!"

She began to brush at the powder, knocking it out of clothing, trying to clean it up. I moved away from her. She followed after, falling into the piles of dust, crawling after me, moaning. "All right, I confess! Those other times, when the Germans came, when the pogroms came, I told them where the hiding places were then, too! I wanted to live! But now I want to *die!*"

She crawled after me like an insect as I moved back away from her. I turned to run off toward the other end of town.

She laughed madly after me. "I know you! I know who you are! I saw your picture on the television! So this is your new world, your world of peace and democracy? Is this what you wanted?"

I ran until I could no longer hear her words, and left the town behind me.

3

So I had learned that the army of the skeletons had already been through here. Perhaps, then, the areas off the main roads would be safe. I passed the rest of the morning in the woods at the edge of the road, hearing the occasional rumble of trucks.

Seeing another small village back off the road, I made my way toward it.

This one proved to be entirely empty. It was much smaller than the previous town, a few small houses, little more than huts, and a dirt-covered square.

One of the huts proved to be stocked with dry goods, and I made a meal, tying up the rest of what I could carry in a sheet and taking it with me. I checked the rest of the dwellings, seeking a working radio or television, but found none, and quickly moved on.

I decided to keep to the countryside. Veering away from the road, I made my way down into a wooded dell. Here, there was no sound save that of birds and the chatter of squirrels. I stopped momentarily to watch a jay attending her eggs in a nest, remembering all the times that nature had been my solace when the world of men became too much to bear.

This idyll was broken by the sight of a skeletal bird veering across my vision to dart viciously into the jay's nest. Feathers exploded, and there was a high, prematurely ended screech. The dead jay fell to the ground, only to transform into a skeletal presence and fly up to join the other aviary skeleton in pecking the eggs and knocking them from the nest. They stopped their work to regard me, the original bird screeching angrily.

I walked on. A brief shiver ran through me. Now I noticed all the churned-up holes in the forest floor, especially near the boles of trees, where the carcasses of dead animals had been renewed.

With relief I left that sight behind, only to break out of the trees at the bottom of the dell and confront a more fantastic one.

In the clearing, which measured roughly the size of a soccer field, lay the ruins of a Soviet MIG jet. It was a dreamlike thing to see, totally out of place in this tight woodland setting. I was reminded of a child's fairy tale, yet the touch of its cold steel was enough to remind me of its reality.

It must have been a fantastic landing. I traced the shorn tops of trees, trailing away from the rear of the plane, as far as the eye could see. The pilot must have glided along the top of the forest until he was dropped into this spot. The jet had been neatly bent in its middle, leaving it otherwise whole.

Always cautious, I approached the cockpit.

The canopy was up. Ready for anything, I put down my burden of food and hoisted myself up to peer inside.

The cockpit was empty.

But there was blood. I took this as neither a good nor a bad sign. It told me only that with all probability a human pilot had landed this plane here. What he might have become . . .

I dropped down, regained my food parcel.

There was matted grass away from the plane, much more of it than would have been caused by one man.

Again, with caution, I followed this trail.

It led into the woods, and then to a cleared path, where there were wagon-wheel tracks.

I followed.

I was led deep into the woods. The trees closed overhead like a canopy. A skeletal squirrel regarded me from a tree branch. I braced for it to jump, but it chittered and ran off.

I saw more skeletal animals—a rabbit, and once, far off, what looked like the bony outlines of a fleeing fox.

Two large skeleton birds, which may have been natural enemies, fought each other in the close skies above. The woods were filled with strange cries.

It occurred to me that the only live animal I had seen had been that jay.

There was sound ahead.

As I approached I bound my food pack to my back and scaled a branching tree. I had learned to be quiet, long ago in Cambodia. A skeletal owl I passed did not note my presence.

The higher I climbed, the more the tree arched over the noises below me. I caught sight of a wooden cart through branches. I climbed out higher. Soon I reached a spot that beautifully arched over the scene below.

There was a crudely covered wagon pulled by a small horse. Three men surrounded it. A woman came into the picture, bearing an armload of what looked like edibles from the surrounding forest. One of the men pulled a pot from the wagon, into which the edibles were dropped. In a moment another woman appeared, bearing a water jug. This she emptied into the pot while two of the men began to arrange a fire.

"This will be a good meal!" one of the men said heartily, in a Russian dialect I could not quite place.

All of them, thankfully, were human.

I made myself as comfortable as possible in my tree perch and watched.

In a little while they had a fire going, the pot suspended over it. They were good woodsmen and, from the smell that drifted up to me, good cooks. I thought of the packages of dried crackers tied to my back and realized it had been more than a day since I had eaten a real meal. Hunger came back to me in a wave.

I held it at bay. It had been many years since I had gone hungry, but like many talents it came back easily to me.

I watched them cook, then watched them eat.

It was during the meal that one of the women went into the covered wagon with a plate of food. I heard moans of pain from within. She reemerged and said, in the same strange dialect, "He will eat nothing."

The man with the hearty voice shrugged. "Then he will die."

Without looking up, but raising his voice, he said, "Perhaps our friend up in the trees would like to eat something!"

They all gazed up at me and laughed. I felt like a pinned spider. At that moment any of them with a weapon could have shot me from the tree. Instead, the hearty one waved his hand and said, "Come down, my friend."

I climbed down from the tree and walked into their clearing.

"You are good, make no mistake about it," the hearty one said. He pinched my shirt. "But you forgot your clothing. You stood out like a child's kite caught in the tree." He shook my hand. "I am Sasha." He turned to the others. The two younger men he introduced as his sons, Tibor and Caspian. The women, who stood back, he did not introduce.

"Sit, and eat," he said.

I squatted by the fire. One of the women, who had long black hair, served me. She did not look at me. The other, whose hair was red and even longer, did, from a distance. I felt examined.

"I know him," the second woman said finally.

"Reesa, it is not your place to speak."

She shrugged and turned away.

Sasha leaned close to me and said, "You are Peter Sun."

"Yes."

"You are a good man. But not always, eh?"

I hesitated before answering. "No, not always."

He patted me on the back. "You are honest."

I thought of how he could know this much about me. They were not Chinese, were not Cambodian. Those days were many years ago. I felt the others regarding me closely.

"Perhaps I'd better move on," I said, putting my food down. I began to rise.

Sasha put his hand on my shoulder and urged me back down.

"Nonsense," he said. "No one here will hurt you. Isn't that right Tibor? Caspian?"

Each of his sons, in turn, nodded, though their eyes were not completely friendly.

The woman with the long red hair regarded me coldly from where she cleaned the pot.

From the wagon came a wail of pain.

"Come with me," Sasha said. "I will prove to you that we mean you no harm."

I walked with him to the wagon.

Inside was a man in a uniform, obviously the pilot from the downed MIG. He lay on his back on a pile of quilts. He was covered with a sheet. He looked to be in a fever, throwing his head from side to side.

Sasha drew back the sheet and pointed to the man's shin. "It was broken, here, when he landed," he said. "It was a spectacular sight to see. He had been shot from the sky by two other MIGs. We took him from the wreckage, and Reesa set his fracture." He looked levelly at me. "In the old days we would have drowned him in the nearest pond, because of the uniform he is wearing." He smiled. "But it's amazing what a difference one day can make, and now he is not an enemy, but a friend. We have a bigger enemy, all of us."

"And what about me?"

His face brightened. "You? You were never an enemy, Peter Sun. Or whatever name you are using today."

"But the way your sons look at me—"

He put his hand on my shoulder. There was a hard kind of sadness in his eyes.

"They don't hate you, my friend. They are in *awe* of you."

I had seen many things in my days, but never something like this. "I don't understand."

His laugh came back. "You don't *have* to! You'll know everything in its time."

"All the same I should be moving along."

"No," Sasha said. "I don't think you want to do that. Even the forest, here, is filled with danger now. A man alone would not last long. We know these woods very well, and we're going east, just like you. Besides," he added, again gaining his sad smile, "we *know* you'll come with us!"

I was about to say something when his hand on my shoulder squeezed and he said, "We have coffee. Come and have some."

After covering the moaning pilot, he led me back to the fire.

4

I stayed. Strangely, it did not seem a wholly conscious decision on my part. Rarely in my life have I been content within a group; even in the days before the present madness, while planning the rally in Moscow, I had never been fully comfortable with those Jon Roberts had assembled. Often I had felt the need to get away, to be alone.

Yet here I was, part of a strange band, and content to be so. There was a kind of comfort in relying on men and women who knew these woods so well.

The first two days I was with them we met no opposition at all. There were many trails through the forest, and Sasha always picked one that best suited us and kept us heading east. Once, we heard a great commotion far off and determined that a battle was taking place, in, Sasha said, the city of Gorki; but, except for the occasional skeletal rabbit, which Sasha and Tibor took great satisfaction in trapping and then slaying to watch it turn to dust, we saw nothing in the way of skeletons.

I saw little of the awe in my companions that Sasha had spoken of. I was treated with deference, perhaps—but it was mixed with what seemed to me like barely veiled contempt. The woman Reesa, especially, took great satisfaction in nearly throwing my meals at me. I saw Sasha, in fact, take her aside a couple of times to scold her. But if anything, her dislike of me only grew. Only when I spoke to her myself about her actions, after she had deliberately spilled a plate of excellent vegetable stew on me while handing it to me, did she show a startling reversal of attitude.

"There was no need to do that," I said testily, brushing what little was left of the stew back into its bowl, the rest of it off myself to the ground.

She turned scarlet red and refused to look at me.

"Did you hear me? I've done nothing to you. There's no reason to treat me this way."

Unaccountably, she turned away and began to weep.

I was at a loss. She dropped the stew pot at her feet and ran off into the woods. I followed. I found her cradled against a tree, covering her eyes, crying.

"You shouldn't be making such noise. You'll give us away," I said.

She rose and tried to run, but I caught her arm.

"What's wrong?" I said. "Why do you treat me as if you hate me?"

"I *do* hate you! Let me go!"

I released her, and she fled deeper into the woods. I looked back toward camp, sure that Sasha or one of the others would have followed by now. But I was alone. Sasha had repeatedly warned us about wandering too far.

"Reesa! Come back here!"

Ahead, I heard her weeping.

And then I heard a sound I had heard once, long ago, in another country.

I ran to the small clearing where she stood frozen against a tree. She had stopped weeping. A wild boar, a vicious creature, stood in the clearing between Reesa and me, regarding her sullenly. It was real, not skeletal, its black eyes and white tusks only adding to its fierceness.

"Don't move, Reesa," I whispered.

She nodded slightly.

The boar snorted angrily, a prelude to attack, its eyes riveted on Reesa.

I searched the woods behind me frantically for a weapon. I found a long, hard stick, but neither end was sharp. I threw it down. I was searching for another when I heard a cry and looked up to see that the boar had charged Reesa.

I grabbed the unsharpened stick and ran into the clearing. Unthinking, I jumped onto the boar's back, looped the hard stick under its throat, and pulled back.

The beast's legs buckled. But I had merely transferred its wrath to myself. In a moment the boar had flipped me over. I held the stick around its throat for dear life, as the boar now poised to thrust at me viciously with its tusks.

Reesa appeared above me, drew a knife out from her boot, and slashed down at the boar, cutting long and deep into the animal's throat.

It gave out a horrible wail, kicked its legs, and as Reesa held the knife to the main vein, the boar suddenly collapsed in a bloody heap.

Only to come back to life a moment later as a skeleton.

But Reesa had anticipated this. When the change came, she brought her knife through the bones in the animal's neck.

Once again it died, its bones turning to dust.

We were thrown into a heap together as the boar disappeared.

We lay panting, and Reesa laughed. "I'm afraid you'll have to put up with my vegetable stew for some time to come."

She raised herself over me, her hair hanging down like a mantle as she studied my face. "More than anything in my life," she said, "I've feared, and wanted, this moment."

She kissed me, pressing her mouth hard against mine. I felt myself respond, enfolding her in my arms, holding her tight against me. It seemed not only right, but strangely inevitable.

I broke the kiss and smiled slightly. "But I thought you hated—"

"Be quiet," Reesa said.

I was, for a time.

5

So the next weeks passed. Reesa and I were lovers. There was nothing but acceptance from the others. Indeed, it had been expected. Sasha was not Reesa's father, as I had thought; neither were Tibor or Caspian her brothers. The other girl, the dark-haired one named Maria, was a cousin of the young men. I gathered from one conversation with Sasha that there had been many more of them at one time. When I pressed him for details, he gave me his sad smile and said, "In time, I'll tell you."

We passed through much country. It had become summer, making our journey more pleasant; the nights, especially, were cool and clear, with stars overhead through the trees. Many evenings I lay with Reesa in my arms, looking at the turning bowl of the Big Dipper, the rising keystone of Hercules with his club, the easily recognized Leo, the huge lion.

We traveled by day, mostly. We met no opposition; the towns and villages we passed through on our journey north and east were deserted of all but skeletal animals. There were plentiful provisions, mostly dry foodstuffs, with an occasional prized can of meat or fish.

During the first few days of this time the pilot in the wagon grew worse. I know that Sasha had been ready for his death; one night when it seemed the young pilot would pass from this world, Sasha stood vigil the entire night, after binding the man hand and foot.

"If he dies," Sasha said, "he will die a second time, quickly."

It was a rough night for Maria, who had come to be the pilot's nurse. But the next morning, after the pilot's fever finally broke and he awakened, it was Maria's and not Sasha's face he saw. There was instant feeling between them, and as the pilot grew stronger he and Maria were inseparable.

One night after dinner the pilot was strong enough to join us as we sat around the fire, talking. He was not a shy young man, but he did wait to be invited. When Sasha bade him sit with us, he wasted no time and pulled out a pack of American cigarettes from his pocket to pass around.

"Marlboros!" Tibor cried happily.

"Ah, wonderful," Sasha said, lighting one. "It's been a long time since I could kill myself slowly and enjoy it."

"You are good people," the pilot said. "I thank you for my life."

"You would have thanked us for your death, had you not recovered," Sasha said.

The young man nodded. "I would have done the same thing." He paused. "I did it for my best friend the day I flew out."

"Was it madness?" Maria said, coming up behind him to put her hands on his shoulders.

"Yes, madness is the word for it," he said. He leaned in closer to the fire. "A nightmare. The sirens went off, but when we got to our planes, half of them were already in the air, with *them* at the controls." He shivered. "It seems the skeletons had attacked the other barracks, turning all of those fellows into . . . those things. We had to fight a battle just to get into the air. We were ordered to fly north, save the planes, regroup. Only four of us got off the ground without being . . . changed."

He gazed into the flames. "My best friend, Mikhail, was turned into one of them before my eyes. One moment he was fighting beside me, the next he was hit by a bullet."

"We all have similar stories," Sasha said.

"Yes," the pilot said, "I suppose you do." He gazed very hard into the fire. "But I *killed* him with my own hands, watched him turn to dust. We had been at flight school together."

Maria hugged him.

"But," the pilot said, looking up from the fire and giving us a hard smile, "we have a new army now, eh?"

Sasha shrugged. "Of sorts. There are things that can be done."

"Such as?" the pilot said bitterly. "Do you know that most of the Red Army was decimated in one day? I listened to the radio when I finally got into the air. My three companions were shot down before me, by men they had known, played cards with the night before. Men made of bones . . ." He snorted, threw his cigarette into the fire. "I'm sorry I'm talking like this. I'm being selfish. It's just that when I awoke, I thought it might all have been a bad dream."

"Did you hear anything about Moscow?" I asked.

He looked at me. "Yes. Total destruction. Half the city in flames. Things went better at Leningrad. Before I crashed, there were reports that Leningrad had become a garrison town, a tough band of fighters holding out in the center of the city. I wish them well."

He pulled another cigarette from his pack, lit it.

Around the fire there was silence.

The pilot said, "Well, what chance do we have? They have the planes, the tanks, most of the soldiers. Thousands of years of bodies to use in battle. What hope is there against them? Nuclear weapons? Where do we drop them, on ourselves? Destroy everything to save our own skins?" He became more angry. "Did you know that that bastard Stalin was in charge in Moscow? He had Lenin killed on the second day. He had already killed most of the czars as they approached the capital. It's said he murdered Nicholas the Second himself, waiting by the grave. It's insane, I tell you."

"As I said, there are ways," Sasha said quietly.

The pilot looked at him sharply. "Do you think anywhere is safe? We heard reports. China, America, the same everywhere. There's not enough vodka in the world to make this nightmare disappear."

Sasha went to the wagon, returned with a dark bottle. "Perhaps this will help," he said.

The pilot took the bottle thankfully, drank long from it. He gave it back to Sasha. "I apologize. I'm afraid I'm not myself. It's just the shock of it all."

The bottle was passed around, came back to the pilot. He took another drink and then yawned.

"He's tired, he must still rest," Maria said.

"I *am* tired," the pilot said. He stood up. Some of his anger had drained away. "You are good people. Please forgive me."

"Go to sleep," Sasha said gently.

"Yes," the pilot said, yawning again.

Maria led him back to the wagon.

"He's right, you know," I said, accepting the bottle and drinking from it. "It does seem hopeless."

"I don't see you giving up," Sasha said.

"No."

"I can't see you offering your throat to become one of them. Can you?"

"But no, I couldn't do that. Someone once said, 'The man without himself is nothing.' "

"Ah," Sasha said. He leaned closer to me. "Tell me," he said, "just who are you?"

He let me drink from the bottle again. I shook my head. "I'm nobody." I looked at him sharply. "Why don't you tell me why you seem to know so much about me, and where we're going?"

Sasha smiled, accepted the bottle back from me. "Ah," he said. "All good things in their time, eh?"

6

A week later the pilot and Maria left us.

It was a parting that Sasha seemed to know was coming. All of them did. Reesa began to fuss over Maria the day before, mending her clothing, helping her gather food. The pilot was sullen and anxious.

The night before their leaving he announced his intentions.

"We wish you well," Sasha said simply. Tibor produced a satchel with weapons in it, opening it for the pilot's inspection. It contained a handgun, a rifle with bayonet, a hunting knife. He rewrapped it, handed it to the pilot.

"It will help," Tibor said.

"Thank you," the pilot said. His nervousness had drained away. "I came here expecting a fight. Maria has agreed to go with me. I thought you would fight to keep her. I don't know what to say."

"Don't say anything," Sasha said. He proffered a dark bottle. "Drink. Your decisions are your own."

The pilot sat with us. "I do want to explain my decision," he said. "I just feel we should be on our own. I want to find a place away from all this madness, perhaps in the Urals. I still hope that one morning I will wake up and all of this will be gone. I just feel in my heart it will end, and I want to come down off my mountain someday and find that the earth has been returned to us."

"That would be a good feeling," Sasha said, looking at me.

"And ... Maria has agreed to come with me. We're going to hide, start a family."

"We wish you well," Sasha said.

"I . . ." He looked down, suddenly angry. "You sound as if you don't believe my intentions. Perhaps you think I'm a coward for not fighting on?"

"Not at all," Sasha said.

"What is it, then? I can tell by your tone of voice alone that you don't think we will succeed."

"Please don't be angry. It has nothing to do with you."

"All right," the pilot said, his anger draining.

Sasha rose, came around the fire to embrace Maria. The pilot rose and shook his hand. They embraced briefly. "You'll be leaving in the morning?"

"Yes."

"Good. We're heading for the Urals ourselves, but our way is slower. We have things to do along the way. Perhaps we'll see you up the road. Two will travel faster alone. I hope you find what you want."

The pilot looked at all of us, filled with emotion. "You are . . . good people," he said.

He turned away, bearing his satchel of weapons, Maria at his side.

At first light the next morning they left.

We saw them off. I turned to Reesa, who stood beside me, and said, half smiling, "Perhaps we should do the same. We could hide in the mountains ourselves, become Adam and Eve."

Her eyes filled with tears, and she broke away from me.

When I caught up to her, she was crying. I held her close.

She cried a long time, and finally told me she was bearing my child, and said, "Don't ever say that to me again."

7

The day after the pilot and Maria left we had a skirmish.

It was over quickly, but it reminded us that the world

was not summer green and free from care. I had almost gotten used to the sight of skeletal birds and animals, even the tiny white insects that infested the earth where real ants and beetles had once crawled. But the sight of skeletal men, after weeks in their absence, proved to me that in no way was I used to this new world.

Caspian and Tibor were out ahead of the wagon, scouting our trail. Caspian came toward us in a hurry, and Sasha immediately drew the wagon to a halt.

"A band, a half kilometer ahead."

"How many?" Sasha asked.

"Nine, perhaps ten. They don't seem to know their way through the woods."

"That will make it easy. And Tibor?"

"Already in place."

"Good. We will follow."

Caspian nodded and slipped back into the foliage. Sasha turned to me. "In the wagon."

I looked at him in surprise. "I'm quite capable—"

"Do as I say. Reesa will come with me. If by any chance—"

"I won't do that," I said. "I'm coming with you."

He considered for a moment. "All right. But do exactly what I say." He smiled. "Perhaps you can be 'invisible' for us."

The three of us followed Caspian's trail into the woods.

We heard the band of skeletons before we saw them. They were thrashing loudly through the underbrush, cursing.

Sasha smiled grimly and whispered, "City people."

He pointed up into the trees, making an arch with his arm. I knew what he wanted of me. Through the trees I could barely make out Tibor, set back off an open space the band would soon reach. Caspian waved to us from another position on its perimeter.

I scaled the nearest tree soundlessly and made my way out until I was over the clear ground, perched like a bird.

Below, I saw Sasha remove his long knife. Reesa, a few meters away, did the same.

I waited for Sasha's signal.

He gave it as the skeletons broke through the trees. I counted nine, all armed with rifles. They were noisy. The one at their head was large. Around his bony frame I could vaguely see the outline of a bearish, bearded man with huge arms and hands.

The bearded one held his arm up, and the band, silenced, stopped.

He seemed to sniff at the air.

Sasha gave his signal.

I swished two leafy branches together. I let those below get a brief look at me, before rolling onto a large branch and hiding myself.

"Get him!" the bearish skeleton shouted.

Three skeletons started for the nearest tree. Tibor was closest, and he dispatched two of them before Caspian appeared to help with the third. The six others reacted by raising their rifles at Tibor and Caspian.

In the tree I made more noise. Two of the rifles swung up at me. A shot sang by me as I ducked back to the safety of my branch.

Meanwhile, Sasha and Reesa had moved on the skeletons from their backs. They caught two immediately, dropping them to dust, and two others as they turned to fight. Caspian and Tibor dispatched the remaining two.

Sasha looked up at me and laughed. "You can come down now!"

Caspian and Tibor bent to gather the skeletons' weapons.

As I was climbing down the tree I saw faint movement in the foliage behind me. I called out a warning as a shot rang out.

Caspian, just standing, was hit and fell.

Sasha said, "Oh, no."

Tibor was already rushing past me in chase as I dropped to the ground. I heard a cry, and a few moments later Tibor reappeared.

"There was an eleventh," he said angrily. Grimly, he pushed on past me. "There are no more."

Caspian was on his back, moaning. Reesa held his head up; Caspian's eyes were closed and he gritted his teeth as Sasha examined a wound on his chest.

"I want all of you to leave," Sasha said.

"Sasha—" Reesa began.

His eyes were dark fire. "Now."

We walked to the edge of the woods. I saw Sasha standing over Caspian, his long knife held loosely in one hand, speaking to him in a whisper. Gritting his teeth, Caspian nodded.

Suddenly Caspian's body stiffened, arched back, and was still.

Quickly, Sasha bent over the body. His hand rested for a moment on the young man's head, and then, even as Caspian's body began to fall away, revealing skeleton, Sasha drew his knife deeply through the throat.

Instantly, the body fell to dust.

Sasha stood, muttered something, head down, and came to us.

"Let's walk on," he said, his lips tight.

We put the rifles in the wagon and went on.

8

Two days later the Ural Mountains rose before us in the distance.

After Caspian's death a pall had dropped upon us. But at this sight, the blue-white, misty rise of peaks, life came back into my companions and me. One word from Sasha put a smile on Tibor's lips, brightened Reesa's beautiful eyes.

She came to me, put her arm around my waist, pulling me close to her and pointing to a spot ahead and slightly to the north, at the base of a towering peak.

"Home," Sasha repeated.

Our pace quickened. Though we were still a day away, our little band seemed to want to make that day pass quickly. Sasha sang a song, in a guttural, non-Russian tongue I did not know. At a chorus Tibor and Reesa joined in.

Reesa looked up at me with tears in her eyes. "You will love this place."

That night we camped in a meadow surrounded by the scent of blossoming flowers. Sasha and Tibor were almost recklessly at ease. For the first time since Caspian's death Sasha drew out one of his dark bottles of wine, and we sat around the fire and talked.

"I used to play in this meadow when I was a young girl," Reesa said, smiling.

"We all did," Sasha said. His face showed contentment. "This was the most beautiful place in the world. We called it the Valley of Blossoms. When all of the flowers bloomed within fifty kilometers of here, the scent all drifted into this place. Look around you. There are no flowers here, but their odor is all around."

"It was a magical place," Tibor said.

"It still is!" Sasha replied.

"Perhaps." Tibor sighed. "But it is not the same."

"Nothing is the same," Sasha said gently, and passed the wine to Tibor, who drank it down.

Later, while the others slept, Reesa lay in my arms and we looked at the sky. The stars were obscured in a lightly perfumed cloud. I felt as if I were drifting in a child's dream.

"This was the place where Tibor married his bride," Reesa said. "Her name was Krista." Her voice was dreamy and sad. "She is dead. This is the place where many of my people married."

I turned her face to look into my eyes. "And you?"

"I waited for you," she said, smiling, and kissed me.

"There were no others? None of your own people?"

"No."

"Why?"

She closed her eyes and lay back against my arm. For a moment I thought she was asleep. A dreaming smile blanketed her lips.

"Because I knew you were coming," she said.

"Would you marry me here?"

"For tonight we will be married."

She looked so sad and happy that I kissed her, and lay my palm on her pregnant belly.

"Tell me what you know, Reesa," I said.

"Soon," she said, "Sasha will tell you everything."

"Reesa, someone must keep watch."

"No . . ."

She would tell me no more, but curled into my arm and slept.

That night I felt movement in the woods surrounding us, but for the first time since I began my journey with these people, I felt no fear. And once again I dreamed the strange dream of the girl with dark skin in the field of petals, opening her mouth and saying to me a single word I could not hear.

9

We reached Sasha's village as night fell the next day.

There were lights, but no people greeted us. At the outskirts was a burial ground on a hill, which we skirted. My companions would not look at it. But as we passed I studied it in the lowering sun. I noticed that all the graves that had been opened had been filled in again, fresh mounds of dirt topping each.

We entered an empty village. But by the time we had reached its square, it was empty no longer. From out of the surrounding hills, down from the slope of the looming mountain to the east, villagers swarmed in.

Though it seemed like a crowd to me, I counted only twenty heads, half of them children.

The sight of children running and laughing filled me with a happiness I had thought was gone.

"You look content," Sasha said.

I laughed. "I think I could stay here forever."

He nodded his head. "If only you could."

An old man in peasant dress approached us, smoking a pipe. Sasha immediately showed him deference.

"Master Yuri," Sasha said, bowing.

The old man waved his pipe. "There's no need for that anymore," he said.

The old man turned his attention to me. Suddenly to my surprise, he bowed.

"It is *I* who should bow," I said.

"Nonsense," he said. Then to Sasha: "We will talk later."

"We are safe for tonight?" Sasha asked.

"For tonight," the old man answered. "Our scouts give us three days." He bowed to me again and left us.

"What did he mean by that?" I asked Sasha.

"Within a week," Sasha said, sweeping his arm around to include both children and village, "all of this will be gone."

I wanted to ask more, but he silenced me by putting his hand on my arm.

"Please," he said, "for my people's sake at least, enjoy tonight."

"All right," I said, feeling my questions, as always with Sasha, silenced. "All right."

There was a feast that started at sundown. First, around a fire in the center of the square, the children danced. There were many gaps in their circle, but they managed not only to be happy but to make onlookers think those gaps were filled with scores of young dancers.

I was accorded a seat of honor, with Reesa beside me. Remarkably, there was a veritable feast of food, with smoked meats and much wine. The festivities, which had a surreal air of finality about them, went on most of the night. There was singing, in the unknown tongue I had heard Sasha use days before.

I found myself becoming increasingly uneasy with the desperate happiness around me, and finally had to excuse myself. Reesa followed me halfway up a nearby hill, where we sat. The night had become cloudy, affording us no stars. I watched the dying, smoky fire below us, listened to the sad, unknown songs.

"Something terrible is going to happen, isn't it?" I said.

"There is an army of skeletons very close. These people survived the first days, Peter," Reesa said. "There used to be almost a thousand of us in this village. There are other villages along the base of the Urals. They are all destroyed."

She listened for a moment to the sad singing that drifted up to us. "They know they will die," she said. "They refuse to become like the skeletons. So tomorrow, after we leave, they will kill themselves, twice. The dust will then be buried, to rest forever."

I looked at her, saw the tears tracking her cheeks in the dim, distant firelight.

"I will kill myself with them, Peter. So will Tibor. Only Sasha will continue with you, after he has twice slain and buried the last of us."

Sasha's voice came close by. "And I will pledge you, Peter Sun, to kill me again, when I am slain at the end of our journey."

I looked from Sasha to Reesa, into their hard, knowing eyes. "You cannot know—"

"These things all will happen, Peter Sun," Sasha said to me. "Or, as you are known to us, Kral Kishkin. We've known they would happen for hundreds of years. Come with me."

Sasha walked past us, farther up the hill.

"Go," Reesa said softly. "I'll wait for you here."

I looked into her tear-filled eyes. "Reesa, I won't let you do these things. Our baby—"

"These things were meant to be. Go with Sasha."

"Reesa—"

"Go."

I rose, and climbed the hill. When I reached Sasha, I turned to look down at Reesa, who had bowed her head and was weeping.

"Sit down with me," Sasha said.

"You cannot let her die like this," I said angrily, looking down at him. "If these fools want to kill themselves, let them, but she must come with us."

"Sit," Sasha said softly.

"No," I said. "I will not let this happen. You can live with your superstitions and legends if you want to, but not Reesa." I drew back away from him and brought out my knife. "I'm willing to fight you, Sasha. I'm willing to die here, if that must happen."

He rose and held out his hand. I stepped farther back and waved my knife at him.

"I mean what I said, Sasha."

The sadness in his eyes was overwhelming. "Listen to me, Peter. Reesa will go with you tomorrow. Only she cannot know it yet." He sat back down, patted the grass beside him. "Please, sit."

Keeping my blade out, I sat, but not close by. "Talk."

A smile came to his lips. "You still haven't learned everything about invisibility, Peter. *Isn't that right, Tibor?*"

I turned quickly to see Tibor just behind me, ready, on command, to take my knife from me and pin me.

"Hello," Tibor said. He walked past me, handed Sasha a dark bottle of wine.

"Is everything well down below?" Sasha asked.

"Yes," Tibor replied. "We've had word from two advance scouts who say tomorrow will be our last free day. All of the others are being told to return."

"I see," Sasha said.

Tibor left, patting me on the shoulder as he passed.

"Sit beside me," Sasha said, holding the bottle out toward me.

I sheathed my knife and moved closer. The clouds had drawn away overhead, showing a sprinkling of stars. Sasha looked up at them for a moment.

"They are old friends," he said. As I watched him he let his gaze drift to the burial hill, visible in starlight to our left. I saw that many fresh holes had been dug, and that Tibor had mounted the hill, picking up a shovel to finish the work.

Sasha took the wine from me and drank deeply.

"You may consider this a child's story if you wish, Peter Sun. Every people has its own version. Ours was passed down by mouth for thousands of years, in a tongue no longer spoken. You heard it sung in our songs."

"Who are you people?" I asked.

He smiled. "Even we don't know. Some called us the Lost Tribe. We used to be called Gypsies, but that is not what we are. The Gypsies are our cousins, I suppose, but long ago we gave up the roads and made villages. When the various pogroms came over the various centuries, it was convenient to call us Gypsies. Enough of our tribe were hunted down and murdered so that we had to be called something."

"And that language, what is it?"

"I can't tell you that, either, Peter. But it is there, and it serves us. It makes us know that we are not Russian in our hearts after all. And made it easier to kill Russians when they tried to kill us back, which was almost always."

He drank wine, passed me the bottle.

"So here is my child's story. It is a simple one. About the beginning of the world, and then the end of the world, and the beginning again."

He waited for me to drink, then began.

"It seems that after making the world, God held it in His hand and looked at it, and all He saw were rocks, and water, and ice. It was a pretty place, but He wasn't happy with it yet, so He passed it through a cloud of perfume. And when He did that, something wonderful happened. The world came alive.

"It's said that the first man and woman that God set His eyes on were our own. He spoke to them in our language and blessed them, and told them to take care of the world. Then He told them that He had other worlds to make and must go away, but that if ever the world needed Him, they should call Him immediately to save them, which would prove that they believed in Him. He then set the world to spinning through space."

Sasha took the bottle, drank.

"So God went away, and forgot about the world, and forgot about His cloud of perfume. And the world spun through space, until such day that it passed back through the cloud of perfume again. Only this time the world became too much alive. What had been dead came back to life, making the world crowded and unbalanced.

"Our own people didn't call God right away, and when they finally did, and God saw what had happened, it was nearly too late, and God was angry. And so He promised to save the world, but at a terrible price."

Again Sasha drank wine, a deep draft.

He looked at me.

" 'A man will come,' God said, 'from both the West and East. To you he will be called Kral Kishkin. But he will not be one of you. And though the only daughter of your strongest father be with him, and flower his seed, this will not be the new flower of the world. But from Kral Kishkin will come the new seed of the world.' He promised that if we did these things, he would once again favor us, but in the next world."

Sasha continued to look at me. "That's it. A good fairy story, eh?"

I took the wine from him and drank. "That's all it is, a fairy story."

He shrugged. "Perhaps. There was a lot more in the texts, about when it would happen, how Kral Kishkin's protection was our sacred duty, all that. I have to say, I didn't believe it myself, until all this happened. Our tribe had become almost secular. My third son, Igor, even went off to school in Leningrad, to become a scientist." His eyes darkened. "I'm sure he's dead now. We knew this was coming, Peter Sun, and we did nothing until it was too late. The prophecy has come true. And Reesa, who is the only daughter of our dead king, has been waiting for you her whole life." He leaned closer, in the near dark, and looked at me with his hard eyes. "But as to how my people handle themselves when this army of skeletons comes, you cannot change that. I only ask that when the time comes, when you see me and know me as a threat, you pledge to kill me."

I said nothing.

He put his hand on my arm and tightened his grip. "This is the way it will be, Kral Kishkin. It is the only way that I can fulfill my sacred duty, and make sure that Reesa, and your baby, have a chance with you. But to do that, you must pledge to me."

I stared at him, mute.

"Tomorrow, before the first soldiers of the army come, I will twice kill the members of my tribe. Then I will kill myself. Reesa will go with you, up into the mountains, to fulfill the duty of your protection. When I tell her, she will not be able to refuse. She knows she is as capable of it as I am. More so, because she loves you."

He gripped me even harder. I could feel the tremble in his hand.

"And there is a chance for my tribe to continue, Peter Sun. One way or another, in this world or the next. If I send her with you, we have the chance in this world."

His grip relaxed. "But for you to save Reesa and your child, you must take an oath to kill me. Because after I kill myself, I will be one of *them,* and I will surely come after you. Do you understand?"

I looked at him. "Yes, I do."

"Do you make the oath?"

My eyes were steady, looking into his. "Yes."

"Good!"

He suddenly laughed, and held his bottle up. He drank some down and then made me drink some down.

Then we sat together in the night and looked down the hill at the dying fire in the village square, and listened to the children singing.

10

The army of skeletons was closer than had been imagined. Apparently they had marched all night and were within sight distance in the next valley the next morning. The rumble of machinery close by could be heard. I was reminded of the progress of locusts, the tremble in the ground, nervous electricity in the air.

Sasha's village was in near chaos of preparation. But Reesa and I were their main concern. We were provided with the finest horse for Sasha's cart, which was loaded with as much food, supplies, and weapons as it could hold. Sasha pressed his own long knife into my hand.

"When the time comes," he said, "use this. My father gave it to me, his father to him. I would like to know that it will continue to be useful. I have offered it to Tibor, but it is his wish also that you have it. He would like to think of you as his brother, and I would like to think of you as my son."

"Thank you, Sasha."

When our actual leaving came, an eerie quiet descended on the village. I felt the weight of their hopes on our shoulders. There were twenty-two of them, in a village that had once held hundreds. They stood watching our cart pull away with hope so palpable it was nearly a physical sensation.

We had gone only a few meters when Reesa made me stop the cart and jumped down to run back to Sasha.

"Isn't there another way?" she cried. "Can't we all rush up into the mountains, hide in the woods? Wouldn't my father have wanted us to *fight?*"

Sasha held her until her crying subsided. Then he

pushed her gently away from him. "We *are* fighting, Reesa. Go."

She ran back to me, crying, and climbed into the cart.

I bade our horse to go, and the cart went on, and Reesa did not look back again.

Sasha waved once to me, then turned and I saw him no more.

We climbed steadily for four hours into the mountain they called Uz-Cur. The Russians called it Konzhakovski Kamen, a richly forested peak capped by a discrete snowy cap. We saw a few skeletal birds, and a single skeletal hawk that circled high overhead but never dropped. The sky became a deep blue.

When we rested, it was on a promontory that Reesa seemed to know well. It provided a beautiful view of the valleys spread beneath us, including her village. We could make out the tiny roofs of the huts, the cleared patch that was the village square.

Reesa sat close by me. Though the day was warm, she drew a shawl tight around her and shivered. She looked somberly into the village below.

"He will have done it by now," she said.

"Look!" I cried.

There, off to the north, was a pall of smoke. There was a dull boom. The village below us erupted in a spurt of fire. There came another explosion, and another. I watched closely and saw one of the rockets, a tiny missile from this height, leave its launcher and arch over the trees to land almost directly in the center of the village. Squinting closely, I could see an array of armaments where the missile was launched. The valley near the village was swarming with tiny white figures, trucks, and tanks. The road, a thin pencil periodically visible through the trees, was clogged with armor. Letting the road lead my eyes north, I saw the blackened remains of two other villages, both smaller than Reesa's; the trees around them had been burned. The villages themselves appeared no more than craters carved out of the foot of the mountains.

Another missile found its target in the village, and

now fire erupted and spread. We heard the thin hollow sounds of gunfire.

"Let's go on," Reesa said, turning away.

The road curled us into a mountain plateau, away from the valleys below. Soon Reesa was herself again. She told me about her childhood, the places where she had played up here, and even higher on the mountain where she and her father had once trained a hawk. The sight of a high circling skeletal eagle brought a pall of sadness over her.

"It seems such a long time ago," she said.

Late in the day Reesa took sick, and I put the wagon into a cove of trees while she went off to vomit into the bushes. When I came to her, concerned, she pushed me away, and when I insisted on standing with her, she turned on me.

"You fool! It's only the baby!"

"I'm ... sorry," I sputtered.

She retched once more, then stumbled out of the bushes and came to rest her head against me. "Don't ever be sorry," she said.

"I—"

"Never," she said.

We climbed into the wagon, and again she put her head against me and closed her eyes.

I studied the sun and saw that we only had an hour or so of sunlight left. "Perhaps we should stay here tonight."

"We should go on," Reesa said. But in a moment she was asleep against me, and my decision had been made.

I laid her down in the wagon, covered her, and made camp.

Our position was more exposed than I would have liked, but after scouting the trees to three sides of us and setting traps, I was sure I could guard the one open area in front.

The sun dropped down and a moon came up, bright and nearly full. I heard the sounds of crickets and wondered if they were real insects or the white ashy ones of this new world.

My eyes betrayed me. One moment I lay watching the rising moon; the next my ears were filled with the

loud sound of one of my traps going off behind me. I
snapped awake, seeing the moon high overhead now. I
had slept for hours.

I had no idea which trap had gone off. I studied the
three flanks behind me with my eyes, my ears. I heard,
saw, nothing. I rose, begging myself to be silent, and
checked the wagon.

Reesa lay sleeping, her breath soft and even.

I backed into the clearing, crouched low, using
nearby bushes for cover. Melting into a stand of them, I
waited.

There was no sound until I heard a voice behind me.

"You still don't know true invisibility, do you, Kral
Kishkin?"

I whirled to see Sasha, or rather his skeleton, standing boldly white in the moonlight.

"Where did you—"

"I hiked through the woods," Sasha said. He laughed.
If I had closed my eyes, it would have seemed he was the
same man I had talked to this morning. But now he was
armed with a short blade, which he held out menacingly
in front of him.

"I'd like my long knife back," he said. Again he
laughed. "Handle first, please."

I drew his blade from my belt and showed him the
blade side. "I'm afraid not, Sasha. I made an oath."

He feigned innocence. "To who?"

"To you, of course."

"I wasn't serious, Kral Kishkin."

He advanced a step on me. I held my position,
poised for a fight.

Suddenly he turned and began to walk toward the
trees. "Come with me," he said, with a trace of his old
sadness.

I stood my ground, and he stopped and turned.

"Follow me to a special place," he said. "We can settle our business out of sight of Reesa. Give me this one
last wish."

He went into the trees, his bones suffused with
moonlight.

Cautiously, I followed.

There was a path. Tensed, with the blade before me,

I trailed Sasha for perhaps twenty meters. I kept him well in front of me. The trees opened up. The ground here was covered with a soft carpet of pine needles. Above, the moon shone down like a lantern. In the air was the faint hint of flowers, as I had smelled that night in the Valley of Blossoms.

"This was a sacred place," Sasha said. "It was a place where we came to pray to God."

He waved his hand, and skeletons appeared all around me, coming out of the woods.

Sasha said coldly, "Take him."

I was besieged. I cut the first two that came at me, watching them fold to dust even as four others moved in. I was grabbed from behind. I slashed my blade back, catching that attacker, but two others held my arms and pinned me as the third remaining held my legs. I felt Sasha's knife knocked from my hand to fall to the ground. The three skeletons held me prone as Sasha approached.

He bent, picked up his knife. He examined it. In the moonlight I saw the ghost of his old features surrounding his bones.

"It was foolish of me," he said, "to ever give this to you. And foolish of me to think that I would not think differently after I had done this to myself." He bent his head back, showing me the long slash on his ghostly neck where he had cut his own throat. "I can only mourn the rest of my tribe who were not allowed to see the world as I do now."

"What do you see, Sasha?"

His eye sockets looked at me. *"This,"* he said, running his hands down his skeleton, "is what God wanted. *This* is the world now. It is foolish to think any other way."

"Have you forgotten that you were human, Sasha?"

"I *am* human!" he said. "I am *me*. Only it is *you* who seem unnatural to me now, Kral Kishkin. It is you who do not belong in this world. Tell him," he said to one of the skeletons holding my arms.

"Hello, Peter Sun."

The voice was that of the MIG pilot Sasha and the others had nursed after his crash, who had set off with Maria to live away from everything. The skeleton turned his face to me and I saw the outline of the pilot's features.

"It's true," Maria's voice said. I looked down and saw that the skeleton who held my legs was, indeed, Maria.

Sasha said, "I, and the four soldiers the army was kind enough to let me have, found their hiding spot, not far from here. It was a place where I knew Maria would go. A cozy little hut, too. But they no longer need it."

"No, we don't," Maria said.

"Hold him tightly," Sasha said. Then to me: "You will see everything differently soon, Kral Kishkin."

He held his blade in front of him, poised for the strike.

A shot sounded.

The MIG pilot gasped, let me go, and dropped to dust. I jerked away from Sasha's knife thrust. A second shot split the night and Maria turned to powder. The third skeleton holding me tried to strike me, but I turned and knocked him down as another shot sounded. He fell to nothingness.

Sasha rushed at me.

I crouched, deflecting his blow, and he fell. He got up quickly.

A gunshot missed him. He slashed at me, just missing my arm, and suddenly he turned and ran into the woods.

Reesa appeared out of the trees and sprinted past me.

"Reesa!" I shouted.

"I will get him," she said, her voice hard.

There followed a mad run through the woods. Both Sasha and Reesa knew this forest better than I. I heard them thrashing through the brush in front of me. I tried to keep up. Far ahead I saw a flash of white bones. A shot rang out. The movement through the woods continued. I heard Sasha curse. In a moment I had broken out into another area free of trees. Sasha had dropped his knife and faced Reesa, who held the rifle up, pointed at him.

Sasha advanced on her slowly, palms open. His voice was gentle. "Reesa, it is I—"

Reesa fired.

Sasha froze, disintegrated to dust, fell to nothingness.

When she turned to me, I expected tears, expected her to drop the rifle and fall into my arms, weeping. Instead, she moved past me, her face set and hard.

"There may be more. We'd better check."

We searched the woods around our camp; there was no one else.

Late in the night, with a hint of dawn coming to the east, Reesa lay in my arms. She was tense and angry.

"Reesa, why are you mad?" I asked.

"I should have been watching you. I should not have been sleeping."

"Reesa—"

"No." She turned to me, anger flaring. "I have a *sacred duty*. I've let myself be overcome by foolishness."

"By love."

Her hands balled into fists, and for a moment I thought she would hit me. "Yes, love. That is the foolishness. I've let myself believe that it can last."

I pulled her close to me. "Of course it can. We'll take care of each other."

"No." She pushed away from me. "Don't you understand? I'm here to take care of you, and then I'll be gone."

"But Sasha said—"

"Sasha only prolonged it! Didn't he tell you everything?"

"He said that you and I had a chance together this way—"

"He told you nothing. The text of the prophecy says the daughter of the highest will conceive the child of Kral Kishkin, but that Kral Kishkin will remake the world with a daughter of another tribe." Now there were tears in her eyes. "You will have another wife, Peter Sun, and you will have other children. But I and my whole tribe will be gone."

"I don't believe it. I won't let it happen."

"It will."

I held her to me, and let her cry until sleep took her. I put my hand on her belly, imagining that I could feel the tiny child, *my* child, move within. I loved Reesa more than life itself, more than all the world and all the living humans on it.

As the sun rose, blanketing the east with beautiful light, I vowed to it that I would not let the things Reesa said happen.

"I vow, on the earth and all the things that live on it," I said.

Next to me Reesa stirred in her sleep, and turned to nestle closer to me, and whispered in her dreams, *"Gone."*

I watched the new day dawn and the world come alive below our mountains, and looked up at the hard, unyielding peak we had to climb, and prayed.

8

From the incredibly shallow life of Roger Garbage

1

What a trip! Hollywood!
How does that Vomits song go again?

> She's such a bitch,
> So loud and so rich
> (HOLLY wood, HOLLY wood)
> She's such a drag
> Like a burned-out hag
> (That's: HOLLY wood, HOLLY wood)
> (Chorus) But in the nighttime, I love her
> That goes unsaid,
> I'd make love to her—
> If only I could put a bag
> Over her head! Yeah!

Then Brutus Johnson's guitar comes in—*brrrrrrrrng, brrrrrrng,* and the place goes wild, and ol' Shark, ol'

Roger, dat's me, advance man, producer, and road man-
ager, collects his check and goes home.

Love it, babe!

God, I hope those bastards are dead.

And Carl Peters, and the rest of them, because, baby,
this is a whole new gig!

Ah, the Grateful Dead *did* know something, didn't
they?

I do wish Rita, ol' Carl's secretary, was still around at
this moment. I'm getting sick of looking at boneheads
through the tinted glass of this Lincoln Town Car. She'd
do all right in this Lincoln, ol' Rita would. She could cut
the coke, and she knows how to use the zipper on these
leather pants. We already know that, oh, yes we do.

Yeah!

But Christ, like any movie that runs too long, this is
getting boring.

I mean, where the hell is the action tonight? All I've
seen is boners marching and stumbling and shooting
guns in the air. I took the old tour through the hills, as
if I couldn't do it by heart with my eyes closed. Remember those days, Rog? Driving that damn tour bus, hair cut
like a Mousketeer, smiling all the time, using that little
hand mike to tell the bluehairs where we were: "Now
that, ladies and gentlemen, is the home of *Bob Hope!* And
just up the street . . ." When what I really wanted to do
was scream at them to go home and die in their
Barcaloungers, huffing out their last cracker-stale breaths
in front of Bob Barker on the tube. Or I wanted at least
to tell them the real story: "Ladies and gents—old farts,
if I might be so bold—see that twenty-room sucker over
there behind the iron fence? Well, it's got enough alarms
on it to wake Fatty Arbuckle from the dead, and ol' John-
ny's hardly ever there, anyway! And if you ever got near
enough to ring the bell, chances are some three-
hundred-and-fifty-pound ex-wrestler would leave off
porking the maid, appear behind you, and blow your
head clean off your shoulders into your outstretched
hands before your finger ever reached the button! See
that TV camera over there? And there, and there and
there? Well, you can wave now, because one of them is

tracking your schnoz even as we ride by! I mean, these
bastards have detectives to watch their detectives!"

Ah, yes, the good old days.

And speaking of Fatty Arbuckle, I swear I saw the fat
fart earlier this evening, walking down the Boulevard.
Those had to be his big bones, and I could just make out
the features. Seemed to be a lot of the old-timers, dead-
timers, if you will, out for a stroll down memory lane tonight, and if I hadn't been so coked, I might have
thought it scary to see Laurel and Hardy and Buster
Keaton—who looked *bad* in bones, even worse than in
life, believe me, I saw the poor old bastard a few times
wandering around, waiting for a part to fall on his
head—and Mary Pickford, walking silently up and down
the Boulevard, passing Grauman's, ogling all the
changes, maybe even crying bone tears. It was like some
horrid silent movie. I even slowed down to watch two of
these dead-timers—think it was John Wayne and Hank
Fonda, but they didn't like each other much in real life
anyway—duking it out right in the middle of the street,
Wayne really womping on Fonda's head until the old
trooper just dropped to white powder and blew away. The
Duke just sauntered down the street, and believe me,
people got out of his tracks. I almost ran him down—
hell, I never liked *him* much in real life, bastard shoved
me out of the way once to get at the bar at one of those
cocktail things Roundabout's parent company, Boil Oil,
was always having, and inviting everyone who wasn't tied
down, or up, from the various entertainment divisions:
Palmer Pictures, Vortex Video, Roundabout itself—but I
let the old cowboy do his thing, thumbing my nose at
him behind the dark glass as I drove by.

Weird, too weird.

And nobody having parties! Up in those hills, and all
the houses dark. What the fu! Boners, boners everywhere, and not a drop to drink! The Stoli's half-gone on
the seat beside me. Hey, I'm even ready to share that with
somebody! Geldorf's house dark, Henley's house dark.

Then at the next house—*bammoo!*

What light in yonder window breaks!

And does break, as I watch, glass shattering, a lamp
out on the lawn, *boomp*, cord trailing behind.

I lower the window a fraction of an inch, listening. . . .

Ah! The magic sound!

Laughter!

Into the driveway, through the open gates, bucko.

Haven't I been here before? It looks vaguely familiar. Long driveway, lots of bushes—*boo!* I keep waiting for a boner to jump out, but maybe they haven't climbed this high into the hills yet. And this one *is* on a hill. Around and around the driveway goes, winding around this friggin' magnificent house. Stone, up to the cupolas. Red tiled roof, lit from the corners. Landscape by Mario. Swimming pool, tennis court, huge guest-house-looking building. Kiss the tips of your fingers, a *beautiful* job.

Exactly what I wanted, and would have had in a couple of years, if not for *friggin'* Carl Peters and his *friggin'* ax.

Later, Carlo.

Look at that parking area!

Beautiful, beautiful. Now I *know* I've been here before. But who? I would have remembered. As plotzed as I am tonight, I must have been more plotzed then. Must have been with Rita, zipped in the front seat. Snatches (including hers) came back to me, a long long night, four or five parties, this was the last stop, me hardies! Rolled out of the car onto the parking tarmac. The world spun. I remember laying there for a while, staring at the roof, the lights lighting the roof. Did I go in?

Who the fu cares. In now, grab the Stoli!

Lock up?

Nah.

I'm not too steady, Eddie. Let me stop a moment, lean against this here hood. I *know* that car. Bobbie Zick, Chin Records.

Is this his house?

Me hardies, argh, I do believe it are.

Aargh, for real.

That's me, throwing up on the hood of ol' Bob's Mercedes. Think he'll mind? Nah. Ol' Bob's got ten 'r 'leven of 'em. Plenty of Mercedes. Heck, this must be his deli car, make a run for a quart of milk, gram of coke. Coke-mobile, maybe.

Ol' Bob.

In now, Zelda?

Now I know. Fitzgerald's place. F. Scott. And the crazy wife. Bob Zick was bragging about what a steal it was, only nine mil, they said it was haunted by Zelda's ghost or something. Ol' Bobbie, always looking for a bargain. And I just barfed on his car.

I hate the frigger, he's got too much money.

Oh, well.

Maybe . . .

Stop the puke presses! I wipe my mouth with my sleeve, rub the sleeve on Bob's car. Revelation! I'll ask ol' Bobbie for a job! Didn't he try to hire me away from Roundabout once? I know, Rita told me, flagrante delicioso. Tried to buy my contract from ol' Carl, to manage a band called . . . *Grapevine!* That was it, Grapevine! They had something, too, could have gone on with a little work. The way they ended up, white fellas doing the black shuffle and turn, Smokey Robinson and the Miracles style, just didn't work. They had one hit, I think, "Heal You":

> *Oh, baby,*
> *You're just so fine (oh, baby)*
> *You're in my dre-eams*
> *All the ti-ime . . . .*

Not bad. But needed work.

Lots of work.

From me!

Bobbie baby, I'm coming!

He likes Stoli, doesn't he? Doesn't everybody? I know he likes coke. Least he did three months ago. But you never know with these Hollywoods, they see Jesus overnight, and bammo, they're off this, off that. No drugs, no alc, no sex, no meat. Communion with fruit— remember that one? Pyramid power. Reincarnation. Buttermilk baths. Save the whales, no nukes, power to the people, give peace a chance, jump off a bridge for Jehovah's Witnesses. Love your neighbor, put up bigger fences. Shit, I *hated* the sixties.

And seventies.

And eighties.

But love them nineties!

Bobbie, baby!

Bring the coke anyway.

So, away from the car. Whoa, the world she spins. Stand still, Rog, let the focus mechanism kick in. Jeez, I smell like puke. Let's stumble to this here bush at the end of the parking area. Nice smell to those blossoms, maybe they'll take the smell out of my sleeve. Rub-a-dub-dub—

Is that a pile of dust I see?

Uh-oh.

Up goes the radar again. I've seen piles like that all night. The double dead. Dance backward, Rog, one-two, one-two—

A hand on my shoulder.

"Taking your job with the Vomits seriously I see, Roger?"

I know that phony-Brit voice!

"Bobbie, babe!" I say, spinning around.

And look right into the eye sockets of a boner.

"Whoa!" I shout. But ol' Bobbie he's got me good and tight. I can see his face now surrounding the skull, just barely, a ghost's grin on ghost lips.

Then he lets me go, and I fall to the ground like a puppet. I wait for the smash on my head, the bullet through my heart, the kick, the punch. I mean, these boners automatically hate our guts, right?

But he just yawns, turns, and walks back toward the house.

"Got any coke, Roger?" he asks.

2

Inside, there's a bone party!

"Bone Party"! I can see it now, new TV show, Saturday mornings after the cartoons. Little stage, big podium with a clock backdrop, couple of legbones for clock hands keeping track of the half hour of fun. Ol' Dick Clark in skeleton drag spinning the hits: and all them young baby boners dancing dancing dancing! I give it a seventy-eight! It's got a great beat, and I can rattle to it! "Bone Party, USA"!

Yeah!

And damned if that's not what we've got on view here. Seems everybody got dead, but nobody stopped the party. If you whacked the pillows on the couch, coke would puff out like dust, that's how much partying has been done in ol' Bobbie's pad.

And the party's not done yet.

Jeez, I see some dead people I knew when. At first it's just a bunch of wild boners dancing, but if you look real close, you can see faces: half the Rolling Stones, a couple of Eagles, various video jockeys. A couple of these bozos actually wave to me as I walk through.

"Yo, Rog."

"Hey, Garbage man, how's it hanging?"

"Roggie, babe!"

Don't they know they're dead?

And then surrealism rears its ugly head higher, and the music pauses . . . before a Vomits CD comes on!

Whoa!

The party goes right on. A boner turns to me and says, "Way to go, Roger Dodger!" The song is "On You," the B side of the Vomits first hit, made it to twenty-one itself, and Brutus's guitar thrums three heavy times, sounding like "Wild Thing," before Randy Pants's voice comes in high, almost screeching:

> *If you won't go*
> *On me,*
> *Then let me go*
> *On you . . . .*

Real Shakespearean-sonnet material, and I stand there, a little dazed by the whole gig.

But now Bobbie Zick is waving to me across the room, near the CD player. While I'm trying to make nice gestures, thanking him for putting on the Vomits on my behalf (even if I wish they were dead), he makes a gesture of his own for me to follow, and turns, mounts the stairs.

I follow like a lapdog, of course.

I mean, if I was going to be dead, I'd already be dead, right?

And the Roger-radar, amazingly, is quiet.

Up the stairs, Roger Dodger!

3

Bobbie's in his office at the end, door open. I pass other doors, bedrooms mostly, but an occasional bathroom, I hear moans, grunts. Now it's coming back to me, that first time I was here. Rita and I used one of these bedrooms. I try to imagine bones screwing. Just doesn't work for the imagination. I mean, they're boners, pun intended, but I just can't see them getting it on.

Bobbie's in his chair, leaning back. It's the kind of office you'd like to have: stereo and video racked floor to ceiling, posters, a big hanging thing behind his desk with the Chin Records logo—a big chin, vaguely reminiscent of a famous rock star's—painted on in Day-Glo colors.

"Close the door, sit down," he says.

"Sure, Bobbie!"

What I really want to do is ask him how a schmuck from Cleveland, Ohio, ended up with a British accent, and why he spells his name B-o-b-b-i-e.

Being in the business, I already know the answer: Why not!

"Hey, Bobbie," I say, sitting down. I put my briefcase on my lap, set the Stoli bottle on his desk.

"Excellent, old boy," he says, taking the Stoli, unscrewing it, dropping some down.

Into nothingness. The skull jaw opens, the bottle sits against the ghost lips, but when the vodka gets to the lips, it just . . . disappears.

He catches me gawking, says, "You get used to it, believe me."

"Yeah," I say.

"So, Roger!" he says, putting the Stoli down. In front of himself, I notice. I also notice he's now looking hard at my briefcase.

"Oh, you bet, Bobbie."

I open the case, open the bag, cut out a line for him

on his blotter. Lots of credit-card edges pressed into that blotter, *old boy.*

Again with the weirdness: the coke gets snorted, disappears, the skull smiles as he leans back in his chair, sniffing.

"Nice," he says.

I line some out for myself, to be polite, and say, "Yeah, it's not bad."

"So I hear Carl Peters dumped your ass," Bobbie says.

He's timed it so the powder is just up my nose, so I almost sneeze my brain out through my nostrils. I lean back in the chair, holding my sinuses with my palms, trying not to die.

"So, yeah," I squeak out.

"He always was a fool."

Immediately some of the coke goes where it can do some good, and I'm feeling much better.

"You can say that again," I say.

Bobbie pauses, partakes of the Stoli bottle.

He puts it down again in front of him and says, "So how would you like to work for me? Remember my offer?"

"I remember," I say, trying to act cool. "Grapevine, right?"

He leans back in the chair and laughs. "Them? They're long gone. Dead, so to speak."

"Oh," I say, not knowing how the hell you answer something like that.

"I'm talking about something much better than that. A whole West Coast thing. *Management.*"

Me? He's saying this to me?

"I have to say," Bobbie continues, "I thought about you from the beginning for this. I thought to myself, if anybody gets through this mess . . . intact, it'll be Roger Garbage."

"Gee, thanks, Bobbie," I say, "I think."

"What I need is . . . a go-between, if you follow me. Let's call it insurance."

"Uh, Bobbie . . ."

He's stopped for some more Stoli. Apparently the

dead can drink, because when this bastard's done, there's only a finger of the stuff left in the friggin' bottle.

He points to the briefcase.

I cut him another line, and he pulls it.

"I say again, old boy, that's *nice.*"

Again he leans back in his chair, puts his bone hands behind his bone head, smiles. "You still don't know what I'm talking about, do you?"

"Not . . . really . . ."

He laughs. "Don't you get it? Don't you see that when the dust settles, so to speak, only one bunch of us, your people or mine, will be in charge?"

"The thought had occurred to me, Bobbie, but mostly I've been running for my life the past twenty-four hours—"

"Exactly!" He stands up, stretches. "And running from what?" He points to himself. "Us! You see, we're probably going to take over the world!"

He snatches up a remote control from his desk, swivels toward a huge TV screen set into one wall, snaps it on. There's a news logo in the bottom right-hand corner, and a reporter is wailing on excitedly about some battle or other. Blurry video, a lot of buildings, rubble in the street, piles of dust. It looks like a hundred other places until the camera pans way back and the Chicago skyline, or what used to be it, is outlined against a sickly looking, smoky orange sky and the shoreline of Lake Michigan. The Sears Tower has a couple of bites out of it, and the Standard Oil Building is mostly gone. A lot of planes are buzzing around and there's gunfire and some louder booming noises.

"Shit, Mama," I say.

And I say it again, because the camera now moves in again close, showing the littered street and then panning right to the face of the reporter, a bonehead holding a microphone.

"So," the boner says, "the battle for the midwest rages on. Provisional Governor Warren Harding has called for a cease-fire to take stock of armaments, but vows to fight on until every last human is 'turned,' as it's now called. As we showed you earlier, the entire Chicago Council of Aldermen, including the mayor, was executed outside City Hall this afternoon. The mayor, after being turned, had this to say—"

Bobbie snaps off the television.

"That's just the beginning," he says, leaning back. "Same thing's going on all over the country. All over the *globe.*"

"Even Britain?" I say, instantly wanting to bite my tongue off for saying it.

"Yes, *old boy,* even Britain," Bobbie says. He leans forward, giving me an even creepier close look at his face. "The point is, you humans are fighting back. There's always an outside chance you could win. And if you do . . ."

He points to me, smiles.

"Uh . . ."

"Don't you get it, Roger? If your people win, you protect me! No matter what, people are going to need music, right? And I'll be the one with the music! If we win, I'll keep you around, turn you, as they say. Either way we work together happily ever after!"

"I'm not too wild about the turning part, Bobbie."

He leans forward. His bogus-Brit voice gets just a tad rough. "No choice on that, Rog. The only reason you're not dead right now is I need you the way you are."

I calm him down by saying, "Uh, right, Bobbie. Tell me about the music."

"That room downstairs," he says, "is filled with enough talent, new and old, to fill the record stores for years. I've signed every one of them. New contracts, iron-clad, for Chin Records. As far as I know, I'm the only producer left in the business."

"Carl Peters?" I ask, knowing that if anybody could survive this nightmare, Peters, the bastard, would be one to do it.

Bobbie replaces his hands back behind his head, rocks back in his chair. "That pile of dust you were standing over in the driveway . . .?"

"Oh," I say, and then I jump out of my chair to lean over the desk and shake Bobbie's hand. "You've got a deal, babe."

"Welcome aboard, old boy," Bobbie says.

4

So for a while it's party time. Each day Bobbie and I make some phone calls when we can get through, do a little discreet driving in the Lincoln Town Car when it's safe. It's getting increasingly *unsafe*, at least for humans, at least in the daytime. So we do a lot of our work at night, leaving the party going at Bobbie Land while we travel to Bel Air or Malibu to close a deal. We close a lot of boner-musician deals. Some of them won't sign when I'm around unless they're really coked up. Hendrix in particular tries to bean me over the head with his Stratocaster, but Bobbie pulls him away just in time. After that I stay in the car behind the tinted windows while Bobbie deals with Mama Cass, who comes out to try to get at me in the car. I make a note to send her a canned ham and a dozen loaves of bread.

At Bobbie's house I get a little more respect. Everyone's so high you could bring the human pope in and they'd cheer. One of Bobbie's phone calls has netted us into a wonderful coke ring, one of many that seems to have sprung up; seems a lot of old dead drug dealers are back in business.

I spend a lot of time in Bobbie's office when he's not around, watching television. The cable reception's gotten wonky; sometimes it's out for hours at a time, and when it comes back on, there's a human at the controls, showing obviously van-shot footage of humans fighting back. These never last long.

"Go, State!" I usually yell, holding my Carta Blanca out in salute, though I don't do this when Bobbie boy is around.

As for boner coverage, I get the feeling I'm only getting their side of the story. But that's nutty enough. The whole world's a mess. The human huntdown has been pushed to the background, and now much of the coverage is about the various boner civil wars going on in every corner of the globe. One particular segment, which I really can't vouch for since I was about as high as I've ever gotten (Bobbie had just reamed me out for making a wrong turn in the Town Car, getting us to Janis Joplin just after she'd been turned into a pile of dust by an angry heroin dealer), showed Simón Bolívar and Ambrose Bierce running away from a pack of wild bone bulls in a Mexico bullring while the place went wild. Just as Bolívar caught it in the back, turning to powder, they went to commercial, and when they came back, Richard Nixon's huge horrible skullhead was filling the screen, sweating from his ghostly upper lip, calmly saying that he had come to China to try to bring peace to the region and to the world.

"China will rise from its ashes and rule the earth," Nixon said, and then he declared war on Vietnam, which was about as much weirdness as I could stand before I turned the set off.

There's a lot of craziness like this. In fact, I keep waiting for my radar to go off, telling me to get in the Lincoln and head for the hills, to get away from Bobbie—who I trust about as much as I ever did, which is not at all. But the radar never snaps on. I mean, where is there a better deal for a human right now? Hiding in a storm drain eating dead rats and plotting revenge?

So I stay and, what the fu, with the dope and music and the job, I'm having about as much fun as possible without being turned.

And then . . . *things get even better!*

Is it possible? You bet, Rhett. Ol' Bobbie, I nearly kiss his friggin' bone head when he makes me cover my eyes one day and then brings me to a corner room on the top floor of the house, where they've been banging around for the past two days or so, pushes me in, turns on the lights, and says, "This, old boy, is your office!"

Office! How do you like that, Dad! You know what you had to do to get an office at Roundabout Records, the millennium of waiting, the lineup of asses to be sucked? I wish I had my old man in a headlock now, let him gawk at the racks of vid-stereo equipment identical to Bobbie's, the desk, the plush rug. How's that, Dad? Did I *make* it now? Am I not garbage anymore?

"Hope you like it, old boy," Bobbie says.

"Like it? Wow—"

"You'll be spending a lot of time in here," he goes on, ignoring my enthusiasm, very businesslike. "Things are getting a bit big at the moment. I'm afraid I'm going

to have to turn the whole music end of it over to you.
Vice-president, old boy, if you like titles." He gives one of
his ghostly Brit grins. "I have another surprise for you, if
you'll follow me down to the studio."

So we tramp downstairs and then outside across the
lawn past the pool to the huge soundproof studio, and go
in, past the ranks of mixing equipment behind glass pan-
els, and when he pushes me into the recording room,
it's . . .

The Vomits! Those four lads in all their lovely bone
splendor, Brutus Johnson with his Stratocaster slung over
his back, Barney Barnes helping Jimmy Klemp with a
cymbal stand—and Randy Pants, sneering as always, one
foot up on a chair, turning to look at me as I stumble in.

"Boys!" I say. Suddenly I love them.

"Hear you wanted us dead, Roger," Randy says in his
baritone growl.

"Well, uh, I . . ."

He smiles, taking his foot off the chair to come over
and shake hands. "Well, you got your wish, pustule."

He embraces me. I see Brutus grinning at me over
his Strat, which he's pulled into playing position.

"We've got some nasty tunes to get out," Randy says,
letting me go.

I turn to Bobbie Zick, who's already leaving.

"They're all yours, old boy," he says, "I've already
signed them for Chin Records. Lifetime contract."

"Great!" I say.

And Brutus grunts, hits a chord, and says, "Yeah."

5

For a time I'm so wrapped up in the Vomits I hardly
know what's going on in the rest of the world. There's
other Chin Records business, of course; but now I've got
a pert little secretary, name of Cheryl, very petite bone
structure, and she handles all but the most important
calls. There's a lot of bullshit to this business, and most
of it comes my way, to the point where I wonder what the
heck Bobbie Zick is up to. I hardly ever see him anymore;
he's either locked in his office or out in his Mercedes,

roaming the hills. I think it must be that Beatle reunion thing, but when *those* calls start coming to me, I know Bobbie really does have other nuts to roast. His own secretary, a porky female monster named Noreen who I'm truly afraid of since I know for a fact she wants to turn me with her own hands, and then possibly eat me, keeps telling me, "He's out, *sir*," giving me her lascivious scowl. Or, when I work up the balls to press her, she says nothing at all, only opening and closing her jaw with a snap, which makes me leave in a hurry. The Beatle reunion thing, by the way, doesn't come off because they're trying their own record company again, and Ringo of all people won't sign.

But the Vomits are doing just *boffo*. Under my hand they've already laid out six new tracks. It's by far the best stuff they've ever done, even if it does have a new morbid streak in it that I don't quite get. Everyone else tells me the boners'll love it, though, as in the best one so far, "Dead Right":

> *(You're) dead right,*
> *'Bout the things that you told me 'bout*
> *Last night,*
> *When you came to me shining in the*
> *Moonlight,*
> *Aoooooooooo! Aooooooooo!*

We had a bit of a fight over that *Aoooooooo!* business, but in the end, after everyone else in the house loved it, including Buddy Holly, who sat in on a couple of tracks, I relented. I'm also high on "Rattle in the Wind," "Rise," which isn't about an erection like I thought but about some guy popping up out of the ground in Utah, where the boys were when they got turned, and a real good acoustic ballad, "Puff," which Randy says is about the same guy after he got wasted the second time—hit by the Vomits tour bus, in fact, as he lurched across the road:

> *And the wind caught you*
> *As you went down*
> *And scattered your bonedust*
> *All over town*

(Chorus): Like a cigarette that's had enough
You went . . . puff . . .

6

So everything's idyllic. Until, one day, just after we get "Puff" the way I think it should be, Brutus's plaintive strumming, the sad, haunting wail of Randy's voice, the Roger-radar goes off.

With a vengeance. I've just had a bad day to start anyway, Noreen, the bony porker, telling me she can't authorize the release of any demo-tape blanks because there *aren't any more*, and then she does that jaw-snap thing and adds, not smarmy like usual but with just a tinge of tremor: "You won't be needing them, anyway." For a moment I think, This is it, and I expect her to rise from her desk, climb over it like Godzilla, and devour me whole. But instead I see she's packing things away in boxes—in fact everything in the whole friggin' place is out of its place and waiting to be packed in boxes.

"What the—" I say, but when I try to move past her to Bobbie's closed door, she blocks my way.

"You *can't* see him."

So I tramp down to my own office, thinking to call ol' Bobbie on my phone, but when I get there, the place is cleaned out, the walls stripped, the equipment gone.

"Yah!" I scream, looking for someone to hit, but even Cheryl's not there at her desk, and when I approach Noreen again, she gives me an even sterner look, so I back away, stunned.

I stumble downstairs. The party goes on, but there's not the same intensity. In fact, a lot of the rockers have left, leaving behind mostly hangers-on, beach scum, and drifters. Still plenty of coke and booze, and when one of the drifters named Keg holds out a magazine with cut lines on it, I decide it's never too early in the day to start, and snort two lines, one for each nose hole.

"Gonna need it, I expect," Keg says, grinning from his skull out to his burned-out ghost features. But when I ask him what he means, he just rolls his eyes and puts his own nose to the magazine.

It's the same all over the grounds. Out in the parking lot most of the shiny cars are gone. I finally get someone to tell me that the Stones and Buddy Holly and the rest cleared out the night before, in their own cars or in buses supplied by Bobbie Zick. When I press for details, the dweeb, a hanger-on named Joe, shrugs and says, showing a ghost of his gap-toothed grin, "Parts unknown, man."

I think of wringing his neck, but leave him behind, a sudden horrible thought entering my head.

Sure enough, the Vomits are gone. I had left them here not four hours ago, work for the night finished, arguing over minor points and drinking Coors. Randy told me to go to my office: "Get some Zs, we'll sack out here for a couple and start fresh tomorrow."

Now they're gone.

Joe, who's shuffled over to the pool and is staring stupidly into it, ignores my question, preferring to scrape a stick at a powdery covering floating on the water's surface near one end.

"Where are the Vomits?" I repeat, a little hysterically.

He continues to stare at the powdery scum.

Horrible thought number two comes my way. I point to the floating powder.

"That's not . . ."

He grins at me. "No, man. Not them. But somebody else. Didn't like the news, I imagine. Party ending and all. Think her name was Cheryl . . ."

My secretary! Yah!

This is the end. I stalk across the lawn, looking up to locate the window outside Bobbie Zick's office. Got it. Nothing so convenient as a ladder nearby, but there's a drainpipe that could stand climbing. A couple of false starts and I find I'm not good at climbing drainpipes. But at that moment I see the porker, Noreen, leave the house, moving toward Bobbie's Mercedes with a stack of cartons in her hands.

Quickly I'm inside. Keg is passed out next to his magazine, but there's still one line of coke on it. I snorkle it up, barely stopping. I toss the magazine aside and stride up the stairs.

The door to Bobbie's office is closed, but I don't

even knock, letting the coke help my foot kick it in for me.

"Hello, Roger."

Bobbie is sitting at his desk, calm as ever, feet up, chair tilted back. One hand is behind his head, the other cradles a telephone lazily to one ear.

"What the fu—" I begin to shout.

"One moment, old boy," Bobbie says to me. He shifts his attention to talk to someone who has entered the room behind me.

"It's all right, Noreen," he says. "He can stay. Just finish loading those papers, will you?"

Noreen angrily slams the door on the way out.

Bobbie points at a chair. I'm sputtering, but I sit down as Bobbie continues his phone conversation.

"No," he says, "nothing to worry about. Just that dividend I told you about. Yes, of course I'll hold on to it, but at this point I don't think we'll need it. Yes, of course, you can never tell."

He listens to some words on the other end, then says, "All right, yes, of course."

He hangs up.

"Now, Roger, old boy," he says, leaning forward and folding his hands. "What can I do for you?"

"Do!" I shout. I know I really shouldn't yell, my radar's at full shriek, but the coke and the fact that my office, career, and secretary are dead has pushed me past the limit. Bobbie, however, seems to take this in stride.

"There's been a slight shift in plans." He smiles calmly.

"Do you mind—"

"Of course I don't mind telling you, old boy. In fact, I rather hope where we're going there'll be more Stoli to drink. You see, if we stay here, we'll all be dust or in jail by tonight."

Now he has my interest.

"It's at the point where you can hear gunfire in the valley," he says, "and that makes me very uncomfortable. We've done just about all we can do from here, so we're moving north."

"North?"

"Suffice it to say that I've had a lot on my mind besides music for the last few weeks, Roger. The world has become a very complicated place. And new . . . opportunities arose. A few like-minded men got together and thought we had a good plan for running the new world. More economics than anything. A kind of . . . super-consumerism." The phone rings. He laughs, ignoring it. "All right, let's call it what it was. A structured monopoly. We'd control all sources of distribution, and more importantly, we'd control all sources of productivity. You saw it on a small scale with the music business. After all, that's where I started out. If we controlled all the artists, then no one could go anywhere else for music, correct? Well, it only made sense to expand this idea to other areas such as food production, water distribution, electronics, media, including publishing and television and radio, transportation . . . well, you get the idea. *Somebody* has to run things, and since nobody seemed to be running anything, we made our play. Unfortunately, Abraham Lincoln came along. That bastard is a genius, I have to give him that. I never thought he'd be able to tie the United States back together, but it looks like he may be doing it."

He looks off to the empty wall of his office where the stereo-video equipment had been stacked.

"Anyway, our little scheme just won't work, not in this country now, anyway. We're going to try to consolidate up north." He smiles. "You realize I'm telling you all this because you're still with me, don't you?"

"Uh, right," I say.

"Good. I hope you understand. Our original pact still stands. You're still VP in charge of music, though I don't know how much of it we'll be able to produce on the run. Until this war thing ends, I don't think people will be buying many records. A shame, I'll always have a soft spot in my heart for this business."

"The Vomits?" I ask.

He waves his bony hand. "Turned loose, like the rest." He stands up. "The party's over, Roger. When the dust settles, we'll see."

Surprisingly, he rises and comes around the desk, making me stand, and puts his arm around my shoulder. He draws me to the window. Together we look out on the grounds, the tennis courts, the parking lot, the recording studio. I try not to look at the pool with its scumy surface.

"The game's not ended yet, Roger. There's a world to be made out there, of wealth, and power, anything you want—if you're on the winning side."

"Right, Bobbie."

I feel his hand move up to my neck and tighten, just a little too much. I turn my head and look into his skull—and at this range, with his human face just a misty vapor surrounding that white bone, it never fails to put a chill up the old back. Two eye sockets that lead into . . . *nada.* I get the uncomfortable feeling I always get with these boners—that they'd much rather kill than talk to you.

His hand tightens just a little more on my neck and then he lets me go.

"Can I ask you something, Bobbie?" I say.

"Anything, old boy."

I look at him and smile, concentrating on the ghostly image of his face and not the skull. "Why me?"

He throws back his head and I think he's going to laugh, but instead he just looks at the ceiling. "Why you?"

Noreen appears in the doorway, scowling, telling Bobbie it's time to go.

"We'll be right down," Bobbie says. Noreen retreats, a final pile of boxes in her huge bony hands.

"Why you, Roger Garbage?" Bobbie asks, continuing our conversation. Again he looks up at the ceiling, then down at me. Once more the chill with the empty eye sockets. "You want the truth?"

"Sure, Bobbie."

He waits a count of five. "Because . . ." He puts his arm around my shoulder again, this time steering me toward the office door and the waiting Lincoln Town Car below. I get the feeling he's looking for just the right words. At the top of the stairs he suddenly stops, and this time he does laugh.

"Because, Roger," he says, "you're one of us."

9

The inner diary of
Claire St. Eve

1

We stayed in Mr. Cary's bomb shelter for a long time. I lost track of days. Occasionally we heard a skeleton rummaging around in the cellar outside; twice, the door was tried and Mrs. Garr stood with her gun ready, but eventually whoever it was went away. We ate, slept, and waited.

Finally, after a whole day with no sounds from beyond our door, Mrs. Garr told me it was time to go.

Mrs. Garr knelt down to talk to me. "This is what we're going to do, Claire. We can't stay here forever. My husband works in New York City. There's a chance—" She stopped, closed her eyes. "There's a *chance* he's all right, and that he got home and is hiding like we hid. There's also a chance he's still in New York. I . . . I've got to try to find him, Claire. Do you understand? I just have to know. And if he's alive, he can help us. We'll have to find a place to go, to hide."

She began to cry, and held on to me. "I just don't know what to do, Claire! I just . . . don't know what to . . . do!"

I put my hand on her shoulder. She looked at me, and smiled a little, and stopped crying.

"You're a good girl, Claire. You're the best girl in the world."

She picked up the gun, and Mr. Cary's ax, and crossed the room, avoiding the two piles of dust that had been Mr. and Mrs. Cary. She listened at the door. Finally she turned the lock and pulled the door open.

The cellar was empty.

Mrs. Garr took my hand. "Come on, Claire."

We went through the cellar and up the steps slowly. Every two steps we stopped to listen.

There was no sound from upstairs.

We went through the house slowly, looking into every corner of every room. Sunlight was falling through the windows.

The house was empty.

Mrs. Garr tried the phone, put it down.

"It's dead," she said.

Finally Mrs. Garr opened the screen door and stepped out onto the porch.

A beautiful summer sun was setting.

Except for far-off crickets, the world was quiet.

2

The car was hidden where Mrs. Garr had left it. We uncovered it, got in, and Mrs. Garr backed it out onto the road and stopped it in front of Mr. Cary's house.

We took all of the food we could find in the house, and filled the water jug from the cellar shelter and took that, too. Then we got in the car and Mrs. Garr turned it toward Withers.

Mrs. Garr drove slowly, hunched over the wheel, studying the road in front of us. We passed the empty graveyard on the left, pulled out of the trees into the area behind Withers.

"Oh, Lord," Mrs. Garr said.

Withers was nearly burned to the ground. The top floors were blackened, caved in, the windows empty of glass. It looked like a skeleton of a building.

Mrs. Garr drove on, out toward the parking lot and the front gate.

The gate was still closed. Mrs. Garr slowly passed Mrs. Page's empty black car and stopped. She got out of the car, pulled the massive iron wings of the gate open, and returned.

As we pulled out into the road, piles of dust were visible, in the gutters near the entrance, in the street. We passed two burned cars, a wrecked bus.

The streets were quiet.

The stoplights flashed red and green. Mrs. Garr ignored them. Cautiously, she drove into the town of Cold Spring Harbor. We saw more wrecked cars, up on curbs or abandoned in the middle of the road. Some of the buildings had been burned. Storefront windows were broken. We passed the harbor front; docks had been searched, boats sunk and blackened.

A light pole had been pulled down, blocking our path. Mrs. Garr edged her car around it.

The sky turned to twilight.

Mrs. Garr stopped the car near the end of one street, in front of a delicatessen.

"Come with me," she said, getting out, taking the gun with her.

We entered the store. The door was unlocked, the lights on. A long deli-counter display window was smashed. There was the odor of rancid milk.

Mrs. Garr looked near the doorway, found a hand basket, and gave it to me.

"Fill this with food, Claire. Whatever will last."

There was a phone in the back of the store, and Mrs. Garr went to it and picked up the receiver.

"It works!" she said.

I watched her push buttons on the phone as I got whatever food I could find. There were two loaves of bread, just going stale, along with canned food and boxes.

Mrs. Garr stood with the receiver pressed to her ear.

"Please, please," she prayed.

Finally she put the receiver back and came back to me.

"Maybe Michael is hiding," she said hopefully.

She took the filled basket from me and we went back to the car.

It was getting darker. Down the street a few lights had gone on. The downed light pole behind us flashed on, sputtered off, flashed on.

We drove away from the delicatessen, toward the edge of town.

Out of my window I heard sounds. Mrs. Garr immediately slowed, stopped the car, and rolled down her window.

Ahead of us were many voices. We heard the bark of a dog.

Mrs. Garr looked at me hopefully.

We got out of the car. Mrs. Garr took my hand, pulled me into the shadows of the buildings. Ahead, the main street ended, opening out onto a little park. I saw the flicker of fire.

We moved closer. A bank stood on the corner, its big pillars hiding us from view. Mrs. Garr pushed me back into the brick, peered around the corner into the park.

She gasped.

I looked around the corner.

There was a large group, all of them skeletons, surrounding a gazebo. A few held torches or flashlights.

A skeletal dog stood patiently next to a skeletal human, wagging its tail.

A skeleton mounted the steps of the gazebo and held up its hands. Faintly, I saw the outline of a man in a brown suit, with white hair.

"That's Mr. Perkins," Mrs. Garr said. "He was on the board of directors of Withers."

Mr. Perkins held his hands up for silence. "I think you all know what to do. As far as I can tell, there aren't many left here in town. There's still Bob Rainer's boy, but we're going to let Bob and Marie handle that themselves. Bob? Marie?"

Two skeletons left the crowd, pulling a young boy with them. The boy was human, dressed in jeans and torn shirt. He was shouting, "No! No!" as his parents dragged him up onto the gazebo.

"Come on, Jimmy!" the boy's father said, annoyed. "It'll only hurt for a minute!"

The boy struggled, shouted.

While his father held him his mother put her hands around his neck.

"No," Mrs. Garr gasped, out loud.

The dog turned and looked right at us. It barked, began to run. Some of the skeletons at the edge of the crowd turned and shouted.

"Claire, run!"

Mrs. Garr took my hand and we rushed back to the car. We got in. The dog rounded the far corner, a half block behind.

Mrs. Garr turned on the engine, threw the car into gear, and shot forward.

The dog leaped at the car. Mrs. Garr hit it full on. Its mouth opened wide. In midhowl it burst into dust.

Two skeletons entered the street in front of us, one of them carrying a length of wood. He swung it at the car, hitting the front as we roared by.

Mrs. Garr turned the corner hard, tires squealing, and headed up over the curb into the park, straight at the startled skeletons.

"Look out!" one of them shouted.

We hit into the crowd, scattering bones, which broke into dust.

Mrs. Garr hit the gazebo. It rocked on its wooden frame. The boy's skeleton parents were thrown to the ground, leaving the boy's inert body sprawled on the floor.

Mrs. Garr started to open her car door. "I'm getting him."

The boy's body suddenly flaked away, turning him to skeleton. He stood.

"Kill them!" he screamed, pointing at us.

Mrs. Garr yanked the car door shut, put the car into reverse, and backed away. Scattered skeletons converged on the car. One grabbed at the door handle on my side, barely missing it.

Mrs. Garr sped up, and we pulled back away from them.

We bounced over the curb, back into the street.

Mrs. Garr turned the car and sped away.

"Oh, Michael, please be there," she said, taking us as fast as she could out of the town of Cold Spring Harbor.

3

The highway was nearly deserted. There were trucks, but they moved fast. I looked up into the cab of one as it passed, and saw a skeleton at the wheel, his arm resting on the frame of the open window.

"Claire, move away from the window and keep down," Mrs. Garr said.

She stayed in the right lane. Three exits after she got on we left the highway. We passed a deserted gas station. There was a blackened hole where the pumps used to be. The front windows were smashed in. Next to it was a supermarket. One large front window was missing, but it was open, the rows of lights on inside, skeleton customers rolling carts. In the parking lot a skeleton loaded bags into the back of a station wagon.

Mrs. Garr reached over, pushed my head down lower in the seat until I could barely peek out the window.

"We'll be there soon."

We went down a short stretch of road, past a closed video store and an open diner. Mrs. Garr made a right turn. Immediately she slowed the car.

"I can't believe what happened here."

I sat up in the seat. It looked as though a battle had taken place. A car and a minivan were completely overturned on one side of the street. The fronts of two facing houses were charred with fire damage. On the lawn of a third house a tree had been felled, completely blocking the view.

Mrs. Garr drove slowly down the street. Street lamps made quiet pools of light. There was a strange silence. A skeleton cat ran out from between two garbage cans, stopped to stare into our headlights, hissed, then ran back behind the garbage cans.

"That's where I live."

Mrs. Garr pointed to the last house on the left. Its front was dark. In the driveway was a car, its hood up.

"Michael," Mrs. Garr whispered.

She parked the car at the curb, took the gun from the seat, and quietly opened the car door.

"Stay close by me, Claire," she said.

We approached the house. Down the block there was a sound. The cat ran out from between the garbage cans and crossed the street, darting into a stand of bushes.

Mrs. Garr pulled me down behind the car in the driveway with its hood up.

There was the sound of footsteps. Into a pool of lamplight in the middle of the block stepped a skeletal figure. It stopped, listening.

It stepped forward, out of the light, and stared at Mrs. Garr's car.

Mrs. Garr held her gun out as the figure stepped forward.

A voice called down the street, "Robert, get in here now!"

The figure hesitated, turned around to look at an open doorway where another bony figure stood outlined.

"I heard—" the figure near the street lamp said.

"You heard nothing. Get in!"

"Oh, all right," the figure said, retracing its steps through the lamplight and then down the street. It entered the house and the door closed.

"The Griersons," Mrs. Garr said. "That was Norm and Joanna Grierson."

We stayed a moment behind the car, then rose and approached Mrs. Garr's house.

She had her key out, ready to use it. But the front door was already partway open.

Mrs. Garr pushed the door all the way open and we entered the darkened house.

"Claire, stay by the door," Mrs. Garr whispered, pressing me to the wall just inside the house. She closed the front door. "If anything happens, run."

She moved through the darkness. There was a flash of light as she turned on a lamp.

The house was a shambles.

The couch had been overturned. A coffee table lay crippled, one leg gone. A television in one corner had been toppled from its stand, the picture tube broken.

Mrs. Garr held one hand to her mouth, moving

through the broken furniture. In her other hand she still held the gun. She moved on, into the kitchen.

I heard her gasp.

I went to the kitchen and looked in. The refrigerator had been overturned, its door opened on its hinges like a trapdoor. I smelled sour odors.

Mrs. Garr left the kitchen, walked through the dining room. A china cabinet had been smashed in. She reached through the shards, took out a small porcelain figure, a boy on a sled, now chipped.

She carefully put it back in the china cabinet and moved on, toward a flight of stairs.

She went upstairs. I followed. There were two rooms under a sloped ceiling. In one room was a large bed, drawers from a dresser broken on top of it, clothes scattered. Next to it was another room.

"Michael," Mrs. Garr said.

She snapped on the light.

A desk and swivel chair were scattered with papers. A computer lay on the floor, its screen smashed through next to a printer. There were books all over the floor, pulled from their shelves lining the walls.

Mrs. Garr stepped gingerly into the room, went to the desk. She brushed papers from the swivel chair and sat down. She placed the gun on the desk. For a moment she put her head in her hands. Then she took a deep breath, reached under the desk, and pulled something out, a black box with wires and buttons that looked like a tape recorder. I saw a foot pedal near the swivel chair, under the desk.

Mrs. Garr pushed a button. I heard a whirr, followed by a click.

Mrs. Garr pushed another button.

A voice came from the tape machine.

"Hello, my little transcriber! As always, Beth, I can't tell you how much I appreciate you getting these dictations of mine into the computer for me. You know me and those keyboard machines just don't get along. I know how tired you are after a day at Withers, and I want you to know I wouldn't be getting anywhere without you. What do I owe you this time? Dinner at the Wild Duck again? Champagne? How about both—"

Mrs. Garr cut off the tape, pushed another button, making a fast whirring sound. She stopped it, pushed the start button again.

"Please make a note there, Beth, for me to refer to Compton again at this point. Now more text: I feel it important to emphasize that at this point Beirut was hardly a political entity at all—"

Again Mrs. Garr fast-forwarded the tape, stopped it.

"Jeez, again?" the voice said. "Hold on, Beth, while I go to the window. That's the third big flash in the last half hour. Maybe you heard the boom with this one. Maybe I'd better cut this off and go watch the news . . . Gee, this is real weird, I just looked out the window and saw some kid or something with a Halloween costume on, dressed like a skeleton. Maybe this is October, Indian summer? I—"

Mrs. Garr fast-forwarded, stopped.

". . . is what I want you to do, Beth." The voice was very serious now. "I want you to go to my brother's place in Pennsylvania. I've already talked with him. You know what he's like. He'll know what to do. Don't even think about doing anything else. I'm going to try to get to you at Withers; if I can't, I'll meet you there myself. Hold on. . . ." There was a blank space, then the voice came back, more urgent. "There's someone in the driveway, Beth, they're opening the hood of my car. What the hell, there's banging on the door, *Jesus*, let me—"

The tape cut off, went blank.

Again, Mrs. Garr put her head in her hands. Then she stood, picked up the gun. Her face looked set.

"Come with me, Claire," she said.

We went down the stairs as a noise sounded below.

The doorway was just closing. Priscilla Ralston, Margaret Gray's toady from Withers, stood inside the house, staring at us. She was dirty, her clothes torn, her eyes bright.

"Priscilla . . . ?" Mrs. Garr said.

"Hello, Mrs. Garr. Margaret sent me to get Claire."

Mrs. Garr held me where I was. "Margaret Gray is alive?"

"A few of us got out, hid in the woods in the shed

near the water pump. We were there a long time." She stared at me. "We dreamed about Claire."

Mrs. Garr's voice was soft. "Priscilla, you look very tired. I think you should sit down."

"That's not what I was told to do."

"Did you follow us?"

Priscilla nodded. "We saw your car leave Withers. Margaret brought me in Mrs. Porter's car, because I know how to drive. Another girl was with us, but the ones in the park opened the door and dragged her out. Margaret is waiting in the car up the block."

Mrs. Garr stepped forward.

"Don't," Priscilla snapped. She produced a long knife and held it out menacingly. "Don't come near me, Mrs. Garr. Just let Claire come with me."

"I won't do that," Mrs. Garr said.

"She has to. Margaret wants her."

"Priscilla," Mrs. Garr said gently. She took a small step forward.

"Margaret told me to kill you—"

Priscilla jumped at Mrs. Garr, her eyes bright and hard. Mrs. Garr held the gun up. As Priscilla slashed down with the knife Mrs. Garr brought the side of the gun up, hitting Priscilla on the side of the head.

Priscilla grunted and fell.

Mrs. Garr knelt to examine Priscilla's prone body. "I must have knocked her out." As she turned Priscilla over she gasped at the sight of the knife thrust through the young woman's stomach in a spreading pool of blood.

Priscilla went stiff in Mrs. Garr's arms and then her body flaked away.

Mrs. Garr stood, held her gun out, hand trembling. She fired.

Priscilla Ralston's body collapsed to dust.

Mrs. Garr took me gently by the arm, led me to a side door, then surreptitiously to the car.

As we drove away I looked through the back window and saw the tall, thin figure of Margaret Gray leave a car far down the block and run like a wraith toward Mrs. Garr's house.

4

We drove into the night. I slouched down in the back seat, kept my head up high enough to see.

At first we drove back roads, but after encountering two bands of skeletons, one on foot and one roving the neighborhoods in cars, Mrs. Garr found the Long Island Expressway. The expressway lights were bright. But mostly there were trucks on the road and they drove very fast, ignoring us. Mrs. Garr kept the windows up and the air conditioner on. She turned the car radio on. There was mostly static, but a few channels were broadcasting. One news network run by skeletons described the battle between two forces in Mexico. Another played slow classical music, interrupted by bulletins from around the world. It, too, was controlled by skeletons. At the far end of the dial Mrs. Garr found a station we could barely hear, broadcast by humans, who sounded scared and rushed. They said they were in a van somewhere in northern New Jersey, transmitting to a satellite. They reported the widespread destruction in that state and said they were going to try to link up to a global network. Abruptly, they went off, leaving only static.

Mrs. Garr switched off the radio.

When we reached the outskirts of Queens on the Long Island Expressway, the traffic thickened. There were more trucks now. Mrs. Garr moved away from the window, toward the center of the front seat. An overhead message sign said there were delays on all the bridges, and that the Lincoln Tunnel was closed.

Mrs. Garr pulled into the right lane and stayed there, getting off when the signs said THROGS NECK/ WHITESTONE BRIDGE. On the Cross Island Expressway, which led to the bridges, the traffic was lighter, especially in the left lane. Mrs. Garr pulled into it.

As we approached the off ramp for the Throgs Neck Bridge, Mrs. Garr studied the thick line of cars and trucks waiting to get off in the right lane.

"We'll take the Whitestone," she said, speeding ahead in the left lane.

The Whitestone Bridge was nearly empty. When we

were halfway over, Mrs. Garr slowed down, driving with one hand as she desperately dug through her bag.

"Oh, please," she said.

She found her change purse, searched through it. Ahead, a truck swerved into our lane, and Mrs. Garr nearly hit it.

She reached back over the seat and pushed the change purse into my hands.

"Claire, *please* find two dollars and fifty cents in change. We *have* to use the exact-change machine."

I dug into the purse. We were hemmed in by trucks, moving toward the pay toll. Mrs. Garr craned her neck, saw that we were in a lane with a skeletal attendant taking money in a booth ahead. She looked to the left and right.

Suddenly she cut hard right in front of a truck in the adjacent lane. It honked its horn but let us in. The sign over the booth said, EXACT CHANGE ONLY. NO PENNIES.

"Claire, please!"

I found six quarters, four dimes, and two nickels. Two dollars. There was nothing else but pennies in the purse.

"Claire!"

I put the change into Mrs. Garr's hand. We were almost to the pay booth. She counted through it.

"This isn't enough!"

The truck in front of us huffed to a stop. A skeletal arm reached out, dropped coins into the pay booth's basket.

"God, we'll have to run through!"

Ahead to the right was parked a blue-and-white police car, a skeletal skull watching the cars as they passed through the gates.

The truck in front of us rumbled into gear as the booth light turned green, the gate went up.

It passed through.

The gate came down behind the truck. The light turned red.

In Mrs. Garr's purse I felt a flap behind the purse with a round flat rise in it. There was a small zipper. I pulled it back and reached in.

Behind us the truck Mrs. Garr had cut off hit its

horn angrily. Mrs. Garr rolled up to the change basket. She looked over at the cop in the blue-and-white car, who was drinking from a Styrofoam cup, steam rising around his skeletal head.

In the little zippered pocket was a large round coin. I pulled it out. It was a half-dollar with John Kennedy's profile on it. I reached over the seat and pressed it into Mrs. Garr's hand.

She looked at it blankly for a moment. The truck behind us hit its horn again.

"Oh, dear God, thank you," Mrs. Garr said. "Claire, get down."

I saw the cop look our way over his coffee cup as I ducked down.

Mrs. Garr turned to the machine, dropped her handful of coins into it, turning her head away from the cop. As soon as the light turned green and the gate went up, she hit the accelerator and we went through.

I looked back surreptitiously at the policeman as we drove on. He was drinking his coffee again, ignoring us.

"That was too close," Mrs. Garr said.

The spans of the Whitestone Bridge retreated behind us. Mrs. Garr stayed to the right. Most of the cars and trucks passed us in the left lanes. I looked back at the water we had passed over. A boat lay half-sunk below, steam rising from its cracked skull. Nearby, a tug pushed a garbage barge as if nothing had happened. The sails of docked yachts dotted the marina shoreline behind us.

In the near distance I saw the Whitestone's sister bridge, the Throgs Neck, jammed with unmoving car lights all across its span.

"You know, Claire," Mrs. Garr said. "I don't believe in miracles. But that Kennedy half-dollar was a little one. When I was a girl, after President Kennedy was shot, my grandmother gave me that coin. It was one of the first minted. She loved John Kennedy. She told me to keep that coin with me always, that someday it would be valuable. I thought she meant it would be worth money. For a long time I kept track of how much it had gone up in value. I forgot it was in there." She turned briefly to look at me, her tired features relaxing in a smile. "Do you

know that coin was worth fourteen times what it originally cost, the last time I looked?"

She turned back to the road, shaking her head. "You
never know—"

There was the scream of a jet engine. I turned my
head just in time to see a silver fighter heading straight
for the bridge behind us.

Mrs. Garr sucked in her breath.

At the last second the jet swooped down, underneath. Quickly I looked to the other side of the bridge
where it streaked out toward the Throgs Neck Bridge.

The pilot in the cockpit was human.

There was a whoosh, and something detached itself
from the jet's wing.

"It's a missile!" Mrs. Garr cried.

The jet banked off to the right as its missile shot
straight toward the Throgs Neck Bridge.

From the left another jet roared beneath the Whitestone Bridge, then another. These two held skeleton pilots. They banked right, chasing the first jet.

The first jet's missile arched toward the Throgs Neck
Bridge and struck it midspan.

There was a white-orange flash. The bridge held,
dreamlike, for a moment and then collapsed into two
falling halves. I watched the span cables collapse, twisting
like strands of spaghetti. I heard the distant honking of
horns and watched tiny truck and car lights spin down
into the night. Where the bridge had been, trucks fell
from the newly made ledges along with debris from the
blasted roadway.

The jet fighters had reached land. The human pilot
angled up. At that moment both of his attackers fired
missiles. The human tried to outrun them. He shot
straight up but the missiles were fast and gained on him.

The pilot slid left as the first missile streaked by. But
almost immediately the second missile found him.

There was a flash, a thudding boom. The human pilot's plane stopped, frozen in the sky, then tumbled to
earth in pieces.

The debris of the plane hit the far shore. There was
one flashing explosion, a rain of fiery shards. A sailboat

lit up, its sail a fiery triangle, before folding in on itself in flames and sinking.

Another jet appeared in the distance behind us, streaking toward the Whitestone Bridge. I saw a flare as its missile fired.

There was a huge explosion in the center of the span behind us. The ground rumbled. A rolling ball of fire rose and rose—and then rolled toward us.

Mrs. Garr stepped on the accelerator and we shot ahead.

The explosion nearly filled the rear window, and then collapsed back on itself. I watched a tanker truck drive out of the flames, on fire. It thumped into explosion. The cab twisted to the side. The truck tumbled over, in flames, consuming nearby cars.

Behind the tanker truck the Whitestone Bridge was gone.

5

We were now on the Cross Bronx Expressway, with increasing traffic. We drove for two miles, until suddenly the traffic thickened to a stop. Mrs. Garr craned her head, trying to see.

She said, "Oh, no."

Ahead of us the two outer lanes of the roadway were blocked by blue-and-white police cars. A flock of skeletal policemen were checking each car as it passed through the bottleneck.

Off to the right, just before the roadblock, was an exit ramp that said BRONX RIVER PARKWAY. There was a service lane, littered with debris, but passable.

Mrs. Garr began to pull into it to get to the exit, until she saw the ramp blocked by police barricades. At the top of the ramp was a huge vehicle, a school bus it looked like, blocking the top of the ramp.

Mrs. Garr got quickly back into lane, sought to push over into the center lane.

Two trucks were close by. Mrs. Garr cut the back one off, moving between them, ignoring the blare of the truck's horn.

She looked desperately into the left lane. It was blocked tight with cars. A little figure, a girl, I could just make out around the eerie little skeleton frame, stared at our car from the back window of a car up front. She had a human doll, stripped naked of clothing and marked all over in crayon with bones.

Mrs. Garr waited for a gap between two cars. One moved up, leaving a bare space before the one behind followed. Mrs. Garr angled her car sharply left, cutting off the car behind, and tried to wedge us in. The car behind, a huge Cadillac, wouldn't let her, moving up so that there were bare inches between our car and that one. Mrs. Garr persisted, until the car behind suddenly braked hard to avoid a collision and Mrs. Garr squeezed in.

The door to the car behind us opened. An angry large skeleton with the vague features of a burly, muscled, black T-shirted man surrounding it got out and slammed his door, heading toward us, yelling.

Mrs. Garr reached for the gun on the front seat.

Cars around us began to honk their horns. Five cars ahead, a cop looked up, yelled at the man to get back into his car. The man stopped near the backdoor of our car, hesitating.

"I said get back in!" the cop yelled.

"What the hell is going on, anyway?" the man yelled.

"We had some humans through here a little while ago, car loaded with weapons. Just get in your car and be quiet."

"Get 'em?" the man asked.

"Yeah, we got them. Now you—"

"Right, right," the burly man said, throwing up his hands. He smacked the back of Mrs. Garr's car hard with the flat of his hand, stalked back to his car, got in.

Neither the cop nor the man had looked in at us. But the little girl in the backseat of the car in front of us was still staring, holding her little doll.

We inched ahead. Four cars ahead, the cops were looking in windows, waving cars on one at a time as they squeezed through the single middle lane.

We were angling toward the center as Mrs. Garr searched the highway divider to our left.

"There."

Just before the bottleneck, a gap in the fenced divider appeared. It looked like it had been punched through by an accident. There was a high curb. As we watched, a car in front of us decided not to wait, jumped the curb, turned around, and drove away from us.

A cop yelled, "Hey!"

Another one said, "Better get that blocked up."

The first cop nodded, moved to get a couple of orange highway cones from a nearby stack.

Cars inched ahead.

"We're turning around, Claire."

The cop found the cones he wanted. We were still a car length behind the hole. The car in front of us jerked ahead, almost hitting the cop returning with the cones, leaving just enough room for us to get by.

Mrs. Garr yanked the car to the left, bumped us up over the curb.

There was a scraping sound under the car. For a moment we were suspended.

Mrs. Garr gunned the engine. The car scraped over the bump and through the hole, turning us around on the other side of the divider. An oncoming car blared its horn at us, swerved around, and sped on.

The cop had stopped to yell at the car in front of us for almost hitting him. In the back window the little girl stared at us. As we pulled onto the roadway and sped off she waved, holding her doll out.

Behind us I watched the cop block up the hole with the pylons.

6

"If we can't get out north, we'll have to go through New York City," Mrs. Garr said. She left the Cross Bronx Expressway for the Deegan Expressway. But the northbound lanes of that road, too, were blocked by police cars. All of the exit ramps leading to northbound routes were closed off or guarded by armed police.

We drove on, toward New York City.

We passed the huge three-quarter circle of Yankee

Stadium, burning on our left. The sign on its front, visible through the lighted smoke, said, YANKS VS. TWINS, JULY 2, 3, 4. FIREWORKS, JULY 4.

As I watched, a top part of the stadium, already chiseled by fire, crumbled in on itself, shooting a stream of sparks into the sky.

There was less traffic now. Mrs. Garr turned on the radio again. From one end nearly to the other there was static. But suddenly a strong station blared out, "We've blown up almost all of the major bridges! This war will not end until the human race once again rules the world!" The breathless voice drew away from the microphone, conferring with other muted voices.

"The George Washington Bridge is gone! We've hit the George Washington Bridge!"

He was interrupted by the rat-tat-tat of gunfire.

He screamed into the microphone. "Close up, get off the road! Get off—"

There was a cutoff shout, a loud hiss, and then nothing.

Mrs. Garr snapped off the radio.

Behind us, in the distance, I saw a glowing ball of fire that might have been the George Washington Bridge.

7

Harlem was in flames. The darkness of the night was lit orange, the streets covered with debris and burned-out vehicles. A phalanx of police cars was burning on one corner, a hole punched through it by a sanitation truck that itself sat burning off to one side.

In the silent streets were stacks of dust. I didn't see one window that had glass in it, not one car without its windshield smashed. We drove through a maze of burning wreckage.

When we reached Ninety-fifth Street, it was no different. No lights were on; the city was lit by fires.

At Ninety-second Street we hit a roadblock that made Second Avenue impassable. It looked deliberate; wrecked cars and overturned buses had been plowed into a solid, high wall that sealed the road.

Mrs. Garr turned west. The same thing had happened at Third Avenue, at Lexington, at Madison. Solid barricades of vehicles had been pushed or parked or jammed across the road.

We continued west. We saw no one. It was as if the city had sealed itself off.

When we reached Broadway, the road was suddenly wide open.

Mrs. Garr turned south.

The shops along Broadway were gutted. I saw an occasional car creeping along, as we were, through the blackened buses, overturned cars, piles of dust. There were no police, no humans.

An endless line of stoplights blinked red, green, yellow, a repeat of what we had seen in the nearly empty village of Cold Spring Harbor.

At Fifty-seventh Street the city came suddenly to life. First, a single skeleton crossed our path, stumbling, a bag with a visible green bottleneck in the top. The figure stopped, ignored us, put the bottle up to its skeletal mouth, and drank. I saw nothing go down into the body, but the skeleton took a long drink.

In the flames from a nearby ladies' shop I saw the vague outline of a man in a three-piece suit around the skeleton.

The figure finished the bottle, dropped it in the street, and stumbled on without looking at us.

I saw more skeletons. Two sat in front of a storefront, the first we had seen with its glass intact. Shotguns on their laps, they studied our car as we drove by. One of them peered closely, trying to see through our windows, but did not get up.

Near Forty-eighth Street there was suddenly light. The poles overhead were on, theater marquees alive with neon. Skeletons were strolling, in twos and threes. Many bore guns.

Some of the movie theaters were smashed and closed, but some were open. A marquee announced, ALL-NIGHT HUMAN REVIEW! LIVE TURNINGS! Another said, DEAD SEX SHOW! XXX!

On some of the light poles overhead, from some of the building fronts, were knotted nooses.

Out of a theater proclaiming LIVE! DEAD! WE'VE GOT IT
ALL! a human woman, barely clad and screaming, ran
into the street, tripped, and fell. A few passersby turned
to watch as a tall skeleton strode from the theater and
aimed a handgun at her back.

"One chance!"

She turned to look at him, sobbing. "I won't! I won't
do it with that *thing*!"

The tall skeleton shrugged, pulled the trigger, putting a bullet into her.

She collapsed, and then a moment later her human
form flaked away, turning her to skeleton. She rose,
laughing. She went to the tall skeleton, attempted to put
her arm around him.

"All right, Clyde, no prob—"

"I said one chance!"

The tall skeleton put another shot into her. She
screamed briefly before turning to dust.

"Damned humans getting scarce," the tall one said
to the dispersing crowd, turning to stride back into the
theater.

We had reached Forty-second Street. The lights were
brilliant, the crowds large. A short skeleton stumbled into
the street, hit the car, tried to hold on. I saw the ghostly
outlines of a needle protruding from his ghostly arm.

"Shi . . ." the figure said blurrily, trying to stand.
Suddenly he looked into the glass, peered closer at Mrs.
Garr, eyes widening.

"Hey . . . you're . . ."

Mrs. Garr gave the car gas, pulled around a yellow taxi, edging to the right, making the next turn as the
figure behind us fell to all fours in the street, attempted
to get up.

A line of theaters, the Shubert, the Nederlander, lay
mostly dark, but one marquee, proclaiming CATS! BROAD-
WAY'S BIGGEST HIT!, with a newly added drawing of a cat in
skeleton form, was lit, with lines of skeletons down the
block waiting to get in.

We encountered another roadblock of junked cars,
forcing us to turn left. Ahead, a crowd milled outside a
hotel, spilling into the street. There were cops among

them. A shot was fired. The crowd moved into the street faster, nearly blocking it.

A few blocks up the street a wide column of military vehicles was making its way in our direction. There were mounted guns, tanks, convoys of soldiers.

Mrs. Garr made another left, down a darker street. A few skeletal figures straggled by, heads down.

On Fifth Avenue we were able to turn downtown again. We passed another huge roadblock with a single plowed lane through it.

The whole lower part of the city looked dark, and suddenly the streets were empty again.

On our right loomed the Empire State Building. It was completely blacked out, its spire pointing into a lonely sky.

Mrs. Garr stopped the car.

"Claire," she said, pointing.

In the doorway to the building appeared a human woman, who looked furtively out at us and ducked back into darkness. Beside her, briefly, I saw a man with a rifle.

Mrs. Garr turned the engine off.

"Quickly, Claire."

Up the street behind us came a dull boom, the chatter of machine guns.

Mrs. Garr took the gun and we ran to the front entrance of the Empire State Building.

It was locked.

Mrs. Garr pounded on the window glass. We peered in.

We saw no one.

"Let us in!" Mrs. Garr shouted. She held her gun up and hit at the glass with it.

Up the street, the gunfire drew closer. Between two buildings I saw a brilliant flash of light followed closely by a whump. The ground shook.

"We have to do something," Mrs. Garr said.

We turned back to the car.

Behind us the door to the building was thrown open, a rifle aimed out at us.

"Get the hell in," a voice said.

8

We entered. Immediately the door was closed and locked by the man holding the rifle. He was about twenty years old, stout. He wore army fatigues, the shirt open at the top.

The young man took Mrs. Garr's gun from her hand, stuck it in his belt. Then he walked briskly past us to an elevator bank. Next to the elevator was a boxy-looking army radio, its dial glowing. The woman we saw was waiting inside an open, dimly lit elevator car.

"In," the man with the rifle said.

We entered the elevator.

"Go." The young man gestured to the woman, and she pushed a button. The man stayed in the lobby. We watched the doors close, leaving him behind.

The elevator rose with a metallic groan.

"It'll take a few minutes to get up, the auxiliary power's weak," the woman said. She was middle-aged, haggard looking. She kept fingering a wedding ring on her left hand.

"Do you—" Mrs. Garr said.

"Please don't talk," the woman said, looking away from us.

We rose in silence. Once or twice the elevator jerked to a halt. We waited for the doors to open, but the car just sat there. The woman looked nonplussed. In a moment the elevator jerked into motion again, rising slowly.

After what seemed an hour, the elevator rocked to a halt and the doors opened.

The woman stepped out into darkness. We followed. There was a window down the hallway, giving flickering light from the distant fires outside. In a few moments my eyes got used to the dimness.

We passed a sign that said, OBSERVATION DECK.

The woman turned into an opening, began to climb a bank of steel stairs.

There was a door at the top; she knocked on it twice.

The door creaked back, and a new face looked in, the face of a young boy of about thirteen with hard eyes.

"Those are the last ones," he said. "The next ones Randy lets in, I'll shoot."

He opened the door all the way, revealing the large handgun he held in one hand.

We walked out onto the observation deck.

There were two others, besides the boy. An old man and woman stood by one of the pay telescopes, taking turns peering through.

"Those two are nuts," the young boy said before he turned away. He sat with his back against the building, cradling the gun in his lap.

The woman who had come up with us in the elevator went back down the steel steps, closed the door behind her.

"She's getting it on with soldier boy downstairs. I *know* it," the young boy said, smirking.

There was a slight wind up here, blowing an acrid odor. The sky was orange black. Surprisingly, overhead a few stars shone steadily.

Mrs. Garr and I began at one corner of the observation deck and made a slow tour, looking out at the city. Far off to the north were the most fires, from the direction we had come. Close by, the city seemed to have been cut into sections, with some completely intact, others burning fiercely. Everything below us was dark.

"The fires have gone out downtown," the young boy said. He had risen from his rest and stood next to us. He still held his gun. "Yesterday they fought all through SoHo and the Village. You could see the guns booming, watch the holes they made. This morning they finished off the Bowery. Most of the action has been uptown today."

He made a disgusted sound as the old man and woman approached. The young man went back to his sitting and closed his eyes again. "Nutty old farts," he said.

The old man's eyes were bright with interest. He wore a tweed sports jacket with patches on the elbows. His tie was neatly knotted. He drew a pipe out of one pocket and attempted to light it, with no success.

"Lawrence, you keep forgetting you're out of tobacco," his wife said mildly.

Lawrence got a disappointed look on his face. He looked at the street below.

"And the Petersen Pipe Shop was only a few blocks away. . . ."

His wife patted his arm.

Lawrence brightened. "But such a small price to pay for such gains," he said. "Do you know—"

"Oh, Christ, here he goes again!" the young man with the gun said.

Lawrence turned to face the young man. "As I've said, Ralph, I just don't understand how young people like yourself cannot see the amazing opportunities this all implies—"

"Can the lecture, Pops," Ralph said, keeping his eyes closed.

Lawrence turned back to us. "The young man has *bullets* for that gun of his. I really can't understand how Randy could allow such a young man—"

"If you don't stuff it, Dad, I'll use two of them on you," Ralph said, covering his ears now, cradling his gun in his lap.

Lawrence shook his head, turned back to us. "But as I was saying," he said, "do you know how remarkable all this is?"

"It's remarkable," Mrs. Garr said, "but horrible."

"Horrible, yes, that's true," Lawrence said thoughtfully. "But you must consider the entire picture. Before my retirement at Columbia University—"

"Christ, here he goes with the history lesson again!" Ralph rose and walked entirely away from us, to the other side of the observation deck.

"Go on, dear, tell them," Lawrence's wife said.

Lawrence watched Ralph leave, then turned back to us. "Unpleasant young man. But as I was saying, this event offers remarkable opportunities. We're actually *living* in the past right now."

"And it's trying to kill us," Mrs. Garr said.

"That's true," Lawrence said. "That's true. But at the same time we're *seeing* it. Did you know that before the television blackout three days ago we were able to *hear* Julius Caesar speak? And Archimedes? There was that one station, what was it, dear?"

"CNN, Lawrence," his wife said.

"Yes, CNN, that actually tried to make sense of this new world for a day or two—"

He was interrupted by a loud, nearby explosion. I looked down and to the right. A tank was moving across Thirty-sixth street, turning onto Fifth Avenue.

"Oh, heavens," said Lawrence, looking briefly but then turning his attention back to us.

"Do you have any thoughts on this, dear?" he said to me. "You look like an *intelligent* young person."

Mrs. Garr drew me close. "Claire doesn't speak."

"Doesn't speak . . ." Lawrence said. "I'm so sorry for you, young lady." He touched my arm briefly, looked sad.

"Tell them, Lawrence," his wife said. "They should know."

"Yes," Lawrence said. "Being so much younger than my wife Katherine or me, you should be made aware that the human race really is doomed."

Mrs. Garr said nothing.

"I'm afraid it's true," Lawrence continued. "Not because the dead outnumber the living. Their numbers have already been reduced significantly by violence. Not even because of the inherent violence they seem to harbor for the living and their wish to turn the living into those like themselves. The reason is, in my opinion, that they just simply have such better *minds* than we do. Better leaders. Even now, in the world capitals, power struggles have been going on. There will be one large war within the ranks of the dead, in which all of the strongest fight it out for world domination. But *think* of these strong minds—Napoleon, Ramses the Second, Henry the Fifth! Many of them will die, and the ones who don't adapt quickly to modern technology, like poor Julius Caesar, who set up catapults inside the walls of the Vatican, and was toppled from power the day after that network . . ."

"CNN, Lawrence," Katherine prodded gently.

"Yes, the day after CNN spoke with him. CNN was shortly taken over by radical groups itself, at first Ku Klux Klansmen from the middle part of this century, whose numbers proved inadequate, and then by the provisional ruling government of Atlanta, which is presently headed by Huey Long."

He stopped, drew out his pipe, patted his pockets.

"If only I had some tobacco . . ."

"Go on, dear," Katherine said.

"Yes . . . well, my point is that a struggle is going on, and those who adapt quickly and well, and with the most intelligence, will prevail. And after the war among the dead is over, they will then begin a new world order, into which I'm afraid we won't fit. So we will be either 'turned,' as the phrase goes, or"—he waved his hand—"wiped out."

"Isn't it terrible?" his wife said.

"Terrible, yes," Lawrence said, "but inevitable, I'm afraid."

Abruptly, Lawrence turned away from us, went to the edge of the observation deck, and looked down. His wife looked sadly after him.

"He's right, you know," she said. "He was right about Japan and World War Two, and about Vietnam. They listened to him then, and he had his journals to publish in. But since his retirement no one listens to him. I think if he just had his tobacco, and somewhere to publish, he'd be so content."

She walked to her husband, put her arm around him.

"There's a battle starting!" Lawrence said excitedly.

There was a bright flash below and a solid boom, followed closely by two others. We went to the edge of the deck. Ralph appeared from the other side of the deck and joined us.

"Holy shit," he said.

Lawrence shook his head. "These young people, this coarse language—"

He was silenced by a brilliant explosion halfway down the side of the Empire State Building. We felt the building rock. I traced the line of fire back to a howitzer that had positioned itself on Fifth Avenue, a half block in front of us.

"They'll be calling in air strikes next," Lawrence said. "It's not us they want. I'll wager they don't even know we exist. What we're seeing here is a battle for the control of New York City, between Theodore Roosevelt's older, less mechanized forces and the more modern ones headed by his cousin Franklin Delano. FDR will win, at least here. I'm afraid he'll find that control of New York is no longer a guarantee for winning national office, though. He should have gone straight to Washington if he wanted that. I *do* miss those early reports from ..."

"CNN, Lawrence," his wife said, without a trace of irritation. "Dear me," she added almost immediately. "Isn't that—"

Her husband had gone to the pay telescope, swiveled it around, and was pointing it up the street, in front of the tanks. He turned away from the machine, patting his pockets furiously.

"I don't suppose you'd happen to have—" he started to ask Mrs. Garr.

"Here, Lawrence," his wife said, putting a quarter into his hand. "But it's our last one."

The professor turned back to the telescope, put the twenty-five-cent piece in eagerly, and re-trained the machine on a now visible column of skeletons marching toward the Empire State Building in perfect ranks.

"Yes, I do believe ..." Lawrence said, peering furiously into the machine. "It is! I can see the bare outline of their uniforms. The Seventeenth Light Dragoons. Magnificent!"

He turned the telescope over to his wife.

"We had heard about this, on the radio," he said to us. "They were General Cornwallis's crack troops stationed in New York City during the Revolutionary War. A marvelous straight-arrow band of fellows." He turned to his wife. "Can you see their buttons, dear? Do you see the shine on those boots?"

"I can see the red of the uniforms distinctly," Katherine replied.

"Let me see, lady," Ralph said, taking over the telescope.

"They're fools, of course," Lawrence said, "and they'll be cut to ribbons by the tanks, which are under Fiorello La Guardia's control, the last we heard. It took La Guardia two weeks to unseat Peter Stuyvesant. For a while it looked as though Stuyvesant had the quick mind necessary to adapt, but when La Guardia retained control of the National Guard, and the Armory on Sixty-sixth Street, and especially after securing an alliance with

Franklin Roosevelt, Stuyvesant was doomed from that moment on. I believe we're seeing that doom come to fruition."

While Lawrence regained the telescope, we peered down into the street. The tanks had turned their turrets from the Empire State Building and trained them on the oncoming troops.

"It won't be long now, I'm afraid," Lawrence said, with a mixture of sadness and excitement.

The tank turrets blossomed fire and smoke. We heard the dull thud of the shots. A moment later the advancing ranks of the dragoons were broken by three huge holes. When the smoke cleared, the column was closing ranks, leaving drifting dust behind.

"Whammo!" Ralph said, laughing

The tanks fired again; again the ranks were broken but quickly mended. There were salvos of gunfire from the flanking buildings now, and we saw the tiny skeletal figures puff into nothingness left and right.

Groups of armed skeletons drifted out of the side streets and streamed toward the dragoons. Still the Britons refused to break ranks. I heard a dim shout of command, and the dragoons fixed their bayonets. Their numbers had been reduced by half.

The battle was joined. As the rear ranks of Dragoons were cut to pieces by tank shells, the front were decimated by M-16 fire, hand grenades, and martial-arts close-up combat. It was soon over.

"Is that it?" Ralph said, turning away to go sit by the door again. "Man that was *boring*."

Lawrence abandoned the telescope, sadly. "They never had a chance," he said.

"There, there, dear," his wife soothed.

In the street below nothing remained of the Seventeenth Dragoons. A drift of smoke sifted piles of dust. Once again the tank turrets turned toward the Empire State Building, and we heard and felt their dull pounding.

The steel door was rapped on twice. Ralph rose and opened it a crack, his gun ready.

He opened the door all the way, revealing the uniformed black man named Randy and the woman who had taken us up in the elevator.

"Have fun?" Ralph said, smirking.

Randy ignored him.

"First the good news," Randy said somberly. He fished in the pocket of his khaki jacket and produced a packet that he tossed to Lawrence. It landed at the professor's feet. He picked it up.

"Tobacco!" the old man cried happily. He peered at the cover of the plastic pouch. "Not my regular brand, but it will do marvelously!"

"Candy store downstairs had it," Randy said. "Now the bad news," he continued. He looked away, and waited for the booming sound of cannon fire to expire below before continuing.

"I got through on the radio downstairs," he said. "They're sending a copter from the heliport like they promised. But it's already half-full. All of us can't go."

He looked at us, but his face was not as hard set as he wanted it to be. The woman next to him still looked at the ground. "Helen and I are going. There'll be room for . . . one more."

He continued quickly. "Settle it among yourselves. draw straws, or whatever you want to do. But be quick about it. The chopper will be here in eight minutes. He's only going to touch down for thirty seconds. Helen and I will be on the other side of the deck."

They walked quickly away.

"I told you he was putting it to her," Ralph said.

"Well, shall we draw straws?" Lawrence said.

"Nah, I've got a better solution," Ralph said. He hefted his gun up. "I'm going."

"But young man—" Lawrence began.

Ralph waved the gun in Lawrence's face. "I'm going, and that's it. Make believe I drew the short straw, if it makes you feel better." He looked at each of us in turn. "And if any one of you says anything to loverboy or Helen, I'll shoot you. Is that clear enough?"

He turned and walked to the other side of the observation deck, looking back once to grin and wave. "Bye-bye."

"Why, I've never—" Lawrence sputtered, starting after Ralph. "In all my years I've never—"

"Lawrence," his wife soothed, holding him back. "Let the boy go. It doesn't matter. You know neither you nor I would have gone without the other, and I'm sure Mrs. Garr here would not have left Claire behind. The only qualm I feel is that Claire didn't get a chance to get on that helicopter."

I shook my head and held on to Mrs. Garr.

"There, you see, Lawrence? It would have turned out this way, anyway. It's all for the best. Let the young man go."

"But the unfairness of it!" Lawrence sputtered.

The tanks fired again. The building shuddered.

There came a new sound, a distant ratcheting that grew in volume. We looked up. Through the pall of smoke covering the city to the east, rode a helicopter, bearing distinctive army markings. It drew closer.

"Hide," Lawrence said suddenly.

Katherine said, "Lawrence, why in heaven's name—"

"Do as I say," Lawrence repeated, leading us to the metal door.

We went down the steps. Lawrence closed the door after us. We were in dim light. Lawrence led us down an echoing hallway to the other side of the building, where we climbed another set of steps.

There was a door there. Lawrence opened it, admitting us to a spacious office with huge curving windows giving a view of the observation deck.

We could see Randy, Helen, and Ralph waiting, looking up.

"Stay in the shadows so we can't be seen," Lawrence cautioned.

We stayed by the back wall and watched.

The helicopter appeared, hanging in the sky, then dropped closer.

Randy waved up to it.

The copter lowered even farther. We could hear the roar of its chopping blades. A door in its side slid back. A rope swing was lowered down.

Randy helped Helen into it, called up something. The sling was raised.

When Helen reached the top, she disappeared quickly into the copter's open door. The sling lowered again, and Randy got on.

The sling went up, and Randy climbed into the copter.

The rope was lowered again, and Ralph was hoisted up.

When he reached the opening, skeletal hands reached out to pull him in.

He struggled. Helen appeared briefly in the doorway, groping for the rope, trying to climb out of the copter. But already her strength was failing, a long wash of red draining from her cut throat. Randy's form appeared, struggling with a skeletal figure who slashed at him repeatedly.

At the top of the rope two figures tried to pull Ralph into the copter. He fired a shot. One of them burst into dust. The copter jerked, then steadied in the air.

Helen, flaking away to skeleton, rose and helped to subdue Randy while he was cut by another bony figure. As Randy turned to skeleton Helen motioned toward the observation deck.

"She's told them about us," Lawrence whispered.

Ralph shot again, hitting Helen in the chest. As Randy rose in skeletal form Helen turned to dust before him.

Holding himself back on the rope, Ralph shot again, into the interior of the copter.

The copter gave a sudden lunge downward. It tilted right.

The rotors hit the edge of the building and snapped. The copter rolled over, chuffing like a giant beast. One of its landing struts caught momentarily on the safety extension at the edge of the observation deck. There was a loud scrape as it twisted free.

Ralph, poised outside the open door, fired off a last shot, stuck his handgun in his jeans, and clung wildly to the rope.

The copter lurched. Ralph was jerked away from it, shaken free of the rope, and hurled out over the edge of the Empire State Building, screaming.

In a moment, as skeletal figures, among them Randy,

tried to climb through the open door, the helicopter gave a mighty, groaning roll and flipped over, sliding away from the building, broken rotors clicking impotently.

In a moment it was gone.

After what seemed like an eternity, we heard a distant thumping roar as it hit below.

"Randy didn't know," Lawrence said. "But when I saw the markings on that helicopter I knew. The entire army group that helicopter was from was taken over by skeletons a week ago. There was a mighty battle, but the human side lost. All the armaments went into the hands of the skeletons. It was all on that television station...."

"CNN, dear," his wife said.

"Of course, CNN. If only Randy had asked me. His friends were treacherous indeed."

We left the office, went out to the observation deck to study the spot where the copter had hit below.

We heard a shout from over the edge of the building.

We looked over. Ralph was clinging to the upward curving metal grating that served as a deterrent to suicidal jumpers.

"Help me!" he shouted.

Below him, very far away, lay the still-burning hulk of the twisted helicopter.

"Hurry up!" Ralph screamed, shifting his weight, trying to gain a better grip on the bars.

"We must help him," Lawrence said.

Mrs. Garr said, "There was a hose in the hallway, wound up."

"Yes," Lawrence said.

Lawrence, Mrs. Garr and I went back to the hallway. Ralph screamed behind us, begging us not to leave.

"We're going to help you!" Katherine called down to him. "They're getting something to pull you up!"

"Jesus, hurry!" Ralph begged.

Mrs. Garr pulled the hose as Lawrence and I unrolled it. It stretched nearly to the edge of the observation deck, then stopped.

"It's not enough!" Mrs. Garr called into the building.

"I'll try to undo it!" Lawrence called.

Ralph begged for help. "I can't hold on!"

"You must hold on!" Katherine shouted down to him. "We'll have you in soon!"

Mrs. Garr stretched the hose taut. Suddenly it moved forward.

"I've taken it off its clamp!" Lawrence shouted.

I watched as Mrs. Garr and Katherine fed the hose out toward Ralph. Lawrence secured the other end to the nearest pay telescope.

The nozzle snaked down toward Ralph. He looked desperately up at it.

"I can't hold on!"

"Just a few seconds more," Lawrence urged. He joined us at the edge of the building. "Just a few seconds and we'll have you up."

The nozzle dangled inches from Ralph's hands. Then it dropped to hit him on the knuckles.

One hand lost its grip, grabbed wildly for the nozzle, got it.

"Good, Ralph! Now hold on!"

Ralph grabbed at the hose with his other hand, wrapped both of his hands tightly around it.

"Good! We'll pull you up!" Lawrence shouted.

Ralph shouted, "Do it!"

The four of us held to the hose and began to pull it over the edge of the building.

Ralph began to laugh. "Yes! I'm gonna make it!" He looked down at the burning wreck of the helicopter. He spat. "Bastards! Tried to fool me! Ha-ha! Bastards!"

"Ralph, pay attention!" Lawrence called. "You have to help yourself over the curve of the safety bars! We can't pull you straight up, you have to climb up around them!"

Ralph was still laughing, looking down.

"Bastards! Nobody fools me!" He held the hose tightly with one hand, pulled his handgun from his jeans. "Know what I'm gonna do when I get back up there?" he called up. "I'm gonna shoot every one of you bastards! You can't trust anybody! You're all dead. You—"

"Ralph!" Lawrence shouted. The hose had become tangled between two of the safety bars.

The hose moved up, pinning Ralph's hand clinging to the hose between the bars. By the time he noticed, his hand was already being crushed against the bar.

"Owwww!" he shouted, pulling his hand free.

He was thrown out away from the building, holding nothing.

"Jesus!" He let go of his gun, which dropped away. He made a wild grab at the hose, but his fingers were inches beyond it.

"Jeeeeeesusssssssss!"

He tumbled away from us, screaming, until he had shrunk to a tiny point, and then vanished altogether into the smoking wreckage of the helicopter below.

The four of us turned from the scene.

"I'm uncharitable for saying this," Lawrence said sadly, "but I believe all of this was for the best. I believed that young man when he said he was going to kill us."

9

That evening, the tanks continued to fire into the Empire State Building and surrounding structures. There was another thrilling, bizarre charge by a regiment that Lawrence thought he could identify as a home-guard unit that had put down the New York City draft riots in 1861. They, too, were crushed. We witnessed an aerial dogfight that ended inconclusively, both jets tearing off to the west after trading streaming rockets in the dark.

Sometime after midnight, with a near-full moon rising high over the decimated city, outlining the cratered streets and jaggedly broken skyscrapers in eerie silver-white light, Lawrence gathered us together and told Mrs. Garr, "You and Claire really cannot stay here."

"Where can we go?" Mrs. Garr said.

"I've been considering that," Lawrence said. "I think automobile transportation would be foolish. Most of the land routes out of the city have been demolished. As of two days ago the Lincoln Tunnel was collapsed and filled with water, and the Holland Tunnel was under attack. I haven't seen a commercial airliner in nearly a week. But the trains . . ."

Mrs. Garr's eyes widened. "You think—"

"At this point it's the only logical choice. If you want to get to Pennsylvania, I can't see any other way of trying." He stopped to pull his pipe from his pocket, pinch some of his precious tobacco from his plastic pouch into it, light it. "Besides, staying with Katherine and me would be foolish."

"You're going to stay here?" Mrs. Garr said.

Lawrence nodded, puffing smoke.

"But why?"

"Katherine and I made a conscious decision some time ago. We're not young, and our love of life is not tied to young things. I'm fascinated by what's going on around me. I want to study it as long as I can. Then . . ."

He puffed his pipe.

"We're going to let the skeletons turn us," Katherine said simply.

"*What?*"

Lawrence nodded. "They will be doing building-to-building searches for humans here soon, if they follow their pattern. I have no intention of letting someone like that unpleasant young man Ralph take me before my time. But when the skeletons come . . ."

"How can you . . . ?" Mrs. Garr said incredulously.

Lawrence patted her hand. "It's easy, my dear. When my time in this life is over, I want to study this other life. I don't mind, really. I would never betray the human race while a part of it, but this second existence presents such marvelous opportunities for starting over, for possibly teaching again—"

"But you'll be one of *them*! You'll want to kill the rest of us!"

"My dear," Lawrence said softly, "we're *all* going to become one of them. That doesn't mean you should give up, but—"

"No!" Mrs. Garr said. "I *won't* think about it! I won't think that they're going to get everyone, my husband . . ."

She began to cry.

Lawrence held her, let her cry on his shoulder, while Katherine looked on with understanding.

"It's just that we've thought it all the way through," Katherine said kindly.

"I won't, I just won't. . . ."

She pulled away from Lawrence and sat hugging herself, and then called me to her and held me while Lawrence and Katherine left us alone.

"Claire, I won't let them do it to you, I won't."

Soon she stopped crying. A set, hard look was left in her eyes. She rose, went to Lawrence and Katherine, who stood hand in hand, looking out over the city.

"Tell me about the trains," Mrs. Garr said.

10

We left between midnight and morning. The last sight we had of Lawrence and Katherine was of them standing side by side, happy, wishing us well as the elevator doors prepared to close to take us down.

"If you were to meet us after our turning, I hope you realize you would have every right to try to destroy us," Lawrence said. He smiled. "You see, we've thought that out, also."

"Remember," Katherine added, "our first allegiance is always to the human race."

"Good-bye," Lawrence said.

"Good-bye," Mrs. Garr said. "Good luck."

The doors closed on the view of Lawrence puffing his pipe, looking thoughtfully after us.

The elevator wheezed and jerked downward. The trip this time took longer than it had before.

As we reached the bottom the doors creaked open on the unknown. Mrs. Garr held my hand very tight.

"Just stay close, Claire," she said.

We passed Randy's abandoned radio, walked to the front glass doors, and looked out.

In the street were the ruins of a destroyed tank, its turret bent at a useless angle, one tread unraveled.

The street appeared empty.

We pushed out through the door, stayed close to the building, and headed west.

We saw no one. The street was deserted, the ruins of

battle left behind. The road was pocked with holes and ruts. Softly blown piles of dust lay everywhere.

We dipped into doorways, walked close to the faces of buildings.

We reached Sixth Avenue, waited in the dark shadows to cross the street.

"Let's go, Claire—"

There was sound north of us. Two blocks up, a tank column rumbled across Sixth Avenue, heading east.

We waited for it to pass. At its rear were two trucks filled with a skeleton army contingent. We crossed the street, ignoring a "Don't Walk" sign flashing at us.

We walked on, moving west and then north.

When we reached Seventh Avenue, we found that we had gone too far north and doubled back.

Abruptly, Mrs. Garr pulled me into the open doorway of a shop whose neon lights flickered inside, on and off, on and off.

"In here, Claire."

We entered the shop. The walls were covered with party goods, costumes, party favors, paper napkins decorated with Mickey Mouse and Bugs Bunny.

I stayed low, thinking Mrs. Garr had spotted someone coming on the street. But instead, she was moving to the front of the shop window, leaning over the waist-high backdrop and trying to reach something. She grunted, strained her hand out, pulled it back clutching two rubber masks.

She handed one to me.

"Put it on," she said.

It was a full-head rubber skeleton mask.

I put it on and watched through the eyeholes as Mrs. Garr put hers on.

When the lights flickered out, she looked like a skeleton. When they flickered on again, she looked like a human wearing a mask.

"In the dark, it will help," she said.

We left the shop. Immediately we saw a figure across the street, a skeleton with an army helmet bearing a rifle.

We walked, hands close to our bodies.

The soldier glanced at us, walked on.

We kept walking.

We passed hotels, the Broadway, Penta, to where Madison Square Garden squatted roundly amid the surrounding buildings.

The white billboard out front read MONSTER TRUCKS TONIGHT!

Another sign nearby bearing an arrow said PENN STATION.

A small crowd of skeletons milled out in front of Madison Square Garden.

"There's another way to get into Penn Station," Mrs. Garr said.

We passed to the right of the crowd, into an entry past the Madison Square Garden sign and under an overpass. There was a half circle where taxis picked up passengers. It was deserted. We found one of a rank of doors that was open.

"Walk fast, keep your head down," Mrs. Garr said.

Out of a small lobby we ran into a swarm of people heading for trains.

Holding me back, Mrs. Garr said, "This won't work." She glanced around furiously. "There's another way, but I don't remember exactly where. I came into the city with Michael once, and we got lost in the tunnels. We saw no one for five minutes. If only I could remember where we came out . . ."

She found a sign overhead that said AMTRAK with an arrow pointing.

"That's it," she said.

We followed the sign. Soon we were in a maze of passenger tunnels under construction. One led us to a dead end. We backed up, made a turn, and found ourselves near a bank of sour-smelling rest rooms. Around a corner were the Amtrak ticket counters, on the wall behind them a huge arrivals and departures sign.

"One more turn . . ." Mrs. Garr said.

We backed past the rest rooms and there was an entry, partly blocked off with a sawhorse.

"This is it," Mrs. Garr said. "Now we have to find a train heading west through Pennsylvania."

We went back to where the ticket counters were visible, long lines of skeletons queuing along.

Mrs. Garr craned her neck, tried to read the arrivals and departures sign. "Stay here, Claire."

She strode slowly out into view and studied the sign. A passenger near the end of one line turned to look at her, looked away, looked back.

Mrs. Garr returned. "Got it."

The curious passenger was about to leave the line to follow us when two other passengers, a man and his wife, arguing, blocked his way.

He tried to get through them, craning his neck. "I saw—" he started to say.

"You saw what, buddy?" the man said.

"Oh, leave him alone, Jeff," his wife snapped. "You're always bothering everybody. Just get me out of this god-damned city before everything turns to dust."

The line moved up. The skeleton who had been staring at us, who wore the vague outlines of a suit and tie, didn't move with it.

"You gonna move or what?" Jeff said.

He shoved the other skeleton, and the two of them started to scuffle as we backed past the rest rooms to the opening blocked by the sawhorse.

We moved past the sawhorse, found ourselves in a black, damp-smelling tunnel.

"The trains are along here somewhere," Mrs. Garr said.

As if in answer, a dirty streak of silver shot past to our left, illuminating the tunnel.

"Let's go, Claire."

There were dim bulbs overhead, barely illuminating the ledge we were on, which led us eventually to a row of train platforms.

"We want platform five," Mrs. Garr said.

Our ledge fronted platform three.

"We have to climb down and across."

Mrs. Garr lowered herself into the pit of the train path, helped me down after her.

We crossed the tracks, stepped carefully over the third rail, climbed up the other side.

Two platforms away sat a silver Amtrak train.

As we crossed the set of tracks on platform four, I

felt a rumble and a headlight appeared down the dark tunnel, bearing down on us.

Mrs. Garr climbed up, held her hand down.

"Claire!"

I held on. She pulled me up as the train passed.

The back of our train confronted us.

We heard voices on the far side. We edged around to where we could see two skeletons, one holding a thermos.

"Last trip for me," the one with the thermos said. "I've got the wife and kids out in Ohio waiting. We're gonna hide in the hills till all this crap blows over."

"You heard about martial law, didn't you? They're shooting anyone who leaves a public-service post."

"Screw it," the one with the thermos said. "I've had enough of this craziness. Did you see they had those old-timers working the northeast corridor. *Steam*-engine men, for Christ's sake. When that guy Fulton broke the union, that was it for me."

"What about the army?"

"Which one? When they figure out who's in charge of everything, then they can call me again."

The other laughed. "Well, they say Lincoln . . ."

We moved around to the other side of the train.

We were confronted by the skeleton from the ticket line upstairs, the one in the suit and tie. He was climbing out of the neighboring train pit, breathing heavily.

"There's a bounty for you humans, you know. It's backed by gold—"

Mrs. Garr rushed forward, pushed him back down into the pit.

He held his balance for a moment, then collapsed, falling and hitting the third rail.

He shrieked, was gone in a cloud of sparks and dust.

Mrs. Garr ran back, pulled me flat against the side of train as the two Amtrak men from the other side appeared.

"What the—"

They walked to the edge of the neighboring pit, looked down.

"Christ," the first one said.

The second one laughed. "Maybe he was a *steam man.*"

The first one laughed, and they went back to the other side of the train. "Time to get this sucker out of here," the first one said; "before somebody blows it up."

Mrs. Garr pulled me along the side of the train. The doors to the rear car were locked. We peered inside. It was an empty passenger car, dark and inviting.

We moved to the next, a baggage car. It, too, was locked.

The first door on the next car was open.

Mrs. Garr climbed up cautiously and looked in. Quickly she came back.

"There are four skeletons at the other end of the car," she whispered.

We adjusted our masks and climbed up. Mrs. Garr immediately pushed the door operator between our car and the baggage car.

I looked down the length of the passenger car. The four skeletons were playing cards. One of them said something and there was a blurt of laughter.

After a moment the door hissed back and opened.

We entered.

The four skeletons at the other end of the car looked up briefly, went back to their card game.

The door slid closed behind us.

Mrs. Garr pushed the door to the baggage car.

The door made a faint rumble, didn't open.

"Damn," Mrs. Garr said.

She tried again.

It didn't open, but there was a faint rumbling sound.

Mrs. Garr hit the door with the flat of her hand.

It groaned, began to slide back.

We pulled the door the rest of the way back. Suddenly it freed, sliding into its jamb.

We entered the baggage car.

The door rumbled shut behind us, plunging us into shadows and bare light entering the two center windows.

"Thank God," Mrs. Garr said.

We took off our masks, felt our way through a maze of boxes and suitcases, sacks of mail, crates of foodstuffs. A tiny skeletal dog in a pet carrier barked feebly; a skeletal bird, in a hanging cage, squawked once, then was silent, following our progress with its tiny eyeless skull.

The backdoor to the car was locked. It was different from the other doors, a huge handle with a double keyhole.

"Enough," Mrs. Garr said suddenly, exhausted. She sank to the floor, pulling her knees up. In a few moments she was asleep.

I sat beside her. And a little while later, as the train rumbled into moving life, I, too, closed my eyes.

11

We awoke suddenly, blinded by sunlight. The car was brightly illuminated. Beneath, I felt the comfortable rumbling roll of the moving train.

We rose and made our way to one of the windows.

The light hurt my eyes, and for a moment I shut them.

When I opened them, I saw what looked like a dream.

"Oh, Claire," Mrs. Garr said.

We were moving through green countryside. The summer trees, the lush growth at the side of the tracks, the rolling unspoiled hills, made such a stark contrast to what we had seen that for a few moments we sat transfixed.

"I wonder where we are," Mrs. Garr said.

We crossed to the window on the other side of the aisle. The tiny skeletal dog began to bark. The bird in its cage cocked its head, followed us with its eyeless gaze. As I moved past its cage it pecked out.

In the far distance, behind the train, were the ruins of a city. Brown smoke spoiled the blue summer sky.

"That's not New York," Mrs. Garr said.

She studied the city skyline for a few moments, then turned away.

"That used to be Philadelphia."

I continued to look. Mrs. Garr rejoined me, pointed up to a high hill where a gutted white building with columns on it that looked vaguely like a Greek temple lay smoldering.

"That was the Museum of Fine Art," she said. "Michael and I were there. They filmed the first *Rocky* movie there."

I remembered now, the long steps, the fighter played by Sylvester Stallone running up, jumping at the top, hands thrust high in the air in triumph.

"Everything's going," Mrs. Garr said wearily. "Soon everything will be gone."

We went back to the other window. The bird squawked once, angrily, adding to the tiny dog's yelps.

We looked out at the hills, spoiled now by what we had just seen and the occasional sights of a rutted country road, a burning farmhouse. In the middle distance a white church sat on a hillock, its steeple knocked askew. Next to it a small patch of a cemetery was churned up, potted with open holes, gravestones pushed over.

"Soon we have to get off the train," Mrs. Garr said. Her voice sounded devoid of hope. She turned away from the window, sat down with her back to it, motioned for me to sit by her.

She took my hand in hers, looked at me with a sad, tired smile.

"I don't know what's going to happen, Claire," she said. "I don't know if Michael's brother will be in Arlentown when we get there, or if he'll be able to help us. I don't know if I'll ever see Michael again. I miss him so much it hurts. . . .

"But I want you to know that whatever happens, I'll try to take care of you. It's the one thing I know I have to do."

She looked closely at me. "You've changed, Claire. I think that seed has begun to sprout inside you."

I nodded.

"You *do* know what I'm talking about, don't you?"

I nodded again, and smiled.

"Oh, Claire," she said, pulling me to her and hugging me. "That seed will bloom into a beautiful flower. I know that. I wish I could tell you—"

She stopped, and looked away from me.

"I will tell you," she said after a moment. "I know

you were never told how you came to be at Withers.
And you were never told who your parents were. In another two years, when you were eighteen and old enough
to leave, you would have been given that information if
you had demanded it."

I waited for her to go on.

"The truth is, Claire, I came to Withers because of
you. Sixteen years ago, when I was just about your age,
long before I met my husband, Michael, I met a man and
I stayed with him for one night. He was black, a colonel
in the air force. The next year I had his baby, a beautiful
brown-skinned girl. Because I was so young, the baby
went into foster care, and I never saw her again. I was
told a good home would be found. After a while I met
Michael and my baby slipped to the back of my mind.

"But then a year ago I began to have dreams. And in
my dreams was a beautiful, young, brown-skinned girl
who wouldn't speak. That young girl was my daughter,
and I knew I had to find her and take care of her. . . ."

She held me and began to cry. "Oh, Claire, I told
Michael about you. He understood everything. There was
paperwork that Mrs. Page at Withers was getting ready
for me. In another six months I would have been able to
take you home. Your real father knew nothing about you,
but we were going to get in touch with him. He was a
good man. I think he'd be very proud of you.

"Claire, why did all of these bad things have to happen before I could take you home?"

Mrs. Garr, my mother, held me very tight, then
turned and looked at the countryside rolling by. There
were tears in her eyes.

There were tears in my eyes, too. The train rolled
on. I stayed with my back to the window, watching the
solemn little skull of the bird in his cage, and he watched
me.

12

Wearing our masks, we left the train at Arlentown.
Only one other passenger got off, a skeleton up toward
the front. The platform didn't reach the baggage car, so

we jumped down and hid behind it while the skeleton passenger walked to a car in the small parking lot, got in, and drove off.

The skeletal conductor leaned out of his compartment, waved at the engineer up front, and the Amtrak train pulled slowly away.

The station, and the surrounding hills, were untouched. It was only when we checked through the few cars in the parking lot that our real world came back to us. In one of them all four doors were locked. The windshield was shattered by a hole on the driver's side. When we looked in, we saw a pile of dry dust on the front seat.

There were two other cars. One was open but empty, the other locked, its keys lying on the front seat near a pile of dust.

My mother searched near the platform, found a large rock, came back, and shattered the driver's-side window.

We brushed out the glass and dust and got in.

The engine turned over once, coughed, died, but on the second try it roared into life.

We pulled out of the parking lot.

We drove through beautiful country. The roads were empty of movement. We passed an overturned mail truck, a bakery delivery truck with all four tires punctured and its backdoors open. The few farmhouses we passed looked quiet and empty.

"Michael's brother's place isn't far," my mother said. She tried the radio. There was only static. She turned it off. I watched her tension mounting as we went on.

We turned down a narrow country road, under a long spread of trees, then into a long dirt path leading behind a hill. A silo was visible.

We passed a burned-out truck.

"That's Jay's," my mother said.

She slowed the car to a crawl as we climbed the hill.

A burned-out farmhouse came into view. A pasture next to it was empty, its rail-and-post fence downed in several spots. The yawning doors of a barn were ajar. The house itself was half-blackened, a charred hole in one corner of the roof.

"Oh, God," my mother said, taking her mask off and

throwing it down. I took mine off, too. My mother's hands began to tremble on the steering wheel.

I saw a flash of movement near the silo. When I looked, there was nothing.

My mother braked the car in the yard, sat gripping the wheel as the dust settled around us.

"What are we going to do?" she said.

Again there was movement by the silo, a quick flash. This time my mother saw it.

She started the car with a cough again and put it into reverse.

Suddenly a human form stepped out of the silo's shadow, rested a rifle against its side, and waved its arms over its head at us.

My mother stopped the car with a jerk. "Jay!"

A human man strode toward us, tall, lanky, with worn features, in his late forties. He smiled, holding his arms out.

"Oh, God, Jay!"

My mother struggled with the door handle, got it open, ran from the car into the man's arms.

He hugged her, laughing.

"Yes, it's me, your old brother-in-law, in the flesh!"

She held him tight, then she looked up at him. "Michael . . ."

"Not yet. But we're expecting him. He got a call in, just before the phones went dead a couple of days ago. Said he was in Philadelphia, on foot. That little brother of mine'll get here one way or another, if I know him. He was looking for you, naturally."

"Oh, Jay!"

He laughed, hugged her again. "Yes, there are still a few of us around. In fact, most of us here are still the way we're supposed to be. Michael's uncle Ron didn't make it, had a heart attack second day all this started. We took care of him the way we thought best. Made sure he was really at rest, if you follow me. But the others . . ."

"Where?"

Jay pointed to the silo. "There. Been empty since last year. Burned the house ourselves. Skeletons came looking a couple of times, once some old friends of ours, once some National Guard types, but we're hid pretty good and they left us alone. Only Hedge Williams, over the next farm, figured out where we were after he got turned, but he was stupid and came alone. Outside of that, been pretty quiet, at least the last few days."

"Claire!" my mother called.

I left the car, came to stand next to my mother.

"This is Claire, Jay. She's . . . my daughter."

Jay blinked, then shook my hand. He looked at my mother and smiled warmly. "Michael told me all about it, Beth." He looked back at me. "Well, you both just come on in, now, and get something to eat, and see everyone else."

He led us to the door of the silo, then said to my mother, "Give me your keys, Beth. Got to move that car out back, mess it up a little more. Don't want anyone nosing around after it."

My mother gave him the keys.

We were met at the door by a woman named Nan, who was introduced to me as Jay's wife. Inside were four others, a man, a woman, and two young girls.

"Oh, my," my mother said as we stepped inside the silo.

It was outfitted like a real house, with furniture, rugs, bookcases, and a television along the curving walls. A washbasin, a tub behind a makeshift curtain, and a stove, vented through the side, lay to the right, and a row of beds and cots and sleeping bags lined the left side of the silo.

High above, two real birds swooped and dived, then settled briefly on a rafter before flying off in mock battle again.

"Don't mind the swallows," Nan said. "We had more, but a couple got killed and turned to bone. Shot those."

We were fed, took short baths, and were given clean clothes.

Jay returned and tried the television. "Got the cable run out from the house," he explained. "Ran an electric line out, too. We've been pretty good for power, only lost it three or four times, not at all in the last three days."

He switched through channels.

"Government station came on this morning, said there'd be an important message tonight. That's *their* government, of course. Haven't seen anything from our people in days. Sometimes those independent stations come on for a few minutes, go off again. Cable company was raided by our people one day. But that didn't last."

He switched off the television.

At the table where we sat, I found my eyes closing, saw my mother sleepy across from me.

"Heavens!" Jay cried. "Get those two to bed 'fore they drop their heads on the table! How long since you got a real sleep, Beth?"

My mother said, "I really don't know."

We were helped from the table and brought to beds.

"No . . ." my mother protested weakly. "Michael . . ."

"Now, don't you worry about Michael," Nan said. "You just go to sleep. If Michael comes, we'll wake you."

Through my own drooping lids I saw my mother close her eyes.

Nan looked at me curiously for a moment, then smiled. "You too, darling," she said. "You know, I've dreamed about you.

She continued to look at me, then turned away.

I lay back and closed my eyes, and as I drifted to sleep I heard Nan say to the others, "Fancy her being Beth's daughter. She's the one I told you about, the one we have to protect. . . ."

13

I awoke suddenly, in darkness. Someone was calling sharply to my mother, trying to wake her up.

I sat up. Our side of the silo was unlit. But across in the living area lamps were on, giving everything a twilight glow. The television was on, showing static.

Nan was bending over my mother, shaking her. "Beth, wake up. Michael is here!"

My mother rose out of sleep, came awake.

Nan said excitedly, "Michael is outside!"

"Oh, Lord," my mother said, rising. "Oh, thank God." There was a crowd by the front door, Jay at its head. He picked up his rifle, which stood next to the door, put it down again. He called out into the darkness,

"Well, come on in! I'm telling you, Mike, there's nothing wrong in here!"

A muffled reply came. Jay cursed in frustration as my mother pushed her way to the doorway.

"He says he can't be sure we're humans in here," Jay said. "I *showed* him myself, for Christ's sake! Michael and some others are over in the barn. He sent out a woman, one of a bunch of people they've been traveling with, to show they're human, too. He says he'll only trust you, Beth."

"Let me go to him!" my mother said. She stepped through the doorway.

"Now, hold on," Jay said worriedly, taking her by the arm. "He sounds real upset. They must have had a hard time out there. I just want to make sure—"

"Let me see him!" my mother said. She twisted her arm away from Jay, stepped out of the silo, and headed for the open barn doors.

"Michael!" she called. "It's me! I'm coming!"

Jay and the rest of us spilled out of the doorway behind her.

I saw nothing.

"Beth, I don't like this—" Jay shouted.

"It's all right!" my mother said. "Michael!" she called out. "It's me!"

A skeleton stepped out of the shadow of the open barn doors, bearing a rifle, which he raised and pointed at my mother.

"Hello, Beth," he said.

"Michael's one of them!" Jay cried.

Behind the skeleton a group of humans appeared, pointing weapons.

At their lead was Margaret Gray.

"Shoot her," Margaret said to Michael.

Michael fired the rifle. My mother stumbled, cried out, and fell.

Michael immediately dropped the rifle and ran to my mother. He bent down, cradled her in his arms. "Oh, God, Beth, don't you see? This is the only way we could be together."

My mother said, "Michael . . ."

"Oh, God, Beth."

My mother looked back at me, held her hand out. "Claire ..."

Her hand fell, and she was still.

She began to turn.

"Shoot both of them," Margaret Gray said.

A short, fat, balding man with wild eyes stepped forward, took up the rifle Michael had dropped, and aimed it.

My mother and Michael, both skeletons, stood up and faced Margaret Gray.

"You promised!" Michael said.

"You're abominations," Margaret Gray said. She nodded to the short man. "Now."

The short fat man fired twice.

My mother and Michael fell to dust where they stood.

"Now kill the rest of them!" Margaret Gray said. "But don't harm the girl!"

The others with her began to fire.

"Damn!" Jay said. He retreated to the silo door and was hit as he reached to pick up his rifle. He fell. Nan grabbed me, drew me inside, and then was hit herself. The others, the man, woman, and two young girls, made it into the silo.

The man was cut down as he reached out to retrieve Jay's rifle. The others cowered near the beds and watched, my back flat against the silo wall.

"Turn them," Margaret Gray said.

There was a halo of gunfire from those entering the room. The woman and girls fell.

"Dust them," Margaret Gray said.

As the bodies turned to bone there came more shots. The skeletons flaked away.

"Hello, Claire," Margaret Gray said, turning to me. "It wasn't hard to find you. The tape Mrs. Garr's husband made was very instructive, though it took me an hour to find the address book with this farm listed in it. I don't approve of what happened to poor Priscilla Ralston." She moved closer to me. The wild brightness in her eyes was even more pronounced. "I've been dreaming about you, Claire. We all have. I always knew there was something ... special about you." She suddenly threw her hands to heaven and looked up. "She is delivered unto me!"

The television static crackled.

The picture cleared, showing a thin skeleton sitting behind a desk. Behind him was an American flag.

"Ladies and gentlemen, the president of the United States," an off-camera voice said.

The others turned to watch.

Margaret Gray smiled thinly and said, "They put me in Withers because of my religious convictions, Claire. All these years, since I was seven years old, I knew something like this was going to happen. I knew I would be at the center of great things." She clenched her hands very tight, and a fierce anger rose in her, threatened to spill, then subsided. When she spoke again, there was almost gentleness in her voice, and she looked at me almost as if I were an object of wonder. I was startled to see a tear pooled in the corner of one eye. "Seven years old, fifteen years ago, and they called me mad, my own mother and father . . ."

Her eyes drifted away from me for a moment, and then she focused again on me with the same look of awe. On the television set a skeleton with the ghostly thin features of Abraham Lincoln was speaking.

"I've had a vision, Claire," she said. "Involving you and me." She straightened and pointed to a chair for me to sit in. Her thin smile returned.

"Let's hear what the president has to say before we do great things, shall we?"

10

From the second life of
Abraham Lincoln

1

"Fellow citizens of the United States:

"Once again I find myself before you to present these brief and customary remarks, and to take in your plain sight the oath taken by the president, as prescribed by the Constitution of the United States 'before he enters on the execution of his office.'

"It has been sixscore and eight years since I last appeared before you in this capacity, and once again this Union finds itself in deep crisis.

"And once again I resolve to you that this Union will not be broken.

"The present course upon which we find ourselves, as in that earlier conflict, can only lead in two directions. Either there will be peace, or peace will be abrogated, and war will continue. There is no middle course.

"Once again the nation is wounded. Yet wounds heal. Once again we find ourselves with an institution, the institution of first life, which threatens to break apart the Union, and with it the hopes and dreams of all its people.

"War is here, and none want it, but neither will it leave until the Union is whole and inviolate.

"As I said in my last address on such an occasion, so many years ago, the Almighty has his own purposes. 'Woe unto the world because of offenses! for it must needs be that offenses come; but woe to that man by whom the offense cometh.' If we suppose that first life is one of those offenses which, in the providence of the Almighty, must needs come, but which, having continued through the Almighty's appointed time, He now wills to remove, and that He gives to us this terrible war, as the woe due to those by whom the offense came, shall we discern therein any departure from those divine attributes which the believers in a living God always ascribe to Him? As I said then, fondly do we hope—fervently do we pray—that this mighty scourge of war may speedily pass away. Yet if God wills that it continue, so be it. And still must it be said, 'The judgments of the Lord are true and righteous altogether.'

"None want war; all want peace. But peace can only come when we welcome the last of our errant brothers into this union of second life. I ask our human citizens to lay down their weapons and open themselves to second life, and so bind the nation's wounds.

"The nations of the world are fighting their own battles in this war. These are tumultuous times. I pray tonight that we will once again, as we did those many years ago, achieve a lasting peace among ourselves and, by so doing, among all the nations of the world."

2

I closed my eyes and prayed to God then that I had said the right things. As always, I feared my voice too weak, too high-pitched, my words ineffective.

It was then that Justice William Douglas, "The best man they could dig up for the job," as he had quipped, administered the oath of office.

I removed my hand from the Bible, and, thankfully, the task was over.

"That was wonderful, Mr. President," Stanton said, beaming beside me.

The cameraman, leaving the back of his giant electronic eye, made a face.

"Didn't look into it straight, did I?" I said, smiling.

He got all flustered and said, "Of course you did, Mr. President. You were ... fine."

"Hogwash. I looked down at the paper I was reading from, just like you told me not to. Don't you worry about it." I rose and clapped him on the back.

Mary, huddled in the corner, looked like she had been crying, so I went to her.

"Happy for me, Mother?" I said, putting my arm around her.

"Happy!" she fumed, pushing away from me.

"It was just a joke," I said gently. "I know how you feel. I feel the same way. But—"

"But nothing, Abraham! You served them once—" She broke off in tears, left the Oval Office, and wouldn't look back at me. "Once again, my heart shall be broken."

I gazed at her sadly.

My sadness didn't last, though. Eddie and Willie were into the room, making a mess of my desk, fooling with the television equipment.

"Father, look!" Willie said, swiveling the lens to point it at me.

I put my hands over my face in mock surprise. "Oh, no! Not the press again!"

"Speaking of the press ..." Stanton said, sidling up to me.

"I know, I know," I said. I could hear their babbling in the outer office. I knew I'd have to face their pens— and cameras—at any moment. "I don't mind most of them. But that CNN ..."

Billy Herndon was next to me. "They're under control, Mr. Lincoln. We've promised Huey Long a cabinet post, perhaps secretary of the treasury."

I guffawed. "That robber!"

Herndon's eyes shone. "Exactly. It will keep him quiet and busy, and we can keep an eye on how much he steals. In exchange he's turned the station over to a man loyal to us."

"All right."

I looked back wistfully at Eddie and Willie. The cameraman was unsuccessfully trying to wrestle his equipment back from their hands. Then Herndon and Stanton led me to the door, and the press beyond.

"We'll deal with other appointments later, Mr. Lincoln," Billy said.

My eyes were still on Eddie and Willie. Then I was nearly pushed through the door, into the waiting arms of the Fourth Estate and its bright lights.

The first question came: "Mr. President, now that there's stability in the country, do you expect the war against the humans to last long?"

"It will last as long as it takes. . . ." I said.

3

Later, as I sat in my office alone, in darkness, waiting for Stanton and Herndon to return, a weariness fell over me. I thought of my speech again. I was sure it was inadequate. I had no doubt I had gotten through to *our* people, but what I had striven for was to make the other side see the rightness of my course. If I could only make them see that the only logical path for them to follow is for them to come over to us, arms open, as brothers . . .

But I doubt they will see that. They fight, just as we fight. No doubt they see the rightness of their course, also.

This was what bothered me. Perhaps this was the root of my own concern. *Were* we in the right? I knew there was a basic animosity in us toward the first-lifers. I felt it myself. Yet it bothered me, just as my deep-seated violence, so adeptly brought out by Herndon and Stanton, bothered me. Were we in the right? Did our mere existence exonerate us from being wrong?

Logic told me that we are here, and this is the way the world is now, *but was this right and just?*

I didn't know. I could only follow the course I had set. And I prayed to God that it was the right one. Because I knew in my heart that we would win, would drive the human race from the earth. . . .

I turned in my chair and looked out the window to

the lawns and lights of Washington beyond. I thought what a different, and in many ways more marvelous, world this was from the one I knew.

The room lights were thrown on. I swiveled around, unbending my long frame from the chair to stand, as an old friend strode into the room, smoking a cigar and smiling through his beard.

"Grant!"

"Yes, sir," Ulysses Grant said, shaking my hand.

Stanton came in behind him, grinning.

"We thought you were dead in Ohio!" I said to Grant.

"I *was*, in a manner of speaking. But no, after I . . . rose, I, uh, had a bit of trouble adjusting." He made a drinking-glass motion with his hand and smiled.

Stanton laughed.

"Didn't we all have trouble! Didn't we all!" I said.

"Well," Grant said, "near as I can figure, I went on a fifteen-day bender. I never did that before, on or off the battlefield."

I said, "Remember when I had complaints about your drinking, and I told 'em to find out what your brand was and deliver barrels of it to all my generals?"

We all laughed.

"My Lord, you sat in this chair of mine, too," I said, suddenly remembering.

Grant waved his hand. "I'm not back here for that, Mr. President. That was bad enough when I had to do it the first time around."

"Ulysses would like to command," Stanton said.

Grant puffed his cigar. "I think we can win this war quickly."

I was not surprised. But I feigned the emotion.

"Excellent! From what Secretary Stanton tells me, the federal armies are in disarray in the southeast and the west. With—"

"Sherman is in the south already, Mr. President," Grant said, "and Phil Sheridan is on an army plane, heading west, as we speak. Some of our own kind in California have tried to form their own little country. They're calling it the New Federation. That won't last long." He paused. "I'm told you know about Dwight Eisenhower heading the new Allied Command Forces. From his record we think he will be excellent in coordinating the campaign with overseas allies. This isn't the same world we knew, Mr. President."

"That's true. And Eisenhower, too, sat behind this desk. . . ."

Grant continued, "The home armies will be in shape within a week. The National Guard has most civilian areas stabilized—"

"New York?"

"New York is quite a mess, to put it mildly. Much of Philadelphia, Chicago, and Boston have been greatly damaged. In the south Atlanta is in flames again—only this time it wasn't our doing, Mr. President. The humans burned the city as they fled. Sherman's men are restoring order."

"Lord, the irony," I said. "If only the first-lifers would let themselves be turned . . ."

Once again that vague feeling of wrongness, of a flaw in my logic, sought to fill me with despair.

"But Mr. President," Stanton said brightly, "we have every reason to believe the war will not be a long one. Almost every major country around the world has stabilized and is now in full movement against the human population. China is turning thousands a day, Russia—the Soviet Union, as they call it now—is making great strides. And you must remember that with each human turned, another soldier is added to our own armies."

"Yes . . ."

"We feel that within a few months, six at most, the job will be done. There will be a stable world order. Then we can get on to other business."

"A world free of war?"

"If not that," Stanton interjected, "then a world making a new start. Our nation will come out of this in a strong position, Mr. President."

"Yes, I suppose it will." I gave them a thin smile. "That reminds me of the possum who ran up the tree. Ever hear this story?"

Both Grant and Stanton looked at me indulgently.

"Can't say I have, Mr. President," Grant said.

"There was this possum whose arse end got struck by

lightning. He knew if he got hit again, he'd be one dead possum. So he ran high up a tree, thinking he'd be safe there. Only, the tree then got hit by lightning, and he fell out of it, and got himself killed anyway." I sighed. "I feel like that possum, gentlemen. I think we all should."

"What do you mean by that, Mr. President?" Stanton asked.

"I fear, Mr. Stanton," I said, "that we are more human now than we ever were. And that *real* peace is something we may never find in this world."

I knew I had been brooding. So I looked up and smiled. I shifted on my own arse on my chair, threw my leg over it to make myself more comfortable. "But anyway, one lightning strike at a time, eh, gentlemen?"

4

Over the next few weeks things did go well. I had some heady conversations with foreign leaders via the telephone, men such as Xeng Lo Pin, the eighth-century leader of China who had emerged on top in that country. He was a remarkable man, one of the few from his era to prosper and adapt to this modern age. He also knew some good ribald stories.

Our own armies became one, and under Grant's administration they turned from petty squabbling to the full business of turning the humans into second-lifers. There was a huge battle in Illinois, where our Fourth Division, under the leadership of George Custer, routed and turned ten thousand humans under the command of General Norman Schwarzkopf. When Schwarzkopf was captured and turned, he immediately assumed command for Custer, who had managed to get himself boxed in and destroyed by an encircling force of desperately noble humans. The humor of the outcome made me wince.

I was obliged to appear on television with uncomfortable regularity. I came to regard the chore as a necessary evil. Television communication had been restored to most of the country. It seemed to give our people strength to see their president on their little boxes, speaking to them directly. I found I had little to say, as usual, but it seemed to be enough. Another revolting modern development, the opinion poll, showed me to have what I was told was an astounding approval rating. I never bothered to find out exactly what that meant, but took Billy Herndon's word that it was a good thing.

Once again the industrial might of the United States, this time the *entire* United States, north and south, was a deciding factor in the progress of the war. Americans were just plain good at making things. Especially things to kill others with. Every soldier in our armies seemed to have two guns and more bullets than he or she knew what to do with. But all of this might was being put to good effect.

Sadly, Mary became more of a problem. She always was sensitive to my black moods, and seemed to feed off them, making herself even more worrisome than she had been. Sometimes she would refuse to see me for days. She was horrible with the White House servants. There were many complaints about her conduct. She could not even concentrate on keeping the White House the way she wanted it. Occasionally she would lock herself in her bedroom and cry, sometimes scream. Even the boys became frightened of her. It became so bad that I took her to my side one day, holding her there with my arm, and pointing from the window of my office to a building in the near distance.

"Do you see that place, Mother? Do you remember what I told you once, the first time we were here? That's an insane asylum, and I fear that if you do not get better, we will have to send you there."

She looked at me with her bright, frightened eyes. "Don't you even know then from now? Don't you know that I ended up in a place like that!"

"Mother . . ."

"I warned you, Abraham! I told you that all I wanted in this new life was for you to be with me and the boys! You gave yourself to the country once!" Her cry turned to a near shriek. *"Why do you have to let them have you again!"*

"Mother, there are things out of our control—"

"There is nothing for me in this life! I thought I was waking up into heaven, and this is *hell!*"

"Mary, you have the boys."

"I have *nothing*! Don't you see that none of this is right! This is not paradise! I want to go home, to Springfield, or back to the ground, oh, Abraham . . ."

She turned into my shoulder, and wept. "I cannot stay in a world like this. . . ."

I patted her, and held her, and tried to remember the girl I had courted, whose face I had seen again after we had both returned from the grave. "Mary, dear . . ."

That night she took her own life, in her room, alone, with a knife to her breast. She left a sealed note, which only I read:

Good-bye, Father, and my darling boys. I know it is selfish of me, but I cannot bear to lose you again. So I go back to where we came from. Hopefully, I will truly, finally, find paradise.

5

That was when I almost lost hope. A blacker depression than I had ever known dropped down upon me. It was not only the loss of Mary, which was as deep as any I had ever known. It was that she had taken with her a part of me that believed that what I was doing was right.

At her funeral, a state affair attended by the myriad politicians who now peopled the Congress and the cabinet, as well as ministers from the various countries of the world, I sat in stone silence. Tad, Eddie, Willie, and Robert sat next to me. I felt as dead as if I had rejoined her in the grave. Her last written words ran through my mind, as truthful and direct as any I had ever penned myself: *I go back to where we came from. Hopefully, I will truly, finally, find paradise.*

Where did we come from? Where had we been, all of us here in this cathedral, all of us seeking to wipe out the human race around the world, before we had risen again? Why were we back here? Did we truly have the right to take possession of this world?

Suddenly the biggest part of me wanted to be with her, in whatever place she had returned to.

I did not go with her remains, the collected dust in

a silver urn, back to Springfield. She was flown there, and Robert went and saw that she was put back to rest in her original spot. The public was told that the pressing needs of the republic bade me stay in Washington. But those closest to me, Billy Herndon in particular, knew that if I went back, I might try to reenter my old tomb myself.

Over the next weeks I took to sitting in my office with the lights darkened, looking out the window, signing whatever papers came across my desk automatically. I ate sporadically, even more so than I always had, not tasting the food, seeing or talking to no one unless it was absolutely necessary. I became so morose that Billy Herndon came in one day, locking the door behind him.

"Mr. Lincoln," he said, "you can't go on like this. It's beginning to affect everyone around you. Soon it will affect the country."

I looked up slowly from my desk. I tried a tired smile. "You don't look so hale yourself, Billy. Have you by any chance joined General Grant's antitemperance league?"

"Mr. Lincoln," he said, "things are going very well. We're almost at the stage where we can call it a mopping-up exercise. General Eisenhower reports that things are even better overseas. Europe is almost at the point of total victory. Some of the smaller countries, such as Romania and Turkey and Greece, have already declared one hundred percent turnings. I doubt there will be any humans left soon."

"Yes . . ." I gave a heavy sigh and looked up at him. "But do you think, Billy, that we're doing the right thing?"

He was startled. "Of course, Mr. Lincoln! We've been over this a hundred times. You yourself told me that you looked into the bottom of your soul, to see what you were, and knew that by our nature we were doing the right thing."

"But is our *nature* correct, Billy?"

He gave me a puzzled look. "Mr. Lincoln, I don't understand—"

"You heard my third inaugural speech, Billy. You heard me quote scripture: 'Woe to any man by whom the offense cometh.' Suppose that humanity is not the offense, but *we* are instead?"

"Mr. Lincoln—"

"Hear me out, Billy. If, for argument's sake, we are the offense . . ." I studied the paper before me, a copy of my address, and read: ". . . which, in the providence of God, must needs come, but which, having continued through the Almighty's appointed time, He now wills to remove."

I looked up at Billy, who stared at me. "Mr. Lincoln, that's preposterous. That's—"

"What if it were true, Billy? What if I—all of us—have it backward?"

Billy had lost all signs of his hangover. "Mr. Lincoln, you cannot deny your own nature. We can only *act* upon our own nature!"

"That's true, that's true. And as far as it goes, there's justice in it." I felt some of my old strength, a new kind of anger, pour into me. "But what if our cause, which seems so just to us, is not, in the larger scheme, just at all?" I pulled another paper from beneath the first, a copy of my second inaugural address. "With malice toward none," I read, "with charity for all; with firmness in the right, as God gives us to see the right, let us strive on to finish the work we are in."

I looked up at Billy. I fear I scared him a bit with the Old Testament fury of my words: "Do you feel malice toward none, Billy? Do you feel charity for all?"

"Mr. Lincoln, as our nature goes . . . As you said, 'with firmness in the right, as God gives us to see the right—' "

"But if your nature is *wrong*, what then! What if it is not God-given!" I pounded upon the table in anger. "*I just don't know why we're here!*"

Billy was speechless for a moment. "Mr. Lincoln—"

"I don't know that we come from God! I *despise* this anger in me, Billy, this hatred toward the human race. I despise the anger I feel toward those of our own who do not bend to our will! I killed John Wilkes Booth with my own hands, because I felt I must, but I *despise* myself for it! I know what I am, I know my nature down to my soul, *and I do not like it!*"

"Mr. Lincoln," Billy said, "you wouldn't. . . ."

I managed to smile feebly. "No, Billy, I don't have it in me. I may be melancholic, but I'm not a fool. There's work for us to do. I don't propose to step out in the middle of it."

"Yes, Mr. Lincoln."

"The thing that truly puzzles and intrigues me, Billy, the thing which poor Mary made me look at for the very first time, is that if we're back here on earth, where did we come from?" I looked at him directly. "And who sent us here, Billy? All I want is a sign. . . ."

He left me then, brooding, in the dark, with only my thoughts for company.

6

More bad news a week later. Grant's campaign in the east went brilliantly, at first. In no time the Atlantic states were solidly in federal hands. He headed inland, with at first similar results. But whether by fate or design, he formed a pincer around a large human force in Pennsylvania, forcing them toward Gettysburg for the final confrontation. By telephone, I tried to convince him to fight where he was and avoid Gettysburg at all costs.

At that moment his transmissions from the front became garbled. I was positive that the drink was upon him again and that now he was partaking even in the heat of battle. But Grant claimed that he wanted to fight on familiar ground.

"Meade had his glory here; now let me have mine!"

The familiar ground was not, of course, familiar, and our forces were routed by a determined human contingent with modern weapons. In his cups Grant had ordered that muskets be used, and I was told that he tried to have cannon on the Gettysburg historic site, which hadn't been used since 1863, loaded and fired, with miserable results. His last telephone call to me came from what he described as the gift shop. I could practically smell the liquor on his breath as he spoke.

"Not going at all as planned, Mr. President," he said.

"General, I must say I'm not surprised."

"There are *picnicking* tables here now, where there used to be pickets! How can a man fight like this!"

"General Grant . . ."

"They're charging, Mr. President! And they have helicopters!"

I heard a strafing sound, heard Grant swear an oath.

"I made all such weaponry available to you, General Grant," I said evenly.

"Damned foolishness! Will Sherman be here soon, Mr. President?"

"Sherman is in the south, and will stay there, General. You were provided everything necessary to secure your area. If . . ." Remembering the great warrior he had been, I softened my tone. "General, perhaps we should talk about a change in command. . . ."

At that moment Grant swore another oath. "Dammit, McClellan, get me another bottle! And—"

That was all I heard. Later they told me that a sniper had hit the general as he stood talking on the phone, and that a moment later he was gone.

At Gettysburg the humans carried the day. They occupied the grounds for the next seventy-two hours, until McClellan, too, was felled, and a low-ranking officer who had tried to hide in the midst of Grant's army was elevated, on his discovery, to ranking officer and brigadier general in the army of the United States of America.

It was then that I traveled to Gettysburg to give a short address and meet my new, and all too modest, army commander, Robert E. Lee.

7

If there has ever been a more melancholy man than myself, Robert E. Lee was that man. I admit I felt instant communion with him. We met in his temporary headquarters, on a ridge overlooking the historic grounds. I felt a chill of memory. Gettysburg, at least, hadn't changed all that much in all these years. The many deep holes where the buried dead had risen to their present state simulated with uncanny accuracy the cannon craters I had seen on my last trip here.

"The battle will be won within the day," Lee said sadly.

"I have no doubt in your abilities, General," I said.

He pointed to a spot to the east, in a valley. It was ringed with the metal carcasses of broken tanks and downed aircraft. I could not make out individual soldiers, but could see the meagerness of their gathering.

"That is what they have left in all the eastern part of the country. There are house-to-house searches under way, mostly in the countryside now. The cities are secure." He pointed to the corners surrounding the valley. "They're surrounded on four sides. I estimate two thousand or so. I've sent surrender terms, but"— he smiled grimly—"they've told me to go to hell."

"They're good men. Is there a ... way to make it quick?"

"Is there ever?" Lee said. "We've thought of gas. . . ."

I shook my head. "That will not do. You know my feelings on the subject, and on all the other horrible weapons we have. These nuclear devices . . ."

"They're ... evil," Lee said.

"Yes. It's all evil, of course."

"But there are degrees of evil, aren't there, Mr. President?"

Our eyes met. "You're bothered by it, too, aren't you, General? By all of it, I mean."

"Yes, I am, sir. But there isn't another way, is there?"

"No, General, there isn't."

"Then let's get on with it."

His blue eyes were tired but set as we shook hands and parted.

My speech was slated for the following hour. I had a few remarks set down on paper, which I had worked over and over on the plane trip down to Pennsylvania. But I was still not happy with them. General Lee had been kind enough to provide a camp stool and table for me to work on as the hour approached. It was while I sat here that a soldier appeared, standing quietly at attention until I noticed him.

"Can I help you, son?" I said, looking up.

The ghostly features surrounding his skeleton were unbearably young. He was perhaps seventeen years old, with longish shaggy hair and the look of the battle worn. He carried a new M-16 rifle but looked as though he'd be more comfortable with a musket.

The young man saluted. "Sir, General Lee thought I should talk to you."

"Go on, son," I said. For the first time in weeks I felt a genuine smile of warmth spread over my features.

"It's just that . . ."

"Don't be tongue-tied. You obviously have a bellyful of words, and if you don't let them out, I'm afraid they'll growl away in that stomach of yours forever."

"Yes, sir," he said nervously.

"That reminds me," I said, "of the man on the rolling log. Ever hear the story?"

"Sir?"

"It's like this. There were some logmen once who cut a big tree and put it out in the middle of the river. One after another they got up on that log, but kept falling off. Then one of them climbed up on the log, started it to rolling, and was able to stand in place and walk at the same time."

The soldier looked baffled.

"Roll your log, son!" I said, laughing.

"Umm, it's just this, sir. I was buried over there." He pointed to a spot near the bottom of the valley in which our present foes waited. "I was here in 1863, during the battle."

"I see. . . ."

"And I just wanted to say, Mr. President, that what you said the first time here was true."

"And what was that?"

He drew a slip of paper from his pocket and opened it. He searched for a moment, then read, "That we here highly resolve that these dead shall not have died in vain; that this nation, under God, shall have a new birth of freedom; and that government of the people, by the people, and for the people shall not perish from the earth."

He looked up at me, and, I admit, there were tears in my eyes.

"It's just that . . ."

"Go on, son," I said.

"I didn't die in vain, sir," he said. "And we all feel you're doing the right thing for everyone."

I stood and shook his hand. There were still tears in my eyes.

"Thank you, son," I said.

I gave my short speech, forgetting the words I had written on the plane trip down. I related instead the short meeting I had had with that soldier, whose name I didn't even know.

Then I went back to Washington, some of my doubts relieved. I learned on the plane that Lee had taken the day, wiping out the last resistance of the humans in the eastern part of the United States.

I learned also that there had been a coup in Washington, and that a former president now occupied the White House.

8

Stanton, with a heavily armed contingent, met me at the airport.

"It's over," he said. "We have the man in custody. It didn't last more than an hour. He had a few others with him, all of whom have been subdued." Stanton paused. "However . . ."

"Yes?" I said, sensing that something had gone wrong.

"I'm afraid Robert and Tad were lost in the attempt. Also Billy Herndon. We feel they should be interred here in Washington. A trip to Springfield would be too dangerous for you now."

"Eddie and Willie?" I asked.

"Safe. We do think this was an isolated incident, and the last threat to your administration. The polls show an overwhelming approval—"

"Damn the polls!" I shouted. "Where is this man?"

He blinked. "Why, he's being held in the basement, in the national security conference room. He'll be—"

"I want to see him, now!"

"But Mr. President, there's a very important—"

"Now!"

He bowed to my wrath. The short helicopter trip to the White House lawn was a silent one. I stalked from the machine as soon as it touched ground and stayed a step ahead of Stanton and the Secret Service, marching to the bank of elevators that would take me to the basement offices.

I stopped them at the elevator. "I'm going down alone," I said.

"Mr. President, there's an extremely important visitor in your office, I really think—"

"He can wait!"

The elevator doors closed, taking me down.

Two marine guards saluted as the doors opened at the bottom. Behind them, at the far end of a long conference table, sat a bound figure.

"Out," I said.

"Mr. President, we have orders—"

"Here is a direct order from the commander in chief! Out!"

They saluted again, stepped into the elevator. I watched as the doors closed, made sure the elevator ascended.

I turned to the man at the end of the conference table, who sat examining me with shifting eyes under his high forehead.

"Why did you do this?" I asked. "Don't you understand this has nothing to do with power? The entire future, for good or ill, is what is at stake here. *Doesn't that mean anything to you?*"

He looked at me, his eyes darting, his jowls hanging loose as he spoke.

"Well," he said, "let me make one thing perfectly clear. They wouldn't have me in China. And Haldeman assured me—*assured me*, mind you—that it would go without a hitch. 'Touchdown,' he said, 'definite touchdown.' Of course, he's been wrong before. . . ."

That was all I let him say. A little while later I went up in the elevator and told the two marine guards waiting there that a dust mop was needed in the national security conference room.

9

From my reading, the man who waited for me in the Oval Office looked familiar. He was a twentieth-century figure, but I had read so much about so many twentieth-century figures that I could not recall him.

He was not well dressed, and favored his pipe, and had such a saddened smile under his bushy gray mop of hair that I immediately took a liking to him.

"Mr. President," Stanton said, "may I present Mr. Albert Einstein."

"Of course!" I said. "The scientist fellow!"

Einstein nodded humbly. "It is a great pleasure meeting you," he said, taking my hand.

"Dr. Einstein has news for us," Stanton said.

"Oh?"

"Enigmatic news, I'm afraid, Mr. President," he said in his German accent.

I looked to Stanton for a clue, but he stood still, his attention focused on Mr. Einstein.

"You know, I came here once before," Einstein said, "to meet another president, Mr. Franklin Roosevelt. That was not a happy meeting, I'm afraid. You see, I urged him then to speed development of what became the atom bomb."

"Yes ..." I said, instantly afraid that Einstein was here to present some new and even more terrible weapon to me.

Einstein smiled, sensing my mood. "Let me assure you, Mr. President, that is not why I am here this time. I think we have all the weapons we need at the moment, thank you."

"I quite agree."

"But I am here with something of a puzzle. You see, I've always been interested in puzzles—for instance, the way the universe is put together. I must admit that this puzzle may even be bigger than that." He looked up at me. "Have you wondered why we're here, Mr. President? Why we're ... back?"

"I've thought about almost nothing else, Mr. Einstein."

He nodded, put his pipe in his mouth, took it out again. "I really do wish I had brought a blackboard."

I took a sheet of paper from my desk, handed it to him along with a pen.

"Thank you."

He began to draw on the paper, a crude picture of what I took to be our sun, along with our own planet and moon circling it.

"This, of course, is us," he said, pointing to the earth. He made a circular motion around the sun. "And this, along with the other planets, is our solar system. And our entire solar system moves through space, around the core of our galaxy, which we call the Milky Way."

He looked up at me. "I understand these things, Mr. Einstein."

"Good." He smiled. "I realize that in your day much of this was not known. But every age has its unknowns. That is the beauty of nature, eh?"

I nodded, smiled myself.

He began to sketch in another corner of the paper, drawing a whirlpoollike object and then a tiny circle on one side of it, about two thirds of the way out from the center. He drew an arrow from the little circle to his picture of our solar system.

He pointed to the whirlpool. "This, then, is the Milky Way, and this," he continued, following the arrow back from the solar system to the tiny circle, "is our solar system's place in the Milky Way."

He turned his shaggy head to me to make sure I understood, and I nodded, scratching my chin.

"Looks like we're rather small turnips in a big garden," I said.

He laughed. "*Rather* small turnips, indeed. There are billions upon billions of galaxies just like our Milky Way—if you want your turnips even smaller!"

"Ha!" I said. "My Lord, Mr. Einstein, but these things I can barely hold in my head. How do you think that big? Did you ever feel like the man wearing a barrel who spent so much time thinking that he forgot where his clothes were? He said, 'If I hadn't been so smart, I wouldn't be so nekkid.' "

Einstein laughed and looked down at himself. "I'm

not such a smart dresser to begin with, Mr. Lincoln. And
it is true that much of the time we don't need to think of
these things to run our daily lives." His manner became
grim. "But I'm afraid that at this time it's necessary."

I kept staring at his diagram, trying to take all this
immensity in. "Go on, sir."

Einstein sketched a cloudy bar across the Milky Way
galaxy, starting at the middle, and out to one edge, going
through the tiny circle representing our solar system.

"This," he said, pointing to the bar, "is the cloud we
are presently in."

I raised my eyebrows. "Our entire system of planets?"

"Everything for a half light-y—" He stopped, smiled.
"For quite a distance."

I stared at the paper, scratched my chin.

Einstein said, "We last went through a cloud twenty-
six million years ago." He paused. "Not coincidentally,
there was an extinction of life on earth at that time. The
first great extinction we have evidence of occurred at the
end of the Permian Age, some two hundred and forty
million years ago. Ninety percent of all species in the
oceans perished; the mass extinction of various land species set the stage for the rise of the dinosaurs."

He began to sketch in other, tinier cloud spokes in
the wheel of the Milky Way. "There have been other,
small extinctions every twenty-six million years or so. One
of those was responsible for wiping out the dinosaurs.
We've now been able to detect other clouds along our
path through the Milky Way."

I stood up straight. "You mean a cloud. . . ?"

"Yes. We believe these clouds have been instrumen-
tal in shaping life on earth. The highly charged particles,
irridium and others, contained in the cloud—"

I held up my hand. "Whoa! Highly charged what?"

He smiled. "That would be physics and chemistry,
Mr. President."

"Let's just say I'm not good at wearing barrels, Mr.
Einstein!"

He laughed, packed his pipe, and lit it. "Do you
know what I wanted more than anything when I . . . returned? To smoke this pipe."

I clapped him on the back. "Well, you go right ahead."

We turned back to the diagram. "To make it simple, Mr. President, there are ... unknown substances in the cloud which made the return of former life to earth possible."

"So that's what brought us back."

"We believe so." He went back to his diagram of the solar system. "Marvelous things have been happening on all the planets. Mars has sprouted vegetation. Incredibly, given the immense pressure and heat on the surface, we have indications of massive vegetative growth on Venus. That planet has become a huge hothouse of sorts, perhaps covered with orchids. The gas clouds of Jupiter are now supporting massive airborne organisms, possibly intelligent. Titan, the moon of Saturn ..."

"Surely, the work of the Almighty," I said, in wonder.

He didn't contradict me. "You might even call this cloud Creation itself, Mr. President. It is marvelous, but it is also fraught with enigma. I have been in consultation with some of the finest minds in the world, at Princeton University and elsewhere. Isaac Newton himself has been working on the problem in England, and Kepler in Germany. These are great men. Here in the United States, at Harvard University, Hubble, who discovered that some nebulae are independent galaxies, by the way, has been at work. He and I and others believe we must initiate a project immediately, to send a rocket at high speed, manned if possible, away from earth in the direction our solar system is heading."

I watched him trace a line away from the tiny circle, through the cloud and out of it.

"You see, Mr. President," Einstein said, puffing on his pipe, producing more fragrant smoke, "in a matter of months, the entire solar system, including earth, is going to leave the cloud. And we have no idea what's going to happen then."

That very night, falling asleep as I pondered the many intriguing questions Dr. Einstein had raised, while simultaneously awash in grief for those I had lost, and feeling very much alone, I had a dream, a vision, the sign I had waited for.

11

The memoirs of Peter Sun

1

At the end of summer, as the first cold winds began to sweep down from the heights of Konzhakovski Kamen, now long behind us, the baby began to show in Reesa's belly.

At my insistence, our progress was slower, though Reesa was strong and called me foolish.

Our wagon was long since gone, broken in the rocks at the summit of the mountain. We had ridden the horse for hundreds of miles until it was hobbled, requiring me to shoot it once, and then again. Near Petropavlovsk, we had found a truck, which had taken us north nearly to Noginski before giving out. We left its rusting, noisy body behind. Now we carried what we could on our backs.

The land provided food, and the night provided stars for our covering. When we felt safe enough, we made a fire, though with the cooler temperatures, and Reesa's condition, there was more need now to take risks.

We had seen no one, human or skeleton, for weeks. In that time a kind of dream had settled over us, a fantasy that the world belonged to us alone, which was broken only occasionally by the sight of a high-flying hawk in skeleton form, or the marks of a skeletal footprint in the dirt. At night the crickets and other night bugs chirped and sang, and though we knew that the sounds came mostly from the white little carcasses of ghosts, again, our fantasy let us think the world was right.

I was content for the first time I could remember. My whole past life seemed like history. All that existed was my wife and my coming child, and the blue sky and brown earth and stars. The moon rose and set for Reesa and me, and changed its shape as the weeks passed. If I lost myself in this living dream, I could make this the world.

Reesa flowered. Her flesh seemed bursting with human life, the ruddy glow as much from what lay within her as from the wind and the night cold. I could not imagine the world, the universe, without her in it.

When we came at last to the long volcanic plains of the central Siberian platform, Reesa stood beside me, holding my hand tight, and pointed north away from their plateau.

"That is where my people came from," she said. "It is said that the tribe was forced east until it ran out of land, and that half of it settled on the Anadyrskoye plateau, near the Bering Sea, and the other half crossed the straits."

I looked at her. "You mean into North America?"

She smiled. "Yes. In our tribe the story is that all of America came from our seed. The American Indians, down through the Central Americas to the south, the Mayans and Aztecs—all of them were once part of our lost tribe."

"That's a rather ambitious statement, don't you think?" I said.

Her face was serious. "It's true."

That night, the pains from the baby were upon her. I stayed awake, guarding, tending the fire, until the cramps passed. I then watched Reesa sleep in the dim firelight.

Off in the distance I heard the echoing bellow of an animal, sounding huge as the earth itself.

I almost awakened Reesa. But the sight of her peaceful sleep made me hesitate. I contented myself with feeling her belly for the kicking baby within and sat the rest of the night alone, with my rifle across my knees, listening to the sounds of roaring and wondering what on this or any earth could make such a thunderous sound.

2

The next day, as dawn lighted the world, my question was answered. In the near distance, out over the plain below our plateau, appeared the giant rumbling skeleton of a brontosaur. It threw its head back and wailed, moving on until it had found a shallow muddy puddle. Its long skeletal head bent to drink. Again it rose, dripping mud, and bellowed again.

"It's hungry," Reesa said. We stood in the open, and I felt, in the presense of such massiveness, suddenly naked and defenseless.

Behind the brontosaur came another, and another, until a herd, led by two giants, was formed. Ponderously, they moved for the mud hole. The large onces sheltered the young ones as they bent to drink, their own mewling cries mingled with the booming roars of their elders.

We headed down into the shallow canyon away from them, leaving the cries behind.

We stumbled into an ancient bed. Around us on the canyon floor lay the churned craters of their burial ground. We came to the thrashed, risen walls of a pit nearly forty feet long and almost as deep.

"I don't want to see what came out of that," I said.

As we made our way to the canyon wall the air was split by the thunderous cry of a monstrous brute. It towered above us a full four stories. Rumbling by on two stout legs, its bony tail swished along the ground, its monstrously large jaw snapped open and shut. Two tiny clawed appendages that served for arms and hands opened and closed.

It whipped its head around, seeming to sniff the air, searching.

Around the bones was the ghostly outline of a tyrannosaurus, pale green lizardlike skin, yellow eyes.

We flattened ourselves against the canyon wall. The monster strode past, making a low noise in the back of its throat. It pawed at the air nervously, turning its head. It looked away, then back—

In the shadows we held our breath.

The monster stepped forward, away from us, toward the mud hole where the brontosaurs drank.

Already some of the brontosaurs were scattering. They herded their young ones away with yelping cries. The tyrannosaurus hastened its gait. There was something horribly graceful about its movements. Its white bones looked like the parts in a monstrous eating machine, fitted together perfectly, bone sliding over bone in balletic motion.

The tyrannosaurus charged for the mud hole.

The brontosaurs lumbered away. One small specimen fell behind, crying piteously. The tyrannosaurus looked down at it, moved forward, growled thunderously, and pushed the brontosaur out of the way, stooping to drink.

The tyrannosaurus pulled muddy water into its jaws, spat it out in anger. Its amber eyes searched for a true water hole.

The small brontosaurus began to lumber away, its larger version waiting to herd it on.

The tyrannosaurus raised its head in fury. It ran fiercely through the mud hole and stopped to tower over the small brontosaur.

Screaming in rage, the tyrannosaurus swooped down with its mouth, took the brontosaur in its teeth, at the same time clawing at it with its tiny hands.

The brontosaurus, giving a piteous cry, dissolved into dust.

The tyrannosaurus clawed at empty air. It raised its head, tried to split the sky with its cry of rage. It angled its head down, charged after the herd of brontosaurs still trying to retreat. In a few moments it had caught those in the rear, clawing them fiendishly, whipping its head from side to side, biting and biting again.

One after another the brontosaurs dissolved to dust.

The tyrannosaurus's rage increased. It leaped into the midst of the herd, tore at one after another of the brontosaurs. Soon there was only one large beast left, shielding two younger brontosaurs behind its bulk.

Screaming in rage, the monster reared up, tore at all three in a single flashing moment, and watched, roaring, as they disappeared.

Against the rock wall I unslung my rifle, checked the clip.

The monster whipped its head around, looked straight at me. Our eyes locked.

The tyrannosaurus charged.

I aimed, shot, and missed. Enraged, the beast threw itself forward. I pushed Reesa behind me, aimed again. The monster was twenty yards away, closing fast, claws scissoring open.

I fired.

The monster's jaw opened wide, the bullet passing in, and in the midst of a ghostly roar it dropped to dust.

Around us came other sounds. More dinosaurs were drawn to the spectacle from the plains around us.

"We'd better get away from this," I said.

We circled the canyon wall, found a slope, and climbed. At the top we found ourselves on a large plateau that rolled gently downward to the east.

The canyon plain below us was alive with dinosaurs.

Four-legged beasts, herds of stegosaurus and a lone triceratops fought over a scrubby plant. Small skeletal things on two legs darted from bush to bush. In the middle distance another brontosaur herd ambled toward a far circle of blue promising water. There was a distant splash. A long, sinuous neck of bone rose from the water, looked left and right, and sank down again. Something that looked like a stunted crocodile fought with another low-slung beast, which reared up on its hind legs, turned, slashed at its foe with a ridged tail. In the far distance a huge beast, a monstrous version of a brontosaur, stood still, either unable or unwilling to move, its relatively tiny head swinging languidly from side to side.

There came a hissing sound behind us. I turned to see a man-sized beast, a smaller version of the tyrannosaurus, facing us, clawlike hands twitching.

I struggled to get the rifle up as the thing charged. But it was on me before I could react. I batted it aside with the stock of the rifle.

It slipped to the edge of the canyon, twisted in the air, unable to regain its balance, and went over.

At the bottom it flashed into a puff of dust.

"We'd better go," I said.

We headed away from the plain of dinosaurs, down the gentle slope of the plateau, and before long the monsters were left far behind.

3

That night Reesa was unable to sleep. As we trekked slowly northward it had grown colder. Our fires had grown bigger. This night we had little shelter. We were surrounded by plains of volcanic rock. At the horizon sat the outline of a village, unreachable till morning. I discovered a little cutout in a low shelf of rock and built our fire at its opening.

"Are you cold?" I asked Reesa.

She snuggled next to me, wrapped me in her blanket with her. Her face was outlined in firelight.

"Not now." She looked up for a moment at the full moon rising in the east, just free of the horizon.

I felt her shiver.

"It is said it will happen on a night of the full moon," she said.

I looked at her, thinking to tell her to stop her foolishness. But she turned to regard me, her face somber and sad, and I said nothing.

"The night I will die," she said.

I felt anger come into me. "Don't talk like that."

"It's true," she said. "It will happen."

I poked at the fire with a stick, angrily.

"Was it the sight of those beasts today?" I said. "You've been so content these last weeks. We both know the world has changed. I just don't want to hear any more about . . . prophecies."

She put my hand on her stomach, rubbed gently where the baby was.

"Tell me about your other life, Kral Kishkin," she said.

"What do you mean?"

"Tell me about your life as an assassin."

I stiffened beside her.

"I've never talked about that. That was another person, not me."

"Tell me," she said softly, looking into my eyes.

For the first time in weeks I thought of my life. How many times had I reinvented myself? How many names had I given myself? Kral Kishkin and Peter Sun were only the latest.

I found myself talking, unmasking myself for the first time in my life for this woman who was my life. Suddenly I wanted her to know me, wanted to speak.

"I was born in Prey Veng, in Kampuchea, across the Mekong River from Pnompenh," I said. I felt her gentle eyes on me, drawing the poison out of me. "I was named Jayavaram after a twelfth-century Angkor king, Jayavaram the Eighth, who built hospitals and rest houses throughout his kingdom.

"My father was a farmer, and he supported Lon Nol, but his younger brother who lived with us was a member of the Khmer Rouge. My father didn't know this. In 1975, when I was seven, I found my uncle meeting with his communist friends, and he swore me to secrecy.

"When the Khmer Rouge seized Pnompenh two months later, my uncle turned my father in, along with my mother and two sisters. They were shot. This happened in front of me while my uncle put his arm around my shoulder. 'This one is ours,' he said. With those words I was spared.

"Most of my village was considered middle class. Whoever wasn't shot was sent to a rural farming community.

"For the next three years I watched everyone I knew die. Except my uncle.

"When I was ten, the Vietnamese invaded the country. I waited until they entered our community, and then I took the gun my uncle kept and tried to shoot him as he rose from his sleeping pallet. The Vietnamese stopped me, and dragged my uncle away.

"I told them my name was Ho Vei. They sent me to Hanoi, and then to Ho Chi Minh City, for study. When I returned to Kampuchea, I helped hunt down and exe-

cute members of the Khmer Rouge. All the while I made
my way slowly toward the Thai border.

"When I was fifteen, I crossed into Thailand. My
name was now Mongkut, after a Thai king and statesman
who resisted colonialism in the nineteenth century. I told
the Thais I had been kidnapped and brought into Cambodia as a child.

"I studied in Thailand for two years. Then I went to
America. In America I told them my name was George,
after Washington."

I smiled, and in the firelight she returned my smile.

"They didn't believe me. So I told them my name
was Peter Sun, a name which I overheard two men talking about. I discovered later they had been talking about
Peter Gunn, the television detective. But Peter Sun I became.

"I thought I had become a different person. I studied the works of Gandhi, and the Transcendentalists. For
a while I lived in my own Walden, a cabin in the woods
with a single bed outside of my university in New York.

"Then my uncle appeared. He had lived as a slave in
Vietnam for seven years. He, too, had escaped, following
my route into Thailand as a refugee. He now called himself Carl Wong. He had told the Americans that he was
Chinese, fleeing the communists, and had been let in.

"He was poor, and had no place to stay. He looked
haunted and old. I gave him my bed.

"We lived like this for a year. He did odd jobs in the
nearby town. I studied and went to school.

"At night he told me stories of what he had been
through, how the Vietnamese had tortured him. He said
he hated the communists now. He wept when he thought
of what he had done to my parents, his family. Sometimes he would prostrate himself on the floor and beg for
my forgiveness. All of this I listened to in silence.

"One night on my way home from classes I bought
a gun. I told the clerk in the store my name was George
Wong. I went back to the woods and shot my uncle while
he slept.

"I buried his body deep in the woods. No one ever
asked for him.

"I worked hard, and studied hard. I found myself in

the middle of a growing movement for world peace. In the beginning I didn't find it ironic. But things grew around me, and I became a focus of attention.

"I had no trouble with my former life in Cambodia as an assassin. Then, I had done the right thing. In the beginning I told myself that what I had done to my uncle was the same.

"But as time went on I came to realize that what I had done to my uncle was different. I had become a monster. I was no better than what he had been. He had come to me broken and old and repentant, and I had murdered him."

I looked at Reesa in the firelight. I loved her more now than I had ever loved anyone in my life. I wanted her to purge what was in me, what had eaten at me and would always eat at me until my death.

I took from my pocket the much-creased piece of paper containing my speech.

"On the day the skeletons came," I said, remembering that faraway time as if it had never happened, "when I was to give my speech in front of all those millions of people, I was going to denounce myself instead. The only thing that would have prevented me from doing this was that it would have been a selfish act. Those people needed me at that moment. It would have been selfish of me to remove myself from their hopes and dreams."

I looked at my piece of paper, then put it away. "So I would have given my speech, with words inspired by Abraham Lincoln. But I would have been wearing a mask while I gave it.

"I thought by now, with all that has happened, all of this would seem irrelevant. But it doesn't."

"Oh, Kral Kishkin," she said gently, putting her hand on my head and drawing it down to her shoulder.

"Reesa, I don't know who I am."

She held me, and as much as she could, she drew out of me the pain that was in me. But the pain was still there. And that night, in the glow of the fire in the cold dark, with my loving wife and growing child beside me, I felt more lonely than I ever had in my life.

4

Reesa took sick the next day.

We had slept together near the fire and had been warm all night. But as the sun lipped the horizon I felt her stir beside me, rise, and walk away to vomit near the rock wall behind us. This had happened many times, with the baby.

When she didn't return, I turned and called, "Reesa, are you all right?"

There was no answer. I sat up, looked for her, found her collapsed near the rock wall where she had stood.

She was barely conscious. I felt her forehead. She was burning with fever.

"Full moon . . ." she whispered.

"Don't say that."

I carried her back to the embers of the fire. The morning was chilly. I built up the flames. Reesa could barely sit up. She began to shiver.

Again she turned and vomited. Her shivering became uncontrollable.

For the next hour she drifted into and out of consciousness. Her fever rose. At one point her eyes became very large.

"Sasha!" she called, staring into the fire. "Sasha!"

She closed her eyes, mumbled to herself, and slept, her body trembling.

All that day and night we stayed where we were. I tried to feed her, but she held nothing down. Frequently I put my hand to her belly, feeling for the baby there. Only when it finally kicked was I content.

During the night she awoke, stared at the rising moon, and cried out.

The next morning she was better, but barely.

"Reesa, can you move?"

"I . . . don't know."

It had grown even colder. Clouds had mounted in the west. I was afraid for bad weather.

"Reesa, we have to make the village," I said.

She swooned, stared hard at me, trying to focus. "Yes ..."

I packed, drew everything up onto my own back, made sure Reesa was as warm as she could be, and set out.

Our pace was agonizingly slow. We rested every five minutes. Then we walked only a matter of yards before we would have to pause for Reesa to regain her breath. Her fever rose as the day wore on, then diminished. She took a small meal at midday. For the first time since the onset of her illness, she kept the food down.

The village grew closer, crawled down off the horizon. Finally it sat a mere kilometer or so from us.

"There it is," I said, pointing.

"Yes ..."

Behind us the weather grew ominous. Black layers of clouds climbed the sky and rolled toward us. The sun shifted through a shadow of haze, then disappeared.

The day grew dark. A chill wind blew at our backs, urging us to hurry.

Finally we entered the town.

Litter and destruction were everywhere. A tractor was planted through the front of one building. Large depressions that proved, on closer inspection, to be dinosaur tracks, peppered the streets. The corners of houses had been torn off. Windows had been smashed, walls staved in. One small automobile lay on the flat roof of a shop, looking as if it had been lifted and thrown there.

I found a shop that was relatively undamaged. One window was broken, but the roof was whole, the door open. We entered. It had been a bakery. There was glass everywhere. Display cases had been smashed, the shelves broken, cabinets overturned. A faint sugary smell permeated everything.

An open door at the back of the shop led up a narrow flight of stairs to a second floor. Here there were living quarters. They were untouched. In one room was a simple bed made up with sheets and a pillow, a wooden table next to it, a tiny window, a crucifix on the wall. A small, round wood stove sat opposite the bed.

I helped Reesa to the bed. I pulled the covers back, laid her down, and covered her.

"You must eat something more, Reesa, for the baby."

"Yes . . ."

She sat up, and I fed her from the pack, some canned vegetables, some crackers.

"All right, Peter," she said. She looked tired, but smiled feebly. She kept the food down. When I felt her temple, it had cooled.

"Sleep," I said, kissing her.

"Yes . . ." She laid her head down and soon was asleep.

I went back downstairs. I looked out of the front window.

The sky was almost black and it had begun to snow.

A chill breeze was whipping through the broken glass. A pantry in the corner of the shop provided a broom and a heavy parka. I swept the broken glass into one corner, then retrieved from the rubble a few planks of wood that had been used as shelves. A crude door led down into a dirt cellar. There was nothing down there of use, save for a few jars of preserves and pickles.

I left the shop, bundled in the baker's parka against the whipping snow, which had already begun to fill the dinosaur tracks.

Two shops down was a hardware shop. Soon I returned to the bakery laden with a hammer and nails and a few more planks of wood.

The next hour I spent sealing the shop window. Snow blew in around me. My hands began to feel numb. In the end, though, I succeeded in closing the shop against the weather.

Outside, around back, I found a small woodpile and gathered an armful.

I climbed the stairs, filled the wood stove in the bedroom, and lit a fire. While the room warmed I sat on the edge of the bed, my hand on Reesa's covered body. I watched the snow fall outside the tiny window.

A sudden weariness overcame me. I lay down next to my wife, my hand on the moving child in her belly, and slept.

5

When I arose, it was dark. A rosy glow from the stove lit the room warmly.

My hand on Reesa's belly felt no movement.

The baby had stopped kicking.

I pulled back the covers and shook my wife. "Wake up!" I shouted. "Reesa, the baby! Wake up!"

She rose out of a deep slumber. I felt her forehead. The fever had broken. When she opened her eyes, they were clear and she knew me.

"Peter . . ."

"The baby!"

She pushed strands of sweaty hair back from her face and sat up. She put her hand to her belly.

"Quickly, Peter," she said. "Listen for it."

I put my ear to her belly and held my breath.

There was nothing: not the tiny snick of heartbeat, the quick moving jab of a kick.

"It's . . ." Reesa said.

"Wait."

Now, out of the silence, I felt something jab out, move, heard the tiny faraway murmur of a tiny heart.

"I felt it!" Reesa said.

I lay back, next to her. "Thank God." I looked at her, felt the coolness of her cheeks.

I said, "You're better."

"Yes. I feel weak, but . . ."

"We'll stay as long as we have to. I'm sure there's food here in the village. There's wood, everything else we need." I pointed to the window, frosted, cuffed with snow.

Reesa examined the room. "I don't even remember coming here."

I kissed her. "This full moon has passed."

"Yes . . ."

She smiled, closed her eyes, and I kissed them.

Suddenly her eyes flew wide and she gasped with pain. "Owwww . . ."

"What is it?"

Her hands wrapped around her belly. She bent forward, fighting for breath.

"Owwwwwww . . ."

I put my hand to her belly. The baby jabbed violently against me.

"Is it all right?"

She clutched my hand, gasping. "Something's . . . wrong."

She lay back. She closed her eyes, gritted her teeth. "My God . . ."

She spread her legs. I watched her belly heave.

"Peter, the baby is coming. . . ."

"Reesa, it's too soon—"

"Inside! It's hurting me inside!"

She arched back. Her face flushed red with pain. She held her breath and then gasped.

"Peter, help me!"

I stripped the bed back. I helped her through the next spasm, pushed the pillows behind her. She screamed, arched, and pushed. Below, I saw her widen, saw the first round tiny white patch of head.

She clutched my hand, arched, screamed. *"Oh, Peter!"*

The baby's head appeared. It was smeared with blood. I reached down to help ease it out as Reesa tensed and pushed again.

"Oh, God, it's hurting me!"

The baby came halfway out. I recoiled. It was a perfect little skeleton, tiny jaw snapping open and closed. It clawed at Reesa with its tiny hands.

"Reesa!"

She looked down, screamed. Then she was overcome by a final spasm of pushing as the baby slid out, followed by a flow of blood and a twisting, dried life cord.

She would not stop bleeding. The baby lay there, blood-covered, eye sockets staring blindly, tiny jaw opening and closing. The faintest of shrouds, the features of a tiny, wrinkled human thing, surrounded it.

" *Oh,* Peter . . ."

The baby clawed at the air, arched, and melted to dust before my eyes, leaving the shriveled life cord behind.

Reesa was white and pale.

"Peter, the blood . . ."

I tried to stop the bleeding. In a rush the birth sack

slid out, followed by a new river of crimson. The sheets, the bed, were dripping red.

"I'm going to die, Peter. . . ."

"No!"

She reached a pale, weak hand down and clutched me. "It will be over in a few minutes."

"I will not let you die!"

She pulled me close to her. In her fading eyes I saw all the love I ever needed. With both of her hands she pulled me close to her and kissed me. She looked deep into my eyes and smiled.

"Kral Kishkin," she said weakly. "It was written; it must happen." Her voice had become a feathery whisper. "Remember that I loved you. There will be another who will be with you, and you must go on. . . ."

"I will die here with you!" I said.

"No!" Her eyes gained life. She tried to rise, still holding me. Then she fell back against the pillows. "There were promises you made to me. You must keep them. You must honor them. There is more than you or me to think of. Kral Kishkin . . ."

She closed her eyes, but continued to hold me.

"I will not let you die!"

For a moment she opened her eyes. "Do what you must." She let one hand fall away from me and pointed weakly to the wood stove. "Now, before it is too late. Before I reawaken. You promised, with your blood. . . ."

"I cannot!"

Her eyes, the love in her eyes, followed me as I stumbled from her grasp, crying, and went to the wood stove. I looked back, and her eyes were watching me.

"Now . . ."

In crying anger I tore at the stove's vent, pulled it savagely from the wall, turned it so that its deadly vapors would exhaust into the room. With blood-soaked sheets from the bed I plugged the hole that vented it to the outside. I opened the grate, put wood in, watched the fire climb to fullness.

I went to Reesa, looked down at her. "There must be another way!"

She reached up, took my arm, shook her head slightly. Already I felt light-headed in the tiny room.

Reesa drew me down to her and kissed me, a kiss I would always remember. "Good-bye, Kral Kishkin, my husband," she whispered. "Believe me, you will find who you are. That was written, also. You have been wearing not masks, but lives. Now it is time for you to wear another life."

She let me go, and closed her eyes.

I stumbled from the room, raging, and pulled the door savagely shut behind me. I lurched down the stairs, threw open the door to the shop, and ran out into the whiteness of the snow, screaming my rage at the sky and resolving not to live.

6

I was in a state of delirium for days. I left the village behind me, climbed up the hills in the teeth of the still-falling snow. I wandered like a madman. I fell into ditches carved by the passage of giant dinosaurs. Once, I heard their roaring cries in the far distance. I tried to match them in rage and thunder. I beat my hands against the sides of rock walls until I drew blood. I chased a skeletal beast for miles, finally catching it and dashing it to dust beneath my hands. The dust I kicked to the four corners, trying to beat it back into the ground. When the storm broke, I screamed at the sun until the clouds returned and new snow began to fall.

Finally, weak with hunger, I collapsed into a ditch under a rock overhang. I fell to mindless sleep. I had dreams of Reesa. In them we had found a new, warm world, and we sat on a mountaintop as the sun rose over us, and surveyed all the land that was ours. It was a new Garden of Eden. There were animals, elephants and deer and lions, and all of them were tame and lived with us and slept by our sides at night. The fruit on the trees was fat and always ripe. In the sky our favorite stars always shone during the evening. The sun danced with fat clouds during the day, and when it rained, the rain was like silver and bathed our bodies and made us alive. There was a stream in our Eden, clear as glass, and a high diamond-colored waterfall, and the fish were orange and plum-colored, and danced near its surface. And we had a son, who grew tall and strong, and with our hands we worked the land and made the world grow fat and bountiful. And Reesa was as ripe as the fruit, bearing children to fill the entire world, and the entire world stretched out from our Eden. In the sky we heard the booming contented laughter of God, who smiled down upon us and pronounced us cleansed of sin, and there was nothing but peace in the world.

Only when I turned to look at Reesa, who stood beside me and shared this dream, it was not Reesa but someone else, a stranger with coffee-colored skin, the girl of my dream in the field outside Moscow, who opened her mouth to speak and said a single word I could not hear—

I awoke with the biting cold stabbing into me like a knife. I could not feel my legs.

For a moment I could not breathe, and panicked. All was dark. I remembered where I was and hit out with my hands, trying to push the too-close darkness away.

My hands sank into long, lush fur.

I screamed. I thought I had lost my mind. I beat at the rock over my head, behind me, trying to dig myself out.

The fur in front of me stirred, pulled away.

A long and shaggy form crept out of my ditch, letting blinding sunlight in.

The absence of warmth assaulted me. I began to shiver madly. My legs, which had been asleep and not frozen, came back to life.

My vision cleared.

Standing, regarding me solemnly in the bright sunlight of a snow-covered world, was the gray, massive, yawning form of a wolf.

We stared at one another. We continued to regard one another while I pulled myself shivering from my prison.

The temperature outside had dropped lower than I had yet felt. There was a crusted, icy surface to the snow. My breath huffed from my nostrils and mouth.

The wolf lumbered toward me and rested against my side.

"I believe you saved my life," I said.

I dug my freezing hand into the warmth of the wolf's coat. The beast looked up at me, waiting.

"All right," I said wearily.

Wrapping myself in my meager clothes, I headed back toward the village, the wolf trailing behind me.

Nearly two feet of snow lay in the streets. The tops of some abandoned vehicles were drifted nearly invisible. The broken fronts of the shops had been covered with an eerily cheery facade of ice and snow.

The blue sky above, the glare of the sun off the ice-white surface, was blinding.

I hesitated at the front door to the bakery. The wolf went in ahead of me, and I followed.

In the pantry I retrieved the jarred fruit and pickles. I was filled with an almost unreasonable hunger. I opened them greedily. I lay a spread of fruit out for the wolf. With barely a sniff he went to it, lapped it from the floor.

I ate two jars of preserves and a half-dozen large pickles before I paused for breath.

It was cold in the shop. I filled the fireplace with wood, stopping for a moment while a memory of my last act with Reesa, loading the wood stove, shot through me. I did not look at the doorway leading to the steps upstairs.

I lit a fire, pulled myself close to it. The wolf followed, curling next to me, its back turned toward the flames.

When the fire was good and high, I found myself sleepy also, and soon lay down on the bare floor, next to the animal, and closed my eyes.

When I awoke, the animal had snuggled closer to me. We shared warmth. My chill was gone. My belly felt half-full, and for the first time in days my brain was not on fire.

I rose, stretched, made another meal of preserves and pickles for the wolf and myself.

"We must find another place to live," I said.

Retrieving the baker's parka from the pantry, I donned it.

The wolf and I went to explore the rest of the village.

We found no lodging better than the bakery until we had reached the outskirts of the village. There, we discovered an untouched cottage. It was hidden in a small square, surrounded by two-story buildings, and had been sheltered from the rages of beast and skeleton. I had to break into the front door.

Inside was relative paradise.

A mantel over the fireplace still stood with dusty photographs and dainty porcelain knickknacks. A wooden nest of figures, enameled fat old women wearing babushkas, sat on a beautifully carved table under a lamp. The furnishings were sparse but settled looking. In the back was a bedroom with a huge, warm-looking bed, topped with a handmade quilt. The kitchen had a pantry stocked with nonperishables, a bucket with some still-usable potatoes, a washbasin, a rough table, and two chairs. There was no television. There was a radio, though, whose batteries immediately ran down when I turned it on. But not before I heard a voice speaking in Russian.

Even without a fire the house seemed warm. Once we had started a fire, there was no reason to leave.

7

The wolf and I lived this way for the next five days. The village belonged to me. Although I avoided the bakery, I explored the rest of the shops. The wolf seemed content just to be with me. He made no demands. He ate what I ate, slept when I slept. When he needed to relieve himself, he left for as long as it took, then returned. I came to accept his presence, just as he had already accepted mine.

I found some tools and winter gear, along with a Kolashnikov rifle to replace my other one. There was plenty of ammunition. We found all this in a dwelling that had been half burned by fire at some time in the near past. It had obviously been home to a local communist official or black marketeer. Probably both. Either that, or this black marketeer had also been dealing in government papers, since we found a hoard of those. Mostly they were boring proclamations from the Central Committee, in a locked box in the attic. There were also some warmer clothes, a good-quality parka a little large for me, which replaced the baker's, and a stash of American candy bars, which had been hidden more carefully than anything else.

Other buildings provided interesting items. Nearly every home had a secret hoard of food, most of it perishable, unfortunately. But occasionally something of use was found. In one dirty cottage I discovered a good-quality tent, a butane heater with five propellant cans that doubled as a cooker, camp blankets, and utensils. In a shed in back of the house was also a dogsled. I eyed my companion and said, "If only there were more of you."

The level gaze the wolf gave me told me that if there had been a hundred of him, it would have made no difference. No proud member of his species was going to pull a dogsled.

Near the end of the week I found the thing I had been praying for, which was hidden better than anything else in the town. Under a tarp in the back of the shed at the rear of the house where I had found the camping gear was a nearly new snowmobile.

It was plain that it had been used for snow removal more than exploration. With some difficulty I was able to remove the plow that had been welded to its front. It started on the second turnover of its engine. It proved to have a half-full tank of fuel. I found two large drums at the extreme rear of the shed and three twenty-liter cans to fill.

As the wolf watched with mild interest I drove the vehicle out into the snow and roared up and down the village street, feeling the cold wind on my face.

8

I made plans to leave the next day. The snow track, filled with gear and food, stood outside waiting for the journey to begin.

That night, as I had every other night, I sat in a comfortable chair in the little cottage and tried the radio. I had been unable to find more batteries. I had picked up snippets of information: that all of the western and central parts of the Soviet Union were in control of the skeletons, which were now under a stable government headed by Nikita Khrushchev. Khrushchev had banned the Communist party altogether and was in the process of forming a republic of sovereign states. I also learned that Soviet armies were pressing eastward, pushing the last remnants of humanity toward me as they were surrounded, pinched off, and destroyed; that most of Europe and all of the Americas had stabilized and were having similar success in wiping out humanity. The news was straightforward and unpropagandistic, which led me to believe that Khrushchev really was doing what he said he was. I found it immensely strange that the world peace I had dedicated myself to was coming about under the sponsorship of a race dedicated to the destruction of humanity.

My twenty seconds of news this night brought me the signing-off of a news program and the beginning of a program of classical music, which promised the live playing of Sergey Rachmaninoff, along with a brand-new orchestral work, the Seventh Symphony of Peter Ilich Tchaikovsky. As the announcer faded to battery death he promised new upcoming works from Brahms and Beethoven, and the possibility of a new work from Mozart—the young composer was completing his Requiem, which had been finished on his death by someone else.

Then the batteries were dead.

I sat with the silent radio in my lap. I looked down at the wolf, who gazed back up at me with his amber, seemingly intelligent eyes.

"This world has a terrible beauty to it," I said.

The wolf stared at me, impassive.

"It occurs to me that you need a name," I said. "Why don't I call you Jack, after Jack London? Would that be all right?"

The wolf seemed to like that as much as anything

else. After a moment of regarding me dispassionately, he turned, walked to the door, and let himself out.

I followed.

While the wolf relieved himself behind the house I studied the quarter-moon-lit sky. The fields of white surrounding me sparkled like silvery glass. The air was cold and clean.

There was an ache in me so deep and pure that I let out a sob. I wanted to feel my missing part, Reesa, next to me, snuggled into my side, seeing this with me. I wanted to see her smile at this scene. I wanted her happiness, to feel the joy she felt when looking at this wonderful world.

Slowly, I began to walk the village street toward the bakery.

When I reached the door to the shop, the wolf was behind me, standing back a few meters, his coat silver in the moonlight.

"I'll be right back," I said.

I went into the shop and up the steps. The wolf stayed behind.

When I opened the door, the room still smelled close and stuffy. The wood stove stood cold, its flue pointed into the room like an accusing finger. It had done its work.

For a startled moment when I looked at the bed, I saw Reesa's form lying there, but actually all that lay on the blood-dried sheets was dust, hers and the baby's.

I walked to the bed, bundled the sheets up, and carried them downstairs with me.

When I passed the wolf, he kept a discreet distance behind me, following me to the top of a hill overlooking the silver distance and the town behind me.

I opened the sheets and let the dust fly out into the dark, lonely, beautiful night.

"This night belongs to you, Reesa and my child," I said.

The dust rose up on the light wind, spread, and settled to the earth. If I closed my eyes, I could see Reesa and my growing son standing silver in the moonlight, smiling at me. When I opened my eyes, they were gone, but in my heart they were still there, would always be there.

Suddenly a kind of burden lifted from me. For the first time I saw that Reesa had been right. Those other masks I had worn had not been masks at all, but lives. I had been Jayavaram, and Ho Vei, and Mongkut, and Peter Sun, and even George Wong. I had been all of them, and all of them had been me. I was who I was, and not a series of playactor's masks. If I had been a patriot, and assassin, and student and peace activist, and even a murderer, that was who I was. The names were all me.

For the first time in my life I knew who I was.

"I am Kral Kishkin," I said to the night, which was now Reesa and my child. "That is who I am. I will not forget, and I will not flinch. I will follow the road that is laid before me, and always I will remember you, and always I will remember what I am. You gave this to me. You gave me myself."

Suddenly, so strongly that I had to close my eyes, the vision of the coffee-skinned girl walking toward me through a field arose before me. Ever east she beckoned me, and she opened her mouth to speak—

And then the vision was gone.

The silver night stood silent and perfect around me. Jack came to stand beside me, and let me bury my hand in his coat.

"It's time for us to go," I said.

We walked down from that hill to the cottage at the edge of the village, and at that moment, in the silvery cold night, with the wolf named Jack curled asleep in the seat behind me, I kicked the snow track into life, and left that place behind, and headed east.

12

The completely miserable existence of Roger Garbage

1

The Great fu-ing White North.

I mean, I've been in better places. Anywhere else, in fact. The forest is something you look at, and piss in, before you go back to the real world. I mean, I'm all for saving the wilds. Why not? They're not good for anything else, right? I remember a Vomits song we were working on for a while, went something like:

> *Green stuff,*
> *Can't get enough (of that)*
> *Green stuff,*
> *I love grass (and that)*
> *Green stuff. . . .*

'Course, we weren't talking about Sierra Club–type nature, per se, but what the hell.

And speaking of *hell*, it hasn't been *all* that, since Bobbie baby was smart enough to bring along the mobile studio. Since I've hooked up with the Vomits again on the road, we've been able to mix a few cuts along the way, when we haven't been hiding in the woods or diving for cover from strafing Apache helicopters.

I mean, Bobbie must have been into some *bad* shit down in California. Won't talk about it, actually he doesn't talk about much of anything anymore. The man looks pale, even for a skel.

I mean, one day here we are, parked in the friggin' Great Something or Other Forest, real "Twin Peaks" type place, summer's ending, bear shit to the left of me, bear shit to the right of me, tall trees, fresh air that makes you want to smoke a carton of cigarettes just to balance things off, and I'm in the studio with Randy Pants and Brutus Johnson, and we're actually getting somewhere for the first time since this little caravan left Cal, and *whammo,* here comes this Apache zooming over like a movie stunt plane, and off go the bullets, and ol' Randy, he just takes one right through the neck, right through the side of the mobile studio, while he's got his mouth open, hitting that beautiful high C of his.

And . . . *poof,* the bastard turns to dust and is gone.

Me and Brutus stop what we're doing and look at the little camp chair Randy was sitting on, and there's only a pile of powder sitting there now, and it's not singing any high C.

"Clean that up, will you?" Brutus says as he dives under the foldout table holding the two-track tape deck. And damned if a nice line of bullets doesn't punch through the side of the studio at that moment, *tat-tat-tat-tat,* and out the other side, leaving two level lines of holes.

"Room under there, Brute?" I say, but he pushes me away. He's pretty wrecked, anyway. Has been, every since we started the Great Caravan. In fact they all have been, the whole bunch of skels who linked up in northern Cal for this Fun Trip to Freedom. Jimmy Klemp, the illustrious Vomits drummer, put it best when he said, "Running for our friggin' second lives, man."

Not Randy Pants, not anymore.

I hear the Apache make a cranking turn and then it strafes us up again on a third pass. Outside, there's lots of yelling and screaming, and little *pffft* sounds like the skels make when they dust themselves.

"Slide me that weed, will you?" Brutus says calmly, pointing to the baggie of grass that's an inch closer to me out in the middle of the floor.

"Fu you," I say, and he scowls.

Suddenly his scowl turns to howl.

"My guitar!"

And there's his Stratocaster, leaning calmly against the wall of the camper studio, as the next line of chopper rounds slices into the wall six inches to its left, straight through its neck, and six inches to the right.

We both watch as the neck teeters, then falls forward, bouncing on its still-strung strings.

"Bad news," I say, sliding out to get the weed and pulling it toward myself.

"Ohhhhhhhh *hhhhhhhhhh!*" Brutus wails.

For a moment I feel his grief, because there was money to be made with that guitar.

"Hey, man, there's always the Fender."

"The *Fender!*" He snorts in disgust.

But the next moment there *isn't* a Fender, because the next Apache round cuts deep and low, just over our noggins, and dices right through the case holding Brutus's backup, which he uses when he wants to sound real sloppy or Ventures-like.

I hear the *boing-boing* sound of popping strings, and know much isn't left.

"What in hell am I going to *do!*" Brutus wails.

"Hey, don't worry, we'll get another one. Plenty of guitar stores in Canada. Maybe even Alaska. Hey," I say, snapping my fingers but still staying close to the floor of the camper, "didn't Big Moe move to Anchorage after that drug bust in seventy-three?"

His eyes light up a little. "Yeah . . ."

"I'm sure he's still there. Didn't Bill Varley from the Frogs see him up there a couple years back?"

Brutus is getting his personality back, he's rolling himself a joint now. "Oooo, yeah . . ."

"That solves it," I say. "Moe'll fix you up with a new Strat. In the meantime we'll work on that acoustic—"

But then the Apache make a final pass, cutting a bullet right in front of my nose, and right into Brutus's Gibson acoustic, making it go *twong!*

Brutus sighs.

"We didn't have a lead singer, anyway," I say.

"Bullshit. *You'll* sing," Brutus says, "and we'll be in Anchorage in four days."

The weed must be very powerful, because I find myself nodding, saying, "Sounds good to me."

2

So I become the lead singer of the Vomits. Luckily the rest of the boys, Jimmy and Barney, made it through the Apache raid and the short battle following, in which the fat bitch Noreen, Bobbie's secretary-bouncer, bit the dust, ha-ha. Some of the other dudes who have hooked up with us, corporate biker types, real homburgs, also go down, stepping on their own claymores or getting shot up by the inadequate force the powers that be have sent against us. By now there are *thousands* of us, and the real U.S. Army boys pull off only because they consider us not much of a threat right now, and, we hear, they have a large, last-ditch-type stand of humans to face somewhere in Washington State.

So we reach Anchorage, and Moe's shop is still there, though Moe himself looks like he got dusted, a big pile of the stuff behind the counter, undisturbed, he was a big guy, his feathered Aussie hat on top of the pile. But though Moe is gone, his guitars aren't, and Brutus has a Christmas-morning-type day, picking four or five out. In the end he goes with a Strat, a National acoustic, and an old Les Paul he finds in the back of the shop, under a bench, that's *never been opened.* How's that for serendipity? The ol' bag of bones nearly dances over that one.

Which, to put it mildly, is a good thing, because it gets ol' Brutus hepped up for a little idea of mine, a nugget of fun that's been growing like a barnacle in my head for the past month or so, and which I very much want to pull off now:

WOODSTOCK II!

And . . . Brutus can be so enthusiastic that soon the idea has taken on a life of its own. Even Bobbie Zick,

man of the worldly mind, comes back down from poli-
ticsville to musicland and gets into it.

"Maybe it would be a way to rally the troops, old
boy," he says, rubbing his bony little chin, sitting behind
his makeshift desk in his trailer.

"Maybe, indeed," I say, smiling.

"All very secret, of course," Bobbie goes on. "There
are lots of deadheads, freaks, old hippies, and such in
this part of the world now." I can almost see the little
gears in Bobbie baby's head working. "Thousands more,
I'd suppose. Makings of an *army*, almost. If we were to arrange weaponry, plenty of drugs, plenty of booze, and
then *organize* these people . . ."

Bobbie smiles, pats me on the back.

"Go to it, old boy," he says.

We both walk away smiling from that conversation.

So the Lonetree Music Festival, as it becomes known,
named after the single runt tree in the middle of the
massive abandoned strip mine we pick for the shindig,
pulls into high gears with you know who at the helm.

And I'm having a *kick*, man! I mean, there're musicians in them thar hills! For the next few weeks, by day I
roam the woods and hills with a skel escort, by night I slip
off alone, with Bobbie's blessing, to find the shy ones, the
ones holed up in caves, in mines, under *rocks*, like I find
Richie Valens. He's drilled himself into a shag quarry and
is squatting in there like a tick, surrounded by guns. I'm
scared to go in there, even with a flashlight.

And speaking of scared, you should see *Elvis* when
he literally rolls on top of me, down from the top of a hill
he's taken over. There's a cabin up there, pigsty-land,
wrappers and empty food boxes all over. Out back there's
a Hostess truck banged into a tree, the back thrown
open.

"You *drove* that up here?" I say.

"You bet, son. Man's gotta eat." He looks at me, and
I gotta say he's one of the few skels who look better if you
just admire the bones: I mean, this guy's *shadow form* is
grotesque-o, rolls of fat, at least six chins, he needs a hair-
cut, his sideburns are about to meet at his neck.

"By the way . . ." he drawls.

"I haven't got any food. But . . ." I tell him about

Mama Cass, holed up a mile away with piles of the
canned hams I sent her, she got the food but I don't
think she got the joke, not that I've tried to approach
her, I remember the last time we met—and Elvis is mine.

"And plenty at the concert, Elvis. Anything you
want."

"Twinkies? Sno balls?" He waves at the open empty
back of the truck, sadly.

"Anything you want."

He shakes my hand. "I'm yours, son." As I walk away
he stops me. "You think ol' Mama Cass is the marrying
kind?"

And there's more. Jim Morrison *does* make it finally
from France, but is incoherent, screaming only for "Bud!
Bud!" He's unable to tell us how he got here. Bobbie gets
him holed up with cases of beer, and soon he's writing
new songs. The Big Bopper bops in. But then I hit a
snag, which is no snag to me, but I keep forgetting that
Bobbie is a *skel.*

"No humans," he says.

"But Bobbie, we're talking Bob Dylan!"

He shakes his bone head. "They won't go for it."

"Are you kidding?"

"No." And now, once again, I see that creepy look
they all get when they're around humans, the slow burn
ready to erupt to violence, the one Bobbie, and all of
them, has been holding in check so long with me. "It . . .
won't work."

"But Bobbie, there's *lots* of humans in this area. Not
only musicians. All types. You wouldn't believe the stories
I'm hearing. There are *soldiers,* even."

His interest picks up. "How many?"

"Maybe twenty, thirty thousand. *Another army,* Bobbie
boy."

Now I've got *him.* He's seriously diddling with it.
Then he shakes his head quickly. "Never work."

"From what I hear, the humans are desperate. You
could hook up with them, drive the federal government
off, make Alaska a separate country. Rock and Roll
Land."

"No."

"A human-bone alliance, Bobbie." I smile. "Make it

... temporary, if you like. Just until you get what you want. Then ..." I look off, shrug.

He's smiling. "You really are a snake, Roger."

"Just keep me around, babe. Let me do what I do."

"It might work," he says, and he's rubbing his chin.

"Sure. Don't forget, alcohol and drugs work on *everybody*. Speaking of which ..."

I eye his pocket, where he's taken to keeping his bag.

"Sure, Roger, sure." Grinning, he cuts me a line of coke on his desk, even holds the straw for me.

"So, what do you think about the human-bone hookup?" I say, sitting back.

"I say yes," he says. "Go to it, old boy."

"You bet, old boy," I say, and we both laugh.

3

So I talk to Dylan, who talks to Billy Joel, who talks to two other guys, who talk to five others guys. And pretty soon I'm ushered into this grand-poobah-type setup in the hills, lots of guards, me in a blindfold, then standing in front of a table with some kind of Council of Five behind it.

"Can he be trusted?" some guy on the end, looks like Mitch Miller, says.

"No," says my escort, who looks government to me, later I realize he was Dan Quayle.

"But it *is* a good idea." This from one of the other deskmen, a woman who I can't immediately place; later I realize it's Quayle's wife.

"Yes ..." Quayle says.

"Can I say something?" I butt in.

They all look at me, wait.

"You can make an alliance with them—then you can fu 'em!"

They continue to look at me.

"Hey, there're thirty thou of you clowns, right? There's only twenty thou of Bobbie Zick's boys! Get in on the concert gig, then wham 'em, get their weapons, their supplies. Then you'll have more stuff to fight the feds with! I mean, Bobbie's planning on doing the same to you. Just leave the music to me!"

They look at each other, and suddenly I see those human smiles I haven't seen in a while, just as creepy as the skel version, that boardroom grin.

I leave with contracts for nearly every live musician in the world, and not one of the dumb shits bothered to read the clause that says they're mine even if they get turned.

I mean, no way I'm gonna side with the humans, the buggers haven't got a chance.

What am I, *stupid*?

4

Not stupid, exactly, but let's say . . . unlucky. So when I'm out the next night by myself, deep in the woods, looking for Muddy Waters who's said to be living in a tent in the vicinity, the Roger-rader goes off just as a lone skel walks out of the dark and puts a Walther blue steel .44 to my head.

"Boo," he says.

"Hey, I'm on your—"

"I know who you are. Shut up."

I feel that cold blue steel at the base of my skull, and I shut up.

"Here's what's going to happen," the skel says. I try to get a look at him, but he's not letting me. He twists the barrel mouth into that soft spot in the back of my neck, just under the skull bone. "Just listen."

I nod.

"Fun time is over. You've got nearly every human left in North America in the ten square miles that surround us. *And* you've got every rebel skeleton in the same area. We want to get rid of both problems at once."

"You're a fed?"

He jams the gun barrel in tighter. I say, "Ugh."

"Just listen. The president wouldn't authorize a nuke like we wanted. So now there's only one way. And your little concert is it.

"We want you to have it, just like you planned. Get

everybody stoned, drunk, whatever you want to do. Just make sure *everybody* comes to that concert. We'll take care of the rest."

He twists the gun even deeper into my neck.

"This is no joke, Garber. Yes, we know your real name. We know lots of things. And make no mistake, the government is coming out on top of this one. Since you like to come out on top, too, do what I say, and we'll make sure you get out of it."

He puts something into my pocket.

"Someone will ask you for this at the appropriate time. When they do, give it to them. Don't turn around, don't open your mouth. Just remember what I told you. We'll be watching. If you screw up, you die. Twice. If you don't screw up, you live, and continue to do music. That's your reward.

"Good-bye."

Finally he hits me with that blue steel .44, sending me to instant black.

When I wake up, he is, natch, gone.

I reach into my pocket and take out the Lincoln penny he's given me. Only where Lincoln should be, it's been ground flat and polished, like a little round copper mirror.

I put it back in the pocket.

I find Muddy Waters, then go back to camp, my night's work done, and do a little of this, a little of that, and sleep like a baby, helped along by enough coke to kill a bull elephant, because I'm at the point where I don't want to think about *anything* anymore.

5

CONCERT TIME!

Man, you want to talk about a high? We're talking about the *biggest* damn thing there ever was! The CD, tape, and album sales alone will put me over the top for life! And Bobbie's managed to get the best equipment spirited up from California, the best amps, and speakers, the whole nine enchiladas. It seems the whole bad dreamworld has gone away for this one day—hell, it's autumn in Alaska and the day comes up bright and sunny, high in the upper seventies! At dawn they're already filling the bowl, blankets on the ground around the stage, a few folding chairs here and there, but mostly we're talking *party*. I've never seen so many drugs in my life. I'm introduced to a skel named Cha-cha, who's spent all of his time since he's been turned coming up with some of the damnedest designer drugs the earth has ever seen. LSD and speed wrapped together like DNA molecules. Cocaine rushes that last for half days. Something called hobbyhorse, or lip smack, a synthetic heroin that leaves no afterburn. Mescatel, you unravel that one: wine and drugs at the same time! Yow!

And I've never sampled such grass! I mean, this plant just about got up and walked out of the ground into my arms! It *smokes* gold!

And talk about ego-boo! Everybody wants a piece of ol' Rog, that's me! By egg McMuffin time, seven in the morning, I'm already flying. The Byrds are here, ready to open the show at seven-thirty, they've *got* to play "Eight Miles High" first, I beg them. Agreement all around, they've worked out their differences, skel and human alike, with only a few fistfights, just like the old days. The Stones will go on next, the first of two gigs for them, followed by Janis Ian for the nostalgia freaks and Chad and Jeremy (hey, I had to let them on, they begged). Procol Harum and the Doors follow, but Morrison has disappeared. Found in a toilet, weeping, surrounded by empties, but he'll do it, he says.

"Don't care if you expose yourself," I say.

"All *right!*" he shouts in that basso growl, and then takes the fresh longneck I hand him and wanders off to a corner singing "Riders on the Storm" to himself.

And I *know* I'm feeling good. I was born for this! No sign of Apache helicopters yet, no mortar rounds into the bowl. For all I know the G-men are rock-and-roll fans, too.

God, I hope so.

Seven o'clock!

Time to rock!

Hours seem to melt by. Jefferson Airplane rolls into a blues set with B. B. and Albert King. The Band has

shown up, another half-and-half act producing an attempted throttling of one human by one skel. But Dylan
has agreed to go out with them before he does his own
thing, which turns out to be a minifest in itself, three
hours with Van Morrison, Joni Mitchell, a virtual replay
of *The Last Waltz*. Then Eric Clapton climbs on stage, and
the rest of them melt away to the background, letting
him do his thing out front for nearly an hour.

Everything's fine until three o'clock, when I have
three frights at once. First, I think I'm dying from something Cha-cha has injected into me, but that turns out all
right; second, I hear the thwack-thwack of a heli blade
overhead, but *that* turns out to be just one of Bobbie's
men with a video camera, tethered to the bottom of an
old Sikorski like a marionette. Video rights! All reet!
Lonetree Music Fest: the Movie!

My God, this is the beautiful end of the world! I love
it!

And then the third fright, which comes during the
most wonderful thing of all—
THE BEATLES REUNION!!!

It happens, just like that. There is sharp disagree-
ment until the end, Lennon waffling between Yoko and
the lads, even Pete Best showing up to claim Ringo's
place once and for all. Best we put in Clapton's backup
band, he's not happy but he's getting paid. And then,
suddenly, Lennon says yes.

I get a brief glimpse of Yoko stalking off, but before
long she's back with both of the Lennon kids and *everybody's* on stage—Linda McCartney, most of Wings including Jimmy McCulloch, the until lately late-lamented
guitarist, George Martin on keyboards, even their man-
ager, Brian Epstein, rattling a tambourine. My God, I
can't believe it! I drop my clipboard, grab the person
nearest me, and begin to weep.

"This can't be real!" I say. "This can't really be happening!"

The person, a skel, who I haven't seen before but
who is wearing a red neck ribbon with a staff tag on it,
supports me and says, "Got a Lincoln penny on you,
buddy?"

I look up in horror, it's the voice of the skel in the woods with the blue steel .44. He's smiling slightly.

"You wouldn't," I say in horror. "You *can't* do it now."

"Good a time as any. Got that coin?"

I fumble the penny out of my pocket, press it into his bony hand. Then suddenly I hear the faint whine of jet engines high overhead and grab his hand, holding it tightly.

"*Please,*" I say. "*Any* other time but now. *Those are the Beatles!*"

And lo and behold, as I say this, as if by magic invocation, the hangers-on and extras have left the stage to John, Paul, George, and Ringo alone, who are beginning to crank into "Let It Be."

The homburg is looking over my shoulder at the stage. There's something back in those deep empty wells of eye sockets, some faintest of glimmers, a memory back when the Bay of Pigs was recent history, when the world was a different, kinder, gentler place, more innocent, when—ah, fu, the man, *thank God,* is a Beatles fan.

"Shit, you're right," he says.

He fumbles into his jacket pocket, pulls out a slim walkie-talkie, yanks the antenna up.

"Six forty-four sweep. This is Antler. Hold. Repeat, hold."

Above, I hear the jet engines give a sour whine, pull off into the ether.

Homburg looks at me. "Who's on next?"

I retrieve my clipboard. "Ummm . . ." Down the list, and it's . . .

Me.

"The"—gulp—"Vomits."

"Great, we'll hit then," Antler says, and relays this information into the walkie-talkie.

"But *I'm* in the Vomits," I say, in a squeaky, weak voice. I'm also thinking, soft heart that I am, of Brutus Johnson, Jimmy Klemp, and Barney Barnes, who I'm about to screw biggest time.

"No problem," says Antler, who's watching the Beatles as if mesmerized. "We'll tell you when, get you out." He gives me the look of a zealot. "Any way you can get me backstage to meet Lennon?"

6

So the next hour and a half of the world belong to the Beatles. They're lighting matches in the strip mine, gathered up to the rim nearly a hundred thousand strong, man and bonehead. There's almost twice as many as we thought, the word got out, they climbed down out of trees, up out of deep mine shafts, had to be part of the biggest love-in of all. Man and bone, the beginning of a new era, not quite, of course. By the end, while Harrison's guitar cries its way through "While My Guitar Gently Weeps," mixed species are crying, holding hands, kissing each other. Even Antler has a tear in his eye as I lead him backstage to wait for the four lads to come off.

"Shit, that was beautiful," he says, and then he slips out his walkie-talkie and informs whomever to be ready.

"When I give you a thumbs-up," he says to me, "get ready to pray."

He pushes me out onto stage, out of his way, as John tramps by.

"Uh, Mr. Lennon?" Antler says.

And then I'm out there with the Vomits.

"You wanted it, shitbrain." Brutus Johnson grins at me from behind his Stratocaster as he tunes it up.

Out there, a hundred thou wait.

"Do one of the new ones, shock the fuggers," Jimmy Klemp says, adjusting his brass-drum pedal. He gives his snare a hit with a stick. "Do it!"

We do it.

At first the crowd is quiet, they've just come off the Beatles, and nobody's going to top that. Plus, they don't know who the fu I am. I may look a little like Randy Pants did in human life, but I'm clearly *not* Randy, and maybe that's good, maybe that's bad. Truth is, they don't know what the fu to think, so we tell them:

> *Hey you!*
> *Sittin' there,*
> *Bone down to your underwear—*
> *Hey you!*
> *Grinnin' back,*
> *When you move you creak and crack—*
> *Hey you!*
> *Lookin' white*
> *DON'T YOU WANNA ROCK ALL NIGHT!*

Brutus comes in with the greatest, longest guitar riff of his career. The song is done in brutal fast time and Brutus, if anything, picks it *up*. He's all over the stage, throwing himself down to his knees, letting them know out there that he is the best, that Clapton can finally move aside.

And suddenly the crowd *agrees*. I get the feeling there were a lot of Vomits fans out there to begin with, at least a lot of Brutus Johnson fans, but suddenly the *whole world* knows it, and Johnson is leaving no doubt. This is his moment, the moment we've all been waiting for for three years. Randy Pants was not the Vomits—Brutus Johnson was—and now everybody knows it!

By the end of the riff a hundred thou have forgotten the Beatles, an amazing feat, Jimmy Klemp backing the end of Brutus's break with vicious boom slams, Barney Barnes knocking deep whumps off his bass like he shot from his Mom's womb playing it—and even Antler and John Lennon have forgotten the Beatles, watching in rapt fascination.

At first I think it's Lennon who's giving me the thumbs-up, but I realize in horror that it's Antler, his arm around Lennon's shoulder.

"Noooooo!" I shout into the mike.

High above, I hear the approaching whine of jets.

Then Brutus's break ends, and it's my turn to sing again:

> *Hey you!*
> *Sittin' in this modern world,*
> *Better grab a boner girl!*
> *Hey you!*

Take her to the nearest bed
'Cause you're not completely dead! Yah!

That last *Yah!* is not part of the song, but part of my panic as the sky above opens up like the mouth of hell. Bright lights, jet fighters, and helicopters up the wazoo. Pray indeed. Brutus could care less, he's gone into his final guitar frenzy and the rest of the Vomits are blithely following. I look side stage for Antler, but he's gone, along with Lennon, and now there are huge speakers in the sky, blaring down at us from blimps, drowning out the huge wonderful sound of our own premium sound system:

"*Stay where you are!* Don't move! Anyone who moves will be immediately shot!"

He's not kidding: up at the rim of the bowl, like Indians in a Custer movie, tanks, howitzers, and men with big guns have appeared. Everything's pointing down. Fish in a barrel.

A squadron of Blue Angels makes a low overpass, making even Brutus stop in midchord—*frunk*—and the whole bunch of them fire rockets in perfect time. The rockets trace a line toward the horizon, trails weaving around one another like ballet dancers, and then, *thoomp*, they explode midair, making quite a brightness, making everyone go temporarily blind.

"*Do not move!*" the speakers blare.

"What the—" Barney Barnes shouts, dropping his bass and running from the stage—but Antler is there, with his trusty .44 Walther out and aiming. He pops one into Barney, and Barney's dusted.

"Shit," Brutus says, dropping his Strat at his feet and just standing there. Suddenly he bursts into tears. "I was just *getting* there. . . ."

Then lights and booms go off all around us, smoke dropping from above, from the rim of the bowl, from *everywhere*, and I'm looking for Antler, but again he's gone, and now I look up.

Pray, indeed!

There it is, though: a tether and ring lowered from a Huey, it's almost over my head before I grab it. Immediately it reverses winch and I'm hauled up, over the rising smoke below.

"Hey, you bastard!" Jimmy Klemp yells at me, throwing one of his sticks. But he's engulfed in smoke and starts coughing. His stick twirls up out of the smoke, just out of my reach, then falls twirling back into the banks of cloud below my feet.

"You bastard . . ."

Up I go.

And then into the belly of the metal Huey beast. I look down. The entire bowl is filled with raspberry-colored smoke, rolling like some caldron. At the edges little figures, skel and human, try to climb out, but they're pushed back down or shot at until they reverse field. The soldiers doing the pushing and shooting are wearing gas masks.

The Huey rises. The little people start to look like ants trying to overflow a hill. But already there are fewer of them, the bowl is eating them up.

"Shit, and the Ramones were on after us," I say.

"Too bad, old boy," Bobbie Zick's voice says behind me.

Yeah, he's there, ol' Bobbie, I should have known, sitting in a comfortable seat. Next to him is Antler, and next to *him* is John Lennon, looking down at the bowl in gaping wonder.

"It's bloody incredible," Lennon says. "And you're *sure. . .?*"

"Yeah, yeah, John, no problem," Antler says. He sounds disappointed. "Just gas. It'll turn the humans and just put the others to sleep for a while. They'll wake up with a big hangover."

Lennon laughs. "Wouldn't be the first time for Ringo."

Bobbie's grinning at me, and now Antler turns to me with a sour look.

"Like I told you, we wanted to use a tactical nuke, but Lincoln said no," Antler says. "Wouldn't even let us use an air burster. What a wuss. If only Bush hadn't gone and got himself dusted in that oil-fire thing in Kuwait . . ." His indignation won't leave. "I *told* Lincoln a neutron bomb would make the damn area safe for picnics in a month. Even that didn't cut it. Well, maybe soon ..."

"Got a few more tricks up your sleeve?" Bobbie Zick asks, and both he and Antler laugh.

"My kind of wuss, that Lincoln," Lennon says.

Antler gives me that hungry skel-to-human glare. "That damn Lincoln. I can't even turn *you.*"

I smile weakly.

"Oh, yes, old boy," Bobbie Zick says, laughing. "You're *still* the valuable commodity."

"You've been working all along with the feds?" I ask.

Bobbie shrugs. "Only since you gave me your idea for this music festival. It was apparent by then our little rebel movement had no chance of success." He smiled. "Better to join the feds than be beaten by them." He spread his hand out at the gas clouds below. "And all these humans were our little present."

"Merry Christmas!" Antler says, with a sly look at Bobbie.

Bobbie says, in his best Brit accent, "I'm just a good American at heart. Your little music fest provided the perfect vehicle for wrapping up everyone's business." He sighs. "And from now on," he says, deliberately using for the first time his real, Brooklyn accent, "I'm afraid I'm gonna hafta concentrate on duh music bizness." His Bobbie Zick Brit accent comes back. "Woe is me, old boy."

"Good bloody American indeed." Lennon laughs sarcastically.

"Good enough to let you start Lennon Records, eh?" Bobbie says. "Two Beatles albums, plus solo efforts for all you moptops. Not bad, eh, old boy?"

Lennon looks out the window. "What can I say? You're no worse than any of them, I suppose. You're all fookin' maggots at heart."

Bobbie shrugs. "She loves you, yeah, yeah, yeah."

"And me?" I say, letting a sliver of hope creep into my voice. "Is there, uh, any possibility of, say, Roger Records? Or maybe, um, at least that, uh, Vomits record getting made? I mean, uh, we could easily replace Barney, and—"

Bobbie shrugs again. "Sorry, old boy. Out of my hands." He looks to Antler.

"Washington's got other plans for you," Antler says. His tone is as flat and unreadable as his eyes.

I smile a phony smile. "Uh ... that's great."

"Yeah, we all got away with one this time," Bobbie Zick says.

"Some of us," Lennon says.

Bobbie and Antler look at each other and laugh, while Lennon and I continue to look out the window, studying the receding, raspberry-smoke-filled bowl below.

7

And ... so I meet Mr. Lincoln of Illinois.

Quite a kick, actually. I mean, this dude is walking history. And after hearing how he refused to dust all those skels and humans in Alaska who refused to bow to his will, well, for the moment at least he's my kind of boner.

But that doesn't make him immune to that same creepy hunger to kill that the other skels have. Only it bothers Mr. L, I can see. When he shakes my hand, there's a momentary hitch, a repulsion that he consciously overcomes. I can see it in his eye sockets, he's fighting himself to like me instead of wring my neck. But this guy always wins, and the handshake is warm—for a skel.

"Mr. Garber," he says.

"Uh, Mr. President."

"I'm going to ask you to help me," he says.

"Uh ... sure."

"There is work that needs to be done. We are very close, after the incident in Anchorage, to the goals we have set."

I know I'm a jerk, he knows I'm a jerk, but, damn, the man has class. "Sure."

Mr. L goes on to explain those goals, maybe hoping that I won't fall asleep. I don't, but I don't know what he's talking about, either. A bunch of jazz about a new world, peace for everybody, a paradise with law and happiness for all. I can see it now. Skels without hell. I feel like telling him about Antler and Bobbie Zick, and how that's probably only the tip of the tomato. Doesn't he know about guys like *me* for cry sakes?

"And that's why, Mr. Garber, we'd like to accomplish this endeavor with as little bloodshed as possible. For the good of all."

"Uh ... right," I say.

He suddenly turns away from me, puts his hands behind his back, and walks to the window of his office. Not a good view out there, it's just about winter now, cold and windy and the trees have dropped their leaves like horses taking a dump. Looks like ol' man winter's getting ready to roar in.

"I'm not a fool, Mr. Garber," Mr. L says.

His voice sounds so sad I suddenly want to friggin' cry, no kidding. I think of my own old man for a minute, the hand, the slap, the drunken bastard. God, I wish this guy had been my father. I would have done anything for him, no slap needed. "I've given up much for this cause. I'm a pragmatic man, not a dreamer. Every one of my ... waking moments has been filled with trying to make sense of what's going on around me.

"I want you to know I'm trying to do the best thing for all. *All*, Mr. Garber. That includes you and me. I used to be human, a long time ago. I ... vaguely remember the feelings I had, and I understand the differences between us. I know I'm different now. This doesn't please me, but I believe there is a purpose to all this, Mr. Garber." He suddenly turns to look at me, and now I *am* crying, what the hell is wrong with me? He's so sad, he's so hard at the same time, it's scary. He's like ... God, almost. Or Solomon. Yeah, I had all that Bible stuff, when I was a kid. Jeez, this is depressing.

"I think in some way you know what I mean," Mr. L continues. He turns away from me again, preferring the window. I don't blame him. This guy's got me ready to pee in my own pants, wanting to fall on the ground and confess my sins. Hell, I'm sure he already knows what they are.

"There's a place in this for you, too," he says. "In exchange for your help, you will be treated with ... respect. I'm told you enjoy the music business. You will be granted a position of some merit in that business, when all this is over—and if you behave yourself. And I give you my word, you will not be turned."

"Working for Bobbie Zick?" I say, suddenly redeemed.

Lincoln turns and scowls at me. "Mr. Zick is in jail. So is the man who was trusted with the mission you were involved in in Anchorage."

"Why?"

Mr. L looks at me as if surprised I asked the question. "Basically, Mr. Garber, though they professed allegiance to the government of the United States, they were trying to overthrow me. The man you knew as Antler, along with others at the Central Intelligence Agency, have been trying to undermine my authority for months. They arranged for a former president to try a coup, they tried to authorize the use of nuclear weapons without my authority, they've tried several other clumsy methods." He reaches into his pocket, shows me the penny with his own likeness burred off. "This was their crude form of humor, Mr. Garber. Needless to say, I've disbanded the CIA. Not that I can honestly see why it was ever needed in the first place."

I feel like cheering for this man.

He gives me a slight smile. "Oh, yes, Mr. Garber, I'm a pretty good politician at heart. In my original time I had to deal with the likes of Salmon Chase and Stephen Douglas. A snake is still a snake, Mr. Garber, and you've got to keep a stick handy.

"Now, Mr. Garber, this is what I'd like you to do. . . ."

We jazz for a while, Mr. L and me. He tells me what he wants, tells me about some dreams he's been having, weird ones about a human black girl who will be the last woman in the whole fu-ing world. It sounds real weird to me, but I can't afford to be impolite. I tell him I can do it, grade-A okey-dokey, no problemo. For a guy without a CIA, this dude knows plenty. Then he shakes my hand again, and he's got real control, because this time I see no hint of that "kill you, sucka" look in his eyes. Only a bit of faint amusement, because we both know he can trust me about as far as you can spread your toes. But that's okay. We're both horse traders. I like this prez. And we both understand that if I don't do what he says, I get turned in a finger snap and find myself warming a bench next to Bobbie Zick in the fed pen.

He's okay, the L Man.

And then the damnedest thing happens. I'm coming out of the Meeting with Mr. L, just sauntering along, and I come to this spot at the top of the staircase outside the O Office where it seems some damage has been done. So I step near the scaffolding to take a look.

Only there isn't any scaffolding, and there isn't any step there, and suddenly I'm hanging by my fingers from the top of a marble hole, looking down at a long drop to hard floor far below. Then my fingers are slipping. I see myself as red squish, then rising again as a skel.

Only now it don't seem so bad. I can actually see myself getting along in this bone world, especially with guys like Mr. L running the show.

So I don't even mind that my fingers are slipping— in fact, I'm kind of helping them along, raising them one by one and thinking about the new and wonderful life to come.

"Geronimo!" I'm starting to say.

Two fingers to go, and I'm letting them slip—

Only then Mr. L is there, looming above me like the tall mast of a ship. He's grabbing my fingers and then my hands, and hauling me up like I'm a log about to slip the wrong way downstream. And he's *strong*.

"We can't have that, Mr. Garber," he says in an almost scolding tone. "That reminds me of the farmer with the nearsighted chicken who couldn't find the feed. All the other chickens got fat and ended up on the farmer's dinner table. Then one day this skinny runt of a nearsighted chicken comes clucking into the kitchen and hops in the frying pan.

"But the farmer takes one look at it, plucks it out, and says, 'I think you're more use to me the way you are!' "

13

The inner diary of
Claire St. Eve

1

Margaret Gray said, "Rise."

I rose from my sleeping mat in Margaret Gray's tent and walked out to see two hundred others rising from their rough beds on the ground.

"Work!" Margaret Gray shouted. "As the Lord commands you, work!"

And so another day began.

We were somewhere in western Iowa, near the Nebraska border. This day, like the other days of the last weeks, we spent in the midst of dried, stripped stalks of corn, gathering missed ears for our meal. We fought skeleton crows to get at some of them. I and the rest had taken to hitting the crows with a long hard stick, watching them burst to dust.

Each ear produced a few kernels of feed corn, and by dinnertime, after the hot sun had slid across the sky like an iron, there was barely enough to make a thick corn gruel, which barely fed everyone.

At dinner, as always, I counted heads. Yesterday there were two hundred and five. But today there was a birth, and two deaths from exhaustion. So the figure should be two hundred and four.

We gather humans as we go. Without the murders we would have doubled our number by now. But if Margaret Gray does not get allegiance, and quickly, the newcomers do not live. The double executions have become standard, and expected, as have the spies, and Margaret's squads of police. When even the police became too zealous, they, too, are subject to Margaret's whims and likely to die.

Four times I have tried to escape, once when we were still in Pennsylvania, making it as far as thirty miles away, stowed in the back of an unknowing Amish skeleton's wagon. For two days I felt the taste of freedom, until Margaret herself found me with a bodyguard of ten. The Amish farmer was turned to dust, begging for his second life on his knees. Margaret administered the gunshot herself. I was taken back in chains.

The chains stayed on me for three days, until I was allowed to go back to work with the others.

Mostly I am shunned, and work alone. Those who try to get close to me have learned that sooner or later it is not a good idea. Margaret Gray comes to think that conspiracy is in the air. Execution cannot be far behind.

"The child belongs to God," she has said of me, and since she thinks of herself as the agent of God, what she means, in effect, is that I belong to her.

I think of my mother all the time. I feel so lonely I want to cry. Yet at the same time I feel that something special is happening to me, just as my mother said it would. Inside, I feel as if I'm opening like a flower.

Margaret Gray hates me, but is also afraid of me. I have become the center of her religious madness. In one sense she reveres me. But this does not exclude me from abuse or from work. Margaret herself has said that no harm will come to me, yet she has not refrained from beating me publicly. There is a rage in her eyes that never dies, and sometimes she looks on me with a kind of hatred that frightens me horribly. But always she holds herself in check, pronounces me "chosen," and no great harm comes to me.

"No matter what, you will be preserved," she says, though I sense she hates saying the words.

In Pennsylvania we started with twenty, and our numbers grew as we progressed. It was as if whatever humans crossed our path naturally gravitated toward us. Margaret did not have to root them out; as we passed through a seemingly abandoned, burning town, the legacy of General Lee's march west, a cellar door would creak open, or a hidden trapdoor would rise, and one or two emaciated human beings would crawl out and join our number. Some proclaimed us their salvation. Many were mad already, ripe for Margaret's teachings and rule.

Those that resisted were executed.

There is no doubt that what Margaret has done is brilliant. She is never without a radio. In each town we first scour for radios and batteries. She then listens with rabid concentration to the local and national news stations, all run by skeletons now, which have unwittingly told us how to proceed. Soon the pattern of the government's campaign became clear. All across the country humans were being choked off and driven south and north toward the center line from New York to California. From the east Lee was plowing westward as the remnants were forced toward his massive army. So Margaret merely held us back, followed well behind Lee, picking up the stragglers, keeping Lee's huge force two hundred miles in front of us.

It worked. We encountered little resistance and avoided those towns that had been quickly resettled with skeletons. We traveled by bus and other transport when possible, abandoning our vehicles when they were spotted and hiding in the hills, scattering and then regrouping again when the crisis was over. Always the radio kept us informed of our own progress.

And slowly our numbers grew.

Although—when I finished counting heads tonight, I came up with only two hundred and two.

I learned later that a man and woman tried to escape earlier in the day, were hunted down and double-executed.

That night Margaret Gray commanded me to lie on

my sleeping pallet in her tent, as she lay rigidly on her cot.

"Sleep," she commanded.

2

When we crossed into Nebraska two days later, Margaret decided that since the last day of summer was near and the harvest moon coming, there would be a celebration.

"For the glory of God," she said.

This was like a release. All of the tension of the last weeks, the constant pressure and fear, was channeled into this event. We were still in corn country, so a harvest feast was planned. Costumes were made for the children from dried corn stalks. The women wore dried cornflowers in their hair. Harvest moon was two days away.

The radio, as if in agreement with our wishes, informed us that there were no troops within two hundred and fifty miles. Ahead of us Lee was pressing westward with rapid speed. The nearest town was forty miles away. We had the sky and hills and corn-filled valleys to ourselves.

The day before the harvest moon we found a haven of sorts. Over a rise we found ourselves confronted with unpicked corn as far as the eye could see.

"A deliverance, from God," Margaret said, raising her hand in blessing.

The fields were ripe. We had never eaten this well. That day the harvest was a happy one, with songs sung and the mounting pile of corn a blessing in the warm sun. Even the skeletal crows were absent. Late in the day we saw the majestic sight of a real hawk circling high overhead.

When the moon rose fat the following night, all was ready. Margaret had decreed that a bonfire could be built. There was dancing, and songs. Then the eating began: corn bread and corn biscuits and corn soup, a bounty of everything. I heard more than one "praise God" and "amen." The little children ran around the bonfire, throwing sticks into it and watching them pop.

As the moon climbed above us Margaret called us to sit. She stood before the fire, with me next to her. Her hand holding my arm dug into me like a claw. All day I had sensed some inner battle taking place within her.

The moon haloed our backs. Crackling sparks shot into the air.

When Margaret finally spoke, it was as if she were tearing the words reluctantly from her soul.

"I can tell you now, my children," she said, her fingers tightening painfully on my arm, "that we are heading toward paradise."

Someone in the back shouted, "Amen!"

"We are heading for paradise, but I tell you that only one of us will see it. For God has commanded that the world be cleansed, and washed clean, so that paradise can come again!"

Again: "Amen!"

"This child," she said, nearly sobbing, pushing me forward for them all to see, "will be the one!"

Silence descended.

Margaret brought herself under control and shouted, "Though we may fall by the wayside, we will fall by God's grace, because the Lord has allowed us to share in His miracle. And this girl is His miracle! Though she does not speak, her life speaks in a multitude of tongues. Though we may look upon her, and see but a girl, she is a woman in God's eyes. And He has put her here to lead us *all* to His light."

"Amen!" And another: "Amen!"

"Hear me!" Margaret Gray said. "For I have had a *vision* from the God of all! *And He had said this girl is our salvation!*"

"*Amen! Amen!*"

"I have had the vision, too!" someone shouted.

"Yes, the dream!"

"Amen!"

"We will head west," Margaret said, "and then we will head north! All who oppose us will be crushed! For we have God as our protector! And God in my vision has shown me paradise." She looked at me, wildness in her eyes, and smiled madly. "And this," she said quietly, "is where the child must go."

"Hallelujah!"

Suddenly I was surrounded by wild faces—faces filled with faith. I was lifted on shoulders and danced around the bonfire. Margaret watched, smoldering with barely concealed rage, but allowed this to go on. Amid shouts of "amen!" and "God be praised!" I was carried aloft, held up.

When I was finally able to, I went off to sit out of the glare of the fire. The celebration went on for most of the night. There was liquor produced, which someone had made from corn. Remarkably, Margaret didn't stop its distribution.

Alone, I thought of my mother, and tears came into my eyes.

Not wanting to watch anymore, I went off and lay on my sleeping pallet. I could not sleep. Outside, the sounds of the revelers had become, if anything, louder. Through the half-open flat of the tent I saw the moon falling slowly toward the western horizon.

The tent flap opened. Margaret Gray stood there, outlined in dark light, tall, fierce, rigid.

Suddenly I became very afraid.

I pretended to be asleep, but watched her through lidded eyes. The silvery lowering moon behind Margaret Gray made her wild hair look like Medusa's mane. The look of vicious madness that had always been there in her eyes was magnified.

She walked slowly to my pallet and stood over me. For a long time she stared down at me. I felt something like electricity flowing from her. I could feel her hatred. I saw her hands flex tightly, the muscles straining, the fingers wanting to choke and rend.

Yet she did nothing.

Finally she gave a strangled, low cry of frustration.

"This is not right!" she hissed.

She bent down closer. She hesitated, then touched my cheek with one long, dry finger.

"So He chooses you, not me," she whispered.

She turned away, went back out into the night and the revelry.

That night the Silent Army of Humanity was born.

3

Humans seemed to know where we were and flocked to us. In twos and threes, as we skirted every bleak prairie town in Nebraska and then Wyoming and Idaho, they rose from their hiding places, traveling sometimes hundreds of miles north or south, and joined us. They were the ones the skeletons had missed, the clever or lucky ones. Like a magnet we drew them to us. Amazingly, the skeletons had not noticed. It was as if we were cloaked, so far behind the advancing skeleton armies that they were blind to us.

But we followed in their wake, and grew.

I became used to people staring, and their deference. No longer did I have to work. Margaret never forbade it. But when I tried to pick up a shovel or bend to pick corn or potatoes, one of the others would appear and, without speaking, take my work from my hands.

Eventually, so gradually that I never noticed, they stopped speaking around me.

Margaret Gray ceased speaking to me, too. She gave me her cot and took to sleeping on the ground pallet. In her sleep she would cry out and thrash from side to side as if in fever. Sometimes during the night she would awaken after these dreams. I would catch her staring at me, eyes wide and unblinking, her face covered with sweat.

In the morning when I awoke, she would still be lying there, eyes wide and staring.

Quickly, I would walk past her to avoid her gaze.

When I finally lost count, our numbers had grown to two thousand. More arrived each day. When we reached the outskirts of Boise, Idaho, our numbers were almost doubled in one day, by a group of nearly eighteen hundred who had come together and were waiting for us.

"We knew you'd come," their leader, a black man named Coine, said, addressing me, ignoring Margaret Gray. "We've dreamed about you."

Silently, taking from the land, acquiring weapons and vehicles as we went, and clothing for the coming cold weather, we moved west.

The new man, Coine, had been a colonel in the air force. Very soon he became Margaret Gray's military commander.

Margaret had changed. In the beginning she would have had Coine executed as a threat. But now she was willing not only to take his advice but to defer to him. She spent most of her time in her tent or wandering the borders of the army by herself.

And, as Margaret stepped back into the shadows, the army held itself together under Coine, and grew strong.

One night in our tent, as I pretended to sleep, Coine and Margaret talked. Coine was a tall man, with a hard face and eyes like stones. But he never raised his voice. The glow of a Coleman lantern lit and softened his features as he bent over a camp table where a map was spread out.

"There will come a time . . . *here,*" Coine said, pointing at the map, "where we will have them vulnerable. We've had indications for months that what Lee is going to do is pause at the California–Oregon border, then turn north. Before they turn is the time to hit them."

Margaret Gray nodded slowly, staring at the map.

"I have a dozen men who can handle what we need," Coine continued. "They were all stationed in Omaha when this started. They know how to work the overrides, and they can locate the codes."

Margaret said nothing.

"You do see, don't you?" Coine said, sounding exasperated. "If we can wipe out Lee, we really do have a chance." He rubbed his hand through his close-cropped hair. "I think it's our last one. If only we could hit Washington . . ."

Margaret looked over at him, looked back down at the map. She nodded.

"Then you approve?" Coine said.

She nodded again.

"Fine," Coine said. He rolled his map, stood. Through lidded eyes, I watched him staring at me.

"Strange girl," he said.

Margaret was staring at me, also.

Coine said, "I was in the air force for ten years. After that the sheriff's office in Topeka, Kansas, for ten more. I thought I was the toughest nut I ever met. But I look at that girl ..." He shook his head. "She makes me melt inside. I dreamed about her, so did most of the others. Everyone I talk to here keeps going, just because of her. She's ... I don't know. It's as if you don't feel like you have to talk around her. And the dreams, the feelings, are getting stronger. If she wasn't here ..." He waved his rolled map. "Well, I don't think any of us would bother."

Margaret kept glaring at me, even after Coine pushed his way through the tent flap and left.

4

Soon Colonel Coine was commanding the Silent Army of Humanity alone.

There was no coup. Margaret Gray merely left everything to him. She became a specter in the camp, seen at its edges, always alone, wrapped in a blanket like a cowl, staring at the sky. Her execution squads and spies seemed to melt into Coine's army and disappear.

Coine was a good leader. He organized the army into work details and training brigades. New men, mostly his own, were put into command.

The weather was growing colder, but because of Colonel Coine's good planning, there was warm clothing for everyone, plenty to eat, and shelters from the cold rains that had begun to sweep the plains. Confident, we marched mostly by day now. We had three scout helicopters, flown by pilots outfitted with specially made skeleton masks that looked real from three feet away. I still thought of my mother a lot, but she was becoming a vague memory to me now, a sadness tucked away in the corner of my heart.

Still, I felt myself changing. Sometimes, when I looked at my hand, I felt a tingle there, and almost imagined a glow. I had grown taller. Somewhere in the middle of this, I realized, I had had a birthday. I had turned sixteen.

I was comfortable with the silence of others around me.
It seemed right. As I walked the camp the children followed me, and I played with them. No one shunned me,
but I was accorded a kind of respect I became used to.

Our numbers swelled to ten thousand.

Everyone had a job. There were details that baked
bread in the open air, and those that mended blankets,
fixed trucks, and gathered fresh water. We were like a
moving hive. Margaret had abandoned her radios. But
Colonel Coine monitored them carefully. The shortwave bands told us that the battle in the rest of the world
was, essentially, over. Canadians who had joined us from
the north, Mexicans and Peruvians and Nicaraguans
from the south, told similar stories of the turning of the
human race.

Coine almost never consulted Margaret anymore.
He had taken to wearing an air-force uniform, open at
the neck. It was rare that he visited my tent. When he
did, it was mostly when I was alone and he thought I was
asleep. He stood in the open doorway, smoking a cigarette and regarding me. I did not have the horrible fear
around him I had when Margaret looked at me. In a way
his visits were comforting. They seemed to give him comfort, too.

One night, while Margaret sat on a nearby hill, wrapped in her silent blanket, staring at a starlit sky, Coine
came to my tent. He stood in the entryway and smoked his
cigarette. But this time, instead of leaving after finishing it, he came inside and closed the flap behind him.

He stood for a while, as if trying to make a decision.

Finally, when I opened my eyes and looked at him,
he strode forward, pulled a stool close to my bed, and sat
down.

"I shouldn't bother you," he said.

I looked at him, smiled, and he suddenly grinned.

"Those are the first words I've said to you since the
day I rolled in here. I haven't done it to be impolite."

He sat there, looking down at his hands.

"I haven't been this tongue-tied since I asked my
wife to marry me twenty years ago."

I waited. Finally he looked up. There was pain in his
eyes. The tall, straight man in charge, who showed only

strength around those he commanded, let himself show weakness.

"I feel like a fool doing this."

I reached out, put my hand on his.

"I had a daughter, and a son," he said. "My little girl was only fourteen. They were all lost to me the day this started."

I kept my hand on his.

His eyes became deep and haunted. "I prided myself my whole life on doing the right thing. They used to call me Straight Arrow. But God help me, what I had to do to my own family!"

He sat looking down.

"When I came home from the sheriff's office, the three of them had been turned. They tried to kill me! My own wife! My children! Since the day it happened, I haven't talked or even dared think about it.

"But there they were when I opened the door to my home, waiting for me in the living room, looking like . . . *that*. I'd prayed they were all right, called on God to spare them, because I knew we could get away, hide.

"When I walked in and saw them like that, sitting in the living room, turned to *bones*, I was stupid enough to think they could still be with us. The dining-room table had been set for dinner. I smelled steak overcooking in the broiler. My wife got up—I could *see* her shadow surrounding that skeleton—and she walked to the table and said calmly, 'Why don't you come and eat, Sam?'

"So I closed the door behind me and walked past my children, who looked at me with those eye sockets, and my wife, Janet, stood at the dining-room table, reached down to my place setting, and took the steak knife from next to my plate.

" 'We had a visit today from my mother, from over the cemetery,' she said, and then she lunged at me and tried to drive the steak knife into my chest!"

He put his hands over his eyes, as if trying to drive out the image.

"I *felt* her in my arms! I felt her cold flesh press into me as those *bones* thrashed at me and tried to stab me! Then my son and daughter held on to my back and tried to pull me down. *Oh, God*—if I close my eyes now, I can still feel them on my back, the coldness, the rub of their bones through the flesh, but just as if they were asking me for a piggyback ride. It was my own son and daughter, *but they were trying to kill me!*"

He took his hands from his eyes. He stared hollowly. "Then my son, Jeremy, put his arms around my neck—God!—and began to choke me.

"I tried to throw them off, drive them away. My wife got the knife partway into my chest. She drew blood. My daughter, Tracy, tried to get my service revolver out. She pulled it from its holster before I knocked it across the room. I pulled at Jeremy's arms, pried them loose, and threw him down."

Again he covered his eyes. "I watched his head hit the corner of a table. He opened his mouth to cry out and then turned to nothing!"

Colonel Coine stood up. He knocked the camp stool back. He kept his hands over his eyes, weeping. "God, how can I live with this!"

He looked down at me. His weeping subsided. He straightened the camp stool and sat back down.

"I pushed my wife away from me," he said hollowly, "and she dropped the knife. Tracy picked it up and drove it into my leg.

"At that moment I almost let them have me. Janet had crawled to the dining-room table, gotten another steak knife, and was stumbling back toward me. Tracy yanked the knife from my leg. I felt hot, searing pain. Then I thought, Let me be with them. I thought that if I let them have me, then I would be with them and they would love me again as I still loved them.

"But instead I . . . *nooooooooooo. . .*"

He put his hands back to his face, covered his eyes, sought to grind the memories out. His knuckles turned white as his fingers dug into the flesh around his eyes. "Oh, Christ, how can I live with this!"

I put both of my hands over his.

"Oh, God . . ."

In a moment the fierce strength had left his hands. He let them fall open.

"I . . . pushed them back away from me and threw myself across the room. I retrieved my service revolver and brought it up"—he hesitated, as if surprised that he was actually saying this——"and I shot my wife and daughter, and watched them turn to dust."

He sat silently in his chair.

"I've said it. I've said what I did. I don't know what kind of man I was then. But I even stayed in that house that night. Outside, the streets were alive with skeletons and screaming. I stayed in my house, locked myself in my own cellar. I sat in a corner with my revolver on my knees and covered my ears. When I got up, it was daylight. I almost put the gun to my mouth and pulled the trigger.

"Almost . . ." he said. "I stayed barricaded in the cellar for two days. No one bothered me. For two days I wept and tried to blot out the memories of what I had done. By the end of the second day I was sitting in the corner, my knees pulled up, the barrel of my service revolver in my mouth, willing myself to pull the trigger.

"But I didn't." He looked at me. "And that night when I slept, I dreamed of you. You were just standing there, unspeaking, staring at me in my dream. And for some reason that made me feel better."

He looked at me hard. "And the next morning, it wasn't so bad. I discovered I could live with myself after all. I unlocked my cellar door and found a few others who had made it through the last two days. We stayed together, and hid, and fought. Some of us died, but slowly our numbers grew.

"And all the while I had dreams with you in them. I felt you were guiding me in some way. Showing me where to go. Whenever it got so bad that I wanted to die, you would be there in my dreams. The dreams have gotten deeper, more detailed. Margaret's had the same kind of dreams. Only she calls them visions. Many of the others have had them, too. I don't know what they are."

His tears had dried. His face was hard-edged again. He learned forward and looked deep into my eyes.

"In my dreams you already know me. I have to tell you this. A long time ago, before I was married, when I was first in the air force, I met a woman. I stayed with her for one night. She was seventeen, and I was only nineteen. Her name was Beth.

"I'm your father, Claire. My dreams told me that."

He waited for my reaction. But I had none. Something deep within me, in the opening flower, had already known this.

"I never knew about you. If I had known, I would have done everything I could to make you happy."

I smiled.

"Now my dreams have brought me to you. Whatever they are, I know they're right. We have to fight for you. If we have to die for you, we'll do that. My own men took a vow a long time ago to do what we had to because we believe you're the only chance the human race has now. In my dreams I saw you traveling with Beth. She must have been a very special person."

I nodded, tears coming into my eyes.

He gave a short laugh, looking down at my hand and at himself on his knees. "I feel like a knight, with his queen!"

I smiled.

He stood up, straightened himself. Again he looked tall and hard-edged.

He stopped at the entrance to the tent and spoke again. "There were some very hard decisions I had to make, Claire. I've made them. Also, I don't completely trust Margaret Gray. I don't know how she'll react to this plan of mine. She's been acting ... strangely. I've been told she's been meeting with some of her old execution-squad people. I don't like that, but there's not much I can do. A lot of people here would still follow her, I'm afraid. I'd arrest her, but that would only start a riot and split the army." He smiled. "Your dad is trying to pull off a high-wire act, Claire. Would you keep your fingers crossed for me?"

I nodded.

His smile widened. "Good."

Opening the tent flap quickly, he left, ramrod straight, walking out into the night.

* * *

5

The humans continued to come down from the hills, from out of their earth-built shelters, to join our army.

When we crossed the Snake River into Oregon, they flowed to us like rivers to a sea. Their stories were the same. They had hidden in their mountains, in their valleys, near lakes and in the woods, and when they knew it was time, they came. Some caught up from behind. Some had come by boat, landing in San Francisco Bay from Australia, continuing by foot eastward, avoiding Lee's army. There was one story of a crashed plane in the California desert, fourteen survivors hiking north, living on a teaspoon of water a day.

The Silent Army of Humanity now numbered fifty thousand.

A place was made for all of them. My father, Sam Coine, moved with confidence. Margaret Gray, meanwhile, became more remote, moving from my tent to sleep alone under the night skies, hiding her face beneath her hooded blanket. The reports of her meetings with her old spies and police, though, continued.

There came a rainy cold day when we caught up with one of Lee's straggling companys who had fallen behind, a force of three hundred skeletons camped near Malheur Lake. My father sought to skirt them, turning our army north, but we were spotted by a scouting party.

My father acted quickly. Five thousand soldiers were sent out. By the afternoon the skeletons had been surrounded and obliterated. With relief my father discovered they had had no radio equipment. Apparently, they had been deserters.

We added their equipment to our own.

The next day, at noon, my father announced his plan on the shores of the lake. The sun had come out. Early winter was in the air. Someone had gathered early chestnuts, and their nutty fragrance wafted through the assembly. A breeze made ripples on the surface of the lake.

My father stood on the back of a truck bed, its gate down. He wore his uniform. Into a microphone he said: "We are very close to a great battle—perhaps the greatest humanity has ever joined. But I know you will do well. Because that battle may decide whether humanity lives or perishes from the face of the earth."

He paused.

"I have decided," he went on, "not to use tactical nuclear weapons as had been planned. This would be a mistake. Also, it would leave us a legacy that the human race does not want to bear. Also," he added, smiling, "it isn't necessary.

"General Lee's army is now camped two hundred miles to the west, near Grants Pass. I find this ironic. It is also where we will engage them.

"Our intelligence tells us that the army will stay there for the next three days. At the dawn of the third day we will attack with a force of thirty thousand. We will not attempt to wipe out Lee's army, but will keep him occupied while the rest of our force, including another ten thousand soldiers and all of our civilians, head north at high speed into the state of Washington and then on to Vancouver. Behind them, units of the army will peel off and hold at bay any of Lee's contingent that is able to follow.

"With luck—"

"No. We will *burn* them!" Margaret Gray's voice said.

She appeared near the bed of the truck and threw her cowl back. She pointed a thin finger at my father. Her face was gaunt, weathered, wrinkled flesh pulled back to show more starkly the madness of her eyes.

My father made a motion for her to be removed. But instead, four burly soldiers climbed up onto the bed of the truck and held my father while he was put into chains.

Margaret Gray climbed up onto the truck while my father was led down. She smiled grimly at him.

"We will *burn* them!" Margaret shouted, throwing her hands up. "The wrath of the Lord will fall on them from heaven! It is now that this false prophet"—she pointed at my father, who stood tall and silent between two guards—"shall be removed from our sight! We have the means to rain *death* upon those who would bring us death, and we will use it!"

A group of soldiers in front stood and brought their

weapons up. Immediately a line of men appeared from behind the truck and joined Margaret's ranks.

"Kill them!" she commanded.

Margaret's men fired on the loyal troops.

"Twice!"

As the soldiers began to turn, Margaret's soldiers fired again, dropping them to dust.

More of Margaret's force appeared. Soon it had surrounded the assembly. From within the circle large groups of soldiers rose to join her.

A small contingent of wavering soldiers was left behind. Reluctantly, they, too, joined her ranks, under force of arms by their comrades. Those who didn't were shot, and shot again.

My father shouted, "This is insanity! If you let her use nuclear weapons, Lee will follow you north and obliterate you!"

Margaret Gray turned to him. "They will burn. And in the morning *you* will burn." She turned, pointed to me. *"And so will you."*

She held her hands up high above the silent crowd. She shouted, "For *I* am the one God has chosen! *I* am the one who will lead all of you to His light! This girl would have led you to death! Your dreams of her are false! Reject them! God has given *me* a *new* vision! It is *I* who will save you!"

"Yes!" someone shouted.

"Amen!"

Soon a cheer had roared through the crowd and taken them over, and amid the wild adulation in their eyes for Margaret Gray, my father and I were dragged off.

6

That night, as wild, drunken, mad celebration swept through the Silent Army of Humanity, my father and I watched the pyres on which we would be burned being built. They were tall masts built to huge rafts, surrounded by a pyramid of dry wood and straw.

"They're all mad," my father said. "If they realized

what they're doing, they would stop now. Margaret Gray is a witch. She'll lead them straight to hell."

They had tied us to a tree, sitting side by side. We had not been fed. Occasionally someone would wander by to hurl insults at us. Some of these were the same people who had treated my father and me with so much respect not a day before. Now a true fever had taken hold of them, a possession from which they might never waken.

"Die!" a small child shouted. He was one of the ones I had played with, a boy with blond hair and deep blue eyes. His face was twisted into an ugly smirk. He picked a stone up, hurled it. It hit my cheek. There was a burning pain.

"Die, witches!" another child, a little girl not five years old, screamed, hurling another stone.

Our guard, a stout middle-aged man with a beard stubble that he continually rubbed, shooed the children away, laughing.

Leaning against a giant tree, the guard said matter-of-factly, "Me, I used to do this for a living. State penitentiary in Nevada. Lethal injection." His face was thick-featured. When he walked, it was almost in a waddle. Suddenly he looked at us, and the madness I expected to see in his eyes wasn't there. "You get to know," he said, rubbing at his thick stubble, "who's guilty and who's not. Most are guilty. It all comes out in the end." He laughed, looking away. "The *end.*"

My father and I looked toward the pyres being built. So did our guard.

"I'll be lighting those tomorrow," he said. "They were my idea, actually. Margaret Gray wanted something . . . exotic." He laughed. "I joined this army back in Illinois. Bet you never noticed me. I've been keeping a low profile. Don't like to get involved. But *this* job I just had to volunteer for."

Again he laughed. "Truth is," he said, his laughter trailing off, "I'm probably the only man left alive who can get you out of this."

My father and I looked at him.

His face was all seriousness. "Oh, yes. I'm not the only one. There is a small band, got wind of what Margaret Gray was going to do. She'd been lining up her people quietly for weeks. This bunch left this morning, before the ruckus. They're waiting about five miles north of here. Pretty well provisioned, too." He looked at my father. "You taught them well, Colonel."

"I'm listening," my father said.

"Thing is," the stout man went on, rubbing his stubble, "if this isn't done right, it won't make a damn bit of difference. I could cut you loose now. But I'd be dead myself in twenty minutes and Margaret Gray would track you down. She'd send the whole army against you if she had to. Specially that little girl, there. She's *very* afraid of that little girl.

"Way I see it, Colonel, when Margaret Gray attacks Lee with nukes in two days, he'll destroy her army where it stands using the air power he's got in California. I'm sure you were counting on that, since your idea all along was to use the bulk of our army as a feint, to draw everything toward it while the rest runs north."

"That's correct," my father said.

The stout man smiled. "I ain't so dumb. Army reserves, fourteen years. Nice way to get away from the pen on weekends. But what Margaret Gray will find is that while she vaporized a whole bunch of skeletons near Grants Pass, she signed her own death warrant, because there's plenty more skeletons to man those bombers and wipe her out where she squats. Even if she tries to run, by then it'll be too late."

The stout man looked straight at me. "Margaret Gray has forgotten the point. It's not to kill skeletons. It's to get this little girl up north, where she's got to go."

My father said nothing.

"Like I said"—the stout man laughed—"I ain't so dumb. It's just that most of these people here, they're scared. They don't want to die, and their dreams tell them they're going to. They'd rather listen to a nut like Margaret Gray, who tells them what they want to hear. Me, I started having dreams of my own, back in Illinois. There's something real special 'bout your little girl here."

"Yes," my father said.

The stout man scratched his stubble. "So anyway, here's what we do. Tomorrow I burn you up." He waddled closer. "Only you don't get burned. We put a big show, everybody cheers. Margaret Gray thinks you're dead, and we all do what has to be done. My name's Earl, by the way."

Again he stared at me.

"Dreams," he said.

7

So the next morning, as the sun was rising with a glow, we were burned at the stake.

There was a great show made of it. Earl had dressed himself in a robe and black hood. His eyes stared dully ahead. We were led from our tree to the shore of Malheur Lake. The tall masts of our pyres stood straight, their platforms on rolled logs waiting to be slid into the water after being set afire.

Margaret Gray watched dispassionately while we were led to the rafts. We were made to climb the tall ladders, to the top of the masts above a pyramid of kindling.

Earl followed me up the ladder, lashed my hands loosely behind me.

"Look down quickly," he said.

I looked down, saw the tunneled hole through the kindling he had fashioned, the hole through the raft beneath it.

"Remember what I told you," he said, squeezing my hand as he climbed down to repeat the procedure with my father.

When he was finished, he stood back. Margaret Gray mounted my pyre and held her hands up. All became quiet.

"This day," Margaret said, "begins the flowering of the new human race!" She gestured at me. "This *child*, who would have led us into death at the hand of this *man*,"—pointing now to my father, lashed atop his pyre—"will now be removed from us! They will be burned! Their bones will be burned!" Her voice rose up in a screech. *"My visions have told me that it is I who will lead you to victory and salvation!"*

A cheer rose. It swept out and back over the army.

Rifles were held aloft, fired. In the rear cannons boomed in salute.

"Let them *burn!*" Margaret Gray screamed, stepping down.

Earl scrambled onto my pyre with a lit taper. He touched it to the bottom of the kindling pile, looked up at me briefly.

He scrambled onto my father's pyre. He lit it, then jumped off as soldiers moved forward and pushed the pyres on their log rolls into the lake.

My pyre splashed into water and drifted lazily away from the shore.

The flames below licked out and around the base of wood. A wash of smoke drifted up over me. When it cleared away, I saw the shoreline choked with cheering soldiers, Margaret Gray among them, watching, arms folded. Earl stood beside her.

As smoke drifted over me again, I watched Earl turn away into the crowd.

My father shouted over to me, "Remember what he told you!"

Flames kicked up the pyre. Billows of smoke rolled up across me. The shrinking shore blinked into vision, was lost in haze. I checked my bonds.

I slipped one hand from the rope, then the other. My feet were loose enough to kick their bonds away. I stood holding the mast, supported by the sticks below my feet. The smoke made me cough.

"Wait until the flames climb high enough to feel the heat!" my father said, choking the words out.

I looked down. Fire had crept halfway up the pyre, jumping from one crackling stick to the next. The hole below me was now filled with rolling smoke. For a horrible instant I had the feeling that the hole was gone, that when I dropped them, sticks would hold me in place while fire trapped me.

"Soon!" my father coughed.

The smoke cleared in front of me. The shore was far off. I heard distant shouts of "Burn! Burn!"

A fire tongue licked at my feet.

"Now, Claire!" my father shouted.

I let go of the mast behind me. I kicked my feet out,

covered my face with my hands, closed my eyes, and dropped.

Sticks scraped at my arms and legs. I gagged on smoke.

For a moment I felt felt suspended.

Then the water hit me. I dropped down below the surface of the lake.

I opened my eyes. Above me the raft bobbed. I kicked out and away from it.

My lungs aching for air, I rose to the surface, put my head up.

I was behind the raft, where I should be. The shore was far away.

To one side I watched my father kick to the surface, wave, and dive back into the water.

I followed.

We swam, leaving the shore far behind, and headed for the distant shore.

8

Listening to the faint, far sounds of cheering, we watched our pyres burn in the middle of the lake.

Black roils of smoke corkscrewed into the sky. The pyres burned furiously, the masts wrapped in fire and smoke.

"Just about now, we should be dying for the second time," my father said. "Are you all right, Claire?"

We lay on the distant bank. My father examined me for cuts and bruises. I had scrapes on my arms, but nothing more. My father had a gash on one leg, and a bruise where he had hit the edge of the hole going into the water. Other than that, he was unhurt.

My father got up. I followed him into the woods, where, back in the trees, marked near the shore where Earl had told us it would be, we found clothing, packs filled with food and supplies, and two bedrolls.

"Earl did his work well," my father said.

After mounting his pack and helping me with mine, my father gave a last look to the Army of Humanity across the lake.

"They'll be destroyed, you know," he said sadly. Then we turned away, heading north.

A skeleton patrol, possibly another group of deserters from Lee's army, crossed our path in late afternoon. They had taken control of a small town nestled between two stands of pine forest. All were obviously drunk. A line of cars stood at the entrance to the town, and two by two, drunken skeletons were racing them up the town's single street. A single stoplight was their starting line. As we watched, a Dodge Caravan and Plymouth Voyager were on the starting line, waiting for the light to turn green. When it did so, amid whoops and laughter, the two vans sped off. They slowly gained speed. At the opposite end of the street, a pile of junked cars attested to finished races. The two cars were even, then the Dodge van pulled ahead. Suddenly, the Voyager began to swerve. It slapped into the side of the Dodge. The two cars separated. The sliding door in the side of the Dodge flew back. A skeleton was thrown out. He spun, hit the ground, flew into dust.

"Whoa!" The drunk spectators laughed. The Voyager roared ahead. The Dodge braked wildly, hitting and jumping the curb. It crashed into the front of a country store.

The Voyager passed the finish line, and braked to a screeching halt. The driver jumped out, climbed atop his van and threw his hands into the air.

The spectators shouted, laughing, and then two more cars, station wagons, pulled up to the starting line.

We skirted the town, walked on.

That night we stayed in an abandoned motel, near a deserted highway. The keys were all neatly hung on a pegboard in the open office. We picked the second-to-last cabin. My father took all the keys, threw them in a drawer except for the one we were using.

"Doesn't look like anyone's been here for a while, but we won't take any chances with someone checking up on us," he said.

It felt good to lie in a bed. My father tried the television in the motel room; only one channel was on, showing cartoons. Later on, before we slept, there was a short

news program, a skeletal announcer talking about reports of imminent action against the humans in the
northwest.

"It is believed," the announcer said, "that the last
large human army is massing for battle. President Lincoln has stated that if this battle is won, the war will, effectively, be over, except for mop-up operations in Alaska.
Now in sports . . ."

My father turned off the television.

We slept.

Early the next morning we moved on. In the next
small town, two miles north of the motel, we found what
we wanted. In a Jeep showroom, partially wrecked, its
front window caved in, sat a 4x4, its tank half-filled with
fuel.

"With this we can stay off the roads," my father said.

The keys were in a cubicle desk near the front of the
showroom. We climbed in. The truck started up immediately.

My father smiled, putting the Jeep into gear.

We climbed over broken glass, through the front
window, and out onto the street.

A skeleton patrol pulled out onto the street in front
of us.

My father killed the engine.

"Down, Claire," he said, pushing me down into the
seat and crouching beside me.

We heard the trucks roll past, moving east, for what
seemed like an hour.

Finally it was quiet outside.

We put our heads up. The last of the patrol was pulling away from us.

"They're heading for Margaret Gray . . ." my father
began.

I heard a sound. When I turned, there was a skeleton soldier, just stepping out of a store, a bag of food
clutched in his hand. An open package of cupcakes was
held halfway to his mouth.

He stopped, stared straight at me.

Next to me my father had vanished.

I froze, looked at the soldier. Slowly, he put the food

down. He stood up straight. Behind him I saw his truck parked next to the store.

"Well, well," he said. "I ain't seen one of *you* people in weeks," he said. He put his hand to his gunbelt. "Might even come in handy."

My father appeared behind him. He caught the soldier from behind in a choke hold.

In a moment there was dust where the soldier had been.

"We've got to be a little more careful," my father said.

We checked the soldier's truck. We found a storehouse of weapons. My father took rifles, a mortar, an antitank weapon, ammunition, loaded them into the 4x4, and we drove off.

At a gasoline station at the edge of town we found four large drums, filled them with gas, and added them to our supplies.

"Into the woods we go, Claire," my father said, pulling off the road.

It was hard riding. There were trails, though, and occasionally a dirt road that felt like smooth pavement in comparison.

In late afternoon we broke out of the woods on a high ridge. My father killed the engine and we got out. There, in a valley below us, was a huge army of skeletons, breaking camp.

"There must be fifty thousand of them," my father said.

Long caissons were rolling out of the valley eastward. The rest were of the camp was packing up. It was an awesome sight, rows of tanks grinding into gear, hundreds of trucks, howitzers, cannons.

"That explains it," my father said. "That group we met before was an advance party. They must have found Margaret Gray."

Below, in the largest tent, a tall figure stepped out to survey the scene. We were not close. But his shroud of features showed a white beard, trimmed close.

"That's Lee," my father said.

A squadron of fighter planes roared overhead in salute, followed by five helicopters cutting the sky. Lee watched them. He turned to look at the snaking line of trucks heading out. Then he ducked back into his tent.

"We've got to get as far away from here as possible, Claire," my father said.

We went back to our 4x4 and turned north.

9

That night, two hundred miles farther north, just over the Columbia River into the state of Washington, we found another motel to stay in.

"Kind of getting used to this good living, you know, Claire?" my father said, smiling. Another abandoned town sat nearby. The television showed Lincoln ending a meeting with his cabinet, an unresponsive secretary of war refusing to answer reporters' questions.

On the way out of the room Lincoln said simply, "Soon, God willing, we will know."

After that the station went off the air.

I slept badly. In the middle of the night I awoke. My father was sitting by the window, staring out. He had such a sad, lonely look on his face that I climbed out of bed, walked to him, and put my hand on his shoulder.

He looked around at me. "It's a sad world now, isn't it, Claire?" he said.

I nodded.

He turned to look outside again.

Abruptly, the world outside flashed to brilliance.

My father cursed. He put his hand over my eyes, threw me to the floor. I had just seen a hint of its outline: a huge cloud, climbing and spreading, roiling out at its head, caught in flashbulb light.

My father held me down. He counted seconds. At twenty there was a boom. The walls of the motel shook. A wave of trembling thunder passed over us.

"My God, that bitch did it," my father said.

Ten minutes later there came another brilliant flash of light. Again my father counted, and at twenty there was a boom and rush of air.

"Sixty miles away," my father said. "Thank God, we can see it and feel it, but it won't hurt us."

A half hour later, there came a third.

Then, silence.

"Stay down, Claire."

My father crawled to the television and turned it on. The picture grew into a scene of a distant helicopter shot, a climbing mushroom cloud, a brilliantly illuminated landscape below in greenish light. The mushroom hung in the air lazily.

". . . and this third explosion"—a frantic voice spoke, over the sounds of the copter—"ten miles away, this one landing in the middle of Lee's third regiment, obliterating it. The earlier two, as we have said, fell short and long. The first destroyed the abandoned town of Harvard, Oregon, the second hit a mill and industrial park, empty for the evening. These are ten-megaton bombs, tactical nuclear weapons. Washington now estimates that the humans were able to get their hands on three, possibly four or even five of these devices. They were taken from the Rocky Flats facility near Omaha, two weeks ago. Up until this time it was not believed that the human army had the manpower, the know-how, or the will to use them. As we said, these nuclear bombs are ten—"

The copter view shook. The voice became even louder, more frantic. "There is . . . another explosion! Off to our right! Get the camera there, get the . . . *my God, look at that!*"

The camera swung wildly. It turned right into the light of the rising explosion. The copter veered away amid shouts from the cameraman, the reporter. "We believe—oh!"

The light brightened. Outside our motel the sky flashed, followed twenty seconds later by a rumble. The television picture cut away to a skeleton at a news desk.

"We have lost our picture from the sight of the fourth nuclear explosion during this great battle." The skeleton put a hand to its ear, listening to the earphone there. "This in, let's switch to Fox Madlin, at the Pentagon."

The picture switched, a skeleton stared right, then turned to the camera.

"This is Fox Madlin, and I've just been told by General Winfield Scott, head of the joint chiefs of staff, that the fourth nuclear explosion came from within the enemy camp itself. That is, it is believed that the fourth nuclear explosion occurred within the human army, as it was firing the missile. I'm told that this was a distinct possibility, that if the warhead was armed incorrectly, or the missile fired incorrectly, the nuclear bomb could go off as the missile was fired. If this is so, then it would seem that most, if not all, of the so-called Army of Humanity has been . . . wait a moment. . . ."

A skeleton appeared in the picture next to the newsman. His vague shroud showed an old cavernous face topped by a huge military hat of 1800s vintage.

Fox Madlin looked into the camera. "We have General Scott with us—"

"It's over," General Scott said bluntly. "I have informed the president. The Army of Humanity has been totally destroyed. There is one more operation in Alaska to be carried out, which I am unable to talk about at the moment, and then—"

The television picture switched suddenly. The original newscaster's voice returned.

"We now have pictures. . . ."

On the screen, a shot from a helicopter, and the helicopter newsman's voice, less frantic, now.

"I do believe . . . yes, are we on? Hello, this is Ralph Bagler, in the air over the sight of the fourth explosion." He laughed. "I have to say we thought we were dust for a few moments there."

Below, a huge crater was surrounded by a familiar landscape: the shore of Malheur Lake. The crater lipped the lake itself. Water was making the crater a shallow lake of its own.

"I believe we have pictures on the ground."

The picture switched again. Now a bouncy camera showed a line of skeletons being helped up from the lip of a great hole. Again, Malheur Lake could be seen in the background, floating with debris and dust.

A microphone was thrust into the face of the nearest skeleton.

"How does it feel to be turned?" a newsman's voice said.

The skeleton looked stunned. "Huh? Oh, fine. After getting blown up by a nuke, anything at all is fine."

The newsman chuckled. "Pretty rough, eh?"

The skeleton shrugged. "Doesn't matter now. We took care of the bastards who got us into this."

"What do you mean?" The microphone was thrust in closer.

The skeleton grinned. "Some crazy woman and her bunch. I'm pretty sure we dusted 'em all. Kept raving about the new birth of humanity and all that." The skeleton shook his head. "No way, José."

"Are you afraid of the long-term effects of radiation?"

The skeleton laughed. "When you're already dead, what the hell's the difference?"

"All right, thank you."

The microphone moved to the next skeleton climbing out of the hole. "And what do you think, ma'am?"

My father switched off the television. "So that's it," he said sadly. "Get some sleep, Claire. We'll be heading north again in the morning."

He watched me go back to bed. "Good night," he said.

Later on I woke out of sleep again, to see him once more at the window, staring sadly out into the lengthening night.

10

In the morning, when I awoke, I thought the room was filled with smoke. I could not see. My eyes registered nothing but vague, indistinct light. When I sat up in bed and rubbed my eyes, the indistinctness gradually faded and I could see.

My father still sat in the chair by the window, with his head in his hands. I thought he was asleep. Instead, when I got out of bed, he lifted his head and said, "I'm blind, Claire. Last night, that first explosion did it. It happened about three hours ago. I've been waiting to see if my sight would come back, but it hasn't."

He stared at me, sightless.

I went and held him.

"Are your eyes all right?" he asked.

I squeezed his hand in answer.

"Good. You're going to have a big job now, Claire."

We ate, drank water, and packed.

Outside, in the 4x4, my father tried to teach me how to drive. But I couldn't. The shifting was too difficult.

"On foot, then," my father said.

We set out, walking in the service lane of the highway, and headed north.

At midday we were passed by a few vehicles manned by skeletons. My father heard them before I did. We easily hid off the side of the road.

"We're going to have to pray for luck, Claire," my father said.

Around noon another car moved toward us from the distance. My father once more warned that we should get off the road. But this one stopped up the road, pulled onto the far shoulder.

A human man got out, humming to himself, looking from side to side. He walked quickly to the far shoulder to relieve himself.

I squeezed my father's hand.

"What is it?" he asked. "Squeeze my hand again if it's a human."

I squeezed his hand.

"Stay close to me."

We climbed out of the hole. I maneuvered my father across the highway toward the man, who was just zipping up his pants.

The man stopped humming, spun around, holding a gun.

"Well, I'll be—" he said.

"Hello," my father said. "We're—"

"I know what the hell you are," the man said. He grinned. "You're the first damned humans I've seen in ten days." He looked hard at me. "And I've seen *you* in my dreams."

He crossed the road and put his hand out. "Glad to—"

When my father didn't hold his hand out, he stopped, frowning. "What's the matter with him?" he said to me.

I looked at him.

My father said, "I can't see."

"And what's the matter with her?" the man asked.

"She doesn't speak."

The man turned, headed back toward his car.

My father said, "Wait!"

The man got into the car, started it up. My father ran forward a few steps, reached out blindly.

"Sorry, I can't—" the man said.

He pulled the car onto the road, sped ahead. Then suddenly he screeched to a halt.

He got out, stood for a moment looking back at us, grinning. "What's the matter, can't you take a joke?" he shouted at last.

My father and I walked to his car and climbed into the back seat, moving aside piles of black cardboard cartons and sample cases. The front seat next to the driver was covered with boxes, too. Cases covered a car phone mounted between the front seats.

The man drove off, fast, and said, "Sorry about the joke. Not very funny." He looked in the rearview mirror, grinned. "You didn't think I'd just leave you there, did you?"

"Yes," my father said.

The man laughed. "It worked! Really, I'm sorry, though. It was a rotten trick to pull. But I just couldn't help it. I've been doing nothing but running for months. Used to be a salesman. Costume jewelry, trinkets, novelties, that sort of crap. Washington, Oregon, Montana, Idaho, parts of Nevada, and northern California. I know every novelty shop and gewgaw joint in a fifth of the USA. One of the best joke shops is up in Seattle, down by the water in the underground market. Great stuff. Always bought a lot from me, too. Open one of those cases back there if you want. Help yourself."

I lifted a slim cardboard carton, started to open it.

"Uh-oh," the driver said. "Hold on."

He looked fiercely in the rearview mirror, swerved suddenly off the road, down to the service-road ditch.

"Just be real quiet for the next minute or so. I'd be grateful if you ducked down a little, too."

He lowered himself in the front seat. We did the same.

Above, I heard a roar and saw the tops of three vehicles fly past.

"Another few seconds, if you please," the salesman said. He counted to ten, then said, "All right! All clear!"

He turned on the engine, pulled the car back onto the highway.

I finished lifting the lid off the box. Inside were sections separated by cardboard fences, wells containing cellophane bags with red clown noses inside, others with blue-and-black noses. The noses were made of foam and had a slit to put them on.

"Go on, keep digging!" the salesman said from the front seat.

Another box contained jokes and tricks, squirting flowers, hand buzzers, snapping gum. Another was filled with plastic children's jewelry, tiny horse and flower charms; another was a box of gumballs.

"Fun stuff, eh?" the salesman said.

Once again he said, "Uh-oh," and darted down into the ditch. We ducked low in our seats.

When the salesman had pulled back onto the road, my father said, "Why are you taking the highways?"

The salesman looked in the rearview mirror. "That's easy to answer. At first I thought to myself, the back roads will be safer. But they're not. First of all only an idiot would drive at this point on a main road. So nobody's got time to look for an idiot. There's army skeletons combing the back roads looking for people like us. First few weeks of this I saw hundreds of them get caught that way. Second of all it doesn't matter much now, because there are hardly any humans left anymore, anyway. And third I know every hidey-hole between here and Vancouver, every cop speed trap, every road that gets traveled and by who. It's my job."

"Where are you planning on going?"

The salesman looked in the mirror. "Mind if we have names?" he said, jovially. "I'm Benny Sullivan. You're. . . ?"

"My name is Coine, and this is Claire," my father said.

The salesman nodded. "Pleased to meet you. To answer your question, I'm going to Coos Bay, where there's a steamer waiting to take me up to northern Canada. Then I'm going to live in the wildest part of the north I can find, and never look at a human or skeleton again."

"You can trust this steamer?" my father asked.

Sullivan guffawed. "Are you kidding? This boat's skippered by my oldest friend. This one's been running junk goods since day one from Taiwan, from the Philippines, from Japan in the old days when they were digging themselves out of World War Two and making great novelties and radios, cheap. We go back forty years. Hell, before this boat steamered trinkets, it ran tobacco from Cameroon, tea from Ceylon, skins from Vancouver. Knows every port from Turkey to Tijuana. Knows how to outrun any coast guard in the world, the ones that haven't been paid off. Skipper's a great character. You'll fall in love."

"How do you know this person isn't a skeleton?"

Sullivan said, with conviction, "I know."

"How?"

"You're a pushy one, for a hitchhiker, you know?" He sighed. "It's easy." He reached over, dug under the cardboard cartons between the seats, held up a carphone receiver.

"When you talk to skeletons, they're different than we are. They sound the same at first. But certain things piss them off. When you tell them you're human, they hit the goddamned ceiling, start foaming at the mouth. It's like they'd like to reach through the line, tear your head off where you sit."

He drove with one hand, hit some buttons on the phone. "Watch."

It buzzed a ring. Then an even voice said, "Hello."

"Jimmy boy, that you?"

There was silence on the other end of the line. Then the voice, a timbre lower, said, *"Sullivan."*

"Yeah, Jimmy, it's me! How're the old bones rattling, babe?"

"Are you still . . ."

"Yeah, Jimmy, still human. You like that sound of that word—*human*?"

There came a strangled sound on the other end. *"Where are you!"*

"Oh, we can't have that, can we, Jimmy? See you."

"I'll *kill*—"

Sullivan hung up the phone, cutting off the enraged voice. "See what I mean?" the salesman said to us. "Now, listen to *this* call."

Sullivan punched new numbers, waited while the phone rang.

"Hello?" a tentative voice said.

"Bert?"

"Benny, that you?" a gruff voice said.

"You bet, Bertie."

The gruff voice laughed. "How they hanging, Benny?"

"Just the way you like 'em."

The laughter continued. "You gonna make it or not? Tomorrow night, or I've got to leave you behind. You know I don't want to do that, Benny."

"I know you don't."

"Hell, I'm five miles out now as it is. Been boarded only twice this week, though. They're getting tired of finding nothing. Tell you the truth, I'm getting tired of hiding in that hold. Hell, Chub's been smelling bad as ever."

Sullivan laughed. "Chub! How is the old gorilla!"

"Fine, just fine. So when we gonna see you, boy?"

"'Bout sundown, I imagine. I'll call. And Bertie, hope you don't mind, but I've got a couple of guests."

There was a pause. "Oh?"

"They're all right, Bertie. Guy and his daughter. Human as they come."

"Well . . . hell, bring 'em along. We can always throw 'em to the sharks. Or sell 'em, right? 'Member Cancún, in sixty-eight?"

Sullivan laughed. "See you tomorrow, Bertie."

"You got a date, boy."

"Bye."

"G-bye, Benny."

Sullivan hung up the phone. "See what I mean?" he asked.

My father was silent for a moment. "You sure it will be all right for us to come along?"

Sullivan laughed. "You heard it, didn't you? What's the matter, don't trust me? Think I'm gonna sell you to the skeletons? Or worse? Wait'll you see Bertie's steamer. It's a mess! And wait'll you see Chub! Hoooeee! I'm telling you. . . ."

He looked in the mirror, smiled, shrugged. "Hey, don't worry about it," he said. "You can trust me. Besides"—he laughed—"what other choice do you have?"

11

Sullivan took a dizzying mix of back and main streets; one moment we were speeding down a deserted main highway; a moment later he made a veering turnoff and bounced us through a badly paved single-lane rut barely worthy of the name road. Only once did he stop, at a gasoline station in a barren landscape; pine trees dotted the near hills, but the bowl we had driven into seemed filled with rocks and dust.

"Bob Miller's place," Sullivan said, with a touch of sadness. He looked over the forlorn front of the gas station. "Thirty years ago, everybody in Millerton, just over the hills there, stopped here." He pointed to the crest of a knobby, pine-strewn rise under the lowering sun, "They named the town for one of Miller's relatives back in the eighteen hundreds. Bob had the first gas in the area. What became the garage was still a country store then. He always was a loner."

Sullivan pumped gas, scoured the dusty station with his eyes. "There," he said, pointing to two open holes just to the right of the garage. "He had his dogs buried there. I imagine there's an open hole up back, too, where his wife, Mary, was buried. I don't know, I wish them all well, in a way." He looked at us. "You know what I mean?

There's ... still part of 'em that's *us*. They were *us* before, and even though they're changed ..."

He shook his head, finished pumping the gas, put
the nozzle back into its holder, and we drove off.

When we reached it at nightfall, Coos Bay was shrouded
in fog.

"Bet you folks are hungry, eh?" Sullivan said. "We've
got a few minutes before Bertie needs us there. I know a
place."

He took us to a restaurant, at one time elegant. But
now its insides were churned up, broken chairs and tables everywhere, smashed glasses littering the floor. On
the wall hung undersea paintings that must have looked
wonderful in low light: drifting fans of sea grass, ranking
hills of alabaster coral, schools of darting sunfish. Now
there were stains on the walls, broken whiskey bottles behind the bar, a sour, damp smell.

"Hell," Sullivan said. "We'll eat something later, on
the boat."

We left the restaurant, and Sullivan was silent as we
drove through the fog-rolled streets.

He stopped. I waited for him to go on. Fog swirled
around the car, broke in clouds as it drifted into the
windshield. I tried to peer through it, find out where we
were, see what corner we had stopped on.

"This is it," Sullivan said.

I helped my father out of the car.

"I can smell the water," he said.

Sullivan said, "Keep your voice down." He leaned
into the car, hit the horn lightly, twice.

We heard nothing.

He repeated the tooting. Then we heard two low,
muffled, foghorn sounds in return.

"She's up the pier," Sullivan whispered.

We brought out equipment from the car. Sullivan
went to the trunk, brought out a battered suitcase. He
closed the trunk, looked into the front seat, rummaged
through the sample cases, brought one out, opened it,
pulled out a long rubber snake.

"Bertie *loves* these things," he said, coiling the snake

and putting it into his pocket. He looked wistfully at the rest of the merchandise in the car. "Too bad . . ."

He walked away, dropping his car keys on the pavement, leaving the car doors open, not looking back.

We followed.

Underfoot, suddenly, was deck planking. I heard the slap of waves against rock or pier below me. I led my father. I could barely see in front of me.

Suddenly Sullivan disappeared into fog. I walked on, feeling through the roiling cloud, leading my father, and bumped into a railing that abruptly ended. Bobbing out of the fog was the pointed bow of a ship, close-tied.

I stumbled back into Sullivan.

"Whoa, take it easy! You're liable to fall into the water!"

I held on to the back of his coat as we walked on.

Faintly, I heard humming. Then it was very close.

"Stand to, friend," a gruff voice said.

Sullivan stopped. "You've got it, Bertie."

"Just stand while I check you over," the gruff voice said.

Suddenly, out of the fog, came a length of skeletal hand, clutching forward—

"My God!" Sullivan gasped, jumping back, into my father and me.

"Ha-*ha!*" a voice cackled. "Got you, Sully! After all these years I finally got you!"

A massive figure leaped out of the fog at us. It was a woman, broad of girth, with an black oilcloth slicker whose hood was thrown back over her head. She was human, with a broad face, close-cropped hair.

She held up the plastic skeleton arm she gripped in her hand.

"You gave me this in eighty-two—don't you remember, Sully? Scared hell out of me, put it in my bed while I was playing cars on deck. Climbed *in* with the friggin' thing! Ha-*ha!* Got you back good with it, didn't I?"

Sullivan, who had begun to recover, nodded and grinned. "You got me back *real* good, Bertie." He took the rubber snake from his pocket, regarded it wistfully, then threw it into the water. "I won't even bother to try this one again, after that."

"Ha-*ha!*"

Sullivan introduced us. "This is Colonel Coine, and this is his daughter, Claire."

"So ..." Bertie examined us, keeping her eyes on me.

"She's the one, all right."

"What do you mean by that?" my father said.

"Been dreaming about her."

Bertie turned, melted into the fog. "Come on, Sully, you and your friends come on board."

We took a step after her, and there, suddenly, was a gangplank with rope handrails, leading to the solid deck of a ship. At the end Bertie waited for us. As soon as we passed onto the deck she dismounted the gangplank and pulled it in. She tramped off into the fog. We heard her mount steps, heard a door close. A moment later there was a *chunk* and a *wish* sound followed by a constant low hum. The ship moved.

"Say good-bye to land," Sullivan said, staring into the fog.

12

We stood a long time on the deck, waiting for Bertie to return. Finally we heard the slam of a door up in the fog again, a grunt, the sound of steps being negotiated.

"What the hell's wrong with you, Sully! Ain't you got no manners!"

Bertie appeared, kept walking past us, returned to the fog.

Sullivan, my father, and I followed.

We walked over dirty deck, around coils of rope, hooks, a mast. Finally we reached a hold. Somewhere I heard chirping, grunting sounds. Bertie took hold of the large door, hefted it up, and pushed it back until it fell with a thump.

"Down you go!" she said.

I peered down into the darkness. I saw nothing, smelled dampness.

"Sully, take 'em on down! I'll be with you shortly."

Bertie disappeared into fog.

Sullivan went down first. We followed. I walked carefully on the steps, my father behind me.

When Sullivan got to the bottom, he fumbled along a wall and hit a switch. Light flared.

What I saw was nothing like what I had imagined. We were in a cozy if cold stateroom, paneled and carpeted. On the walls were mariner's charts and prints of modern art. At the far wall, next to a small bar, nestled a couch fronted by a coffee table, sided by comfortable-looking chairs; in the middle of the room, under a hanging lamp, was a pool table, racked for play.

"Chilly down here!" Sully said. He walked to the thermostat on the wall, turned a knob.

Instantly, heat ticked up from baseboard heaters with electric coils.

I led my father to the couch and we sat down.

From above, Bertie's voice boomed down. "Get 'em somethin' t' eat and drink, Sully! There's beer in the fridge! I'll be down—got to check the autopilot!"

Sullivan walked behind the bar, produced two bottles of beer and a can of soda.

"Colonel, when was the last time you had a Carta Blanca?"

My father laughed. "I can't believe it. Is the rest of this room as comfortable as this couch?"

"You bet. Bertie likes her nice things. Earned 'em, too."

My father took the frosted beer, swallowed some. He shook his head. "And cold, too!"

Sullivan was already back behind the bar, laying out cold cuts from the refrigerator.

Soon we had eaten, more and better than we had in days. Bertie joined us.

"Get me one of them Mexican Millers, will you, Sully?"

He handed her a beer. She sat in a chair beside the couch. She drank from the bottle, made a satisfied sound.

"Best investment I ever made, hauling this stuff up from Azatlán." She grinned. "Never got to make that last delivery to San Diego, zoo animals *or* beer. So if you get thirsty, I've got two hundred more cases of the stuff."

My father laughed, a sound I hadn't heard him make since I had first seen him.

Bertie stared at her bottle. "Wouldn't be a bad way to ride all this out, too, locked in the hold with cold cases of beer . . ."

She looked up at me, stared. "So you're the dream girl."

"She doesn't talk," Sully said.

"She didn't talk in my dream, either," Bertie said. She kept her eyes on me.

"In mine I found her on the side of the road, just like I did," Sully said.

My father said, "I dreamed about her, too. That I would find her."

Bertie nodded solemnly. "What we got is a mystery. When I started having these dreams, 'bout a week after those skeletons started popping up, I asked around. I never had dreams like that before, ones that kept coming back. I asked Nate Sherman," she said to Sully, who nodded, "and Jimmy the Macedonian, who we lost just a week ago. I called anybody I could think of. When I called Pete the Greek—remember Pete the Greek, Sully?"

Sullivan laughed. "I remember him."

"He was skeleton when I reached him. Started screaming at me, hissing like a snake."

Sullivan shook his head.

"Anyway, nobody I talked to had these dreams. Least, not that they remembered. A couple of 'em, Charlie Franks for one, remembered vague things, a girl in the back of his dreams, and when I mentioned this to Nate and Jimmy, they remembered the same kind of things. Like someone watching in the back of their dreams. Sully was the only one who had started having the dreams with the girl in them, and his were even stronger than mine. Until a couple of days ago, when mine got even stronger."

"The night before I found Claire and the Colonel," Sullivan said, "when I was sleeping in the back of my car, I woke up and it was like she was standing right in front of me."

Bertie nodded. "That was the way I felt last night.

Like she was standing in front of me." Again she looked at me. "And now here she is."

Sullivan said, "Yep."

"I think it means somebody's on our side," Bertie said. She nodded her head with finality.

Sullivan said, "I don't know what it means. But it felt like the right thing, picking her up and bringing her here."

"Bringing her up north," Bertie said. "That's what I had to do in the dream, bring her up north."

Sullivan nodded.

My father said, "All the time we were fighting, I felt that the most important thing was to get Claire to a certain place. Even when I dreamed about her before I found her, I knew that I had to move her west across the country, then north."

Bertie and Sullivan were looking at me, waiting. I had nothing to give them. I knew inside that what had happened was what was meant to happen. But they looked at me as if waiting for a sign. I had none to give them.

"It's a mystery," Bertie said. She slapped her knees, getting up. "Well, it's time to get Chub his dinner." She looked at me. "Want to come along?"

My father said, "Well . . ."

Sully said, "Oh, let her go." He laughed. "I think they thought we were going to throw them over the side, sell them as white slaves."

Bertie laughed. "Still might do that! Come on," she said to me, "come and see Chub. You'll get a kick out of him. He likes youngsters."

She looked at Sully, who laughed, got up, and walked back around the bar. He uncapped two more Carta Blancas, came back, and put one in my father's hand. He leaned over, whispered something in my father's ear.

"Chub is *what!*"

Sully whispered some more.

My father said, "You can go along, Claire. But be careful!" He laughed along with Sully and Bertie.

Bertie led the way up the steps. Out into the fog we went again.

"Stay close, the deck's slippery," Bertie said.

We walked forward, amid the sounds of cackling and animal cries and chirps and growls, passing the tall cold metal walls of the wheelhouse. I nearly tripped over a coil of rope. Bertie grabbed and steadied me.

"Got to get your sea legs, Claire," she said.

There were more sounds around us, chitterings and squawks and cheeps. We passed very close to a crate with small holes in it and I heard what sounded like a pig's snort.

"Shut up, you guys!" Bertie shouted. "Chub'll take care of you tomorrow morning!"

The animal sounds increased, and Bertie laughed.

"Ate an hour ago and they're hungry again already," she said.

Near the bow of the ship was another hold. Bertie lifted and threw it back.

"Be careful climbing down," Bertie said, descending first into the darkness. "These steps are steep."

From below, came rumbling sounds.

"Pipe down, Chub, we're comin'!"

At the bottom of the steps Bertie stopped me. "Stand there."

In the darkness came the sound of a television set; I saw its low purple flicker at the far side of the room. It was angled so that I could just see part of the picture: one of the *Star Wars* movies. In front of the television, shadowed in its glow, was a tall, wide chair with its back to me.

From the chair came a grumbling complaint.

"All right, Chub, we're coming! Hold tight!"

Bertie found a light switch, threw it on. The hold was bathed in light.

The figure in the chair turned around to look at us.

"Chub! I brought a friend!" Bertie said.

A huge, African ape stood out of the chair, regarded me with its massive, intelligent dark eyes, then smiled from ear to ear.

"He likes you!" Bertie cried.

She rushed forward, took the ape in a hug, and danced him around. Chub followed her playful lead, but kept turning his head to look at me.

"So what you watching?" Bertie asked, stopping in front of the TV. "That space junk again?"

Chub looked away from me, made excited grunts at the screen.

"I know, I know." Bertie turned to me. "He loves that Princess Leia. Thinks he's Hans Solo or somethin'." She turned back to the ape, nuzzled his head. "Ain't that right, Chub?"

Chub made excited sounds, nudged Bertie out of the way as Princess Leia came onto the television screen, leading Skywalker and the Wookie down a corridor. Chub eased himself back into his chair and continued to watch.

Bertie waved a hand at the ape. "Keep an eye on him, will you? I'll get his dinner."

She crossed the room, unlocked a bolted door, and went into a far room.

Chub looked at me, then looked at Princess Leia on the television screen. He looked back and me and smiled, taking my hand.

The room was similar to Bertie's stateroom, and nearly as neat: carpeting on the floor, some prints, mostly movie posters, including one huge one of Darth Vader's masked head, on the paneled walls, a floor-to-ceiling bookshelf stuffed with children's books and videocassettes, some toys, a sleeping pallet, a small tray table.

When Princess Leia disappeared from the scene, Chub excitedly rummaged around his chair, produced a VCR remote, and rewound the tape until the previous scene was repeated.

"Found the big goon in Hawaii, on one of the smaller islands," Bertie said, returning with an armful of food—potato chips, a small canned ham, pickles. She locked the storage-room door behind her, put the food down on the tray table, began to prepare it. "He was just a baby. Some jackass movie producer had left him alone in a beach house for a week. He wrecked the place. When I was passing a mile offshore, I saw the bum beating Chub with a stick out on the beach. I almost shot the guy.

"Anyway," she continued, "I took a dinghy to shore, bartered Chub away, and he's been with me nearly fifteen

years. Smart as a whip. He could even pilot the boat if he
had to. And he's cleaner than any mate I ever had on
ship." She pointed to a door on the far side of the room
with a cutout sickle moon on it. "That's his bathroom.
He does all his business in there, just like you and me.
Watches movies when he's not working."

She finished with the food on the table, which Chub
eyed with interest, and carried the entire tray over to the
ape, putting it down in front of him.

He lost interest in me and the television and began
to eat.

"He'll be busy for a while," Bertie said. "Almost his
bedtime, anyway. Tomorrow I'll let him up on deck, you
can see him do his thing."

We went to the stairs, mounted them. I took a last
look at Chub. He had stopped eating to give me a close
look.

Up on deck Bertie closed the hatch and secured it.
The fog was even thicker. When we reached midships,
Bertie began to climb the steps to the wheelhouse.

"Come on up," she said. "Got to check the instruments."

I followed her into a snug, warm, half-circle-shaped
room bathed in green-and-red instrument light. I
watched while Bertie checked over her instruments,
made an adjustment.

"She's on autopilot. We shouldn't pass near anything
tonight. Got enough alarm bells rigged around this
bucket to go off if anyone comes within five miles."

Suddenly tired, I yawned.

"Somebody needs a good night's sleep. We'll get you
into a bunk below, little gal."

She put her arm around my shoulder, led me out of
the wheelhouse, back into the fog, down the steps.

At the hold door aft she paused.

"I imagine they're on the way to being good and
drunk down there by now. Good for 'em. I'll get their
stories later. I bet the two of 'em have had a hard time.
Bet you have, too."

Sleepily, I nodded.

"I just want to tell you one thing, between you and
me. Can you keep a secret?"

I looked at her, felt a sudden warm trust. I smiled and nodded.

"Good. Just wanted to tell you about those dreams of mine."

She paused.

"Damnedest thing, but I didn't want to worry anyone else. In the dream it was you and me and your father and Sully. 'Course at the time Sully was the only one I knew. But now we're all here. We were on this boat, and you looked at me, and I knew I was going to die.

"Funny thing is," Bertie went on, "the way it happened, it was all right. It wasn't scary or anything. Like it was supposed to be that way. You looked at me, and I knew that Sully and me and your father were just about the last humans on earth. And the three of us were going to die. And when I saw you get on the ship, it was like the dream came true. You looked at me, and I knew I was going to die. Somehow that didn't bother me."

She shook her head. "Just thought I'd tell you that. I'm not scared, and I have no intention of going down without a fight, but for some reason all of this just seems right. As long as you're safe, everything's gonna be just fine."

She put her hand on my shoulder, then opened the hold, with fog swirling around us like dreams.

"Time to get you some sleep, little gal."

13

The next morning the fog lifted, and Chub came up on deck.

"How do you like my little bucket of bolts?" Bertie asked jovially. "She's slow but who's in a hurry? Named her the *Arc* because I always seem to be carrying two of everything, including electrical equipment. Get it?"

The *Arc*, which proved to be brightly painted in red and green, and not the dull, dirty scow I had expected, was even more laden than I had thought, with cages, wooden crates, huge coils of rope and chains. Every free space on deck was covered with caged animals. Chub cavorted around, checking ropes, tugging them to make

sure they were tight. When he found one that had loosened, he called out in a loud, excited growl and Bertie
came to tighten it.

"All right!" Bertie shouted. "Time to eat!"

At once every animal on deck began to chatter and
cry. Some of the cages rocked with excitement. Chub,
who had already eaten his breakfast below, ran to the
open storage hold while Bertie climbed down, handing
food up to him.

"All right, Chub, do your thing!"

Chub sorted and distributed the food. "They love
'im!" Bertie cried. The noise level was overwhelming.
Gradually it diminished, as each cage and crate was dealt
the appropriate meal. Soon the *Arc* was almost quiet.

"Ah, peace," Bertie said. "It won't last five minutes,
but it's something to look forward to."

In less than five minutes it was over, but Bertie's expression of bliss didn't evaporate. I helped her and Chub
clean some of the cages. I admired the happy, sleek birds
and foxes and all the other animals within. There were
even two lions. By then it was time for the humans to eat
lunch. We went belowdecks, Chub back to his own quarters to watch a movie.

"You blowhards drinking again?" Bertie yelled good-
naturedly at my father and Sully, who were sitting on the
couch with open bottles of beer.

"Saving you a seat, gal," Sully said, getting up to get
Bertie her own beer. Bertie sat in Sully's vacated spot,
sighing contentedly.

"This is the life."

"Yes, it is," Sully said.

"Don't know about the rest of you, but I could stay
on this ship forever," my father said.

"If you could stand the smell!" Sully said.

"Hah!" Bertie said. "Smell indeed! Never mind the
animals, you three could use a change of clothing yourselves. We'll have to go through the forward hold later,
see if we can't find some of those Hawaiian tourist outfits
I was bringing to San Francisco."

These words cast a pall over the party. Sully said,
"Wonder what San Francisco is like now?"

Bertie said, "I skirted it about a week into this mess.

The Transamerica Pyramid was shot up, but Ghiardelli Square looked pretty intact. They . . . seemed to be going about business as usual."

Sully gave a weak grin. "You always said it was a *dead* town, Bertie!"

"Ha!"

"Actually, it was a great town," Sully said.

Bertie got up, took her beer to the bookcase, and turned on the radio there. "Might as well see what the world is up to."

The radio came on, a voice advertising chewing gum.

"What the hell they do with chewing gum?" Bertie said.

"Chew it," Sully said. "The bastards seem to have everything under control, don't they?"

"Different world . . ." Bertie said.

The commercial ended. A broadcaster's voice said, "And now a wrap-up of the top stories: The White House announced today that after consultation with foreign leaders, it can be stated with certainty that no more than a handful of humans are left. The United Nations Security Council, which began meeting again two weeks ago, concurs in this statement. President Lincoln, meanwhile, has been in closed-door meetings with NASA and top scientists, discussing an upcoming space shot. We have learned that a manned mission, termed 'very hazardous,' is being mounted. NASA insiders say a launch date will be set soon. In other news Mark Twain has caused something of a stir in book circles by calling the accidental-drowning death of Ernest Hemingway last week 'a fortuitous day for American Literature,' and 'no monumental loss.' Twain, whose comments were made from his Connecticut home where he lives with his wife and daughters, and where he is reportedly working on a sequel to *Huckleberry Finn*, went on to say, 'The dumb fellow took care of himself the first time around, and this time Providence was kind enough to lend a hand.' Hemingway was yanked from the rear deck chair of his boat last Tuesday when a giant pliosaur took the marlin bait from his trolling fishing line. Hemingway had boasted to friends on board that he didn't need to strap himself into the chair. In the world of sports the World Series *will* be played this year, albeit a little late. Baseball Commissioner Mountain Landis has announced that the series will start on November fourteenth—"

Bertie snapped off the radio.

My father said, "They going to find us, Bertie?"

She took her beer back to the couch, sat down. She was silent.

"I know the answer to that one," Sully said.

"Sully and I were talking, just before you came in," my father went on. "We both had an interesting dream last night."

Bertie looked from one to the other. "I had a dream, too. . . ." she said slowly. "There were some new parts in it."

My father said, "Yes . . ."

"When do you figure?" Bertie asked.

My father looked ahead sightlessly. "One day, maybe two."

Sully said, "Sounds about right."

Bertie got up, collected the empty beer bottles, and replaced them with fresh ones. "Drink up, mates. We've got planning to do."

My father said to me, "Claire, would you mind leaving us alone?"

Bertie put her hand on my shoulder. "Go on over and see Chub, darlin'," she said.

I got up and left.

14

Neither my father, nor Bertie, nor Sully told me what had been discussed in their meeting. But that same afternoon Bertie took me to Chub's food hold and turned on the light within. It was a small closet, four or five feet deep, with shelves stocked with packages of potato chips, canned hams, institutional-size cans of tuna, and other foods. Outside in the stateroom Chub sat watching *Return of the Jedi*, looking up to regard us now and again.

"Here's what you need to know," Bertie said. She

reached under the fourth shelf down from the top. "Look under here."

I stooped to look at a tiny switch.

"Hit this," Bertie said, "and watch what happens."

I hit the switch. The right-hand wall of the closet moved back and pulled aside. Musty cold air wafted out.

Bertie squeezed into the opening, fumbled around, hit another switch.

The interior of a small room was lit. There were wooden pallets on the floor, a couple of folded blankets, a crate to sit on. The far wall was the metallic inside hull of the *Arc*.

"It ain't much, but it's home if it's gotta be," Bertie said. "I hid Chub in here a couple times when the Coast Guard decided I shouldn't have a gorilla on board. Endangered species and all that. Most of the Coast Guard boys were all right about it, but one tightbutt from the port of Los Angeles decided he was going to run for office. He never did find Chub in here. Lost the election, too."

We had a partial view of Chub outside. He looked up at us, grinned widely.

Bertie said, "Had to ride in here with Chub myself in eighty-six, when I was boarded by pirates."

She watched my expression. "Oh, yes, there's still such a thing. Now they got high-tech speedboats, sonar, lots of big guns. Would have killed me if they found me. Instead, they just took every carton and beast on board. Even stole Chub's videocassette collection."

Outside, Chub made a grunting sound.

"So you listen to me good. When and if things start hopping around here, this room is where you run to." She showed me the switch on the wall, how to make the door close and open. "And don't you worry about your father, Sully, and me. We'll be in here with you, if we can."

We left the secret room. Chub was moving excitedly in his chair. Once again Princess Leia had appeared on the screen.

Bertie shook her head, patted Chub as we walked by. The ape smiled up at her, at me, looked back at the television, screeched with delight.

"Darn monkey," Bertie said.

15

The next day there was a little rain, but we still had clear sailing.

"We're just about . . . here," Bertie said, pointing to a chart in her stateroom. "Due west of Queen Charlotte Island. Good old Canada. Must have a lot of skeleton moose running around up here now. I had a moose on board, once. Dumber than a cow. You never saw so much dung in your life! Anyway," she continued, tracing her finger due west from that point, till she reached a thin line of islands strung out like tiny beads from the bottom of Alaska, "these here are the Aleutians, and *these,*" she said, isolating a section of the beads, "are the Fox Islands. That's where we make our turn north. Once we get there this ship could steer itself, right up the Bering Strait to Seward Peninsula. Just north of Nome, just west of this little protrusion here," she said, fingering the most western part of the Alaska mainland, "that's where we're going." She moved her finger over into the water between the two continents of Asia and North America. There was a little dot of land there. "There it is. Little Diomede Island. Right in the middle of the Bering Strait. Right smack in the middle of the West and East."

Sully, my father, and Bertie were looking at me. It was Bertie again who spoke. "This is what the dreams say, Claire. This is where you're supposed to go. Do you have any idea why?"

I shook my head.

"Well," Bertie said, "whatever it is, we'll get you there."

An alarm sounded in the room. All over the ship bells were going off, animals screeching.

"Uh-oh," Bertie said. "Looks like we've got company coming. That's the five-mile alarm. Let's see what we've got to deal with."

It was another beautiful day on deck, winds calm, the smoke from the *Arc*'s stacks rising straight up and drifting behind us as we chugged north. The sky was a deep, clear blue, the air cold, smelling of clean, deep water.

Bertie scanned the sky with binoculars, then the four horizons of the sea. The bells continued to sound.

"Better get up to the bridge. I don't like this at all. I don't see a damn thing."

We climbed up after her. It was a tight fit in the little wheelhouse.

Bertie studied her instruments. At night the green screens filled the wheelhouse with eerie light, but here at midday, with bright sunlight filling the tall windows, Bertie had to bend close, shielding her eyes to study the screens.

"Hell," she said, squinting. "Nothing in the air or on the surface. It's below us, but it's fairly small." She hit a switch. The alarm bells immediately went silent, leaving the screechings of the animals the only alarm. "If I had to guess, I'd say maybe we've got us a baby blue whale for a companion—hell!" she said. "It's no whale. I know what that is!"

As she finished speaking a sleek yellow metallic form rose in front of our bow. In its tiny conning tower a water-streaked window showed a skeletal face. The machine tilted back in the water, showing two long mechanical arms with grip claws on the ends.

The entire machine dropped below the surface.

"Get on deck! Sully, you know where the big guns are! Get me that surface-to-surface thing and a couple of depth charges! If we don't sink that thing, it'll put a hole in us!"

As she spoke the *Arc* rocked dully. There was a deep thump on the right side.

"Move, Sully!"

Sully was already out of the bridge, taking the steps down two at a time. He scampered across the deck.

Another thump sounded.

"That thing's from San Diego," Bertie said frantically. "It's a research sub called the *Crab*. Navy demonstrated it once when I was there. It hasn't got torpedoes. It doesn't need them to hurt you. It tore a hole in the side of a scuttled ship as big as your face. Sunk the thing in five minutes."

Again there was a bump at our side. The *Arc* listed slightly to the left before steadying.

We followed Bertie out of the wheelhouse and down to the deck. Over the right rail we could just make out the bubble top of the sub, below the waterline.

Sully came back bearing a long, awkward tube and a canvas sack. He laid them on deck. Bertie began to work with the tube, loading and checking it.

"We've got to get the damn thing away from the ship before we can use this on it," she said.

Sully rummaged in the canvas sack, brought out two hand grenades.

"Poor man's depth charges," Bertie said. She grabbed one, leaned over the rail, pulled the ring, and counted to three, then dropped it out away from the ship.

The grenade hit the water and went off, far above the submarine.

Immediately the yellow sub sank down out of sight, undamaged.

"Damn!"

A few moments later there was a rocking, thumping sound from the other side of the *Arc.*

Chub appeared on deck, looking curiously out of the top of the hatch and then climbing out. He went to the nearby cages, tried to calm the frantic animals within.

"If only I could see," my father said.

We moved to the other side of the ship, looked over the rail. There was the yellow sub, a little lower the water, working at the hull.

Sully grinned. "If he puts a hole there, it'll ruin the beer in the hold below." He climbed onto the top of the rail. "Can't let that happen."

"Sully, get down!" Bertie shouted. "If anybody goes, I will. That thing's got a rudder in the back, between its propeller and tail. Foul the rudder up, and it goes nowhere. But how . . ."

Sully was already over the rail, two pineapple grenades clutched in one hand. "Got to save that beer!" he said.

"Sully!"

Bertie reached out for him, but the salesman dropped down into the water.

"Oh, Lordy," Bertie said.

Sully's form disappeared below the waves. We saw him hit the area by the minisub's conning tower, then begin to slide back. With one hand he grasped at the yellow sub's minitail, then he was lost to view beneath the machine.

The sub rocked at the *Arc*'s side again. A shiver went through the ship.

"It's breached us in the forward hold," Bertie said. She moved down the rail, returned with a life preserver tied to a long coil of rope. "If Sully comes up, throw him this." With reluctance she moved away from the rail and ran to the forward hatch. "Got to see how bad the damage is, close it off if I can."

She climbed down into the hold.

A moment later there was a rocking explosion. A gusher of water rose up from the rear of the minisub.

When the water cleared, the sub had moved off and back. A violent whirring came from its engine.

A human form rose to the surface, popped through. "Think I got her!" Sully shouted.

With my father's help I lifted the life preserver over the rail, let it splash down to the water in front of Sully.

He took hold of it.

Below him, the *Crab* rose up.

As Sully grabbed the life preserver one of the minisub's front hands twisted, opened, took him by the middle.

Sully screamed.

The sub's conning tower bobbed out of the water momentarily. Behind the glass the skeletal head stared straight at Scully, grinning.

Scully grasped at the life preserver, tried to pull himself free of the claw. We pulled the rope tightly.

Bertie returned carrying an armful of rifles. She dropped them on deck. She looked over the side and shouted, "Sully!"

The claw tightened around Sully's middle. He arched back, crying out, and let go of the life preserver. Blood washed from his middle into the water.

The claw closed tighter. Sully looked up at us, held his arms out, his mouth open.

His arms dropped lifelessly.

The claw held him up, half out of the water.

He turned to skeleton, flesh dropping away, and as he stirred to life again the claw closed hard on him.

Arching a final time, giving a ghostly yell, Sully turned to dust and dropped away into the waves.

"Sully . . ." Bertie said.

The minisub's empty claw moved down into the water. A clanking grind still rose from the machine's rear. It bumped against the side of the *Arc*, bounced away, bumped into the ship again.

Angrily, Bertie reached into the canvas sack of hand grenades, brought one out, and pulled the pin. "Down you go, bastard," she said, dropping the explosive on top of the minisub.

It went off. The glass in the conning tower shattered. Water lapped into the opening. The machine rolled partway over, drifting away from the *Arc*. After a few moments it nosed up and began to sink back into the waves, grinding noisily.

"Poor Sully," Bertie said. She turned away. "The hole below was in a compartment I was able to seal off," she said. She smiled sadly. "It's where the Carta Blanca was. The patch won't hold forever. We'll be taking water on slowly. But it'll get us to where we've got to go."

The minisub slipped out of sight. Its clanking was silenced by the waves.

I saw in the water, well away from it and heading to the bow of the *Arc*, the kick of a swimming skeletal form.

I pointed.

"They got out, dammit," Bertie said.

At the rear of the ship the animal chattering increased. There was a gunshot.

"Quick, move forward," Bertie said. She put a rifle in my father's hand, took one herself. "We've got to draw them away from the aft so we can get to that closet in Chub's stateroom."

I picked up a rifle.

A shot rang out over our heads. We moved toward the front of the ship.

"That sub holds two, if I remember right," Bertie said.

An armed skeleton appeared amidships, moving

from one crate to the next. Bertie aimed and quickly fired. The skeleton shouted, threw its hands up, and burst to dust.

"That's one."

A voice called out, "Claire? Colonel Coine?" It paused and then said, "Remember me? Your executioner?"

It was the voice of the man named Earl, who had helped my father and me escape Margaret Gray.

"Of course you remember me," Earl went on. "You just killed the navy-sub pilot. He was a good . . . man." Earl laughed. "You were right, by the way, Colonel, about that battle. But everything turned out for the best. It's amazing how differently things look after you've been turned. I felt terrible over what I did, letting you go like that."

Bertie whispered, "Keep him talking. I'll get around behind him."

She moved off.

Earl said, "Why don't you just come with me, Claire? There are an awful lot of people interested in you. You're some kind of celebrity, believe me."

At the spot where the navy pilot had been I saw a skeletal shape step out, jerk quickly back.

"Are you the only ones they sent out?" my father said.

"Colonel Coine! So good to hear you! To answer your question, yes, we're the only ones. It was hell convincing them to let us look. It seems President Lincoln believes it was a waste of time trying to find Claire this way." His voice was reasonable, calm. "If you come out, I promise you you'll meet Lincoln—wouldn't that be a thrill?"

"Yes, it would," my father said.

"If only—"

A shot sounded. I saw in the space between the two crates the skeletal form fall as it vanished to dust.

"It's all right!" Bertie called out. "It's over!"

We joined her, and watched her kick at the pile of dust that had been Earl.

"Poor Sully," she said. She took my father by the arm. "I propose we drink the last of the cold Carta

Blancas down in my stateroom, to Sully's health. He was a damned good fella. I also think we have a little celebrating to do, since it seems, in our case at least, that dreams don't come true."

16

"I want you in here every night until we get to Little Diomede Island," Bertie said, standing at the doorway to the secret closet in Chub's stateroom while I arranged the blankets on the bed. "That fellow Earl may have been lying when he said the *Crab* was the only ship they sent out after us. At the very least the *Crab* may have radioed back our position. There might be others out after us."

I climbed into bed. Beyond Bertie's form I saw Chub in his chair, his happy face shadowed bluely in the glare of the television. The theme from *Star Wars* was playing.

"G'night, gal," Bertie said.

I reached up and kissed her on the cheek.

Bertie trundled back into Chub's stateroom. As she closed the closet door on me I heard her say, "C'mon, Chub, up on deck. You can watch more've that junk later. Got to tend to a couple of them critters. Tomorrow we sail through the Straits!"

The door closed.

I slept.

Then awoke.

I had the definite feeling that I had only slept a few moments. Yet the air felt different. Everything felt different.

I rose from my bed and opened the door. Chub's stateroom was empty, the *Star Wars* tape still running.

I climbed the steps to the deck.

All was quiet. The stars were out above, and a faint flowing mist had settled on the surface of the sea, making it dreamlike.

I decided I was foolish. I turned to climb back down into the stateroom.

"It ain't so bad, Claire."

I turned to see Bertie in skeletal form. Her bones showed cut marks across her neck. Beside her stood a skeletal Margaret Gray, her bones faintly glowing green in the darkness.

"Yes, me," Margaret Gray said. She held her hands, one of them bearing a long knife, to the sky. "The Lord will deliver me! And lo, I will rise again to heaven!"

"That submarine had three passengers," Bertie explained. "But like I said, Claire, it ain't so ba—"

"You'll like this even better," Margaret Gray said savagely, sweepin her knife down across Bertie's neck.

"Oh—" Bertie said, her hands rising to her throat as she turned to powder.

"Your father is the same," Margaret said. She threw back her head and howled. "Vengeance is mine!"

She advanced on me.

I scampered down the walkway to the stateroom below. I ran to the secret closet, acitvated the door, entered, locked the door and crouched in the darkness.

The door to the room opened, and Margaret Gray was there, her bones pulsing a sickly lime color.

"Don't you think your fat friend Bertie told me about your hiding spot, child?" she said.

Her hand tightened around the knife handle, and she stepped into the secret room.

"Don't let my glowing bones bother you. Standing five thousand feet from a nuclear explosion will do that to you. Now we will see who the *chosen* one is," Margaret hissed.

Behind her the volume on the television was drowned by an angry, booming animal shriek.

Margaret whirled to see Chub standing massive and angry behind her.

"Abomination!"

She swung the knife down, but the ape clutched her arm and squeezed.

Margaret shouted and dropped the knife.

They moved out into Chub's stateroom. Margaret pulled away from Chub, dived for the knife. Grunting with anger, the ape moved after her. He caught her as she reached futilely for the weapon. The ape lifted her body over his head.

Margaret was turned toward the opposite wall and

looked straight at Chub's huge poster of Darth Vader's head as Chub heaved her at it.

"*Noooo!*" Margaret shrieked, holding her hands out, trying to twist in midair.

She hit the poster screaming, her neck bent at an odd angle, burst to dust, and was gone.

Chub came to me, looked at me with his sad, knowing eyes. Tentatively, he held a hand out, grunted softly.

On the television Princes Leia had appeared again.

I cried, and let Chub hold me.

Later that night we gathered Bertie's remains, and my father's, and stood at the rail at the stern of the ship, looking at the wisps of fog playing over the liquid waves. First Chub scattered Bertie's dust, and then I let my father's go. We watched them drift, scatter, and disappear. The ship moved on, leaving the ashes behind.

Chub went up front to the wheelhouse. I stayed behind, and watched the waves and the drifting fog. Sometime during the night Chub sailed us through the Aleutian Islands, and I watched their dim, distant coasts slip by.

All the next day Chub stayed in the wheelhouse and sailed the ship.

At the eastern horizon the vague coast of Alaska slipped massively past.

That night, as a beautiful sunset fell, and as every animal on board began to chatter and screech with excitement, the wooded mound of Little Diomede Island came into view and grew before us.

And I wept, because something in the open seed of my flowering heart told me I was home.

14

The Memoirs of Peter Sun

1

Cold.

I could not remember a time when I had not been cold. It seemed natural now: one's hands were always cold, one's fingers always moved like creaking icicles, one's feet had never felt any other way but leaden and dead. Numbness was natural. Deep within me, there might have been a place that harbored warmth, but I could not be convinced. If I had been told that I had been turned to ice and snow, the way a petrified tree is turned to stone, I would have believed it. I could not believe there was running blood in me any longer.

If it hadn't been for the wolf I named Jack, I would have died the first day out. He not only provided a measure of protection from the cold at night, he was also smart, and led me to the natural formations in the white, snowy world that provided the most protection from the killing wind and drifting snow. He was my guide and teacher. When I began to set up our tent at the end of the first day, he sat on his haunches and watched critically. When I was finished, he calmly rose, trotted to one corner, and leaned on the staked rope with his body. The stake immediately popped out of the ground.

I stood huffing breath, frustrated. And then I laughed. "Well, how do I do it?"

Jack sat down and regarded me calmly, his tongue lolling out.

I tried it again. Once more Jack knocked the stake from the ground easily.

"Come on, Jack, show me how!"

The wolf merely sat regarding me.

I put the stake back into the ground, as deep and fast as I could. This time when Jack moved to knock it out, I stopped him and said, "No!"

He looked at me, then turned and walked away.

I nodded, finishing the job, and stored all our gear inside, laying blankets for a floor.

After some trouble with the heater I finally was able to get it started. It formed a tiny circle of warmth within the tent.

Proud of myself, I began to peel off my outer layers of clothes, letting the warmth make me sweat.

Jack came to the flap of the tent, looked at me critically.

"Well, come on in!" I said.

He refused to enter.

"You don't like the heater, either? Don't you want to be warm?"

The wolf regarded me blankly.

The gusting wind rattled the tent, but it held firm.

"Ha! The hell with you, then," I said, turning my back on him.

I ate a meal of hot beans, turned the heater to its lowest setting, then wrapped myself inside one of the sleeping bags and went to sleep.

I awoke, with Jack nudging me.

I blinked snowflakes from my lids.

I sat up, half-frozen, hugging myself. My sleeping bag was covered with snow that had been melted by the heater, then refrozen into ice.

"Christ!"

There were stars overhead. A quarter moon lit the world silver white. The tent was gone, ripped from the ground by the cold wind. Everything surrounding me was covered with a glaze of ice topped by a dusting of snow.

I found my outer garments. I shook the snow from them and climbed into them. They were cold inside. I pulled the zippers up.

The wolf turned, trotted away from me.

"Dammit! Now what!"

Shivering, I rose and followed.

The tent was a half mile away, snugged and twisted into a crevice that had stopped its slide over the ice. It was frozen in place. I had to tug it out and then slide it back as if it were a sheet of twisted metal.

The stakes were nowhere to be found.

"No big loss, eh, Jack?" I said.

It was impossible to re-erect the tent that night. Jack trotted around our creviced wall, lay down in a spot where the wind didn't reach, and went to sleep.

I brought my sleeping bag, lay down beside him.

Silently, the wolf edged his body closer to mine, half covering me.

In a little while I was warm, and asleep.

2

The next day we made almost a hundred miles. The clouds lifted a little, and with them the wind. Flurries danced, whirled like dervishes.

We passed no towns. The world was an endless sheet of white. Jack sometimes rode in the snowmobile with me; at other times he would suddenly leap out to dash over the snow ahead. Sometimes on these jaunts he would be lost to view in the misty swirls of cloud. But always he would let me catch back up.

"Scouting, eh?"

Tongue lolling, he would jump back into the snowmobile as I slowed down for him, then curl up in the back.

At the end of the day I once more attempted to erect the tent. During our ride, I had let it hang out the back of the snowmobile. The sun and wind had acted to soften it to the point where I could fold and store it. When I was ready to use it again, it was manageable.

Again Jack watched me critically. He had stopped us

near another rock outcropping. I managed to pry a couple of large stones free and sought to weigh down the corners of the tent with them. When Jack moved to one corner that I had staked in this way, I stopped him and yelled, "All right, I get the point!" I put my hands on my hips. "What should I do?"

The wolf went to the snowmobile, edged his nose into the back.

I lifted the equipment back there, rummaged around. There was nothing useful I could see.

The tip of something long was poking out. Jack pawed at it.

I pushed the wolf back, uncovered a clutch of long stakes. "So this is it, eh?"

The wolf turned, trotted back to the tent.

Laughing, I followed with the stakes.

I began to pound one into a corner, straight down. Once again Jack stopped me. He nudged at the stake, pawed at it, trying to pull it back.

"At an angle, right?"

I yanked the stake out, angled it away from the tent then pounded it down.

Jack let me finish the work.

"Want to try it out?" I said, standing back. I waited for him to try to knock the stakes loose.

Instead, he went to the flap of the tent, nudged it aside, and went in.

"Crazy wolf," I said, shaking my head. I laughed and followed Jack into the tent.

When he objected to my lighting the heater, I complied. Instead, I took it outside, cooked a meal for both of us, then stored it in the snowmobile. The blanket floor Jack let me keep. He didn't object when I lit the Coleman lamp for a little while, just to stave off the darkness. When I finally turned it out and lay down to sleep, Jack once again edged in close.

That night, out of the wind completely, with the animal's warm body next to me, I slept soundly, and the next morning I was so comfortable I didn't want to get up.

3

The next day the flurries intensified. By midmorning gray clouds had darkened, fat with snow, and the wind picked up.

Jack made me stop before the brunt of the storm hit. I was praying there was a town nearby. I thought Jack had found one when he went well ahead on one of his scouting missions. But when I caught up with him, he merely refused to get into the snowmobile and made me halt.

"Come on, boy, we'll keep going, maybe there's shelter up ahead.

He looked at me with his calm eyes.

"All right, dammit."

I gunned the snowmobile's engine and followed slowly as Jack turned and trotted off into the foggy whiteness.

There was barely enough time to set the tent up in the hollow of a rock outcropping before the storm hit with full force. It was like nothing I had ever seen before. The very air turned white. Snow fell in sheets, inches at a time.

I crawled into the tent. Jack followed. I threw back my parka hood, began to pull my gloves off to open a can of beans. But Jack closed his mouth over my glove, preventing me.

"What, no food?"

He waited until I had put the hood back on, then nudged me down into a curled sleeping position.

"Is this it, Jack? We sleep until it's over?"

In answer I felt his heavy, strong body snuggle close to mind, heard him give a heavy sigh of relaxation. Soon he was asleep.

Though I was weary, sleep did not come so easily to me. I lay staring at the side of the tent, hearing the swishing wash of heavy snowflakes against the fabric. By the shadow of outside light I could see the snow piling up against it. The world held a soft, hissing sound.

I tried to remember what had happened to me. Beyond being cold, I could remember little. Reesa's face rose into my mind. For a moment I saw her smile distinctly, felt the curve of her body against me. But already she was fading into memory. It frightened me that she was so easily gone.

"Am I really Kral Kishkin?" I asked myself. The name Peter Sun, and all the other names, didn't seem to mean anything.

Yes, you are Kral Kishkin.

And then suddenly I was asleep, and just on the cusp of consciousness, as I drifted down, the dream of the young girl with brown skin came, so real I could almost touch her, could almost smell the flowers in the meadow around her. Behind her, outlined against the sky, was a huge ship tilted at an angle, and around her as she opened her mouth to speak were the cries of animals and birds. . . .

4

Through the dim changes of light sky against dark, by which I calculated the passing of day to night and back again, the storm lasted three days.

The first day Jack would not let me rise. It was not hard to refuse him. I had an acute physical awareness of the cold. I knew that if I left the warm cocoon the wolf and I had made, even for an instant, the cold would get into me and never leave again. When the first hunger pangs passed, it was easy to stay where I was. I watched the movement of light across the top of the wall of the tent. Everything else became as a living dream. Time seemed suspended. I discovered that my mind could mold time, if I willed it to, make the day seem to pass faster, suspend itself in the continuum. Night came after day, and then day came again, and it all seemed like minutes to my numb consciousness.

But toward the end of the second day hunger became something that could not be ignored. The wolf let me sit up. Immediately I wanted to lie down again, find that spot of warmth. My shivering gloved hands grasped a can of beans, sought to open its top.

It took a long time. But finally, shaking with cold, I scooped some of the cold beans out in front of Jack and sat hunched and trembling to eat the rest myself. The vision of tea rose into my mind and would not leave. Ready to bear Jack's wrath, I fired up the heater to low, relishing its glow of warmth, and melted some snow. To my surprise the wolf ignored my actions and accepted a plate of steaming water when I placed it in front of him. For myself I brewed a mug of tea, and sat cross-legged, sipping it furiously, rocking to and fro, muttering to myself.

When his water had cooled, Jack drank it, then stared at me until I had turned off the heater.

"You're a h-h-h-hard master, J-J-J-Jack," I stuttered. He only regarded me calmly, and curled back down to sleep again.

I followed him.

The next morning the storm broke. I was so attuned to the swishing sound of snow brushing the tent that when it was gone, I was instantly aware.

I tried to get up. But the wolf growled, low in his throat, and made me stay.

In midafternoon Jack let me rise. The top of the tent was ringed in brilliant light. By the rise of snow on the tent nearly two feet had fallen.

More than two feet. Our little hollow had protected us from all but the hard swirl of snow that made its way in. Without this protection the snowmobile would have been buried. As it was, I spent an hour and a half digging it out.

Beyond our hollow half the world had disappeared. There was not a cloud in the blue sky. The ground was a plain of whiteness. Even the ruts and hills we had passed on our journey here had been all but obliterated by the all-covering snow. To the east our path looked like a stretch of colorless eternity, with no break in the landscape, no refuge from the whiteness.

Jack trotted off a short distance, stopped, and relieved himself. Then he returned, nudged me toward the snowmobile.

He made off east until he was but a dot on the landscape.

"You're the boss," I muttered, and broke camp.

5

Over flat nothingness we covered two hundred more miles.

The snow, where the line of the storm had cut north, finally began to thin. The world was still blindingly white. But now the tops of hillocks and trees became visible. Mountains rose to our left, disappeared as we left them behind. This country was rugged but not as fierce. I began to have thoughts of humanity again.

Once, and only once, did we see a sign of other intelligent life. A lone balloon, bright red and green, passed high overhead, its shape a dreamlike intrusion on the blue and white that had come to be my world. It was soundless, too high to make out anyone in the basket. Jack made sure we hid ourselves in the shadow of a conifer, until the apparition had moved in a silent line down the sky's horizon.

For the rest of the day I thought about the balloon, wished that it would rise back into my sight, bringing a connection, colorful if tenuous, to the rest of the world. As for Jack, he, too, seemed aware of the apparition, and kept us near covering and shelter.

Four days passed. The weather warmed perceptibly, from bone-numbing cold to a bearable chill. The wind also had died. At night, sleep was almost peaceful.

Jack, though, seemed restless. His scouting trips became more lengthy.

Once, when he didn't return after nearly a day, I thought I had lost him. It was then that a true despair entered into me. The thought of navigating this white wasteland by myself was abhorrent. I had come to rely on the animal as more than a guide. I feared that without him, without that connection to the world of the living, I might go mad.

But he did return. I had never seen him so excited. Though night was falling, he growled and pushed at me until I agreed to repack camp and ride.

Our headlight cut a beam through the falling darkness. Jack made me turn it out. We drove by the light of a near-full moon.

"I don't understand why this can't wait till morning,"

I said. There was anything but scolding in my voice, though. At that moment, happy as I was to see Jack again, I would have attempted to follow him up to the moon.

We rode for hours. If Jack had done this on his own, he was truly a remarkable creature. But apparently he had. When I sought to stray from the path he wanted me to ride, he would growl and nudge me right or left. There, inevitably, would be Jack's paw tracks in the snow, picked out by the headlight, to guide us.

After half the night and fifty miles had passed, a city rose in front of us like a majestic vision.

Jack sat back on his haunches and howled.

It was a beautiful sight, and became more beautiful as we approached. Minarets rose from the floor of a plain as flat and wide as the eye could see. Snow swirled through the streets, untrammeled save for Jack's paw prints. The dreamy colors in the moonlight—orange, red, blue—were breathtaking. Every building was topped by a swirling, colorful tower. Windows sparkled with gem-like glass cut into intricate patterns. The city was a page out of the *Arabian Nights*.

We followed Jack's footprint trail up the main street. There was some damage to the buildings. Mostly there was silence. Shop doors stood open. A breeze whistled through the open crack of a bejeweled church window.

Jack threw back his head and howled again.

In answer there was the hint of a cry, which echoed past us, whispering along the streets and into the alleys.

Again Jack howled.

Again he was answered by that ghostly cry.

Jack regarded me solemnly.

"What is it?" I asked. "Who is calling?"

Jack nudged me ahead.

Down the silent street we rode, our track churning into the snow like an interloper. The shops thinned, transmogrified into rows of brightly painted houses. Windows were hexagonal, diamond-shaped, octagonal, painted in enameled borders, filled with rose-and-yellow glass.

I stopped, idled the engine.

Jack howled again.

The cry came, very close to our left.

I turned the engine off.

Jack jumped from the snowmobile, trotted ahead of me.

I followed, taking the Coleman lantern and a rifle.

The door of the second-to-last row house on the left stood ajar. From inside came the unearthly cry. Jack seemed unconcerned, nosed the door open, trotted in.

I turned the lantern up.

Inside was a storybook room, with carved furniture neatly arranged. One curious-looking chair was pulled out to the center of the room. It held ropes. One of the ropes was tied in a knot around the trigger of a hunter's rife.

In one corner of the room, woven of strong twigs, was a large basket.

Jack howled, an unearthly sound in the little room.

I approached the basket. In it, barely alive, was a wolf.

I bent down and examined it.

It was a female. It was frighteningly thin, its ribs hollow bellows. It looked up at me with the same calm stare as Jack did, its tongue lolling out.

I went back to the snowmobile. In a little while I had heated water, and was spooning the warm liquid into the wolf's mouth while Jack sat by, watching closely.

I tried to feed the wolf, but the animal would not keep beans down.

In the wood stove I built a small fire. Soon we were warm and snug.

"How did this happen, Jack?"

The wolf regarded me solemnly, then padded to the table next to the roped chair. There was a notebook on the table. I picked it up.

I could find nothing remarkable with the man's name on it. But he must have been remarkable. In the notebook was a record of the day he had been hunting in the surrounding hills and discovered the remains of a massacre. Other hunters, it seemed, had come across a wolf pack and nearly killed them all. The only two alive were two young ones, Jack, whom the man had named Chee-na, and a female, whom he named Ra-see. The words meant "light" and "clouds." Both animals had been wounded.

The man took them home, nursed them to health. At first his neighbors thought him crazy. There had even been a movement to make him give up the beasts. But after Chee-na had saved a local girl from being killed by a mountain lion, the opinion of the locals changed. Chee-na and Ra-see became local celebrities, pampered and respected.

The notebook was filled with stories about Chee-na and Ra-see.

Then its tone became dark when the time of the skeletons came.

The man, and most of the town, held off the invaders for days. The skeletons were isolated, and most they were able to kill. Then a local man, who was superstitious, got it into his head that the skeletons must not be stopped, committed suicide, becoming skeleton, and opened the town to attack.

Most of the townspeople were killed. The rest fled. Only the wolves' owner and a few others held out. For a while they were left alone.

Then word came that the local imperial guard, now all skeletons, had been ordered to sweep through every town and village and wipe out any remaining opposition. It was only a matter of time. It was during the first of these skeleton raids that Ra-see was wounded, and became sick.

The next entry in the notebook was dated four weeks ago. It told how Chee-na had run off during the night. The skeleton forces were due in numbers in the next few days. The village had been visited by a spotter's balloon, green and red, which flew high overhead, distributing pamphlets ordering them to lay down their arms and be turned.

The final entry told of how the wolves' owner would not allow himself to be turned. He had rigged a contraption in a chair that would kill him twice, and thus spare him the indignity of bowing to the skeletons' wishes.

The chair in the center of the room, covered with dust, tied with ropes to the rifle trigger, told the rest of the story.

I put the notebook down. Jack sat near the wood stove, alert, eyes on the basket.

The female wolf slept.

I rubbed my eyes, found another chair near the fire, and sat in it, staring into the flames.

Sometime toward dawn I slept, too, but Jack was still awake, keeping vigil, the lowering moon gleaming through the windows as I closed my eyes.

6

In two days Ra-see grew stronger. In another she began to walk.

The third day she kept beans down, along with a little beef broth I made from bouillon cubes in the cottage's cupboard.

I began to feel better myself. The nights in the cottage were snugly warm, the days bearable. I explored the city. Much of the food had been stripped away. There were larders with enough crackers and dried fruit so that a man who had eaten beans for a week thought himself a king. There was also some petrol. I was able to refill my nearly empty fuel reserves.

I was in no hurry to leave. But on the morning of the fourth day Jack gave me indications that it was time to move on.

"We should stay another day or two, Jack. I don't think Ra-see is ready to travel. *I'm* not ready to travel." I looked out past the boundaries of our magical city, at the flat, rolling whiteness.

Jack growled.

"Sorry, mate. This time I draw the line. We stay."

I walked away from him. I felt vaguely apprehensive for not listening to his whims. But at the same time my reluctance to leave overcame my reluctance to stay.

Jack stayed in the same spot, quietly looking at the far, rolling snow plains.

That night I found him still there, studying the sky under the stars.

"Jack, this is ridiculous. Come in now."

I tried to pull him. He resisted, quietly but firmly. When I insisted, he gave a low growl in his throat.

Finally I gave up and went back to the warmth of the wood stove in the house, and tended to Ra-see.

7

In the morning, Jack had made his way back to us. He lay curled next to Ra-see, who had abandoned her basket during the night. Jack regarded me inscrutably. When Ra-see stood, it was on strong legs. I was ready to pronounce her well.

"See, Jack? An extra day didn't hurt."

When I opened the door to our home, another brilliant day met me.

"What's this?"

The beauty of the day, and of the brilliant, metallic many-colored buildings and minarets surrounding me, was marred by the sight of thousands of leaflets that covered the ground, the buildings. They nested on slanted rooftops, angled out of gutters, peppered the roads.

I bent and picked one up.

On its cover was a death's-head, grinning. Beneath was a message in many languages: Chinese, Russian, English, French, Italian, tens of others, many of which I did not recognize. When I found my own original language, Cambodian, my eyes stopped, at last, to read. It was a simple message, direct and chilling:

PEOPLE OF HUMANITY! YOUR CAUSE IS LOST! BUT WE WAIT TO GREET YOU WITH OPEN ARMS! DEATH AND RE-BIRTH ARE YOUR FUTURE! LOOK TO THE SKIES! YOUR SALVATION WILL COME FOR YOU!

I could well imagine that lone, high balloon, sailing over during the night, a tiny dot against a cloudless, moonlit, starry sky—and Jack silently bearing witness, his eyes following the balloon's progress as the leaflets fluttered down like snowflakes.

I dropped the pamphlet and came inside.

"Jack, you were right," I said.

He gave no indication of smugness. He only went

past me, walked to our snowmobile, parked nearby, and stood next to it.

"All right, Jack," I said.

In ten minutes we were tracking our way out of the magical city, not looking back.

8

East, and slowly north. In two days we had crossed the Anabar River. In another two days of swift travel, the Olenek and Lena. The Anabar was frozen, as was the Olenek. We crossed them easily. But the Lena, a wide, swift waterway, was a mass of floes, forcing us to turn north until we found a bridge.

The days were cold and clear, as were the nights. But winter had eased its icy claws from this area. Here and there a patch of brown or dried green poked through the hillsides.

At first Ra-see traveled behind me, wrapped in blankets. Near the end of that week she took to foot, setting out on a short probing mission with her mate. I missed their company, however briefly they were gone. At night Jack and I watched the skies.

The Verkhoyansk Range rose before us. It was a sturdy low line of mountains. Even in my inexperience I knew this crossing would be difficult. A stream we waded showed a thin line of ice on top. Just beneath the surface the water tumbled and gurgled. One step of a boot broke through.

"We're going to have to move slowly, Jack," I said. My words were more to remind myself than because the wolf needed telling. He had taken to walking a hundred yards in front of us, marking our path as we rose into the mountains.

It was snowier, and colder, as we climbed. But still the balance between thaw and freeze was precarious. I feared a false ice bridge most of all. Once, our path seemingly laid, Jack trotted back to dissuade me from attempting a safe-looking stretch of ice and snow. Sure enough, as his weight left it, the snow collapsed in cracking folds, exposing a deep hole.

In thanks I put my hand into the deep fur on his back and rubbed.

He took this compliment in stride, then cut out across our new path away from me.

There came a day, though, when our luck and Jack's skill ran out.

Even Jack could not have prevented our mishap. A quick storm, which rose over the mountains, dropped an inch of snow and then was gone during the night. It obliterated all signs of passage the next day. Then the sun warmed. The new snow began to melt. That afternoon the temperature dropped as suddenly as it rose, and continued to drop.

The next morning a smooth sheet of ice covered our path.

We had been making a straight passage through the deep crack between two peaks. But now the land rose before us. Our smooth path was a false one. At each step Jack's forefoot broke through the thin ice to meet the real path below. At one point the ice cracked. He sank to his forelimbs. He had to push himself back on his hind legs to free himself.

As he did so the flat stretch of ice the snowmobile had been on gave way.

What had been solid and smooth now became cracked and broken. I cried out. The snowmobile lurched. It sank ominously to the right. I was nearly thrown out. Ra-see stood helpless nearby.

The snowmobile stabilized for two heartbeats. Then there was a whoosh as the area in front of me collapsed.

The snowmobile sank forward. It straightened for a moment and then angled sharply down. I held the wheel tightly, afraid to breathe. A hole at least two hundred feet deep opened below me.

The snow track creaked forward, stopped. A chunk of ice that had a moment ago helped support the weight of the machine slid past and down into the hole. I watched it tumble and break against the sides of the ice cliff.

I held on, fearing to move.

The snowmobile slid forward.

I held my breath. The machine crunched to a halt, its rear runners snagged in snow. Then, ever so slowly, its weight began to pull it forward and down.

I looked at Jack, who stood stock-still at the edge of the hole, staring at me, and quickly, I made a decision. Whirling around, I began to throw our stocks of food out of the snowmobile, as far as I could. The tent followed. I heaved supplies above the lip of the hole.

I stood up in the seat as the snowmobile slid another few inches. I reached up to the top of the hole.

My hands found no purchase on the slippery ice.

Beneath me the snowmobile, with a sliding crunch, twisted down, began to slide out from under me.

Frantically, I boosted myself on the top of the seat as it fell away. My hands dug into the snow and ice.

Something hard was there, the lip of a crag. I grabbed onto it and held as the snowmobile fell.

I looked after it. I gasped.

The hole behind me had widened. Now I was staring down into a nearly bottomless crevice, watching the snow-mobile tumble and smash itself against the icy walls of rock.

In a moment it was lost in swirls of snow below.

I closed my eyes, looked back up.

Jack had moved to my position at the edge of the hole. Without a sound he opened his mouth, dug his hind legs into the snow, bent, and took my sleeve in his teeth.

"All right, Jack," I whispered, "all right, I'll try."

I pulled myself up. I tried to kick out at the rock wall to assist myself. There was no rock wall, only crusted snow. As I kicked at it it collapsed, leaving me hanging in air on the edge of a cliff.

Growling with effort, Jack held on to my sleeve.

I closed my eyes. I took a deep breath and pulled myself up.

I nearly made it. One arm went up and over the top of the hole. Then I began to slide back down.

Ra-see appeared. She closed her mouth over my other sleeve, holding me in place.

Again I rested. Then, holding firm with my outstretched arm, I hauled myself up, moving the sleeve that Jack held until it, too, was up and out of the hold.

My feet dangled. Then my knees found the crag, closed around it, and I threw myself up and over the edge.

I crawled forward, away from the hole. I lay gasping. I rolled over, looked at the sky.

I saw the two wolves standing at a respectful distance, regarding me impassively.

"Come here," I said. I took them both in my arms, nuzzled them to my face.

I laughed, my body still trembling with the nearness of death, and then I cried out, hearing my voice echo hollowly in the canyons around us, "I'm alive!"

9

Now we were on foot. I had saved the tent, but not the deep tent stakes Jack had so patiently taught me to use. I had one blanket. The heater was gone. I had one weapon, a handgun, loaded with six shells. And only half our food stores, perhaps enough for a week, were left. With an irrational curse I noted that they were all beans.

Still, with Jack looking at me without so much as a hint of loss of resolve, I found it hard to be mad for very long.

"We've made it this far," I said, "we'll make it all the way.

That night was not as difficult as I had feared. A mountain stream brought us fresh water. For some reason the beans tasted fine. There was no wind. The tent was set up easily, with no objection from Jack, in the hollow of two mountain walls with stones for anchors on its corners. The weather had warmed perceptibly again. We were nearly through the mountains. In another few days, with luck, we might come on a town or village on the other side and replenish our stocks. Perhaps we might even find another snowmobile.

I slept that night as soundly as I had slept in weeks.

In the morning I awoke to find Jack and his mate gone. I assumed they had scouted ahead. I set to making breakfast. It looked to be another blue day, with a hint of cumulus clouds to break up the beautiful tedium of the sky. I was thirsty. I walked to the stream to get water.

I cupped my hand in the cold water and brought it to my mouth.

"Human! You will stand, please!"

For a moment I thought I was dreaming. I thought the voice must be in my head.

"Human!"

I stood slowly and turned, water dripping from my still-cupped hand.

"Yes, you! Welcome to the world!"

I faced a skeleton. But the angle of the morning light showed me the outline of a thin, wiry Oriental with long hands. He wore robes. They were dazzling bright. I marveled at the wash of colors. It was as if he were wearing a rainbow.

"You admire me! Please do not! No man deserves admiration!"

His voice was thin and reedy, but strong. He bowed.

"I am Yu Fon, of the eleventh century B.C." He held his hands out, palms up. "You?" he said.

"I am ..." I said nothing.

"No matter. You are who you are. Follow."

He turned and walked away. "If you seek flight, do not waste energy. I know your position. I would merely return. Neither can you kill me."

I did not follow him, but circled around the rock formation he had walked into.

On the far side, in a small, flat rock plain, stood the green-and-red balloon Jack and I had spotted. It stood tethered to a stake in the ground, bobbing languidly a few feet off the ground. Its basket was intricately woven of colored rushes in the form of pictures: suns, a smiling moon, an inscrutable cloud above a lapping sea. These pictures were separated by tiny drawings of the balloon itself, in intricate detail.

"*Things* you may admire, for they are handiwork which rises through our hands, from God."

Yu Fon stood on the top of the rock formation I had seen him disappear into.

I turned and ran toward the tent.

"Flight is a waste of energy!"

I looked back. He was gone from the top of the rock formation.

Breathing heavily, I rushed into the tent, went through our remaining stores, locating the handgun. I carried it outside.

Yu Fon waited for me outside the tent. He bowed. "Human—"

I aimed at him, fired the gun. A hollow click sounded.

"I took the liberty," Yu Fon said. He held open his palm, revealing the bullets.

Giving a shout, I charged him.

He easily sidestepped me. When I whirled around to face him, he was not where I had seen him go, but on the opposite side, standing before the tent.

"Will you follow now?" he said. "The balloon awaits!"

I shouted a curse, charged him again.

He was not there when I grabbed for him.

"Movement is elusive!" he said. I turned in a circle, not locating him. After a moment I saw him stand on top of the rock formation.

He turned away, began to climb down the far side, toward his balloon. "I will wait!" he said.

I packed quickly, mounted my gear on my back, and moved away from the balloon. Putting a fair mile between myself and my camping spot, I looked back to see the balloon gone from its mooring. I frantically checked the sky, but found no sign of it.

I turned and walked on.

By midday I expected to come across Jack and his mate. But they did not appear. It occurred to me that Yu Fon may have done something to them. Suddenly I wanted to see the skeleton again, to choke him to death if need be to make him tell me what he had done to my companions.

That day and night were lonely ones. I set up the tent under a rock overhang, watched the dripping water of the day turn to halfhearted icicles on the lip during night cold. I ate, realizing that my food would soon be gone.

During the night I waited for the howl of wolves, but heard nothing.

The next morning, the ground around my campsite was strewn with Yu Fon's pamphlets:

PEOPLE OF HUMANITY! YOUR CAUSE IS LOST! BUT WE WAIT TO GREET YOU WITH OPEN ARMS! DEATH AND RE-BIRTH ARE YOUR FUTURE! LOOK TO THE SKIES! YOUR SALVATION WILL COME FOR YOU!

I tore the one I held to shreds and threw it down.

"Impolite!" Yu Fon's voice said.

I looked to the top of my rock overhang. There he stood, his balloon tethered thirty feet behind him.

"Come! We have wasted enough time on the ground. The skies await!"

He turned toward his balloon.

I stalked the incline of the rock overhang and ran after him.

"What did you do to those wolves!"

He easily avoided my attacks, leaving me breathless.

"I would not worry about wolves," Yu Fon said. "Wolves are from God. They provide for themselves, on heaven or earth."

"Did you kill them?" I shouted. Again I tried to grab at him, again felt only air.

When I gave up, he stood a yard to my right, arms folded.

"It is time," he said, and turned again to walk toward his balloon.

I sprinted away from him, packed, moved on.

So it went for four days. During this time I made scant progress, worried about Jack and Ra-see, and ran out of stores. The tent became snagged on a sharp rock, ripped down one side, and became useless. I slept on the ground. By the evening of the fourth night I had eaten the last half can of beans and begun to feel a gnawing in my belly.

Yu Fon landed his balloon, eclipsing the moon, a hundred yards away from me. I watched his slim skeletal figure climb from the basket, tether the balloon, climb back in.

"I won't fly with you!" I shouted. I walked in moonlit darkness to get away from him.

The next day I found a stand of berries and some roots similar to turnip. The berries, though, turned out to be inedible. I spent the day doubled over in pain. The cramps did not pass until evening. During my illness I had visions—the balloon dancing in the skies overhead, making circles and ballet movements, Yu Fon throwing colors into the sky from a stick, which merged and danced among the scant clouds.

That night, as I sought sleep, I heard Yu Fon whisper in my ear, "Come, it is time!"

I opened my eyes. He was already walking back toward his balloon.

I looked at what I had, what I could gain. I had nothing. My food was gone, my shelter gone, my companions gone. I would not last on my own in this unfamiliar territory, with its unfamiliar foods. On the horizon no town or village had appeared. I might wander for days or weeks. Eventually I would go mad.

I stumbled to Yu Fon's balloon and looked into the basket.

"You wonder," Yu Fon said in the darkness, "if I will kill you."

"Yes."

"You wonder if I will turn you into a creature such as I, because it is in my nature to do so."

"Yes."

He said, "Time will tell."

I climbed into the basket, feeling the softness of the pillows and straw in its bottom. Yu Fon released the tether and the balloon rose, kissing the clouds and the soft dark sky. Yu Fon began to sing, a soft Chinese melody that made me remember my childhood so long ago in Cambodia, and down I went to soft sleep.

11

I woke up human.

The light of day was bright. Overhead, I saw the opening in the balloon for hot air to flow in, the metallic gas blower beneath it. Yu Fon's skeletal hand reached for the lever.

A blowing hiss of fire stormed up into the balloon. I felt us bump the sky and rise perceptibly.

I sat up. The basket was large, nearly the size of a small room. There were chairs against its perimeter, a small table covered with instruments and rolled charts to one side. Next to it was a black enameled case, covered in yellow pictures of the stars and sickle moons. Next to that was another box. Next to that box were piles of pamphlets. Books were strewn over the pillowed floor.

"You slept well?" Yu Fon said.

"Yes."

"Good! 'The tired mind craves sleep, as the rested mind craves knowledge.' " He smiled slightly. "That was something I said three thousand years ago!"

I felt my stomach growl.

"And so, too," he said, "does the hungry stomach crave food."

He opened the box next to the enameled case. He brought out vegetables and a box of crackers. He distributed them, giving me the lion's share.

After I had eyed the food suspiciously, my hunger overcame my suspicion and I ate.

"Now the stomach, too, is happy!"

I stood, feeling the basket shift slightly. I looked over the side. Below, the earth moved like a quilt, rivers and streams cutting the green, brown, and white land into patches and strips.

"I came from the south, when I was born," Yu Fon said. "The province of Qinghai, as it is called now. We had beautiful lakes, not as many in number as Xizang Zizhaqu, but more pleasing to the eyes. I was born near a lake, and grew up swimming in it. Later, with my balloons, I learned to swim in the sky."

I looked around at him. "Why haven't you tried to kill me?"

"Kill is not the right word," he said. "I have pondered this long and hard. In my mind I am serene in this knowledge. *Turn*, which denotes change and not death, is a more correct term."

I snorted. "Kill is the right word."

"Not so," he said. "This we can argue. If we were both human, and I were to strike you, you would go elsewhere, and that would be murder. But if I were to strike you now, you would go nowhere. You would stay here. Only your flesh would drop away. You would wear a new appearance, perhaps, but you would still be here."

"How many have you killed?" I asked. "I read your pamphlet. How many have you hunted down?"

"As I said—"

"*Turned*, then!" I said, annoyed by his calm tone.

"Ah." He looked at me. "Thousands. But only when they were ready, and asked it of me."

"What!"

"Long ago, in my first life, I resolved to live a life of peace and tranquillity. For a time I was a magician. My era, as all eras, was a troubled one. Men sought to gain advantage over other men, and men killed other men for their possessions. This, I resolved, was not correct. I sought a life of contemplation, and so set out from my home province for the north, where I heard men of contemplation lived. I found them in what you now call Mongolia. In my balloon I landed there, and lived among them, and learned to think. In time I set out on my own, not wishing to be among men any longer, and lived in the sky alone, closer to God. Here my thoughts were more serene, and purer.

"Alas, one day my balloon crashed to earth, and I was killed. So ended my days of contemplation!

"But no! Suddenly I found myself on this earth again!

"My only obligation, I resolved, was to once more think purely. So I set out in this new balloon, made in this age, and sought to unlock the mysteries of this new existence."

I snorted. "And what have you found?"

"Much. Not all. I found in myself an innate wish to destroy humans. When I awoke, and pushed myself from the ground, I found myself near a road. On the road walked a human boy with a stick over his shoulder, tied to which was a cloth filled with food. I had an overwhelming compulsion to strike him. I confronted him, and hovered over him, my fist ready to hit. This at first puzzled and troubled me. I had never harbored any wish to harm a thing before. I saw this urge in all of those like myself. I resolved there must be a reason, and to the good. A thing's nature is itself, and it's true nature is always for the good.

"But I did not strike the boy. I asked him, instead, if he wished to be struck.

"He cried, 'No!' and ran off.

"During those first days and weeks, in the chaos that was around me, I thought long and hard about this wish of mine. All around me others were indulging in it at will. This, I thought, was wrong, though the urge itself must stem from something right.

"Eventually I aligned myself with a warlord of the fifth century B.C. who was triumphant in his area. He took me on as his court magician. He began to ask me for my thoughts. I studied many books, modern and ancient. I imparted my thoughts to him. He deemed me wise. Then he granted me my wish of having a balloon, so to spread my thoughts throughout China.

"Here, then, is what I learned, and what so intrigued my warlord, so that he allowed me to spread my word. For me to be here now I must have come from somewhere else. A place, frankly, I do not remember. This is the case for all of those like me.

"I went to this place when my balloon crashed to earth in the eleventh century B.C. Does it not make sense that to arrive in a place, you must have come from some other place? Obviously, there is a reason for me to be here now. And if it is my nature to want to—"

"Enough," I said, tired of his reasoning. I thought only of Reesa, and my infant son, and all the others I had seen slaughtered since the beginning of this madness. Yu Fon trying to make sense of it all annoyed and frightened me.

"Perhaps later—"

"I don't want any more of your prattle," I said. "Just

as long as you won't kill me, or *turn* me, while I'm with you."

"To do so without your consent would be sinful!"

"Just don't commit any sins."

I turned back to the view below, losing myself in its beauty, and later, when Yu Fon opened his black enameled box, and performed magic for me, and spread colors among the clouds as we drifted past them, as he obviously had when I thought I had been seeing visions, I didn't protest.

Later still, by the light of a sinking orange sun, Yu Fon bent to contemplation, reading, I noted with a wry laugh, a book I had read in college, *Moby Dick*. "The eternal struggle between good and evil runs thorugh all ages and cultures," he said, noting my interest.

And later still, as he put his book aside in the fading light and leaned back to rest his skull against the side of his balloon and close his eyes, before I closed my own eyes to sleep, I looked on him for a moment with almost fondness, knowing that some strong, vital part of him wanted to destroy me, but that some other, stronger, more human part, his mind and intellect, would not let him do that.

That night I slept more soundly than I had since before the madness came, and dreamed again of the brown-skinned girl and the huge tilted ship.

12

The following day, as we slid above a drift of thin clouds that made the earth below look as if it were covered with a baby blanket, it occurred to me that Yu Fon had not dropped any more pamphlets.

"There is no need," he said.

"Why?"

"There are no more humans in this province. There are no more in all of China and Russia. There are no more in America, Europe, and Australia, too, for that matter."

This thought struck me like a thunderbolt. *"The human race is gone?"*

He shook his head. "There are a few. The Americans, always an inventive race, have perfected an airborne machine to find those remaining. Soon . . ."

"Soon it will be the end," I said.

Yu Fon looked at me dispassionately.

"Where are you taking me?" I asked.

"Where fate brings us," he said cryptically.

Later I asked him, "Yu Fon, have you heard of Kral Kishkin?"

"All races have heard of Kral Kishkin, in one form or another. In China we called him Fo Yin, the One Who Starts Again."

"You asked me who I am."

"Yes."

"I am Kral Kishkin."

"Ah."

"What do you mean by that?"

He said nothing.

The remainder of the day he was silent, tending to his balloon, reading, arranging a meal for us. The rest of the time he sat lost in thought, his back against the basket of the balloon. When I spoke to him, he put his finger to his lips, begging my silence.

In the late afternoon a thin smile came to his lips. He began suddenly to sing, the gentle Chinese song I had heard on my first night in the balloon.

He smiled at me. "All is clear!" he said. He closed his eyes and sang for the next hour.

As the sun lowered through the haze he studied his charts, made adjustments, dropping a sandbag so that we rose higher.

He called me to his side at the gas jet. "There is something you must learn," he said. "When the balloon lands, you must have your hand on this lever, Keep it light and ready! Try!"

"Why?"

"It is necessary!"

He took my hand. I flinched slightly at his cold, ghostly touch. He placed my hand upon the gas jet's lever, guided me with sharp words while I practiced using it.

"Good!"

He taught me the use of sandbags, how to gauge the wind, how to alter the direction of the balloon and use the sky.

"Again, good!"

He sat back down, leaned his skull against the wall of the basket once more, and sang contentedly, his thin voice trailing over the clouds as night turned upon us.

13

The next morning I awoke to find Yu Fon looming over me. I lay curled on the floor of the basket. I came awake, suddenly afraid of the depthless skull eyes, the merciless straight grin of the skull jaw.

It was only when the faint, gauzy outline of his human features became evident to me that I beheld him as more than a monster.

"It is time," he said.

I studied his calm features. I looked for the fiery rage that would herald his surrender to his instincts and attempt to turn me. But instead he rose and went to the side of the basket. He stood studying the northern horizon.

I joined him.

"The winds are good!" he said. "You will have little trouble. You are hungry!" He pointed to a meal on his chart table, laid for one.

He put his hand briefly on my shoulder.

Without a word he climbed over the side of the basket and jumped.

In shock I watched his garments flutter out like a parachute, turning him onto his back.

"Why have you done this!" I shouted down.

He held his hands out, retreating toward the beautiful earth, and smiled his calm smile.

"*Why!*" I shouted.

"When one visits a place," he shouted back faintly, "one always returns home!"

"Don't speak in riddles! Tell me!"

"Fly to your destiny . . . !" he said, in a trailing whisper.

"Yu Fon!"

But he was gone, down through the clouds to the patchwork earth, and I was alone, missing him already.

14

Yu Fon was right; the winds were good. My one mistake in navigation brought me closer to the earth. Rather than regret it, I savored it, studying the trees, watching the reflection of the balloon in sparkling cold lakes. The world was like an unreeling movie beneath me.

As the sun passed its zenith a flock of skeleton gulls appeared, squawking. They studied the balloon. I thought they might attack. I stood ready with a rolled chart to fend them off. But they were only looking for food. When none was offered, they flew off.

It turned out they were a herald of water. Soon I saw the northern horizon spread out in a rocky, ice-flecked coast that spread rapidly toward me.

I studied the approaching coastline.

"Jack!"

There was the wolf and his mate, standing high on a rocky cliff, looking up at the balloon as it drifted over.

"Jack!" I called down.

The wolf arched his head back and howled, joined, a moment later, by his mate.

Desperately, I tried to follow Yu Fon's instructions for descent. The thin, sandy beach below the cliffs grew close. I dropped, but too slowly. I would drift out over the water before landing.

I glanced back. Jack and his mate were making their way down the cliffs to the beach.

The water approached.

And then, abruptly, the wind, blocked by the rocky cliffs, slackened. I dropped down to a bumpy landing yards from the lapping waves.

I jumped from the basket, carrying the coil of thick tethering rope in my arms, and sought to secure the balloon. Instead, the wind picked up. The balloon bobbed up, leaving me desperately holding the rope taut so that the balloon would not drift away without me.

Jack and Ra-see ran down along the beach toward me. I gave a mighty pull on the rope. The balloon touched beach again.

"Jack! Quickly! Jump in!"

I pointed to the balloon. I bent over, giving Jack my back. I felt his weight spring off me, and then Ra-see followed, vaulting into the balloon.

A sudden gust of wind pulled the balloon up and over the water, and me with it.

I hung on to the tether rope for dear life. The balloon rose, then fell, dipping me into the waves.

Hand over hand, I pulled myself up, grabbed at the basket, and pulled myself up and over the wall.

Immediately I went for the lever on the gas burner. I threw a jet of fire up into the balloon opening.

We rose.

The water receded below. Behind us the land fell back, and then disappeared. We flew onward to the east.

The world, suddenly, was made of water.

15

It was Jack, standing watch, propped on a chair, his tongue lolling, his fur blowing forward by the wind, who saw the island and the ship first. Ra-see, who had not had an easy journey, lay curled on the softest part of the basket's floor, sleeping. Both she and Jack showed signs of having been in at least one fight, with what sort of beast, probably skeletal, I could only imagine. Neither, though, had been badly hurt. Ra-see's hearty appetite had done much to assure me that there was little wrong with her.

I had pronounced the she-wolf healthy, and was rising to join Jack at the helm when he howled. I stood beside him and studied the horizon. I saw nothing but a line of low haze spreading to the water.

Soon, though, the haze resolved itself and grew, rounding into the coastline of an island.

Jack gave another howl. There, just visible to my

straining eyes, was the long form of a beached ship, the
one I had seen in my dreams.

"Jack!" I said.

I began our descent. The island spread. It looked a
virtual paradise, a deep green expanse of trees edged in
white sandy beach. A rocky promontory rose along the
far end, showing the view of a high waterfall cutting
down one side, reflecting light like a crystal ribbon, dropping to a clear pool of water.

We dropped lower. The ship became clear. Etched
on its bow was the word *Arc.* It lay slightly tilted, just as in
my dream, and looked as though it had been driven up
onto the beach as far as it would go. I could see the
ragged markings of a hole in her side.

Soon the water would leave us behind and give us to
the beach.

I saw a shaggy figure appear near the ship and point
excitedly in our direction. The figure lumbered behind
the *Arc.* A moment later it returned and pointed something at us. As I realized it was a rifle a shot went off.

The balloon gave a little jerk and then dropped.

Suddenly we were losing altitude. More shots were
fired. I turned up the gas jet, but it could not keep us up.
We drifted over the water.

The balloon faltered and collasped, and we fell in.

The basket tipped over as we hit. As it filled with water I saw Jack fall into place next to Ra-see. The two
wolves began to swim.

I went under. When I rose to the surface, I located
the beach, about two hundred yards away.

I kicked and swam.

The two wolves were well ahead of me. As I approached the shoreline one leg, and then the other,
cramped up.

Suddenly I was like a stone. Gulping for air, I went
under the waves. Unable to kick, I sank.

I attempted to claw my way up. My lungs wanted air.
I rose perceptibly, saw light on the water a few feet above
me.

I knew I wouldn't make it. I began to slide back
down as my lungs prepared to give up.

Then Jack was under me, driving me up. Now my

arms came alive again. With Jack pushing at my legs, I clawed for the surface. My lungs were about to burst as I came up to air. I threw water out of my mouth, pulled oxygen in. I felt myself blacking out.

Jack stayed with me. Now my leaden legs found the bottom. The water shallowed out.

I staggered to the beach, trying to regain my breath, and collapsed.

Someone was standing over me. I heard a grunt. I tried desperately to come awake, but suddenly fell to unconsciousness.

When I awoke, I had been rolled onto my back. I lay staring up the long barrel of a rifle held by a very angry ape.

I turned my head.

There was the outline of the beached ship, and there in front of it was the brown-skinned woman from my dreams.

She took a step toward me. The ape became very disturbed. The girl came quickly forward, calmed the ape, and moved him back.

She stood looking down at me wordlessly, and then knelt down, gazing into my eyes. She looked very young and new, like a rose that had just opened.

"I am Kral Kishkin," I said.

She nodded, reached out a tentative finger, and touched my face.

And suddenly both of us knew everything.

15

The repulsively desolate, nearly but not quite redeemed existence of Roger Garbage

1

Flying high.
I've got the world by the bon-er!
In the sky,
I'm no longer a lon-er!
People always said that I was a skel,
Now I don't have to say, "How can you tell?"
(Chorus) Because we're all Ba-Ba-Ba-Ba-Ba-Ba-Ba-Ba-BONES!

Repeat the last line, lots of drum snap, maybe get the audience involved, clap their bone hands in time. Great tune, if I do say so myself. Maybe I was cut out to write songs all along, you know? I even sang it for Mr. L, over the sky phone, but he didn't have much to say. I mean, the guy's got a lot of catching up to do to get to rock and roll, right? And with this big human crisis and all, I figure we'll give him time. For now, like I told him, he can leave all the rock and roll to me.

Yeah!

I mean, is this the life, or what? Twenty thousand feet high, a big jumbo jet, fuselage crammed cockpit to tail with all kinds of weird antennas and radio equipment. I told the pilot first day up, though he's one of these Secret Service types who wouldn't laugh if his mother-in-law slipped on a banana peel, what I told him is we need a motto for this plane.

"How 'bout: 'We finds 'em, you turns 'em'?"

He just kept looking through the windshield, studying the sky. I tried to come up with another: "How 'bout: 'As the world turns'?"

This time he kicked me out, said, "Get back to work," and locked the cabin door behind me.

"Another Cap'n Bob!" I muttered.

But they're not all so ramrod. One guy, name of Paul Piper, I call him Pipeman, though I haven't shared any of my stash with him yet—let's face it, this whole bunch is G-man and I'm scared boneless one of them is going to stumble across one of my straws or something and throw me out a hatch or tell Mr. L—anyway, Pipeman acts like somebody who might like the stuff. Rather weird, by his shroud looks: skinny and dorky, with those black glasses you want to put on the pavement and step on, but he's definitely got a sick mind. And likes rock and roll, because the first thing he did when we got off shift the first day is start hot-wiring some of the equipment into a stereo receiver. Next thing you know we've got two hundred watts of an R.E.M. CD blasting through the belly of this monster, and Cap'n Bob is roaring at us down the aisle, screaming at Pipeman to "Turn that shit down!"

"Okay, Mommy," I say, and Pipeman grins sheepishly and notches the volume down until Cap'n Bob goes back to his cabin. Then we crank it up again.

It's then I come real close to sharing my stash, until Pipeman tells me he learned all this gizmo stuff in a room so deep in the Pentagon you could feel the pressure pop in your ears. "We were working on all kinds of neat-o stuff, before Lincoln busted up the Company. The man hated the secrecy, but he sure loved the toys," he says, grinning. "Little lasers that could burn your eyeballs out, leave the rest of you fresh as a baby's butt. That would have been a good one on the battlefield—if the suckers are blind, they can't fight, right?"

"Uh, right," I say.

"We had another one that could give you headaches, *bad* bangers, through four feet of cement wall. Pretty cool. I mean, this stuff we're using here," he said, patting our human finder like it was some sort of pet dog, "is just a variation on something we came up with for scoring drug users. It's little more than a supersensitive heat sensor, okay? The way we originally had it tuned, it could tell if you were using drugs. The body metabolism gets screwy when you've loaded it up with, say, cocaine. This baby could pick that up. Now all we've done with it is tune it to a general human metabolism, which is different than ours, and boom! Like shooting fish in a barrel!"

He isn't kidding. This sucker of his digs humans out like ticks from a dog's back. One overfly of the grid pattern Pipeman has programmed into his toy and—whammo—what looked like empty office buildings, deserted cellars, streets devoid of people, becomes a pinperfect map of every hiding human there is. We found one guy four hundred feet underground, drooling on himself in an anthracite mine, laughing over how he'd fooled the skels.

Uh-uh.

But back to the drug thing, I turn to Pipeman when he tells me all this stuff, try to keep a straight smile on me, and say, "Um, I mean, like, this thing can't pick up drugs anymore, can it?"

"Nah. Not unless I want it to." And then, to my proverbial horror, Pipeman taps a few keys, singing *my* new tune to himself while he does it, "I got the world by the bon-er!" and then turns to me with his sheep grin and says, "There. Now it's tuned for coke." And slyly, turning a nearby sensor my way: "Now if I was to train this baby on you . . ."

"Hey!" I say, pushing the little beeper away as Pipeman starts laughing like a loon.

"Just kidding, Rog," he says, doing away with the sensor and punching the original codes back into Big Skel; and once again I can't tell if this is Pipeman humor, or skel humor, or if that little glint in the back of his eye sockets is that all-present boner wish to make anything nearby that looks human into a Halloween cutout. "Just kidding."

"Uh, right," I say, swiveling my seat back to the console, and the human hunt on terra firma, twenty thou below, continues.

2

With amazing progress.

In four weeks we've covered all the continental U.S. In another four weeks Europe is clean, as well as Australia. Then it's South America's turn. I like that one, because we make our landing in Rio, which I haven't seen in a while and which looks exactly the same to me as it always did. Lots of record deals always got done in Rio. Great convention town. I mean, they were always carnival dudes down there anyway, and what's the dif if instead of wearing skeleton costumes they actually wear the skeletons? They're still all drunks and crazies. Even Pipeman gets into it, permanent Mardi Gras, complete with fruit hats and drunken stupor. Only Cap'n Bob seems unaffected, though I do spy him one night, after a coded message has come through, which Pipeman has of course decoded for our own personal fun, which is from Stanton, Mr. L's warmonger. The message is glowing with praise for our little mission. There's even mention of me—KEEP DINNER WARM, the message says, and I already know that my code name is Dinner so that means they aren't planning on turning me boner, at least not yet. And that same night, lo and behold, I see Cap'n Bob with not one but *two* skel ladies on his arm, both of them with legs up to *there*, if you squint and look at the shrouds and not the bones. Not bad. He even has a Carta Blanca in his hand, the old rascal, and gives Pipeman and me a solemn wink as he passes us on the street.

Finger on the side of the nose, Cap'n Bob. Your secret is safe with us, unless we can use it against you.

It's in Rio, this same night, in fact, that I see a little business springing up that it seems is getting popular everywhere, and which, frankly, gives me the willies.

It's Pipeman who stumbles on the shop first, because
he's drunker than *I've* ever been and looking for a fight.
I've already had to keep him out of two, which is strange
because he's supposed to be protecting *me*. The word has
gone out that I'm not to be touched, but that hasn't
stopped a few hombres from wanting to impress their
bone chiquitas by tearing the only human left in the dis-
trict apart with their bare fingers. I mean, fun is fun. But
always we get out of it, I don't know how, because what
starts out as hostility with a capital "H" toward me always
ends up with Pipeman trying to steal some hombre's
woman and me having to haul him into an alley before he
gets dusted. A dust wish is what Pipeman seems to have.

So when we pass this little shop with a crowd around
it, Pipe-o naturally figures it's another fight scene. He
barrels through, me in tow, screaming, "Lemme at 'em!
Lemme at 'em!"

But there ain't no fight, only to shop with a big cli-
entele.

Creep city. I mean, I should have turned and run
right away. But there was a crawly fascination to the
whole thing. Even Ricki Scum, the late (I imagine) and
great (some say) and (definitely) unlamented lead singer
of Pustule never got as weird as this.

Walls and walls of human stuff. And I mean *stuff*.
We're talking heads, and not all of them shrunken, and
limbs of all kinds. Jars and jars on shelves up to the ceiling, everything neatly labeled. Ears must be in this year,
because there's a woman in a fancy shroud outfit,
screams money, maybe Tahoe or at least Bev Hills, who's
fighting with another woman over a jar containing a human hearing organ. It's just floating in alcohol, like some
gnarly little flounder.

"Wha?" I say.

"Famous ear," says some hombre next to me, who's
suddenly studying me like I'm a crayfish under his fifth-
grade microscope. "Notice the small bite out of the lobe.
It's said to have belonged to Van Gogh." A chuckle. I
know that sound, the sound of a merchant. "It's not the
first of its kind to be sold this week. The women, they
think that if they bring the ear back to Van Gogh, who's

rumored to be alive in Brussels, he will paint them, make them immortal."

I turn to look at this skel, who's smaller than me, but that makes me feel no better, the way he's staring at me.

"Ever think of selling?" he says.

"Huh?"

He suddenly pinches my arm. Testing, I suppose. "A whole specimen, I could fetch a pretty price indeed. Keep you whole, of course."

"I don't really . . ." I say, knowing I've gone white, sidling like a crab away from the man who's following me through the crowd, his lust apparent and growing. There are two huge goons behind him, who now appear to be attached to him, in a very musclelike way.

Then the Roger-radar goes off, full blast, and I know I'm in trouble.

Not that he tried, but Pipeman takes care of it for me. He would have gotten in a melee anyway, condition he was in. It's just that his timing was perfect. Watching the two women wrangling over the ear in drunken fascination, Pipeman has suddenly decided that *he* has to have it. So he makes a lunge, which happens to cut across the path between the shop proprietor and myself. Then, in another four seconds, the whole shop is alive with bony fists flying and colorful Brazilian curses.

We get out, but I don't know how. At one point I find myself face-to-face with one of the owner's goons, who puts a surprisingly gentle and large bone hand on my head and starts to lift me off the ground.

"Don't harm him!" the little man shouts from across the room, where one of the two ladies who has been left high and dry on the ear deal is pummeling him with her pocketbook. "Raoul, don't harm a hair on his head!"

Which is about the only thing Raoul is harming, since he is picking me up by my spike hair.

"You heard the man, Raoul!" I shout, but then Pipeman has burst on the scene.

"You heard the man!" P-man shouts, ducking between Raoul and me and coming up swinging. Raoul drops me after the second punch and turns his goon attention to Pipeman, who's grabbed me by the arm.

"Out!" he shouts. We flog our way through the

crowd toward the front door. The human wedge that is Pipeman and his knuckles of rage gets us to the door before the curious skel crowd outside blocks our path.

P-man stops, opens his mouth wide, and shouts, "*Conga!*"

And that's how we escape. Pipeman is suddenly behind me, his hands on my hips, swaying to an unheard melody, kicking his feet out to one side and then the next. And this crowd, no crowd, at least not one in Rio with this amount of craziness and alcohol in their blood, can resist. They're all lining up behind *him*. Soon we're kicking and snaking our way out into the street as the police cars arrive, sirens screaming—only to have the Brazilian cops join the line!

And then *real* music appears, rising out of the streets, one-two-three-four-one-*cha*, one-two-three-four-one-*cha*, and we're snaking around the entire city, me at the lead, skels pressing Carta Blancas into my hand, rum and Cokes into my other hand. And I'm into it, celebrity of the night, yeah! and we're congoing through the whole city of Rio, thousands and then *millions* of skels behind me, Pipeman waving his finger in the air, one-two-three-four-one-*cha*, music everywhere, guitars, marimbas now thrust into my hands, *cha-cha-boom, cha-cha-boom!* and then the Philharmonic, pulled out of the opera house, carrying their instruments, dancing in the streets, joining our manic line, the *entire city of Rio*, which by the way has hardly been wrecked at all, I mean, it's always been party time here and I doubt they knew the difference when the boners came, every skel in sight, and I find out later that the news had come out that Brazil, and all of S. America, is free of humans, which only fed the frenzy of Mardi Gras, the biggest party of all, *and me at the head*!

I hear later, from an unreliable source named Pipeman, that Cap'n Bob was seen at the very end of the line, with both his bone bimbos, something I'd give mucho dineros to see a picture of, but alas.

3

Our mission continues. After Rio there are other places, other grids. We are the vacuum cleaner of boner world, which is what earth's becoming. We sweep over every tiny square inch of China. I gotta tell you, no fun there. I mean, there were billions of Chinese before, there are billions of Chinese boners now. If there's a difference, I can't tell. Beijing is a bust, most of it's been torn up. I think they still hold it against us for that Nixon thing. The food stinks. I mean, I've had better Chinese back on Rodeo Drive at three in the morning. I can't say I'm sorry to go. Even Pipeman is morose here, they've taken to outlawing beer, they need the grain to feed the people or some such swill.

Canada is a little better. It's cold, late winter, but here they're still playing hockey and there's a beer tap every three feet. Pipeman likes it just fine. He even gets himself a little girlfriend, which makes me kind of lonely since I'll be damned if I'm gonna date one of these bone babes. Makes me real nostalgic for ol' Rita.

Pretty soon I'm so hepped up horny that even Cap'n Bob notices. We're going to be in Calgary a week while they do engine work on the plane. When Pipeman illegally decodes the next message from Stanton to Cap'n Bob, there's a real puzzler there in the middle of all the praise and good news: MAKE DINNER HOT.

Pipeman smiles, slaps me on the back. "Looks like they listened to me for once, Rog boy," he says.

"Wha?"

"Never mind, Rog, never mind. Let's just say the captain and I had a little idea."

That night, when Pipeman gets ready for his nightly jaunt into town, he invites me along to dinner.

"You sure?" I say.

"No intrusion at all," he says. He's still whistling, slicking himself up. I figure, what he hell, I'll go along, and get dressed up myself. Clean the ol' boots, slick up the ol' spikes, brush the ol' teeth. After having a meal with P-man and his doll, I can always hit one of the bars and drink Canadian until my eyeballs roll up into my head.

Only when we get to the restaurant, P-man's girlfriend, Maureen, isn't alone. First thing I notice is that there's heavy security at all the doors, big beefcakes with guns and straight mouths. The next thing I notice that sitting at the table, looking like a scared rabbit next to skinny, bony Maureen, is a ... *human woman.*

"Wha?"

"Merry Christmas, Rog!" Pipeman shouts. "And happy birthday! And jolly Groundhog Day, and the effing Fourth of July!"

I'm still staring. I've been up in the air so long with skels, dealing so long with skels, it's been months since I've seen another human face up close except my own lovely one in the morning mirror. And *she's beautiful!*

"Meet the last human woman in Canada!" Pipeman says, by way of introduction. Then he pulls a piece of paper from his pocket and says, "Her name's ... Adelaid Moore. Lately of—" P-man breaks off here to laugh, taken with his own skel humor. "Edmonton." He turns to me. "And this, Adelaid, is our own Roger Garber, alias big-time rock promoter, lead singer, and songwriter, Roger Garbage!"

There's fire in this beautiful girl's beautiful eyes. I stammer out, "Uh, hi."

She spits at me, bull's-eye, right on the ol' face.

Pipeman laughs and sits down. "Great beginning! Waiter!" he calls, and two skels are instantly bowing and scraping, I feel the long white arm of the government here, *give them anything they want, take care of 'em, they're important honchos, do it, bub.* Now I understand the goons at the exits.

"Listen," I say to the girl, but once again she spits on me, a leather-jacket shot. When I sit down anyway, she reaches out and tries to tear my eyes out with her nails.

"Hey!" Pipeman scolds. Now he's not laughing. It disturbs me, the jerk is showing off for his girlfriend, playing the big G-man.

Two goons are at our side in a shot, responding to Pipeman's scowl. He looks at Adelaid and says, "Didn't our little chat mean anything?"

She's like a tied tiger, though, fury in those green eyes, those beautiful, deep, green eyes. But she stays in her seat and leans back. She'd obviously rather be fighting with anyone here—me, the skels, anyone she could get those claws into.

"Good girl," P-man says, waving the goons back to their posts. He says brightly, still showing off for his runty, adoring, geeky girlfriend, "Let's eat!"

The waiter brings menus. Pipeman's watching me slyly as I open mine. I don't disappoint him as my eyes pop.

Meat listed! Pheasant, beef Tatar, club steaks, leg of lamb—*meat!*

I look up at Pipeman in disbelief. He says, taking in the whole table with his show-off magnanimity, "*Everything* on the menu is available!"

"How . . . ?"

P-man grins. "Prewar," he says. "Well preserved. All of it was frozen, of course. But I can tell you the breast of pheasant is *excellent*." He looks at his girlfriend, Maureen, and winks. At that moment I want to dust him.

Adelaid has glanced at her menu, showing some of my own surprise, and then closed it on the table.

The waiter is back, waiting.

"Rog?" P-man says, playing the smarmy host.

I'm looking at Adelaid. "Um, I, um . . ."

"The heck with it!" Pipeman shouts gaily. "Filet mignon for everybody! And buckets of Dom Perignon!"

His girlfriend, Maureen, gives a delighted giggle. Once more I picture my hands around P-man's neck, giving a good twist, watching him puff away to talc. . . .

The champagne, the first of many bottles, arrives pronto. Pipeman holds his glass up before the waiter has even filled mine.

"A toast!" he says. "To love!" He looks at me and Adelaid, then at Maureen, who giggles and, I swear, blushes.

I hold my glass up weakly. But suddenly I'm feeling very uncomfortable. It's not a feeling I know, or like. This isn't like that gong that goes off when ol' Rog is in trouble. It's something—dare I say it?—deeper and more disturbing. I mean, here I am in this room full of skels, this *world* full of skels, with the only living woman left in all of Canada, and suddenly *I'm not happy about it*. I mean, this party isn't really for Adelaid and me or the human race, is it? I mean, it's not our celebration, you know? We're talking *bone* appétit.

What the fu . . .

"Drink!" Pipeman all but orders. He's bubbling with dorky stupidity and puppy love.

"Hurrah," I say lamely, holding my glass up. As I look over at Adelaid she's watching me carefully, her green eyes slitted. I try to grin at her, but know how sick it looks.

Suddenly she holds her glass up and drinks it down quickly, then looks at me again and gives a tiny, extremely cynical, and very knowing smile.

4

So this dinner deal goes on. And on. Pipeman makes it a point to tell us how wonderful, and rare, everything is, from the asparagus—"You know, those asparagus fields in California were pretty chewed up for a while, it was tough to get these suckers, it seems a lot of Indians were buried in those ruts, but I made a *special* effort to get this rare item here tonight, for this *special* occasion"—to the dessert—"I'm telling you, a lot of the sorbet equipment was banged up in the early days of the war, but I made *special* arrangements for *new* equipment to be assembled, just so we could have this lemon wonderfulness on this *very special* evening." I feel like telling him how special it is, because I haven't eaten a damn thing. It all just lays there on my plate while one skel toady waiter after another whisks it in front of me and then, eight minutes later, whisks it away. My stomach's all in knots. I can't really figure out why, it's not the hormones, with that gorgeous redhead sitting a yard away, it's not that the food is too rich. What I really want to do is shove a plateful of coke up my nose and forget the whole thing. Maybe slap a Stones tape on, some of the early London Records stuff, and wander around talking to myself. Anything but this.

But Adelaid the Gorgeous seems to be having a wonderful time now. Suddenly she's not only got an appetite

but a mouth, and she's scarfing down every morsel in-
sight, and drinking everything put in front of her. I stop
counting at four glasses of champagne, and we're talking
Mr. D here, which of course Pipeman has told us is *extremely* hard to get now because many of the existing cases
were either smashed or more likely drunk by nasty humans, and much of the grape vineyards were plowed up
by stretching skels or torn up in The War. Blah-blah-blah.
He goes on and on, but I'm amazed at this human
woman, who's not only won my groin but my heart, and
now seems drunk as a pig, clinking glasses with the inane
Maureen, who has stopped giving her and me that I-want-
to-kill-you skel look as her own alcohol level has risen as-
tronomically. I don't get it! They're all having a jolly time
but me!

Me, Mr. Party!

"C'mon, Rog! C'mon!" Pipeman scolds. And I try,
really try, but it's just the way Adelaid keeps looking at
me, giving me that tiny little sharp smile, all the time
she's putting on this wonderful party-girl act.

Suddenly I want to throw up.

And no kidding. I push myself up from the table,
mumble some sort of excuse, and stumble away, noticing
how Pipeman motions to the goons that it's okay before
they let me pass. I push through the men's-room door,
just make it to the sink before everything that isn't in my
stomach because I haven't eaten any of it, comes pushing
up. It's bile mostly. I'm standing there, heaving over the
sink like a sick schoolboy, wishing I was anywhere else in
the world. Wishing I was seeing anybody else's face in my
head but that redhead outside, whose hoot of phony
laughter I now hear as Pipeman finishes one of his stupid
former-CIA G-man stories . . .

I mean, jeez, this is bad news, me, the Party Man. I
can't even put the coke up my nose; when I take it out
and look at it in the bag I just want to heave some more,
and quickly get my wish. I barely get my stash back in my
pocket without watching it fly all over the place.

Powder, just like I'd suddenly like to see all these
skels: powder . . .

"Hey, Rog!" P-man's voice comes booming through
the opening swinging doors just then. And he's striding

in, the little gimp, putting his chilly arm around my shoulder.

"Hey, Rog, babe, what's the problemo!"

"Leave me . . . alone," I spit out.

It must be my tone, or that he doesn't care, because he stumbles back, chuckles, and says, "Okay okay, we're done with this gig anyway, let's go, it's hotel-room time."

He strides out, whistling. When I wipe my sleeve across my mouth and follow him, they're all getting up from the table and getting ready to leave.

Adelaid is waiting for me. The look on her face hasn't changed. She might have downed a gallon of Dom Perignon, she might have sucked down three stingers after dinner, but she's sober as a fox, and both of us know it.

"Come on, sugar pie," she purrs, taking my arm as I lurch up to her.

Then we're out into the night, into Pipeman's rented white limo, into the back where P-man and his bone babe are already pawing at each other and giggling. I sit with my head hunched down. Inexplicably, Adelaid begins combing the back of my neck with her soft fingers, digging in with those fingernails just a little bit, just a little *scratch*, until we arrive, minutes that seem like hours later, at the Hotel Maurice, the finest in all of Calgary, a night-lit castle with turrets and a beautiful crystal-chandeliered entranceway. We're out of the limo and moving over the red carpet with black-and-red-dressed skel busboys bowing us into all that light, and past the front desk, and into the polished brass elevator, big as a bedroom, with mahogany rails all around, and up to some floor or other and out. P-man and Maureen, already half out of their clothes and laughing like high-school idiots in the back of a Chevy, are bidding us a giggling good night. Then Adelaid and I are into our own suite and the door slams shut.

"Now," Adelaid says, not at all purring. It's like she's waited the whole night to say it this way, and of course she has. All I can do is sink to the floor and groan, still wondering what the hell is wrong with me and with my brain.

"Did you drug me?" I say.

"No."

"Did anybody drug me?"

"Stand up, you lizard."

I rise to my knees, in an appropriate begging position. I look up at her. I get the blazing eyes back, the fox returned to tiger.

"Oh, Jesus," I say, looking down at the rug, wanting to vomit again.

She laughs.

When I look up again, I see, almost with relief, that she's managed to conceal some sort of weapon, a letter opener or slim stiletto. I can't explain it, but all I want her to do right now is dice me into little pieces with it and make this stinking *pain* go away.

"You really don't know, do you?" she says.

"Huh?"

"You really don't realize how low you are, what you've done."

"Wha? Who? *Me?*"

I look up through sudden tears—where the hell did *they* come from?—and I see her rear one foot back and kick me. I actually see the foot approaching my face like a cartoon. Almost with pleasure I feel the pain of physical hurt whack aside that other pain. I fall back and down, weeping.

"Jesus . . ."

"He won't help you, you bastard," she says. "Maybe you didn't hear but there was even a cult that searched for him, to see if he came back to life along with everybody else. Of course that would only prove that he wasn't God, wouldn't it? They didn't find him. After that there were more cult members than ever. Isn't that *comical?*"

I try to rise a little, and again she kicks me, that cartoon foot growing larger as it approaches my face. I think I grunt with pleasure.

"Let me tell you about myself," she says. I've never heard a person with so much venom in her voice, not even Carl Peters at Roundabout Records when he was reaming out Randy Pants and Brutus Johnson after they got caught with two nubile lovelies of, incidentally, my procurement, and who happened, it turned out, to be thirteen years old, a fact that threatened to end their careers. "Are you ready?"

I rise up on my elbows, wanting another kick. Mercifully, it comes. "Yes," I say, through the coppery taste of blood.

"Good. It's a simple story. There were lots more, billions more, just like it. I was fifty feet underground in a Canadian Treasury gold vault when your wonderful skyplane found me. Five months ago I had a husband in the trade commission and a nice house and two little boys. You can imagine what happened to all that when the skeletons came. By the time I reached the vault, there were four other people with me. We actually were in contact with three other cells and were making plans for guerrilla action. We'd already blown up a couple of their banks. We were making progress. By our estimate, two weeks ago, there were still thousands of humans left in the province. There were maybe fifty thousand in all of Canada. More than enough to keep fighting.

"Then a strange thing began to happen. One by one the cells began to disappear. Those that were in touch with us, those that were in touch with others. Like dominoes. And the dominoes began to fall in a line. And then there was just silence, until skeleton soldiers knocked on our door two days ago, then blew it in.

"Two of the three I was with committed something the underground came up with called real suicide. That's a double dose of cyanide that gets you once and then gets you again. The third was turned on the spot and told the soldiers where I was hiding.

"It took them a while to find me, but they got to me this morning and yanked me out of my hole. I was going to take my cyanide until they told me they were going to clean me up to meet a very important man, a *human*, who had done a lot for them, and who now had a very important mission, and needed to be comforted."

Again she kicks me. I lay there weeping.

"All I did was . . ."

"All you did was *what?*" she screams. She's thrown herself on the floor beside me now, holding the stiletto in her whitening knuckles, close to my face, yanking my spiky hair back with her other hand.

"I . . . oh, Jesus," I whine, "all I did was survive . . ."

There comes a knock on the door. I hear Pipeman's voice, a bit of concern through the cheeriness.

"Everything okay in there, Rog?"

I pull in a snuffling breath and say, as normally as I can, "Everything's all right, Pipeman."

He pauses, then laughs. "Okay, buddy," he says. "Don't do anything *I* wouldn't do!"

He's gone, and I'm looking up at Adelaid, who's kneeling over me, staring balefully down.

"What it is you're going to do for them?"

"I don't know . . ."

"What's this 'important mission'?"

"Something to do with a vision Lincoln had, something to do with the last humans . . ."

One of her hands tightens very hard on the stiletto. The other pulls very hard on my hair. She bares her teeth, beautiful little straight things, capped and very white. One of those caps looks too high. I have an insane thought that she would have made a great advance lady in the music biz, a little chat, a few drinks, pull out the contract, and sign the acts for an incredibly low advance, she's got the right temperament—

And then the door booms in, showing the big boot of one of Pipeman's goons. Two of them jump into the room commando style and pump bullets into Adelaid. She drops her stiletto and staggers back, the blade grazing my throat as it falls to the rug. She's biting on something, staring straight at me, and I know what that bumpy cap in her mouth contains. She keeps staring at me as the bullets make her fold and then the cyanide gets to her.

She collapses, that little smile meant for me collapsing with her. Her body heaves and is still and then heaves again, and she drops to powder.

"Damn," one of the goons says.

Pipeman strides into the room, pushing the goons aside. He's wrapped in a natty silk robe. He looks down at the pile of dust and says, "Damn," too. He turns to one of the goons and says, "Get a cleaning lady up here." Then he looks at me. "You okay, Rog?"

I look at him, still tasting blood, and run my finger

lightly across the line where Adelaid's stiletto just cut a little slice of neck, not even drawing the red stuff. I look up at Pipeman, shudder, and say myself, "Damn."

5

And before you know it, after a few days of recovery, we're back in the sky again.

Only now things are different. First of all with Pipeman, whose bone babe, Maureen, not only left him for one of the goons, but who caught hell for the whole mess he got me into and is now on swab duty. I have to say I enjoy seeing his hound-dog look as he cleans the toilet and serves dinner to Cap'n Bob and me and the others. I'm especially grateful that he's been ordered not to talk to me. I'm afraid if he said anything, anything at all, I'd pry open the nearest triple-paned airplane window and jam him through it.

And secondly, things are different with me, too. Not that I'm freaked or anything, a couple of days in bed without Adelaid staring at me seemed to do the trick, I'm not even having nightmares about her anymore. I mean, I still don't know what got into me. Wanting her to kill me like that. I should see a shrink.

The coke and Carta Blanca help. I spend most of my time zipped now. Having mashed potatoes between the ears makes the days fly. Cap'n Bob doesn't seem to mind. He's had the whole rear cabin of the plane soundproofed while it was in for repairs, and now I can play Pipeman's sound system as loud as I want. The Cap'n was even so kind as to stock the room with a wall of CDs, everything from jazz to metal, a little gesture, he says with a solemn wink, for that conga line back in Rio.

Ah, loyalty.

But something *is* still wrong with me, because nothing—not the music, the drugs, the alcohol—seems to make me partylike. I mean, scientists say that even vegetables, like what I've tried to turn myself into, have feelings, right?

I think what I am is . . . *lonely.*

Is that the deal? That with all this humanity being

peeled off the earth layer by layer, I'm feeling lonely for
the human race? Is that a hoot, or what? I mean, what
did the human race ever do for me, or anybody, except
piss on 'em? Millions of years of evolution: and the end
product is some two-legged geek who picks up the first
long stick he sees and beats the geek next to him to a
bloody pulp. And that geek is what I miss?

Fu me.

Throw on another CD, first one I grab. Close my
eyes, take a slug of Carta Blanca, slam that disc into the
player, turn up the volume—and what do you know.
There's Brutus Johnson's shoulda-been-famous edgy guitar opening to the Vomits song "Beat Me," the perfect
antidote. With any luck, as soon as this air gig is over I'll
be working with the Vomits again, last I heard they're
doing the bars in Vancouver, still mad at me over that
Lone Tree thing. But when they see the deal I've got for
them, they'll come around. Soon I'm hip-hopping
around this little soundproofed universe, bouncing off
the walls like a Spaulding rubber ball, yelling and screaming, practicing those licks on an air guitar while up front
they send those zonker rays down to earth and dig the
last humans out of Nome, Alaska, out of everywhere, for
all I know, because I'm told that very soon, within the
week in fact, there'll only be three, *count 'em, three, human
beings left in the whole friggin' world*:

> *Beat me!*
> *Yeah baby baby baby*
> *Beat me!*
> *You gotta gotta gotta gotta*
> *Beat me!*
> *Hey daddy daddy daddy*
> *Beat me. . . .*

6

And so, four days later, earlier than schedule, it's
"Mission Impossible" time. I feel like Peter Graves before
he turns on the tape. Only instead of the tape I've got
Cap'n Bob, and unfortunately he won't turn to smoke

when the telling's over. He'll still be a pee-rick, ramrod straight, an arrow of American justice, ready to go anywhere, stick his head up any hole. Only now he's turned the piloting over to Cap'n Bob Jr., and is telling me, finally, what my little gig is in this thing.

"They're down there on the island somewhere!" he shouts. He's insisted that we hold this little historic meeting in the cabin, from which I've so long been banished. Lucky me. The jet whine on this baby is noisy as hell, and the cabin, I see to my surprise, is knee-deep in empty snack-food wrappers: cheese puffs, chips of every corn and potato kind and consistency, pretzels. Well, well, maybe Cap'n Bob ain't so ramrod after all. Now I know why he didn't want me up here, would have ruined his image.

"What you have to do!" Cap'n Bob shouts, his voice rising as Cap'n Bob Jr. makes the engines whine even louder by making a tight circle; we've been doing this for hours, tilting and turning, circling the little island below, one each turn passing the beached ship and the ragged, deflated balloon tethered next to it, making me dizzy and airsick. "What you have to do is get under cover immediately! We'll drop you on the far side of the island! When you make contact, get to a high point and advise over this radio!"

He hands me a thin, long thing, is trying to show me how it straps to my side under my shirt, but all I can focus on is one word he said.

"Did you say *drop*?"

"Yes! It's the only way! We can't land in water! And to get you to the mainland and then back out on a boat would take days! This is the way they want it!"

"No way, bubba," I say, but he's already got me in the John Wayne shoulder grip, two hands, looking straight into my eyes. I'm trying hard not to shiver, to concentrate on the Cap'n Bob shroud, his Cap'n Bob hat, and not the skeleton eye sockets under the visor.

"You're going down, with or without a parachute!" he says. "Your choice! I'll throw you out myself!"

The look in those eyes, the feel of that grip, and I believe him.

And so, two hours later, I'm in the back belly of this

wonder plane, with Pipeman bowing and scraping in front of Cap'n Bob, sweeping the door in front of the hatch with his broom, opening the hatch himself, almost falling out in the process. Cap'n Bob, meanwhile, is explaining to me, very badly, how to make a parachute landing after jumping out of a huge jet. At least I can hear him back here, though I don't much like what I hear.

"You have to do *nothing*!" he says. "The chute will open for you, after I attach the rip cord to this ring!" He shows me a big ring near the top of the hatch. "When you land, it'll be on beach sand, but try to bend your knees slightly, take the bump in a soft position! It'll cushion your fall!"

He's waiting for me to acknowledge all this gobble, but all I'm doing is looking out that hatch at that little island we're circling, and wanting to get sick.

"You understand?" Cap'n Bob says.

We're coming around toward that beach, and I just want to make them keep circling so I never have to jump.

"I don't understand," I say.

"What!"

"Why don't they just turn these two?"

"This is the way the president wants it! He'll be here himself tomorrow!"

"I still don't get—"

A beep goes off and Cap'n Bob Jr.'s voice, lost in jet scream, comes over the intercom.

"Nearing target, Captain!"

"Right-o!" Cap'n Bob says. He turns to me. "Just find them, and radio back! Make contact, if you want! You're human, they won't mind. Keep them in sight until tomorrow morning. *That's all you have to do!*"

Worlds are spoken in that sentence. We both know that if I do this, Mr. L has promised certain things, and that those promises will be kept. And if I don't . . .

The intercom crackles.

"Over target, Captain!"

"Got it!" Cap'n Bob says. To me he says, "Time to go, soldier!"

"Soldier, my crotch," I say. I'm so coked and drunk

that it comes as a complete shock to find that I'm still so
scared I want to relieve my bladder. "No fu-ing way."

"It's D day, son!"

Without speaking, in a smooth motion I have to admire, Cap'n Bob, who keeps his promises, snaps my rip
cord to the ring, swoops me up like a sack of beets and
hoists me out into . . .

NOTHINGNESS!

Oh, God, I think, *it's finally time to die.* Only, I'm not
doing much thinking at all. I'm spending all my time
screaming and tumbling. I turn on my back and suddenly
stabilize, seeing the hatch pulling away from me, a long
thin rope like an umbilical, Pipeman's smirking face in
the hatch opening.

"So long, Rog! You son of a bitch!"

I twist away, facing down. By now I'm sure the parachute won't open, because the island has anchored itself
below me like the hard bottom of an elevator shaft and
I'm falling toward it.

"Oh, Jesus, I'm gonna die!"

But then there's a sharp tug, I feel for a moment like
Cap'n Bob has yanked me back into the plane, and will
pat me on the back and say, "Just joking, son!" but instead I straighten out into the classic drop position, and
look up to see the bright white bloom of a parachute
overhead. Up around it I see the belly of our plane bank-
ing away, climbing.

What do you know. And I didn't even soil myself.

Below, the ground is still coming up fast. But now I
think I can handle it. There's a bunch of trees which I
don't like so much, but they slide out from under me,
leaving a nice fat strip of beach. I come down *whoosh*
right in the middle of it. Bless the cap'n and his little
beef-filled head. I should have listened to him, because I
keep my legs stiff as ironing boards and come down on
one of them, feeling it more or less contract. If there's
anyone on the island, they hear my womanly yelp.

A moment later I'm writhing in the sand in pain, sure
that my leg has snapped in two. That bastard Cap'n Bob. I
want to dust him, mix what's left with water, mold him into
a little statue of himself, and stomp him all over again.

But no, the leg ain't broken. Just a little pulled at the

ankle, I can even get up and walk like Walter Brennan in "The Real McCoys."

Which is what I do.

I'm halfway toward the trees, approaching all kinds of animal noise, when the radio under my shirt comes on, the speaker talking right into my ribs, tickling me like hell and making me fall down laughing.

It keeps talking, and I'm on the ground now, fighting for breath, trying to pull the damn thing from its Velcro straps so I don't die laughing.

"Ye-yes?" I finally gasp out, yanking the radio from my side and putting it to my mouth.

"Everything under control down there!" comes Cap'n Bob's ramrod voice.

"Y-yes, fine."

"Good! Call us when you make contact! Over!"

Without even a thanks or good-bye, or waiting to let me say all the tender things in my heart, the radio is silent.

Just because I want to, I push the call button, and when Cap'n Bob comes on immediately, sounding concerned, saying, "What is it, soldier!" I say, "Fu you."

7

Under the moonlight,
Won't you be true?
Because if you're not,
I'll have to unman you!

Under the moonli-i-i-ight (wop-wop-wop-wop)
You'd better kiss me! (wop-wop-wop-wop)
Or I'll make an inci-i-i-ision (wop-wop-wop-wop)
Around where you pee! (wop-wop-wop . . . wop!)

Great song, great girl band name of the Joylettes, circa 1979. Ah, those were the days. Punk-o-la rock. And I'm feeling great myself, the ol' Rog returned, maybe it's the nearness of those humans on this island, or getting away from all those skels. Who the hell cares why? I think what it really was, was being away from what I really dig, the music. Ah, my work as a secret agent is almost done, then back to the bands, get some new acts together, write some songs, do some promo, some production, the noise, the babes, the booze, the drugs—yeah!

Ah, those thoughts are like a breath of fresh air. Ol' Adelaid is just a bad drug trip now. I know what's best, and that's what's best for Roger. No joke, Moe. Just get this little sideshow out of the way, and it's home free on Mr. L's coattails for the rest of my natural life and after. Because what these skels don't realize is that I'll be the only human in the whole world, the only cat who gets *two lives*! Fantastic. Like having a spare in your pants. Won-der-ful.

And these humans, they didn't take long to spot. I mean, they've got this island set up like a circus. Animals, *real* animals, everywhere, and a gorilla who I'm going to steer clear of. One *mean*-looking hairball. The two humes, Mr. and Mrs., everywhere they go there are two wolves with them, as well as various parrots and gazelles and gerbils splashing and frisking around. Mr. and Mrs. I can't quite figure out, she looks just beyond jailbait, and he's an Oriental dude, skinny and tough, vaguely familiar. They look like they're walking on eggshells around each other. Part of me wants to know their story, the rest of me, which is ninety-nine percent, doesn't give a flip.

I've radioed in, and kept an eye on them all through the afternoon, and now that night's fallen they've built a fire and done a little cooking. Now the Mrs. is cleaning up. Real "Leave It to Beaver" stuff. The Oriental has gone to get more firewood or take a leak, but it's the gorilla I'm keeping my eye on while I eat my own dinner, wonderful G-man rations out of foil packets. Another reason for me to want to see Cap'n Bob and Co. again.

The gorilla's amazing. He's nearly human himself, carrying dishes to the water pot they've got set up, poking sticks at the fire to make it flare up, dancing around the Mrs. like she's some sort of queen. She seems to treat him with regal deference. I watch with envy as the big monkey scrapes off some of the good-smelling veggie stew they had into a bin for some of the other animals to fight over. Could have used some of that myself—

"Hello," a voice says by my ear.

I should have known he'd come around behind me.

The two of them would have had to be blind not to see the plane, my parachute, or heard me screaming around as I came down. Very classy, they were, to rely on my stupidity.

I turn around and give the Oriental dude the patented Rog-grin. " 'Lo yourself."

He sits down beside me. Not at all threatening. But I get the feeling he'd break me in half if I did anything stupid. The monkey and woman below are now looking up at us, also.

"Care to join us?" he says calmly, friendly as can be.

"You bet!" I say, getting up.

He gets up, too, holds his hand out. "You might know me as Peter Sun."

Pete Sun! Now I know why he looked familiar. I shake his hand like mad. "Hey, you're the dude that ran that gig in Moscow! All those bands, Peace Day, the whole thing! I'm Roger Garbage, Roundabout Records, we tried to get one of our acts, the Vomits, into that show, but you said you were only booking folk acts, and only paying transportation. *Bad* idea, man . . ."

He nods vaguely, as if trying to remember. "Sure," he says.

It's okay, it's okay, it was a long time ago, a lot of vodka under the bridge, and I'm impressed with this guy. Pulled off a commie Woodstock, great coup for the West, rock and roll and all that.

He makes his way down to the camp, and hobbling, I follow.

"Looks like that's broken," Pete says, nodding toward my swollen leg, putting a hand out to help me.

"Nah, just a bruise," I say, taking the help anyway. A free ride's a free ride. "Injured it in a miniature-golfing accident."

The Mrs. is waiting for me. Silently, she hands me a plate of veggie stew. Apparently they knew all along I'd be down. I mumble thanks and lace into the food, all the while yakking at the two of them, getting polite words from Pete Sun and no words at all from the babe. The two of them sit close but not close, if you know what I mean.

Finally, after I make a brilliant observation to the Mrs., waiting for an answer as she stares at me mutely, ol'

Pete rests a hand on the lady's knee for a brief moment, removes it immediately, and says, "Claire doesn't speak."

"Oh, right, sorry. Hey," I add, "great stew, though."

Pete smiles vaguely, lets me finish.

I mean, it's like I'm not there. There's some sort of bubble around these two. Three's a crowd, you know? It's fine if I'm around, fine if I'm not. The ape doesn't seem to like me much, which makes me kind of sad 'cause he'd make a great showpiece in an act, maybe even teach him to keep time with a tambourine. Remember the New Monkees? Hey, why not?

So I finish my stew, and ol' Pete's obviously been very polite in letting me eat and chat. There's a question in the air that's obvious to all of us, and finally, after I've had a cup of real coffee the Mrs. has made for me, ol' Pete asks it, albeit in an eerily calm fashion.

"May I ask why you're here?"

"Me? I, uh . . ."

"We saw the plane. I've got binoculars, saw the skeletons in the hatchway with you."

"Uh . . ."

"I also saw your radio."

I wish he would scream, get mad, show craziness, but he just looks at me with that *calm* friggin' face.

"I, um, well . . ."

Finally I shrug.

"Did they send you here to find us?"

And then I blurt it out, not really knowing why: "You're the last ones."

He looks at the ground and says, so quiet I almost don't hear him: "Yes."

"Hey, no big deal." I try to be jolly, but now memories of that night with Adelaid are coming back, all the wonky stuff I felt, the friggin' pain.

Pete Sun looks up at me and smiles slightly. "You mean the *three* of us are the last ones."

"Uhhhh. . ."

He's right, of course.

"What are you going to do?" he asks me, nodding at the radio under my shirt.

"Uh, well . . . I don't know."

I can't stand it. The woman is looking at me with the

same poor puppy gaze. I can't think. I get up, spilling the last of the coffee, mumbling some sort of apology. I stagger away. My head feels like it's spinning like a gyro. What the hell is wrong with me? *Why can't I think clearly?*

I stumble back up the hillside, away from the campsite, hobbling on my leg until I'm well into the woods. Finally I stop to bang my head on a tree, but it doesn't help. I still can't get my thoughts one in front of the other. Adelaid's face is there in front of me, mocking me with her smile. Now I realize that her look was only a more cynical version of what Peter Sun and his girlfriend were giving me.

Judas.

So that's it. I continue to hobble up the hillside. Jeez, this leg hurts. I keep thinking of all those old movies, Jeffrey Hunter, Max von Sydow as Jesus, the hard, pitying look on their faces when they tell Judas to do what he must. *What are you going to do?* ol' Pete asked me, and he had that same look on his face.

I stop to bang my head against another tree, but the pain is still in there, thick and soupy and not about to leave. I climb on. Suddenly the night opens up above me, a spread of stars, I didn't realize how *dark* it was here. I'm up high, and realize I'm at the top of the big hill on this island. A cool breeze cuts into me. There's the sound of rushing water nearby. Jeez, the sky is beautiful.

I stumble on, trees behind me, rock underfoot now. The water sound gets louder, a rushing splash. The coolness on my face is highlighted by water spray. And now suddenly I'm at the edge of the island's waterfall. It's gorgeous under starlight, like rushing diamonds into the depths below. I pull out my coke, then shove it back in my pocket. I don't need, don't *want* coke for this one.

Jeez, for the first time in months I'm straight, no coke or booze, and I'm seeing something I like. Amazing.

I stare at it, mesmerized, and then suddenly realize that we could get to the point where no human eyes ever see this sight again. Truly amazing.

What are you going to do?

That's easy, now. I'm no Judas. Suddenly Adelaid's face is really smiling in front of me, the pain is gone, and everything is clear. No way I'm going to let humanity get wiped off the butt of the earth. Not if I can help it. I've still got a couple of angles, can fool the skel boys for a while, and work some deals.

No way I'm a Judas, no way. Not me.

My radio gives a beep. It must be time for me to check in.

I'll check in, all right. I'll make these boners dance *my* dance. Ol' Roger Garbage, the fixer, the man who saved humanity! That's me, bub.

One final time I drink in the scene around me. I feel *human.* I let the beauty of it all seep into my real skin and real eyes and let the feel of water spray over my real face and hands.

The radio beeps discreetly again, signaling me to check in, to betray the human race, to be *Judas.*

Sorry to disappoint you, boners.

Already there's a plan in my head, I'm cooking, I'll have Cap'n Bob and Stanton and Mr. L and ol' Pipeman and the rest of them looking for Pete Sun and his wife for months. I'll kick the coke, stop drinking.

Adelaid's face is before me, blowing kisses. Even my old man is there, his hand frozen as he raises it to smack me one, a look of puzzled pride crossing his drunken features as he says, "Maybe you're not such a worthless shit after all. . . ."

Roger Garbage, savior of humanity, champion of the world!

Heh-heh.

"Dammit, Garber, come in!" the radio squawks, forgoing the discreet beep for Cap'n Bob's jet-noise-impregnated shout.

I reach beneath my shirt to pull the radio out, jam my finger into the call button.

"Oh, yeah, you f—"

My leg collapses beneath me, and with a grunt I fall forward, sliding over the lip of the rocks and over the waterfall as the Roger-radar gives the loudest blast I've ever heard.

I actually watch myself go over, feeling that cool spray on my face. I only realize about three quarters of the way down, as the rocky surface rises up to me, what's happened and what's about to happen.

I give myself just enough time to get off a good loud scream.

"Fuuuuuuuuuuu. . . !"

Then I hit the rocks, *hard*, headfirst, splat city right in the center of a big flat one.

I'm dead as a doornail for above five seconds, like a fade-out in a movie.

And then . . .

I'm back!

Heeeeeeere's Roger!

What was all the fuss about. Hey, these bones aren't bad. I honestly can't say I feel much different. One thing I do notice, as I make myself comfortable on my flat rock, is that ol' Pete was right, my leg *was* broken, a nice straight fracture you can see right below the shin. Oh, well. Works just fine now.

I have a sudden horrible thought, reach a shaking boner hand into my pocket—

Hallelujah! My stash is still safe.

I cut a nice line right there on the rock and snorkle it up.

Ahhh.

The radio, still strapped to my side and having been saved from smashing when the rest of my body cushioned its collision, is squawking again. Then Cap'n Bob's voice is shouting, "Goddammit, Garber! Come in, soldier!"

I pull it out. I hesitate a moment before pushing the return-call button. I look up at the top of the waterfall, the ledge from where I just made my swan dive.

I shake my head, wondering what the hell I was doing up there in the first place.

"Shit, man, I must have been crazy."

What are you going to do?

That's an easy one, bub.

Laughing, the coke hitting my head just as I hit the call button on the radio, I cut off Cap'n Bob's loud shouting to say, feeling more like ol' Rog than ever, "Hey babies, Mr. and Mrs. are ready for the picking! Ol' Rog is in the Dodge! It's party time! We're talking last-human soufflé! Do it! I'm ready, Freddie! Wipeout time! Ya-hoo!

"COME AND SQUASH THESE SUCKERS FLAT!"

16

From the second life of Abraham Lincoln

1

My dreams used to scare Mary. I miss her, sometimes terribly. I know she was a bother with her frets and all, but she was what I had, and as the saying goes, "You don't miss your water till the well is dry."

Well, I'm afraid my well is pretty much bone-dry, these days. My brooding has gotten completely out of hand, to the point where it even bothers *me*. That's a very analytical thing to say, I know, but I must confess that much of my interest and pleasure these last weeks has come from my study of the so-called science of the mind. Though I can't say I hold much with this Freud fellow, whom I met a few weeks ago in Washington, I think he was on the right track.

Seems I'm what's called a manic-depressive. Heck, if that's what they call a brooder, then I'm guilty. One of the doctors here, a man named Linus Pauling, quite well-known in his own right, has suggested on the television that I be given some sort of drug to cheer me up. I called that doctor on the phone and told him that there was no pill made that could cheer up my problem.

"The only pill," I said, "is the end of this war."

"But Mr. President," he said, "the war is going well!"

"Wars never go well," I answered. And then I couldn't resist, and repeated one of the most comical sayings I've heard, from an American baseball player named Yogi Berra who reminds me of one of my favorite wits, Thomas Hood: "It ain't over, Mr. Pauling, till it's over."

Fact is, it *is* almost over. But I find the brood upon me greater than ever. Because my doubts are still upon me. We have turned nearly every human on earth, and yet I don't feel that this great task is over. I feel that this is only the second act of the play.

"Nonsense," Stanton has said to me. Thank the Almighty for Stanton, who has proved to be a needfully ruthless secretary of war. Even better at it than he was the first time. Whenever I have wavered, he was there, hard as a rock, pushing forward. "Do we prefer a state of perpetual civil war?" he is fond of saying, using my own most persuasive argument. "Is there an alternative?"

No, I must say, there still does seem to be no alternative. Which is why Stanton has so vigorously opposed my acting on my dream.

"Poppycock!" he roared at me, when I first proposed the idea. "Turn them *all*, and as soon as possible! Without that there can be no unity!"

"And yet," I countered, "these dreams have not been mine alone. We have the testimony of many humans who say the vision of this young human girl has guided them."

"Guided them to *what*?" Stanton stormed around the Oval Office, bristling with rage, stroking his beard. He looked ready to hit someone, perhaps me.

"You look like the bear who can't get at the honey pot," I said, not being able to resist smiling at his antics.

"I repeat," he said, "guided to what? To our embrace! All of them have been turned. Even if this ... *girl* exists, what of it? I say she, too, must be turned. And then this conflict will end!"

"I agree with you," I said firmly, "but I would like to do it in my own fashion."

"By sending this *fool* ..." He made a quite comical impression of Mr. Garber's strange hair, pulling his own hair up from the top of his head so that it stood up. "This *human* fool . . ."

"I feel it is right."

"But—"

"In my dream I meet this woman, the last of all humanity, and the man with her."

"And then?"

"I don't know. I only know that it is significant. Don't you remember the dream I had before each victory in the other war? The phantom ship approaching the indistinct shore? It proved significant, did it not?"

"If I remember correctly, you had it the night before your assassination," he responded bluntly. He frowned. "The longer we wait—"

At that moment Eddie and Willie burst in, playing human and skeleton. Eddie chased Willie around my desk, shouting, "Take that, you rascal, take that. . . ."

Eddie stopped a moment to salute Stanton. "Lieutenant Lincoln reporting, sir!"

I looked up at Stanton, smiled, and shrugged.

"Mr. President, you are impossible."

Stanton stormed out, muttering, the matter settled.

2

And so as the weeks went on, and early winter passed into late winter, and the air force used its marvelous machine to find the rest of humanity and search for the girl, my dreams became more distinct and numerous. Always they were the same. I was to meet the young woman and her young man on an island. A warm feeling always embraced me in the dream when I did this. And then I would wake up.

Around the world a measure of stability had arrived along with this turning of the last vestiges of humanity. But along with it came an uncertainty, a waiting. It was as if the whole of our skeletal race were holding its breath. Even Stanton, who pooh-poohed the idea, had to admit that though he still felt I was wrong, he, too, felt an edginess about the future.

One day, as early March snow was melting outside

my office window and the cherry blossoms of Washington were trying to make themselves bloom, I finally discovered the source of this edginess. Down across the grounds I could see Willie being led on his beloved pony, gesturing to the Secret Service man who led the horse to make it clop faster. Behind me I heard a sound. I swiveled in my chair to see Eddie enter the room, a picture book dangling in one hand.

"Will you read to me, sir?" he said, saluting.

"I certainly will, Lieutenant," I said, dropping my long leg from the arm of the chair and making room on my lap.

Eddie picked up his book and sat. But I noticed a rather forlorn look about him.

"Something got its stinger in you, Lieutenant?" I said.

He shrugged.

"You miss your mother?"

"Some."

"Something more than that?"

Hanging his head, he nodded.

"Hmm, what could it be?"

Again he shrugged.

"I see. That reminds me of the man who lost his tongue—ever hear of him?"

I detected interest, so I continued, cuddling the boy in a more comfortable position on my lap.

"I thought this might be your kind of yarn. Seems there was once this man who heard one man say to another, 'Cat got your tongue?' He resolved to see what it was all about. So the dang fool went and got himself a cat, and an ax. He sat the cat down, then laid his tongue out nice and neat on the top of a tree stump, and whacked it right off!

"Well, this started him hollering plenty, and hopping up and down. Only no one could hear him! And to add insult to injury, the cat ran away with his tongue!

"He says to himself, 'Now I know what that man was talking about, and it's not a pleasant thing!'

"So he chased down the cat, wrestled his tongue away from it, and ran to the doctor, who sewed it back on. Only that doctor was a bit nearsighted, and had never sewn a tongue on anybody before, and put it on upside down!

"Ever after, that man talked backward when he talked at all!"

Eddie looked up at me, skeptical, but he was smiling, and that was what I wanted.

"Now, want to tell me what's eating you, backward or forward?"

He hung his head and nodded. "I want to know where we go."

"What's that?"

"I want to know where we go when we ... *go*."

"Ah." Suddenly I got his drift. "You mean, where did mother go?"

He nodded. "And where did we go ... that first time."

"I see." I reached up to scratch my beard. "Now *that*, Lieutenant, is about the toughest one of all."

His eyes were wide and direct as only, I've found, a child's can be. "Why?"

"Well, some of these scientist fellows, they think maybe just this cloud we're in picked up some—what did they call it?—*genetic ghost* from traces of our bones left where we were interred, and that these gene particles were then sprung up into us. I don't hold with that, myself. The way I figure it, we must have come from someplace to get back to here. Now, if that's true, that's pretty good news, because it means that no matter what, we've got it made."

"You mean we'll see Mother again?"

I scratched my chin, hard. "Now, that one's what I like to think of as a secret. I can't recollect this other place we must have been myself, and I have yet to meet anybody with any sense who can, but I have to believe that if it's there, it must be all right. I think we'd remember if it wasn't, and wouldn't be in any hurry to get back." I cocked an eye down at him. "What do *you* think about it?"

My little son put his head to my breast, almost breaking my heart, and I felt him tremble. "I'm scared, Father."

"Why, you rascal, there's nothing to be frightened about!"

"But I am. I heard you talking to those men about the spaceman you were sending to find out what happens when the earth comes out of the cloud. You said you didn't know what was going to happen. I didn't like going that ... other time. I remember getting sick, and moaning. ..."

Suddenly my little boy was blubbering, holding me tighter than a barnacle on a ship. And I, president of the United States, so-called hero for prosecuting a successful war and stabilizing my country and most of the world, felt as helpless as I ever had, unable to tell a little boy that everything in the world was all right.

I let him cry a bit. To tell the truth I felt like blubbering myself. Then I held Eddie out from me, just a little sternly, and said, looking into his eyes, "Lieutenant, your papa is on the case. You believe that, don't you?"

He wiped away tears and nodded.

"And you believe that if I can't handle it, nobody can, right?"

"Y-y-yes, Papa."

"Well, that's settled, then, isn't it?"

"Yes, Papa."

"Good. Then let's get down to important business." I took up the book he had brought with him, something by this whimsical fellow Dr. Seuss, and began to read from it, with great flourishes at the dramatic and comical parts. When Eddie left, it was as if nothing had ever bothered him. He marched out like a good little soldier to join his brother, whom he fought lustily with over some toy or other not an hour after we had had our very serious little talk, which I, of course, had not forgotten.

3

Not a week after this incident Stanton told me that the search for the young woman in my dreams was concentrated now in an area of Alaska, and that our space experiment was about to come off. He suggested that I should go to California to be ready for both events.

It seemed a good idea, so I agreed. There was a speech I had begun working on. The ride in *Air Force One* would provide me the time to do that. Also, Professor Einstein had invited me to meet him at the Mount Palomar Observatory, which was something I looked forward to greatly.

Eddie and Willie begged to come, too. Finally I gave in to their wishes. As soon as we were airborne, they pretty much took control of the plane, much to the chagrin of the pilot and crew. They were quite the rascals, and if I hadn't been so used to their antics, I would have gotten no work done at all. I thought they would drive poor Stanton to distraction, but I did much work on my speech, and when I showed it in draft form to the war secretary, he approved of its contents.

"It's very fine, Mr. President," he said.

"I have some doubts about this speech," I said. "But I think it will be needed."

"Oh, no doubt about that, Mr. President," Stanton said. He paused to look out the window. "It is marvelous to be flying like a bird, isn't it, though?"

I chuckled. "I have mixed feelings on that one. I'm afraid I keep waiting for all this heavy machinery to go crashing to earth. I've been told it's the weight of two ironclads like the *Monitor.* You remember how heavy that was, don't you? How can something this massive possibly stay in the air?"

Stanton turned from the window. "As to your speech, though, it will be appropriate to speak when the girl is found and hung."

"It will be an historic occasion."

"That it will."

I gave a deep nod. "I'm still not convinced I have the whole story."

Stanton smiled. "Your dreams again? But it *is* rather eerie, don't you think, Mr. President, the way everything has come to a head at once?"

"It is rather . . . strange."

Eddie chased Willie up the aisle, a tired-looking Secret Service man loping after the two of them.

"I must say though," Stanton said, "that I never for

one moment thought we were following the wrong course."

"Once I was on it, neither did I. Though I wish I could see what was at the end of the path!"

Stanton nodded. He turned to look out the window once more. "I've never been one for doubts, but thinking about our little space experiment, it would be tragic if this war was all for nothing."

"That," I said, giving a deep sigh, "is not something I am prepared to believe. It is why I place so much importance on the young human woman. I feel that someone—something—has guided, and will continue to guide us, on this course."

"I hope you're right, Mr. President. And your remarks will be perfect when the human girl is turned."

I looked with him out the window to the beautiful world below, before turning once again to my speech.

4

My time at Mount Palomar with Professor Einstein was exceptionally enjoyable. He met me at dusk. We shooed away the Secret Service, letting them guard the perimeter of the dome, and locked the door to the observatory behind us. Eddie and Willie's bedraggled Secret Service man was still with them at Disneyland. Stanton was nearby, monitoring the military situation, and would call us with news if it arrived.

"I am glad you could come, Mr. President," Einstein said as we climbed the steps to the telescope room.

"I wouldn't have missed it for the world," I said. "You know, I had quite a fancy for the stars in my other days. I used to go to the observatory in Washington occasionally to study them. Of course, they didn't have toys this marvelous to look at them with, then!"

"True," Einstein said. The two of us stopped to admire the huge, thick tube pointed through the open, slitted dome above us. A wash of stars filled the slit.

"Before light pollution, this was the finest observatory in the world!" Einstein said. He preceded me into the observing cage, which would rise and take us to the eyepieces.

We ascended slowly. I watched the stars seem to get closer.

"Marvelous," I said.

"I'm told you've been having dreams," Einstein said. He consulted a white-faced clock on the wall, over the door we had come through. I enjoyed his company so much because he was not only intelligent, but possessed a sense of humor. The corners of his eyes crinkled up when he was being wry.

"Yes," I said, chuckling. "Some of those around me think I'm silly to put stock in them."

Einstein said seriously, "I think *they* are the silly ones. "These dreams could be a kind of communication, you know. There has always been a school of thought that has maintained that dreams are messages from another physical realm, or universe, and that the sleeping mind is merely a receiver tuned to receive those messages. I think in this case it would be foolish to discount that theory."

"I think you're quite right, Professor."

"Besides"—he chuckled—"I've been having them myself!"

I laughed as the cage stopped.

We were before an instrument with two optical eyepieces attached to it, one for Einstein, and one for me, which the scientist adjusted for me.

"Have a look, Mr. President."

He watched me as I gazed through the instrument.

A thick, deep, glorious wash of stars, like millions of tiny diamonds, filled the view of the eyepiece, set against a backdrop of velvet black.

"You know, Professor, I often wondered how all of those stars got up there. I know I may sound naive on this, since you yourself tried to figure out just that question, but I think it was one of the things that got me to thinking about Providence. When I was younger, I didn't give it much thought, because I was busy with other things. But looking up at the stars got me to pondering. It just seemed too beautiful, too vast, to pop into existence all by itself."

"I know exactly what you mean, Mr. President.

That's the same question that got me to thinking how it all got there, and why it does what it does. I wanted to see how God performs his tricks!"

"I used to love the magic shows! We had a man named Herman the Magician who came to the White House. I'd make him do all his tricks in slow motion so I could see how they were done. It used to drive Mother to distraction! She couldn't understand why I would want to know the secret behind the magic!"

"I think that's all you or I really want, Mr. President—to glimpse how it's done. It would take some of the mystery out of life, perhaps. But it certainly would remove a lot of the fear!"

"I quite agree with you, Professor."

While I was admiring the view the telephone in the cage rang. Einstein picked it up.

"It's for you, Mr. President."

I took the receiver. While Einstein swung the telescope to another target I spoke with Stanton.

"They've been found!" Stanton said.

"That's good," I said.

"A tiny island off the coast of Alaska. It will be secured by tomorrow."

"Thank you, Mr. Stanton."

I hung up.

"It seems the stage is set for Act Three of our little drama," I said to Einstein.

"The last humans have been found?"

"Yes."

Einstein had taken out his pipe and was stuffing it with tobacco. "Well, perhaps tonight we will get a preview of the denouement."

He nodded toward the eyepiece, and I looked in. There, surrounded by stars, was a sharp dot of light.

"Is that your fellow?"

"Yes," Einstein said. "And very brave he is, too. It took NASA and the Soviets long enough to put together the mission. But he wasn't the only one who wanted it. They were fighting for the job. Our Grissom wanted it badly. But, in the end, they let Gagarin have it, since he had been first into space."

"The first shall be last, eh?" I said, looking at Einstein.

The corners of his eyes crinkled.

Once again, Einstein consulted the white-faced clock over the entrance door. "I'm expecting a phone call of my own soon. I thought it might be instructive if we actually watched while it happened."

He turned back to his eyepiece and I to mine.

I watched carefully. There was a dot of light, and it continued to be a dot of light. Einstein pulled himself away from his own eyepiece, consulted the wall clock, and announced, "It's happened."

"He's out of the cloud?"

"As of now. And the earth will be out tomorrow."

"Darned if I saw any difference in that dot of light when it happened."

"We'll have to wait—"

The phone rang then. I must admit my heart came up into my throat.

Einstein took the call, and said once, then again, "I see."

I waited for the results, and when he had slowly hung up the phone and paused to light his pipe, he told me.

"Hmmm," I said.

Einstein said, "I once stated that God doesn't play dice."

"No, but he certainly does play chess, doesn't he?"

The corners of Einstein's eyes crinkled up. "He certainly does. Perhaps we are due for another dream, eh?"

"Perhaps."

For a few more minutes we lingered over the stars, watched their place in the universe. Then I went back to where I was staying and took my speech out of my hat, read slowly through it, still not convinced that the words were exactly right.

Finally I gave up, and slept.

That night, as if in answer to a prayer, both my old dream of a ship approaching an unseen shore and the new one of the young woman with brown skin came to me. Only now I was on the ship, and I could see the shore, and I knew suddenly who the young girl was, what was going to happen, and what I was supposed to do.

5

And so, finally, began the most momentous day in the history of life on earth. I had spent the later hours of the night in a long limousine, speeding amidst a caravan of cars containing Stanton and others north to Seattle, Washington, where a navy ship waited to take me to sea. There was a quick side trip to the Seattle Zoo, effected only after many presidential orders and with Stanton ultimately throwing his hands in the air and sputtering, "Dreams!" Eddie and Willie slept beside me in the car, Eddie snuggling over during the night to rest his head on my lap. Willie had wedged himself into the far corner of the seat against the door, but I managed to pull him over close to me as I stared at the passing lights in the sleepless night.

As dawn broke we reached the Seattle shipyard. I stretched myself out of the limousine and walked the gangplank to the ship's deck. It was a sleek, long thing, covered in turrets and saluting midshipmen. The sun was rising on what looked to be a beautiful morning.

"Welcome aboard, sir," Admiral John Paul Jones said.

I waved off his salute, smiled, and slapped him on the shoulder. "No need to salute, Admiral," I said. "Just get me to that island by three this afternoon."

"Will do, Mr. President!"

Eddie and Willie scooted past me, preparing to wreak havoc on the ship. Admiral Jones merely smiled. Soon he had us steaming north by west at high speed, toward Little Diomede Island, with five destroyers in tow.

"Think we'll need 'em?" I laughed, pointing out the trail of ships to Stanton.

He scowled.

I laughed, and turned my face to feel the salt spray, and watch the waves break behind us.

We reached the island before noon. We anchored well off, in sight of a beached ship. The seas were calm.

An advance party of armed men hit the beach before us, making me wonder what all the fuss was about. The two humans we were looking for, along with a very changed Roger Garber, were waiting calmly for us on the sand.

"Just in case," Stanton growled, and I'm afraid I annoyed him again with my laugh.

Eddie and Willie had pretty much destroyed the admiral's ship in the short time we were aboard, and they did their best to scuttle the launch that brought us to shore. Finally, yards from landing, the admiral let them roll up their pants and lowered them over the side so they could splash to the beach.

"Look, Father, humans!" Eddie said, stopping dead, with water still lapping around his ankles. He pointed to the young man and woman who, side by side, stood regarding our party calmly. Nearby were a sleek pair of wolves, who watched us noncommittally.

My bones creaking, I got out of the launch and lowered Eddie's finger with my hand.

"It's not polite to point," I said. Then reserving as always that understandable revulsion we have for these humans, I held out my hand and said, "How do you do?"

The young man stepped forward. "Hello, Mr. President. My name is Kral Kishkin." He took my hand in a surprisingly warm grasp. "It's very nice to meet you." He introduced the young woman standing next to him. "This is Claire St. Eve."

"Yes, it is," I said, taking the hand of the young woman, whose face looked as though it were lit from within.

I turned to our spy, Mr. Garber, and said, "Well, I see you've decided to join the ranks!"

He grinned sheepishly and said, "Well, uh, yeah, kind of an accident, but I still hope we have a deal. . . ."

"Good work, Mr. Garber. I'm sure something will be worked out."

Eddie and Willie were circling the hull of the beached ship, throwing sand. The wolves had sat themselves down to watch these antics. Behind me other launches containing the television equipment, a huge dish for transmission to an overhead satellite, cameras, lights, were being unloaded along with an army of technicians to man them.

"This promises to be quite a day," I said.

"Yes, it does, Mr. President," Kral Kishkin said. "May I show you our home?"

We walked up the beach. He showed me the charming bungalow he and Claire had built, nestled in a cove, surrounded by waterfalls, springs, and lush spring vegetation. The air was filled with the cries of animals. As we entered the bungalow I saw a huge, hairy form in a chair, watching a television screen. A video machine ran from a portable generator. As we approached, the form straightened itself and stood, a great ape. It regarded me solemnly.

"I do believe I've found my brother at last!" I said, laughing, remembering what they had called me during my campaigns.

To my surprise the ape trod forward and took my hand.

I threw my head back and laughed even harder. "I think he knows what we have for him!"

I turned and spoke to one of the Secret Service men. He nodded and returned to the ship.

"This certainly is a cozy spot," I said.

"Thank you," Kral Kishkin said.

I regarded the young lady. She was very much as I had dreamed her, though in person her aura was even stronger. Though she didn't speak, I felt as if she were saying volumes.

"Remarkable," I said.

The Secret Service man returned with his surprise. The great ape had returned to his chair and his video movie. In it a young woman in a princess's outfit was firing some sort of space gun.

When the Secret Service agent came in trailing a female ape, my friend in the chair looked up, looked back at his television screen, then jumped up, knocking the television over and chattering like mad.

The female took this for foolishness, naturally. But the ape fellow recovered quickly. Soon the two of them were chattering away together in a corner of the bungalow, as if nothing else in the world existed.

"Shall we go outside?" I offered. I checked my watch, seeing that we had plenty of time before four o'clock and resolving to enjoy it.

We toured the island. We left Stanton, Mr. Garber, the television people, the admiral, and his men behind on the beach. It was like being in another world. Early spring had bloomed all over, and huge, nearly tropical plants were throwing their lush flowerings at the sky. The air was fragrant with oxygen. It reminded me of certain springs in my youth, when the world was still ahead of me.

We sat on a flat rock near the bottom of the island's tallest waterfall and spread out a lunch. Eddie and Willie, their pants still rolled up, splashed in the water.

"Mr. Kishkin," I said to the young man, "I was briefed about your work. I must say I approve mightily. I'd now like to explain to you, if I may, why I have taken the actions I've taken the last months."

"Mr. President," the young man replied, "I understand. There were times in the past weeks and months when I didn't understand, and I hated all of you for what you were doing. But I know you did what you thought was right. I now know that there was no malice in it."

"It's very good of you to say that, Mr. Kishkin."

"It's true."

I nodded. "It's the slaughter that's always weighed heavily on me."

"But now we know its meaning, don't we, Mr. President?"

I gave him a slow smile. "Yes, we do. I take it we've both had the same dream. May I tell you what I have in mind?"

"Please, Mr. President."

We ate our lunch, and I told him my plan. At the end of it I told him of my difficulty with the speech I had written.

"It's rather inappropriate now," I said.

"Perhaps I can help you, Mr. President."

He drew a much-folded piece of paper from deep out of his pocket and handed it to me. "These are words I wrote a long time ago based on your own words."

I unfolded the paper and read it. At its creases it had

been so worn through that the words were nearly illegible.

"I would be proud to use these words, Mr. Kishkin," I said, and felt tears rise into my eyes.

Through them I saw Kral Kishkin and the young woman smiling.

It was time to walk back. Once more I admired the lushness of this place, the green budding, the cries of the animals. As we broke through the foliage onto the beach I saw one of the television technicians bending over a live goose as if to harm it. I shooed him away.

"I've met so many marvelous people!" I said to no one in particular.

I turned to Kral Kishkin and Claire St. Eve. "Are you ready?"

The young woman nodded. Kral Kishkin said, "Yes."

"All right, then."

We walked forward, onto the beach, toward the tall gallows that had been erected there.

6

The television lights went on. For a moment they blinded me, taking away the beautiful day, the blue sky, the waving tops of tress. I fumbled for my hat, took it off, fumbled around for the piece of paper in there, found it, and put my hat back on. Then my eyes adjusted to the glare, and I looked out into the cameras, as I had been taught, and made believe they were my old cronies back in Springfield.

"Friends," I began. On the gallows platforms behind me Kral Kishkin and Claire St. Eve stood waiting, nooses knotted around their necks. The television cameras swiveled to take their picture, then came back to me.

"On this momentous day," I said, "I welcome you.

"Many days and weeks have passed since the prosecution of our cause. These have been long and difficult times, with much hardship for us, and for our human brethren.

"Now these hard days are past. *The war is over.*"

I looked down at Mr. Kishkin's piece of paper, and spoke slowly.

"In each man war and peace are joined. Each man is a battlefield. It is the sum of these battlefields that makes a nation, a world, great or bankrupt. If a man, if many men, opt for war within themselves, then war, surely, will follow in the world. But if men fight the battle within and choose peace, then there is surely hope for this, or any, world.

"As each man is a battlefield, so, too, is each nation. And if the many nations that are men choose peace, then so, too, will the world choose peace."

I folded Kral Kishkin's paper and put it down. I checked my watch. It was two minutes to the hour of four.

"Those words are not mine. They are those of the young human behind me. He has sought to make his own world a better place."

I signaled to Kral Kishkin and Claire St. Eve.

They removed the nooses from their necks, dismounted from the gallows, and came to stand beside me.

"Mr. President!" Stanton shouted.

"It's all right," I said, smiling at the Secretary of War. I looked at my watch. It was one minute to four.

"Today," I said to the television cameras, "we have achieved our goal. For, my friends, our work upon this world is done. In less than sixty seconds the earth will leave behind the cloud that brought us here. All of us, all of our race, will be gone from this world.

"But we will not be gone! For this is a day of joy for both skeleton and human. This is not an apocalypse, but a birth.

"A long time ago, at the beginning of human time on earth, there was a man and a woman. And from them grew the human race, until by war and corruption a great flood was sent. Noah, in his Ark, made a new beginning.

"Once again, war and corruption have filled the earth. By whatever Greater Power, physical or spiritual, it is time again for a new beginning. That is why we were sent back to earth; that was our task. We leave behind a new Adam and Eve, to make a new start on earth. The rest of the human race has moved on.

"Each man goes to his own next world. For those filled with corruption it will not be the easiest of worlds, for an accounting must be made. But for the rest it will be . . ."

By my watch there were twenty seconds more. Eddie and Willie ran to me. I held them tight. Already I could feel the change coming on me, the breaking up of my essence in this world.

Eddie said, "I'm scared, Papa."

"Don't be, you rascal!"

There was a pull as of a receding tide. Around me those of us began to turn to powder.

My eyes suddenly could not focus on the distant waterfall, the bright blue sky. I saw another sky, another color, other vegetation waiting for me, growing more distinct and familiar.

Remembrance of this world flooded through me.

"Mother!" Eddie shouted, pulling away from me to run ahead.

Roger Garber ran on, crying, "Carl! Is it really you? Can we talk? Jeez, it's hot in here."

"Paradise!" I shouted joyfully.

I saw Kral Kishkin and Claire St. Eve standing before me. Then they faded until only their bones were visible to me. I looked down, and my own body was whole.

And there around me was my world. . . .

"Good-bye, my friends!" I shouted to Kral Kishkin and Claire St. Eve.

I saw their ghosts wave—and then they were gone, and I was home!

17

The inner diary of
Claire St. Eve

Winter is coming again.

It has been a good spring and summer. The land has provided for us here. Next spring we will plant even more than this year. The animals have bred plentifully, to the point where there is some meat. But still, we are careful of the stocks we must tend ourselves.

Chub has provided us with a surprise. During the summer he disappeared with his mate. Though we searched the island, we were unable to find him. Fearing his loss, I mourned. But soon other things filled my thoughts. His memory was a distant, pleasant one I always would keep.

Then early one morning Kral woke me to say he had sighted a ship.

I arose quickly and went with him to the beach. We watched with some trepidation as the yellow form of an inflatable dinghy approached. Kral, ever vigilant, bore a rifle.

The boat headed straight for us. Even before it had beached, I saw Chub's form gesturing to us from its bow. With him was his mate, whom we had named Leia. She was very much with child. They had gone off alone, as etiquette apparently called for in their culture. Now they had returned. As these things are reckoned, the baby should be born sometime after the new year.

Cold began to seep into this place in early October. By the end of the summer Kral and I had built a good cabin of heavy logs. There is plenty of wood already stacked for fires. Kral was cannibalized the *Arc* for oil-heating equipment, a stove, anything else we might possibly need. Chub and his bride continue to make use of the videotape collection.

Next spring Kral plans on repairing the *Arc*. He says that we will fill this island with game in a year or so, and that it will then be time to move on. Already the wolves are restless, and have taken their litter to the farthest part of Little Diomede Island to raise them. Kral goes to visit them often.

Lately, Kral has begun to brood. I know he is waiting. There is an understanding between us. He has begun to grow impatient. He wants to make a world overnight. It is hard for him, I know. When he gets like this, he works with his hands, and he has driven himself to distraction building more hutches than the rabbits will ever need, feeders for the birds, fences on the eastern part of the island for the lions' preserve. I watch him now from this field-topped hill between our home and the fertile valley where he is planting winter wheat. Occasionally he stops the strong oxen pulling the plow to look up at me and wave. Finally, as the sun is lowering toward sunset, he puts his tools down and makes the long climb up the hill across the late-flowered field toward me.

"Is something wrong?" he asks, concern etched in his face. His yellow skin has nearly browned from the sun and outdoor life. His muscles have grown hard and strong.

I shake my head no.

"Why are you here? Why are you looking at me like that?"

I am smiling. I can't stop. Something is welling inside me. Now, at this moment, I feel complete. The flower that is me is fully bloomed.

Gently, I take his callused hand and place it on my belly.

He is puzzled. But after a short moment realization grows on him. His smile becomes wide.

"You mean . . . in the spring. . . ?"

A look of complete joy comes over him. Already I know it will be a boy. This boy will be followed by many others, both girls and boys. Down across the generations, our children will cover the face of this world. With their fear taken away they will lead good lives. Kral and I will teach them.

I take Kral's hand in my own, looking into his beaming face, part my smiling lips, and say, finally, "*Yes.*"

The legacy of horror is about to be passed on....

NIGHT
by
Alan Rodgers

Tim Fischer knew his grandfather's terrible secret. As a boy, he'd stumbled into the attic room where the Cross was kept...and saw the vision of the Crucified One. That day Tim glimpsed something of the awesome power his family had been chosen to protect for nearly two millennia. Now he must retrace his grandfather's last days to learn the truth about the old man's death and his own strange inheritance. What he discovers is a miracle that will stretch his sanity to the breaking point -- and a dark, ancient brotherhood that will unlock the horrors of hell itself to stop him.

Buy *Night* and Alan Rodgers' other horror novels wherever Bantam Books are sold, or use this page for ordering: